ORISHADAON
To the Ends of the Urth

BRANDON R.J. BOWLING

This is a work of fiction. Names, characters, places, and incidents either are the product of the author's imagination or are used fictitiously, and any resemblance to any persons, living or dead, business establishments, events, or locals is entirely coincidental.

ORISHADAON: TO THE ENDS OF THE URTH

Published by Brandon R.J. Bowling

Cover art by RJ Palmer

Printed in the United States of America

For Zane. Dreams do come true.

CONTENTS

ACKNOWLEDGMENTS

Over the years a great many people have helped and inspired me. It would be foolish to try and name them all. Rather than risk leaving anyone out I offer my heartfelt thanks to everyone who had a hand in making this novel happen.
There are a few people who deserve special mention for their outstanding contributions: Andre "Earthdawn" Morin, Trent Rogers, Rick Weiss and Alicia Barnes. If not for the four of you, Orishadaon would still be languishing on a hardrive, never to be released.

PART I

REVOLUTION OF THE SELF

1.
ALIVE OUT OF HABIT

"I can't believe they're dead," Dayn muttered, stumbling over the reptilian corpse of an annaru as he stared blankly at the bodies lying amongst the muddy undergrowth. He blinked in disbelief and tightened his grip on Agidyne, the blood-soaked blade in his trembling hand.

The shadow of a large winged beast passed overhead, drawing his attention. It soared just above the canopy of rustling leaves, opening its beak to emit a mournful shriek that echoed hauntingly through the humid air.

"I can't believe we aren't," Ryl remarked, startling Dayn from his reverie. "Are ya alright?" he asked anxiously.

Dayn waved off his concern. "I . . . I killed it." Preserve life, never take it, that was his oath. He surveyed the carnage in horror, ashamed of what he had done. "Where is she? What happened to Alis?"

Ryl looked away when Dayn met his gaze. The bigger man reverently lowered his tattooed head and ran a nervous hand across the necklace of bones and karda teeth he wore. "She sent two annaru to the Aether, the bodies are over there," he said, pointing.

Dayn stared at the pair of annaru corpses and grimaced, shaking his head in denial. Grief tightened his throat. "I'd expect nothing less," he whispered, hoarse voice barely audible over the shrieks and howls of the jungle. He silently prayed for Alis' soul, touching his fist to his heart in honor of her memory. "What happened to her?"

"The rest of the war-pack won't be far behind," Ryl said, ignoring the question. He banged a heavy fist against his shield, testing its durability. The thick outer layer of bark split with a resounding *crack*, prompting him to toss it away. "If they catch us now they'll kill us both."

Dayn clenched his fists in frustration.

Ryl tentatively held up a vial of blue liquid. "Ya want this?"

"Keep it," Dayn told him, barely acknowledging the item, acquired through great hardship in a place far away.

Ryl gingerly stuck the vial back into one of many pouches on his belt. "We should go," he urged. "We need to worry about ourselves."

Dayn ignored Ryl's remark and nudged one of the fallen annaru with his foot, half expecting the creature to spring to life and attack. Instead, it lay unmoving on the ground, elongated jaw agape and its three-fingered hand still clutching a cruelly barbed spear.

Annaru were strange creatures made up of a blend of human and reptile anatomy. Possessing the feral instincts of an animal coupled with the cunning intelligence of a man, annaru were a fearsome enemy that Dayn's faraway tribe struggled against almost every lunar.

This particular annaru had stood seven paces tall before a blow from Agidyne's sacred blade cleaved its burly form in half. Its saurian head and thick, muscular arms lay at Dayn's feet, while its lower half rested some distance away.

Satisfied that his foe was truly dead, he turned away from the body and glanced up at the three red slashes tattooed across his companion's scalp. Dayn was not a short tribesman, yet Ryl stood half a head taller, and was much broader as well. Ryl was of the hunter caste, and he exemplified the virtues of strength and honor. Dayn could think of no one he trusted more.

"We should go," Ryl repeated, more forcefully this time.

"What happened to Alis?" Dayn asked while wiping blood off the notched and rusting blade of his sword, another relic from an age long past.

Ryl looked around nervously. "I don't know, more annaru came outta' nowhere durin' the fight and she led 'em away. I didn't see where she went. Dayn, we really have to go," he insisted. "That couldn't have been the entire war-pack, the rest will be here soon."

"You mean she's still alive!?" Dayn instantly perked up. "We have to find her." He squinted into the surrounding underbrush, guessing where she might have gone.

"We'll never find her in all this," Ryl complained.

"You're a hunter, you can find her."

Alis' name lodged itself in the forefront of Dayn's thoughts and he couldn't help blaming himself for her current plight. She followed him into this jungle because she cared about him and wanted to make sure he stayed safe, but where was he when she needed protection? She might be dead now, he realized. No, he shook his head. She could not be dead, Alis was too strong to let this jungle take her soul.

While Dayn mused on Alis' fate, Ryl was busy prying his spear from the stiffening jaws of an annaru. The shaft had lodged itself in the back of the saurian's throat after being rammed into its open mouth.

Once free, Ryl inspected the spearhead, which, according to tribal legend, was made of skyfire rock from the shattered third moon. The Swift Claw tribe considered the spearhead a holy relic, but Ryl seemed indifferent to its blessed history as he took a practice jab.

Content with the weapon, he got down on all fours and rooted through the undergrowth, sniffing the air for signs of Alis' passage. "The jungle cleared away some of her smell. I don't know if I can find . . ." His eyes narrowed as he caught her scent. "This way."

"After you," Dayn said with a wave of his hand.

Ryl, forcing a grim smile, ducked beneath a fallen log and stepped around a cluster of ferns as he led the way.

The trees all around were tall and spindly, their trunks towering above even the largest long-necked karda. A thick canopy of tangled vegetation blotted out the sun and left the jungle in perpetual gloom.

Muddy earth covered the forest floor, blanketed by a thin veil of mist left behind by the early morning rains. The footing was treacherous at best. A myriad collection of deadly predators inhabited the Tresslevale, all of them hidden from view by the spidery tendrils of mist that snaked between the tree trunks and coiled around Dayn's legs. It was hard to draw breath in the oppressively humid air, and clouds of biting insects constantly buzzed around his head. The unending hoots and howls of the jungle began to wear on his already frayed nerves until he was jumping at every noise, sure that it was an annaru about to spring out of the fog and attack.

Not for the first time Dayn cast a worried glance over his shoulder, unused to the claustrophobic nature of the deep jungle. Before now he had spent his entire life on the fringes of this strange, green world, under the light of the sun and the watchful gaze of the ancestors. The unhallowed jungle assaulted his senses with sights, sounds, and smells that were all totally unfamiliar to him. The place put him on edge.

He trudged through the muck and tangled vegetation for an incredibly long time, lamenting his failure to protect Alis all the while, before Ryl motioned for him to stop.

"I need to rest," the big man gasped, sagging to the ground with a hand around his stomach.

"You can't be tired already," Dayn scoffed, wiping beads of sweat from his own brow. He slumped down beside Ryl and shook his head. "Every time we stop we let Alis get that much further away." He kicked off some of the grime that had accumulated on his bare feet before turning back to Ryl. "What's got you so tired anyway? You usually have the endurance of a horn-face."

"It's this heat," Ryl grumbled as he leaned against a nearby tree. "If I sweat any more, I'll shrivel up like dried leather."

A slight smile turned the corner of Dayn's lip. Even after everything that had just happened, Ryl could still find time to complain about something as trivial as the weather. Not that he was wrong; the Tresslevale was hotter than a savanna brushfire during high sun. Even so, Dayn suspected that more than the heat was bothering his friend, and he voiced his concerns.

"It's just, seein' ya back there . . . I didn't know ya could kill so, so . . .," Ryl trailed off, sucking in a deep breath. The words carried a tone of fearful reverence, something Dayn had never before heard from his friend. "I'll be fine," Ryl assured. "Forget it, I'm just tired."

Dayn uncorked his waterskin and took a long drink of the

brackish, lukewarm liquid inside. He grimaced at the awful taste it left in his mouth, offered it to Ryl when he finished and turned his attention to the jungle.

A dragonfly the size of his hand flitted past on incandescent wings and landed on a gnarled tree branch. Nearby, a pack of hopper lizards scurried through the underbrush, squawking noisily as they fought over some insignificant scrap of bug meat.

The sweet scent of morayth reached his nostrils and he quickly scanned the area for the source of the tantalizing smell. To his surprise, a tangle of the vines was close by, and it held a veritable bounty of the plump red berries. His stomach grumbled just thinking about the fruit. It might not be horn-face meat, but after two lunars of nothing it would be enough to take the edge off his hunger. "How about some morayth," he offered, licking his lips.

Dayn concentrated on a particularly large berry and envisioned it in his palm. For a brief moment nothing happened. Upon focusing his efforts he caused the vine holding the fruit to tremble. The juicy morayth leaped from its vine and floated into his waiting hand.

As he wrapped his fingers around the morayth a jumble of images flickered before his startled eyes. He saw a flock of tiny winged reptiles take flight from their perches, and a massive form barrel through the jungle. Next came a dark gaping maw ringed with teeth, followed by utter darkness. A haunting scream echoed through his thoughts as the vision came to an abrupt end, snapping him out of his trance.

He turned to Ryl, who stared at him expectantly.

"Are ya gonna' pass me any of that morayth?" his companion grumbled impatiently.

Dayn rubbed at his eyes. "What was that?"

"What was what?" Ryl replied quizzically, his thick brow furrowing in puzzlement.

"I saw . . . something," Dayn shook his head. "A vision, maybe."

Ryl reached over and plucked the morayth from Dayn's grasp. "What kinda' vision?" he asked before dropping the berry into his mouth.

"I don't know," Dayn frowned. "I think maybe we should move on." He eyed the surrounding jungle suspiciously.

"Something doesn't feel right about this place."

Ryl shrugged and stood up, wiping off the back of his legs. "At least give me another moment," he pleaded, leaning against a nearby tree for support.

Dayn stared into the jungle with apprehension, unsure of what to do next. He nervously ran a hand through his closely cropped, sweat-matted hair. What should he do? If there was something dangerous out there, he and Ryl could be walking to their doom. He would take no chances this time, no one else was going to pay for his mistakes.

"I have to use the soul weave," he stated matter-of-factly.

Ryl frowned and rolled his eyes. "I thought Sharna told ya it was too dangerous."

"I know what she said, but this is important."

"The ancestors forgive yer foolishness Dayn."

"Not likely."

Ryl's frown deepened. For a moment, Dayn thought he was going to argue further, but then he asked, "Whadda' ya need me to do?"

"Just watch over my body, make sure nothing happens to it while I'm gone," he instructed.

Ryl conceded with a shrug of his broad shoulders.

The orishadaon brushed leaves away from his feet and sat down cross-legged. After driving his sword into the ground, he took a deep breath and used his finger to trace the symbol of the mind's eye in the muddy earth. Humming to help his concentration, he placed a hand against his forehead and closed both eyes, shutting himself off from the world as he focused on releasing his mind. To navigate the soul weave was no easy task, made all the more difficult because he had never fully mastered the technique.

"The ancestors watch over ya," he faintly heard Ryl's prayer.

A wave of euphoria passed through Dayn when his soul floated free of its imprisoning shell. His pale and fragile body remained chained to the earth as an interwoven web of multicolored energy blossomed into view, extending infinitely in every direction. To Dayn, the shimmering energy appeared as a spider's web, with every living creature connected to one another by the strands.

He cautiously grasped a glowing strand of the web and pulled his awareness away. He moved slowly in the beginning, still unsteady in the strange new environment. Before long, however, his mind raced across the strand as he searched the sensitive web for the creature in his vision.

At first the intruder eluded him, but he refused to give up. He readied his senses and tried again. Time almost stood still as he probed deeper, dragging out his discomfort as he held the soul weave together with sheer force of will.

The longer he used his abilities the more they hurt him by sucking him dry of life-giving soul energy, his orishadai.

Under normal circumstances, he would not have taken such a chance as this, but the vision had disturbed him to such a degree that he felt the risks were worth it. Even so, his continued trek across the weave drained him quickly.

Just before rejoining his body he sensed something so subtle that it almost went overlooked. A small strand of brilliance shone on the weave. Dayn followed the strand to its source, expecting to find the minds of an annaru war-pack waiting in ambush. Instead, a ball of crimson brilliance blossomed before him.

What he found was a ferocious presence that halted him in terror, a savage beast with a single-minded desire to kill.

He touched on something else in that dark place, a presence so vile that the slightest contact with it sickened Dayn and dealt a staggering blow to his senses.

How could it have hidden itself all this time? his horrified mind wondered as he reeled from the discovery. The shock shattered his concentration and abruptly hurled his awareness back into its prison.

Dayn's first sensation was that of a trickle from his nose. He reached up to wipe it, only to have his fingers come away covered in blood. The sight of it made him shiver despite the searing heat coursing through his veins.

"Ya weren't gone more than an eye blink, this time," Ryl commented.

"It's a karda, a blade-nose," Dayn blurted.

The color instantly drained from Ryl's face. "By the blood of my ancestors!" he choked on the words. He opened his mouth to speak again but nothing came out.

"We must be away from here now," Dayn said firmly, backing up a step as the jungle seemed to close in around him. He heard the snap of a twig and spun around, grasping Agidyne and swinging it at whatever had crept up on him.

2.
ANYWHERE BUT HERE

It was no blade-nose lying in ambush that snapped the twig, but a tall, lithe woman wearing nothing except a karda skin belt strapped around her waist and holding half of a broken branch in each hand.

Surprised, Dayn forced his rusted blade to a halt less than a finger-width from the mane of tangled hair dangling across the woman's neck. Alis never flinched.

"Thank the ancestors you're alive!" Dayn beamed.

Sweat glistened on her naked flesh, beading around numerous fresh scars, but Alis wore a smirk on her mud-streaked face. "Was there ever any doubt?" she teased, gesturing to the three red slashes tattooed across her exposed breast. "Takes more than a couple annaru to kill a Swift Claw."

"It'd take more than a whole war-pack to stop you," Dayn said proudly. There were few members of the scout caste with matching skills, and fewer still who surpassed hers. Alis could move across the savanna without leaving a single bent blade of grass in her wake, quiet as a whisper and invisible as the wind.

Ryl interrupted the joyous reunion with a grunt of irritation and put a hand over his lips, motioning for quiet. "Have ya forgot about the blade-nose?" he whispered.

"Blade-nose?" Alis arched an eyebrow, amber eyes sparkling with curiosity.

Dayn was in the midst of recounting his journey across the

weave when a rumbling growl silenced him, along with the rest of the jungle. He spun in a panicked circle, not knowing which direction the sound had come from. The loud crash of a falling tree had his leg muscles tensing in anticipation.

Ryl grabbed Alis by the arm, cringing when his hand brushed across a patch of dainty oval scales, and pushed her into motion. "Run!" he yelled and dashed into the undergrowth behind her. Another thunderous *crack*, this one much closer than the last, sent Dayn running after the pair.

Ahead, Alis' sinewy form melted into the surrounding jungle and Ryl pulled away, moving faster than his size and earlier exhaustion would suggest he could.

The jungle blurred into mixed shades of green and brown as Dayn increased his pace. His heart skipped a beat as he stumbled over some unseen obstacle beneath the cover of mist. He saved himself from a nasty tumble and continued running with renewed urgency.

Branches groped him as he fled, ensnaring his arms and legs, slowing his desperate run. His mind screamed for him to hurry as he darted around a patch of protruding roots. The harsh glare of the blade-nose fell across his back and some sixth sense told him to duck.

He did so a moment before a tremendous *crunch* sounded and the carnivore's massive jaws clapped together above his head. He lunged to the side, hoping the karda's momentum would carry it past him. His hopes were realized an instant later when it barreled past, snarling angrily as it dug in its heels and splattered him with mud.

He tried to push himself up but lost his footing on the bed of slippery leaves covering the misty forest floor. Alarmed, he scrambled away on all fours, grabbing onto everything he could for support. On the verge of panic, he looked over his shoulder, instantly regretting his decision to get a better view of the beast.

He caught a glimpse of it on the other side of a tight patch of brambles. The blade-nose stomped through the thorns on two massive hind legs, protected from the spines by its thick hide. Muscles bulged against a coat of stripped, azure scales shimmering in the dim rays of light that pierced the canopy. At thirty-five paces long and double his own height, it was the largest of its kind that

Dayn had ever seen. The huge horn on its bobbing snout was terrifying enough, but the heart-stopping bellow it let out as it locked eyes with him made his blood run cold.

Dayn wrenched his gaze away from the beast as he pushed through a copse of squat cycads, startling a flock of winged reptiles that quickly took to the air. Blindly, he swatted at them, and in his rush bumped against the remains of a low stone wall. Dayn hopped over it, absently wondering why anyone would build a wall in the middle of the jungle.

The blade-nose was no longer right behind him, but he could still hear it moving just out of sight. He wiped at the sweat running into his eyes and nearly collided with another stone wall, this one slightly higher than the last. Without slowing down, he leaped up, caught hold of the top edge and pulled himself over in one easy move. While in the air he noticed more of the odd structures, and caught sight of Ryl further ahead. He hit the ground running.

It wasn't until he again spotted Ryl, this time through a perfectly circular hole, that Dayn realized he was looking through a window in what remained of the side of a building. This must have been a village once, and a big one, judging by the number of walls he had passed.

He pushed through a thick patch of hanging vines and suddenly the blade-nose was there, towering over him like an angry mountain. He crashed headlong into its open muzzle, staggering backwards as he prepared to meet his ancestors.

Cold, unblinking eyes bored into him and he stared back, too terrified to move. The blade-nose remained motionless, watching him with lifeless gray eyes. It didn't breathe or close its jaw around him because it wasn't alive. The massive edifice was nothing more than an over-sized statue resembling the karda. Carved in the form of Kor, the annaru god, the statue directed its baleful gaze across the city.

Dayn let out the breathe he had been holding and gave the carving's snout a pat, peering into the back of its cavernous mouth where a slab of black obsidian blocked his view. He could almost feel the vengeful god's breath upon his cheeks, even though he knew it to be impossible. Kor was dead, praise the ancestors, and had been for hundreds of cycles of the seasons.

Behind the monolith, the jungle gave way to narrow streets

and buildings encrusted in sheets of bright moss. Sunlight breached the canopy and Dayn put up a hand to shield his eyes from the dazzling light. Before him lay the crumbling remnants of a sprawling, ancient city, fallen into ruin after many seasons of neglect.

Something in the distance caught his attention and he pushed aside a wide cycad leaf to get a clearer view. A temple rose up amidst the ruins, towering over the tallest trees in the surrounding jungle. The structure's tiered mass blocked out the sun and cast a perpetual shadow across half the city.

"Impossible," Dayn mumbled, wondering if it was an illusion conjured by his fatigued mind.

"Look out!" a familiar voice hissed in warning. Ryl darted from his hiding place behind a pile of rubble and hastily pulled Dayn aside.

"What are you doing?" Dayn protested, startled by his friend's sudden appearance. Ryl yanked him into an alley just as an azure-scaled snout pushed through the tree line. A moment later the blade-nose stalked out of the jungle and onto the open street.

Dayn ducked down and cursed himself for so easily forgetting about the karda.

Ryl glared at him and motioned with his spear to a group of crumbling buildings where Alis waved from inside a web-covered window.

The orishadaon stole a peek at the blade-nose. It milled about for a moment, then lowered its massive head to sniff the ground. The karda's nostrils flared when it aimed its head in his direction, and he quickly ducked out of sight.

"We're not going to make it."

"We'll be fine, just follow me," Ryl said quietly as he wormed his way through the rubble.

Dayn had to do something, but after using the soul weave he scarcely had a drop of orishadai left, certainly not enough for anything meaningful. Not surprisingly, he found himself recalling one of Sharna's many lectures.

"The body is a vessel for the soul's energy," she had told him when he was in his eighth season. "Imagine a full water jug. You are the jug, your orishadai is the water. Each time you sip its contents you drain a little more, until there is nothing left. Wasting your abilities on lesser tasks leaves you empty when you need the power most. Do not grow dependent on your unique skills, child."

Only eight seasons old at the time of the lesson, and already on the path to becoming a true orishadaon. He remembered the words, but never truly understood them until now. Curse the old witch! Even when she wasn't around, she still forced her teachings on him.

"Okay," he whispered to himself. "Let's see what I can do without my power." Dayn stepped out of the alley and into plain view before he had a chance to rethink his decision.

Ryl gaped at him. "What in the Aether are ya doin'?!"

"Go." Dayn waved him back as the blade-nose swiveled its head around and fixed him in its triumphant glare. "Meet me at the big temple," he hurriedly added. He shouted at the top of his lungs, whether in fear or for courage he didn't know, and ran into the overgrown city. "Damn you karda, come and get me!" he yelled over his shoulder, darting behind a collapsed building.

The blade-nose stomped after him.

Dayn ducked down an alley, winding his way through piles of rubble and narrow corridors. He put some added distance between the beast and himself by weaving amongst the wreckage, but the karda's frustrated roars remained dangerously close.

He came to the edge of the building cluster and hid in the shadows of an entryway, checking up and down the wide thoroughfare ahead for signs of better cover. After a moment of observation he dashed towards a two-story building across the way.

The karda burst through the rubble to his right, sending hunks of rock bouncing across the cobblestone street. With his pursuer snapping at his heels, Dayn offered a prayer to the ancestors and dove through a window half concealed by a curtain of vines. He came down hard but did not falter, rolling to his feet and darting through the cluttered interior without slowing down.

Ducking behind a sagging wall, he pressed himself just out of sight of the blade-nose as it peered through the same vine-choked window he had used to enter the building. He held his breath, not daring to make a sound as it gazed inside. A low growl echoed through the building, followed by utter silence.

He stood with his back pressed tightly against the damp stone wall until he felt sure the karda had moved on. A tiny green snake slithered across his foot as he waited, its smooth belly scales tickling his skin. A cool breeze rustled patches of dangling leaves. Nothing else moved. He slowly exhaled, the sound like an earthquake in the eerie quiet that had settled around him.

Mustering his courage, he glanced out the window. The karda was no longer there, or anywhere else within sight.

"I should get to the temple."

He stepped towards a large hole in the wall, stopping to brush a beetle the size of his fist out of the way. It landed on its back, kicking its legs and snapping its oversized pincers.

As he lifted his leg through the open space a dark shadow fell across him. The orishadaon instinctively froze. A giant, tooth filled maw loomed overhead, only paces away from his outstretched leg. The karda's lip curled into a cruel sneer as it looked down on him pitilessly. Dayn barely had time to scream before it drove its head through the window.

The force of the blow knocked him and a large section of the surrounding wall across the room, crushing his leg between the stone and the animal's snout. His back hit the opposite wall with enough force to drive the breath from his lungs as his head smacked against the unyielding stone. Bright lights exploded before his eyes.

Half blind, disoriented, and struggling for breath, he stubbornly tried to stand. To his credit, he made it almost a full pace off the ground before collapsing.

The karda slammed its considerable bulk into the dilapidated building, raining chunks of masonry down on his cringing form. The beast roared its fury, sending a wave of dust and fetid breath sweeping across the room.

"Get up," he groaned, pressing a hand against his throbbing head. "Get up," he repeated more firmly when his body refused to move. The orishadaon struggled onto his hands and knees. By the time he managed to prop himself up against the wall the karda had hit the building again, causing portions of the ceiling to collapse in a shower of rubble. One more hit like that and this place would be his burial mound. Dayn cringed, but pushed the pain to the back of his overburdened mind in the way he had been trained to do.

"Time to go," he said in a raspy voice, throat clogged by

clouds of wafting dust. He choked back a startled cry, wincing when his battered right leg refused to hold his weight. One shoulder against the wall to hold himself up, Dayn slid towards the opposite side of the building. He refused to die here. Not in a place like this.

He moved on, one arm outstretched to keep from toppling over. A vine-choked window waited on the opposite side of the building. Once he reached it, Dayn stole a quick glance outside and clambered through. The ruins ahead looked clear enough, and he wasted no time putting the house and the blade-nose as far behind him as possible.

Within moments a roar sounded, followed by a loud *crash*.

He had to move faster. He grabbed the back of his injured leg and swung it forward. "One foot in front of the other," he said, gritting his teeth against the flash of pain each step brought him.

3.
THE UNRAVELING

Many of the buildings on either side of the thoroughfare stood intact, albeit thickly carpeted with twisting vegetation. The deserted homes leant an eerie, lifeless feeling to the ruins, and Dayn could almost hear the restless spirits moaning from the Aether. The living jungle had pushed out the old inhabitants and was slowly reclaiming the land they had taken from it so long ago.

"Why did you bring me here?" Dayn asked the ancestors. "Why did Sharna send me to find my destiny, here?"

He wandered amidst the ruins, avoiding thick patches of weeds and upturned stones as he waited for an answer that would not come. He desperately wanted to find his friends and be away from this place.

Dayn licked his parched lips, suddenly in need of a drink of water. He slid the waterskin from its loop on his belt and uncorked it. As he drank he spied something moving out of the corner of his eye. The remaining water spilled across his chin when he twisted his head around to get a better look.

"Ryl?" he asked tentatively. "Is that you?"

There was no answer but the wind howling down the empty street.

If it was anything at all, it had not set off his psychic alarm. Of all his strange, often unstable powers, his psychic alarm was most reliable. Nevertheless, he cast a nervous glance at the tightly packed buildings lining both sides of the street. Better to be sure he told himself.

Finding nothing out of the ordinary, he moved on.

He made it another few paces when, again, he caught a glimpse of something moving at the edge of his vision. This time he was sure he had seen it, yet he received no mental alert, no warning of its presence.

"Who's there? I said who's there?" he persisted, glaring into an adjacent window. A formless shadow stalked past the opening and he inadvertently backed away.

His mind was playing tricks on him, it had to be. That thing couldn't be real, he would have been warned if it were. It was not real.

When another shadowy form skittered across a rooftop further down the street, Dayn limped away as fast as his leg would allow. He put a hand on Agidyne as it bounced wildly against his hip, keeping the sacred relic close as he begged the ancestors to banish the false demons.

More indistinct figures appeared, moving silently within the gloom of ruined buildings. "There's nothing there, they aren't real," he told himself, conviction waning as more and more of the monsters made themselves visible in spite of his denial.

He pulled Agidyne from its scabbard and waved the rusty blade through the air, as if to show the demons he had a means to defend himself. It did nothing to stall them, and he hurried on towards the temple with grim determination.

He came to an abrupt halt, heart freezing in his chest when more of the creatures appeared on the street ahead, blocking his way. He spun around to retrace his footsteps, and discovered that the demons had cut off any hopes of retreat.

"No, no, no," he shook his head. "You aren't real," he fell to his knees, murmuring sorrowfully.

Not a sound from his psychic alarm or the ghostly stalkers.

"They aren't there, they aren't real," he repeated again and again as if the words were another of Sharna's lessons to be memorized. He cringed away as the nearest creature reached out, its clawed hand missing him by less than half a pace. He dropped his sword and pounded the sides of his skull to drive away the dreadful images. "You are not real!" he screamed at the top of his lungs, closing his eyes against the horror that had befallen him.

He expected the cold claws of the demons to wrap around his flesh at any moment, but he never felt their touch. Not daring to hope that they would be gone, he slowly opened an eye to glance around.

Nothing.

Not a trace of the horde of shadows looming over him only a moment before. His mind *was* playing tricks on him, again.

Such visions had plagued him in the past, but never had they been so intensely real. Dayn resolved to talk with Sharna about his unstable powers when he got back to the village, but for now he had to meet his friends and figure out what they were going to do next.

He had only just stood up when a firm hand grasped his shoulder and spun him around. Another unyielding hand slapped across his mouth to silence his startled cry, and Dayn found himself staring into a pair of stygian eyes. He struggled in vain against his attacker, until he recognized the eyes. After he calmed himself the hand slowly released its grip.

Dayn cleared his throat. "Ryl, where have you been?"

"Shhhh," Ryl pointed to the ruins behind him. "Yer screamin' gave us away. The blade-nose is just over there." He motioned Dayn to follow him in the opposite direction.

The orishadaon obeyed, stopping briefly to gather up his sword. "Where are we going?" he asked.

"The temple seems to be the safest place," Ryl replied without looking back. "Alis is already inside. She wanted to come after ya too, but I sent her back."

Dayn didn't have to ask why. His overgrown friend didn't trust Alis. She was a 'half-blood' he said. Annaru blood flowed through her veins, and though it was barely enough to make her heritage noticeable, it gave most tribesmen a reason to distrust her. Ryl refused to accept her presence in the tribe, claiming that she and her father (who was half annaru himself) would be the death of the Swift Claw people.

As the temple's shadow fell over him, Dayn forgot all about Alis' lineage.

He had to crane his neck to see the top of the mammoth structure. A dark entrance gaped open in the side of its fifth tier, from which a steep staircase led down to the third tier and a forbidding altar. From there the stairs split in two and wound like twin serpents around the altar, down to the first tier where another huge entrance loomed dark and dangerous. Serpentine columns and statues of long dead annaru surrounded this last entrance, the one Ryl directed him towards.

Dayn had a sudden, inexplicable bad feeling about the place. Awful things would happen if they went inside. He knew it to be true, knew it the same as he knew the blade-nose would catch them and kill them if they didn't. He shook his head. "We can't go in there. This is bad."

"Quiet!" Ryl silenced him with a pleading look. Dayn wanted to tell his friend that they had to find somewhere else to hide, anywhere else, but before he could he was interrupted by the wild blaring of his mental alarm. At the same instant, Ryl's eyes opened wide and, panic stricken, he stumbled backwards. "The blade-nose! Right behind us!"

All arguments forgotten, Dayn scrambled towards the opening without looking to see if his friend was telling the truth.

"Faster!" Ryl called, but Dayn was already going as quickly as he could. Piercing agony shot up his leg each time he put weight on the knee.

The roar of his psychic alarm deafened him, drowning out everything but the sound of his own labored breathing. He offered a prayer to the ancestors, though they seemed to be ignoring his prayers as of late.

"Get inside!" Dayn shouted, sprinting past a pair of annaru statues standing guard on either side of the entrance.

The karda lunged for him. Its massive bulk knocked over one of the statues with as much effort as it might take a man to bend a blade of grass.

Dayn cursed his luck as he landed hard on his chest and sprawled out on the solid stone. Even as the breath burst from his lungs and his vision swam with darkness, he threw an arm forward and dug his fingers into a crack.

Something behind him cast a long shadow down the tunnel ahead. His body went rigid, hands reflexively clenching into white-knuckled fists as a knot of fear tightened his chest. The shadow quickly filled the narrow tunnel.

It seemed he was not fated to escape the jaws of this karda.

Dayn inhaled, put a hand on his sword, and hesitantly rolled over to meet his doom.

He found himself face to gaping maw with the blade-nose, and let out a cry of terror despite himself. The karda's head shot forward and Dayn threw up his arms in a futile attempt to ward off the blow. He squeezed his eyes shut as fetid breath washed over him in a nauseating wave. The jaws slammed together with a deafening *crunch*.

If his nostrils did not still burn from the stench of rotten meat carried on the karda's breath he might have believed he was dead. Could the blade-nose have missed? he wondered, and tentatively opened his eyes.

He pulled back in shock, not quite believing what he saw before him.

The blade-nose lay on its stomach, head sticking into the tunnel, shoulders pressed hard against the bowing column on either side of the entrance. It squirmed against the groaning, ancient stone, but the columns held.

Dayn's eyes watered as the beast's violent thrashing released a clinging haze of dust. "By the ancestors," he rasped when the horn on the end of its snout slashed through the billowing cloud right in front of him. In shock, he reached up and probed his nose, only to find it whole and undamaged.

"Maybe my luck is changing," he said with a grin. Then he felt something warm and wet trickle down the side of his head, and a single drop of blood spattered the cold stone at his feet. As he watched, another droplet landed beside the first. "Or maybe not." He sagged against the wall and placed a hand over the side of his face. "Alis?" he called out hoarsely. "Ryl?"

The teeth and bones on Ryl's necklace rattled together as he stepped out of the shadows with Alis right behind him. He gave Dayn only a cursory glance at first, amazed as he was by the sight of the blade-nose, but quickly snapped his head around for another look. "Ya look like ya just got tossed into the Aether and spat out by an angry demon."

Dayn laughed weakly, steadying himself with an elbow against the wall while he tried to staunch the flow of blood from his head. "So I look like I feel," he replied after a pause.

"Ya haven't lost yer sense of humor," Ryl grinned.

"Don't encourage him." Alis pushed the hulking hunter aside and pointed an accusing finger at Dayn. "What in the Aether were you thinking trying to fight a blade-nose by yourself? You could have been killed."

"I'm glad you're not hurt," Dayn said, taking care to avoid eye-contact.

"What would happen to Nesthome and the tribe if they lost their orishadaon?" She was practically shaking with anger. "What would I do if I lost you?"

"Bah, those annaru-lovers would get along just fine on their own," Ryl said and gave Dayn a hearty clap across the shoulder.

Weakened as he was, Dayn bowed under the blow. He slumped to the ground and his hand fell away from the wound.

"Let me see that." Alis knelt down beside him and gently prodded his temple.

Dayn winced. "Ow."

"Don't whine, this is your fault," she chided while inspecting the cut. "Besides, I've seen you take worse than this."

The blade-nose gave up trying to force its way inside the tight confines of the tunnel. It wriggled free and took to pacing in front of the entrance.

Dayn wiped away the sweat beading on his forehead and reached for his waterskin, then remembered he had spilled its contents in the street. Frowning, he pushed Alis' hand aside and pressed his own tighter against the wound. "Forget about it, it's nothing." He started to shiver.

"That looks bad." Ryl crouched next to Dayn.

Alis shoved him aside a second time. "Just stay out of my way."

"Oh, calm yerself. Ya aren't mad about that annaru-lover comment are ya?"

She ignored him while untying the belt around her waist.

"What are you doing?" Dayn asked in confusion.

"So yer father is half annaru," Ryl said with a shrug. "Ya know I didn't mean anythin' by it."

"Hey!" Dayn's lips twitched upwards when she pulled his belt off too. "We don't have time for that." He smirked groggily, not really caring if she continued or not. He'd caught sight of his tattoo and was staring at it as if it were the first time he'd ever seen the seemingly random series of spirals and dots on his flesh that marked him as an orishadaon. The markings began on his right shoulder, snaked to his elbow, and covered half his chest, neck and back as well.

Alis hurriedly yanked all the pouches off both belts. "I'm making bandages," she stated bluntly, wiping the smile off Dayn's bemused face. She dumped the contents of her waterskin onto the side of his face before wrapping both strips of karda hide around the sputtering orishadaon's wound. Once finished, she nodded her approval. "Just lie there a while. I'm worried about you Dayn, you look paler than usual."

"I'm just a bit winded." He struggled to rise, but was forced down by a firm hand pressed against his shoulder.

"You need to rest," Alis insisted. "We can't have you running around the jungle like this."

Dayn tried in vain to push her hand away. "I have to go."

"Go where?" She motioned to the blade-nose pacing in front of the sole entrance. "You can't get past that thing you stubborn, sun-baked idiot."

He cringed inwardly at the harshness of her words. She was really angry with him this time.

"The karda *is* blockin' the only exit," Ryl agreed. "We aren't goin' anywhere until it leaves."

Dayn couldn't help but chuckle at that last remark.

"What's so funny?" Alis asked in obvious annoyance.

"You think we should wait for the blade-nose to leave?" His head drooped lazily until his chin rested against his tattooed chest. "Well, you'll be waiting a long time because as far as stubborn is concerned, that thing has me beat. It'll wait out there until we're dead. We need to find another way."

"Ya got a point there," Ryl agreed with Dayn this time.

"Oh, quiet yourself!" Alis found a new outlet for her ire. "You always agree with him. Why do you always have to agree with him?"

"Because he isn't part lizard!" the offended hunter practically yelled in her face.

Almost as soon as Ryl spat out the words, Alis drove her fist into his jaw.

Dayn gasped.

Alis didn't pull her punch at all, and the blow was more than powerful enough to stagger a normal man. Ryl, however, did not even flinch. It was as if Alis had slammed her fist into a solid mud brick wall.

"Stop it." Dayn feebly raised a trembling hand between the two. There was little else he could do in his present condition.

"Damn you, Ryl," she snarled, dropping her hand.

The bigger man's lip curled upwards, revealing a row of yellowed teeth. "Feel better?" he sneered.

Alis turned to Dayn, her body rigid with fury. Something akin to bloodlust burned in the depths of her amber eyes. "Another way out?" she hissed between barred teeth. "Stay here and I'll find us another way out." She pointed a trembling finger at Ryl. "You. Make sure nothing happens to the orishadaon."

"Wait," Dayn called after her as she stalked off.

"What?!" She whirled, nostrils flared and eyes blazing, causing his heart to catch in his throat.

He gulped. "There's no light back there, shouldn't you take a torch?" he asked meekly.

She made sure he met her steely gaze before answering. Her slitted, serpentine pupils expanded into wide orbs, surrounded by gently glowing irises. "No need for one. I am part lizard, after all."

4.
AS DAYLIGHT DIES

"She's been gone a long time," Dayn observed. The sunlight shining through the end of the tunnel had dimmed since her departure, leaving a dusky veil of shadows in its wake. With nightfall steadily approaching, he worried more and more.

"Ya look terrible. Are ya okay?"

"No."

Cold sweat drenched his shivering flesh. He wrapped his arms around himself to ward off the air's dank chill. Nothing he did, however, eased the relentless pounding in his temples. Dayn felt just a little bit dizzy as he leaned against the unnaturally cold stone of the nearest wall.

"I'm sorry about what I said," Ryl mumbled. He shifted uneasily when Dayn remained quiet, waiting for a response.

"Apologizing to the wrong person," Dayn finally replied in a dry rasp. He felt nauseous. His stomach cartwheeled like a winged karda caught in a storm. A moan escaped his lips as he reached up to massage his aching temples, only to find the side of his bandage-swathed face swollen and tender to the touch. "Where is she?"

The hunter hung his tattooed head in shame. "I don't like being yelled at. I didn't mean what I said. She's not all that bad, it's her father ya gotta' worry about."

Dayn turned to stare at Ryl, causing an explosion of pain inside his skull that sent the world spinning in erratic circles. A few moments of struggling to stay conscious followed, after which, his sense of up and down returned to normal.

"Why are you lookin' at me like that?" Ryl finally noticed him glaring.

"I don't blame you for hating annaru, not after what happened to your parents."

His friend's face morphed into a mask of remembered pain.

"I was there and I saw it, but Alis isn't annaru. She had nothing to do with it."

Ryl breathed a deep, calming breath, then nodded slowly.

In the following silence, Dayn reached down to test the bruised and swollen flesh around his knee, flinching from the gentlest tap.

Ryl pointed past sheets of dangling cobwebs to the karda, now lying in front of the tunnel's entrance. "I assume it was Spike that hurt ya."

"Spike?" Dayn glanced up at him questioningly.

Ryl shrugged. "Thought I'd give our new friend a name. Spike seemed good enough." He shook his head at Dayn knowingly. "Don't even think of movin'. Ya hurt yerself and Alis will slit my throat. Get some more rest."

"I'm fine," Dayn shuddered as his sweaty back came into contact with the cold stone wall. What he really needed was to speak with Sharna about the events of the past few lunars. It was becoming increasingly difficult to keep his powers, not to mention his sanity, in check, and he needed to know why.

He reached a hand towards his companion. "Help me up."

Ryl sighed in dismay and offered a prayer as he grabbed Dayn's outstretched hand and hauled him to his feet. "Here." He thrust an uncorked waterskin into his hands. "Ya should take things a bit slower than ya are," he cautioned as Dayn gulped down a mouthful of the warm and dirty water.

Ryl dug the vial of blue liquid out of one of his many pouches. "Ya want it? Ya look like ya could use it." He gazed down the tunnel at the blade-nose as he offered it to Dayn, who shook his head.

"Save it in case you or Alis needs it. I'm not hurt *that* bad."

The hunter shrugged and placed the vial back in its pouch. "Whatever ya say."

"I hope she comes back soon." Dayn took a tentative step. Stumbling, he caught hold of the wall to keep from falling over.

Ryl shot him a worried glance but said nothing about the slip. "Ya really care about her don't ya?"

The bluntness of the remark caught Dayn off guard.

Ryl shrugged. "She cares about ya too, that's why she always worries."

Dayn listened to the wind hissing through the forgotten halls of the temple. If he tried hard enough, he could almost imagine he heard a voice carried on the gusts. "Sometimes, sometimes I wonder if it's really me she cares about, or just the thought of having me around to help the tribe."

"She doesn't need yer help," Ryl replied.

"What?"

The big man ran a nervous hand across his necklace. "What I mean is, no one else could take on as many annaru as she did and survive. Ya keep treatin' her like she's fragile and weak, but she's tough. She has to be, with a father like hers."

Dayn thought about that for a moment and nodded to himself. She did manage to distract the annaru, and elude them in their own jungle. "I still don't know what matters to her."

"Don't worry yerself about it. She's here isn't she? That should say somethin'."

"You're here too."

"Bah, I couldn't let ya have all this fun by yerself," Ryl laughed awkwardly.

Dayn grinned. His friend had always been terrible at accepting gratitude.

Without warning, Dayn's head twisted sideways as if struck, wiping the grin from his face. His psychic alarm blared, instinctively sending his hand to Agidyne.

"Be calm, it's only me." He heard Alis' voice moments before she appeared at the edge of the dim light. Her bare feet padded silently across the stone, bringing her out of the shadows. "I guess you're feeling better." She seemed much more in control of herself now than during her abrupt exit, though she still refused to meet Ryl's apologetic gaze. "There's a whole maze of tunnels down there," the scout explained to Dayn. "I'm sure there's another way out. Thought I'd come back and see if we could put that memory of yours to work."

The orishadaon understood her meaning immediately. "Let's get moving then, no sense wasting any more time here."

He pulled his sword from its scabbard. Placing a hand on the blade, Dayn concentrated on summoning what little orishadai he could. The tiny spark that he managed to draw forth was focused into a tight ball which he placed inside the sword, causing the weapon to glow with the intensity of a torch so long as it remained in his hand. "That should do. Let's go."

Alis led them down the narrow passageway. Strange carvings covered its entire length, all depicting what looked like important moments in annaru history. While Dayn couldn't read any of the writing, the images showed human sacrifices, appearances of the dark god Kor, and brutal battles between annaru and beings in odd-looking clothes.

It took him a moment to realize the beings were humans, and the odd-looking clothes were actually suits of interlocking metal plates. There were a few damaged scraps of armor amidst the tribe's relics, but he had never imagined how a full suit might look when put together. It reminded him of an insect's carapace.

One particular image stood out amongst the rest. It depicted a single, naked human standing before an army of annaru, with an image of Kor hanging in the air above. The figure looked to be leading the army, or perhaps standing alone against it. The vagueness of the carving made it impossible to tell.

"There's no time for that," Alis said as she guided them deeper into the temple.

"But it's interesting," he protested, realizing immediately how childish he must sound. He allowed himself to be led along without further complaint.

The passage ended at an archway that opened into a circular room devoid of any remarkable features save for a spiraling staircase leading deep into the earth.

Alis paused when they entered the chamber, listening.

"What's she doin'?" Ryl whispered.

Dayn shrugged.

After a few moments of staring off into space, Alis blinked and focused on her companions. "Oh." She blinked again. "It's nothing. I thought I heard something."

Dayn tightened his grip on Agidyne. The sword reminded him of his duty to the tribe, a duty he inherited from Sharna after completing his Succession. Metal was an unholy tool of the ancestors, and before that the annaru. Only orishadaons, with their fortitude and control of orishadai, could touch metal without risk to their souls.

Alis motioned for him to follow and descended the stairs without looking back. Ryl waited a few moments for her to get ahead and then went down next. Dayn, however, stopped to give the eerie chamber a final look. He felt as if he was being watched, although what in the long-forgotten place could be watching him was a question he did not have an answer for. Maybe, he thought, it would be better if he never found out.

"Wait for me," he called and hurried to catch up.

5.
MENTAL TORMENTS

As he followed the spiraling stairs into the heart of the world he couldn't help but think he was descending into the shadow of the Aether itself. By the time he finally stumbled out into a hallway at the bottom he had to grit his teeth against the stabbing pain in his knee. A quick breath of the stagnant air brought back the nausea he'd felt earlier.

"Not much choice," Ryl remarked, then plodded off in the only direction he could.

Agidyne's glowing blade illuminated a long hallway, littered with fallen masonry, crumbling statues, and the skeletons of many annaru. A vile odor rose from the skeletons, like the sickly sweet aroma of meat left to rot in the sun.

Water dripped onto Dayn's head from a crack in the ceiling as he inspected the nearest skeleton. "What happened here?"

"Who cares?" Ryl walked around the dusty bones.

"I can't understand why Sharna sent me out here," the orishadaon wondered aloud as he peered through an adjacent archway. The light revealed a small, pungent smelling room with a low ceiling and more annaru writing on the walls. "What does all this," he threw out his arms to indicate the temple and its lifeless inhabitants, "have to do with finding my destiny?"

Ryl shrugged, splashing through a puddle as he walked. "Maybe yer destiny's in this temple somewhere?"

"Don't second guess the ancestors," Alis cut in. "They have a

31

path for all of us to follow. When it's your time, you'll know your destiny."

Dayn picked up a cracked skull. The brittle bones shattered into splinters the instant he tightened his grip. He froze as the sound echoed through the abandoned halls like a thunderclap, calming down only after all returned to silence. "The ancestors can keep my destiny."

Ryl casually stepped over a fallen column, unfazed by the jarring noise. "I don't think that's yer choice to make."

"It's my destiny and my life. I'll live it however I want."

"So you have completely ignored Sharna's teachings." Alis shook her head in disappointment, then brushed aside a strand of dark hair that had fallen across her face.

Ryl stopped at an intersection, his bare feet less than a pace from the skeleton of an annaru that had been ripped in half at the waist. "Which way does destiny lead us?" he grinned.

Alis leveled an intense glare at the larger man, forcing him to lower his head in shame. "That isn't funny."

Dayn looked yearningly over his shoulder, back the way they had come, to the way out. "Maybe we should go back, we don't want to get lost down here."

"No." Alis shook her head, slitted pupils narrowing as she turned to face Dayn and Agidyne's glow reflected off her eyes. "If we keep going we'll find something, I can feel it."

"I thought I was the only one here who could see the future," Dayn quipped.

Alis rolled her eyes. "Just pick a way."

Ryl decided for them, turning down the tunnel to their right without a second thought. They went left at the next junction. "Right, left," he said, keeping track of their progress. After half a dozen more twists in the dank, unknowably old tunnel, Ryl's memory began to wane. "Right, left, left, right, left, right, no wait, left, uh . . ."

"You mean left and then right," Dayn corrected with a sly grin.

"How do you do that?" Alis wondered curiously as Ryl tried to recite what Dayn had just said.

"It's all in here." He pointed to his skull. "I was born with a good memory." The memory of an orishadaon, he added silently.

Sharna trained him to master his memory through dozens of mental tests, many of which involved remembering a long sequence of words, such as, in this case, directions.

"Maybe Sharna's teachings aren't completely wasted on you after all," Alis commented.

They passed through a circular archway and Dayn nearly crashed into Ryl as his friend came to an abrupt halt. "What is it?" Dayn leaned around Ryl's massive frame for a better look.

The room ahead lay in chaos.

Six meticulously carved statues, now nothing but piles of shattered stone, were set into the walls of the circular room. A massive slab of cracked obsidian sat in the chamber's center, serving as a table of sorts. A human skeleton lay across it, impaled through its tattered ribs by a well-placed spear. The dusty bones of a single annaru slumped against the table's base, clawed fingers still clutching the wooden haft of the spear.

"By the blood of my ancestors!" Dayn gasped.

"I know," Ryl agreed in a hushed whisper.

Alis surveyed the scene without expression.

Dayn was mortified. In seasons past, the scaled ones waged a bloody war against humankind, a war which led to his people becoming little more than slaves to the annaru. Later, the descendants of those slaves rebelled, bringing down the annaru empire to give humanity a chance at survival.

His jaw tightened as he glared at the lifeless annaru bones. "What happened here?"

"Something terrible," Ryl offered, his explanation vague. He reached out and dragged a finger across the dusty obsidian slab, revealing the black, oily surface beneath. "A long time ago," he added, wiping the thick coat of dust from his finger.

"The annaru are monsters." Dayn angrily snatched the spear from the deceased creature's claws. "They're all monsters." He snapped the brittle weapon over his knee and tossed the pieces away.

The annaru continued to stare up at him mockingly through its empty eye sockets.

He stalked towards the skeleton and gave it a mighty kick, scattering the bones about the chamber. "You kill our tribes! Our people!" He vented his frustration by shattering the ribcage with another kick. "You tried to kill us!" The annaru's skull landed with a heavy *thunk* beside the obsidian slab, but remarkably it did not break.

Dayn lifted his foot to crush it into oblivion, but Alis halted him. "Let it go," she advised, placing a calming hand on his shoulder. "These bones aren't worth the effort."

The corner of Dayn's eye twitched. He summoned all the willpower he possessed to restrain himself. Anger welled up within him like a massive, red wave about to crash down and smother his senses. He had to suppress the hate. If he let his emotions take control, the raging energies within his soul would overpower him. He couldn't allow another breach in his mental barriers, especially not when other people were close enough to be caught in the backlash.

Ryl took a step back. "Maybe we should be movin'."

The orishadaon couldn't blame him for his caution. Of course, if he did lose control of his powers, as he had once before, in a place he dared not remember, Ryl was going to need more than a step to be safe from the blast.

Dayn took a deep breath and focused on calming his soul. He concentrated on the comfort of Alis' presence and the weapon in his hand.

For some strange reason he recalled his father, a tall, muscle-bound hunter with strapping shoulders and a barrel chest. The three red slashes of the Swift Claw were tattooed on his bald scalp, in much the same manner as Ryl's. It was customary for all hunters to shave their heads and be marked there, to set their caste apart from the rest of the tribe.

"Your first duty is to protect the tribe," his father had told him on many occasions. "Never do anything that might bring harm to your people. You and your brother must use your gifts to help your people. It won't always be easy, but you must be strong enough for everyone."

He had endeavored to be strong every lunar of his life, to live up to his father's expectations, especially at times like these. It took all his willpower to prevail, but he refused to let the inexorable tide of fury and blood red emotion drown his senses as it had once before, when he had given up control and let the rage course through him. With a supreme effort, he fought down the upwelling of anger, banishing it to the deepest part of his soul.

Alis gave his sagging shoulder a final squeeze of reassurance before letting him go. "You've learned some self-control," she said.

Dayn might have been mistaken, but he thought he detected a hint of admiration in her voice.

"What are we gonna' do?" Ryl wondered aloud.

Dayn sighed wearily and sat on the edge of the obsidian slab, keeping as far away from the skeletons as possible. "We have to find a way out of here," he said after the last hints of the red tide drained away.

Ryl inspected a nearby statue, brushing aside a pile of rubble with his foot.

"There has to be an exit somewhere," Alis agreed.

Dayn didn't want to spend another minute in this chamber with the scattered remnants of the annaru skeleton; too many restless spirits resided here. The claustrophobic confines of the temple blocked him off from the open sky and the light of the sun, and he could stand it no longer. To him, this forsaken place felt like a tomb.

"Ya sure yer up for this?" Ryl's thick brow furrowed with concern. "Yer not lookin' any better than before."

"Don't coddle him," Alis chided. "He'll be fine, he always is."

Dayn waved off Ryl's concern. "She's right, we don't have time to wait for me to get better." He rose and moved purposefully towards the next room, showing them both that he could manage well enough to get by.

Alis nudged him with her elbow. "You never give up do you?" They were just about to leave when she motioned for quiet. "Wait." She cocked her head to the side as she had when first entering the tunnels. "What's that sound?"

"What sound?" Dayn and Ryl asked in unison.

"I don't hear anythin' but wind," Ryl said.

"It's like . . . I don't know . . . whispering."

"Whispering?" Dayn asked incredulously. "All I hear is the wind."

"No, not wind," she insisted, looking around. "I keep hearing it, and it's coming from that way." She started towards a passage across the room.

35

Dayn grabbed her by the arm before she could get through the archway. "You're just going to wander off down some dark tunnel because you think you hear something?"

"I *know* I hear something," Alis replied, pulling her arm from Dayn's grasp.

6.
FOLLOW

"That's exactly why we shouldn't go that way," Dayn interjected. "If something down here is still making noise I don't want to run into it."

"Ya know, he's got a point."

Ryl's remark served only to infuriate Alis, and encouraged her to go off on her own.

Dayn chased after the scout, sidestepping a puddle of rank water and frowning in disgust when he brushed against a trickle of slime on the wall.

She led him down one twisting corridor after another until even his trained orishadaon memory had difficulty remembering where he was.

They passed into sections of tunnel that were more ravaged than elsewhere in the catacombs. Time and a fierce battle had reduced the once grand architecture to a warren of tunnels that ended in collapses, branched at seemingly random intervals, twisted back on themselves, or stretched endlessly into the depths of the earth. Headless annaru corpses littered the winding corridors, left to rot beside other, less recognizable *things*.

One such thing was a bulky, eight-pace tall horror with a ridge of bony protrusions growing from its spine. Next to it laid a skeleton with long, dangling arms that would have dragged across the ground when it walked. Another had walked on all fours like a horn-face, its mouth many times too large for its head. There were others, some exotic and others almost plain. All of the infernal beings were hideous, possessing vaguely human features twisted into monstrous visages.

While Ryl stumbled along in stupefied silence, Dayn's mind struggled to comprehend all of what it took in. Alis, however, pressed ever onward, oblivious to each new scene of carnage as she deftly navigated through the labyrinthine network of tunnels.

"Is the sound getting any closer?" Dayn wanted to know. "Because if it isn't, I think we should go back."

"She's not even listenin' to ya anymore."

"It's louder up ahead," Alis answered Dayn's question, likely just to prove Ryl wrong. "Just a bit further."

Dayn regretted ever descending into this accursed place. He tried listening for the sound Alis was so intent on finding. There was the ever-present wind howling through the halls, and the *drip drip drip* of water from the ceiling, but no whispering, which made him worry more than if he had heard it.

"Can we turn back yet?" he asked, trying again to convince Alis of her folly.

"It's louder up ahead."

Dayn cursed under his breath.

Ryl looked about uneasily. "Comin' down here was yer idea ya know."

Dayn's head ached. The swelling around his knee made walking difficult, and he regretted not resting more before leaving the upper reaches of the temple.

The obsessive scout turned at the next bend and went down a short side-corridor before stopping beneath a massive obsidian archway almost twice her height. Grotesque heaps of annaru skulls were piled on either side of the arches.

"By the blood of my ancestors," Dayn gagged.

"It's so close, just in there." It came as no surprise when Alis pointed through the archway. "I just want to take a look," she pleaded. "I think I spotted some stairs back the way we came, let me see what's in here and we can get out of this place for good."

Ryl puffed out his chest indignantly. "Why didn't ya say somethin' earlier if ya saw a way out?"

His tone caused Alis' slitted pupils to narrow threateningly. "Because I knew I'd never get to find out what's making that sound if I did," she replied with forced calm.

The big man turned his tattooed head to Dayn, who shrugged.

There was something horrible on the other side of those arches, something that bristled the hair on the back of his neck and sent shivers up his spine, something that clenched his guts with icy fingers and held on tight. He could feel the wrongness of it. "Alis . . ."

"Dayn!" she said with such force that he knew she would go in, with or without him.

"All right, but we're leaving as soon as we're done here." He made sure Alis agreed before letting anyone step through the arch yawning open before them like a hungry mouth.

He pinched his nose shut when the reek of countless corpses assailed his nostrils. Annaru skeletons, all headless but otherwise unscathed by the catastrophe that had felled them, surrounded a six-sided platform at the center of a massive room.

Bizarre swirling patterns that matched Dayn's orishadaon brands covered the walls and what he could see of the floor. He craned his neck to take in the vaulted ceiling and rib-like columns that connected to a giant 'spine' far above him. It gave the impression of being inside a karda's stomach.

Curiously, no sign remained of the annaru's demonic attackers.

Alis waded through the sea of tangled bodies towards a short set of stairs chiseled into one side of the hexagonal platform. Ryl followed, leaving Dayn alone at the entrance.

"Wait," he called in a hushed voice, carefully limping his way through piles of yellowed bone, every step sending a jolt of pain radiating up his side.

Strange energy infused the entire chamber. It caused a sensation similar to when he was around other orishadai users, yet not quite the same. This energy was more . . . sinister, filled with undeniable malice.

Dayn climbed to the top of the platform where a circle of sneering statues waited. Agidyne's light flickered briefly, twisting the statues' shadows, making them dance and jump as if they were alive.

Sprawled out across the very center of the raised platform was a towering skeleton seven paces tall. It looked like the partially preserved form of—Dayn couldn't believe what he was seeing—a hybrid of human and karda anatomy. Scaly skin gave way to leathery hide, and the human lips had long since withered away, revealing still gleaming rows of needle-like teeth inside a bony, misshapen maw. The hybrid held a giant, curving sword in one skeletal claw and clutched a battle-scarred gauntlet in the other. The gauntlet was made of blood red metal, with a ruby the size of a clenched fist fixed into its back.

Dayn could only guess at the hybrid's importance to whatever had killed the gathered annaru.

Alis nodded absently, transfixed by the dead warrior and the gauntlet it carried. "This is amazing," she whispered and stepped closer. "We have to bring that back to Toran, he'll want it."

"Is your brain sun-baked?" Dayn snapped at her, but Alis wasn't paying attention. She reached out and placed a reverent hand on the gauntlet. "Don't touch that!"

Ryl stepped over a headless corpse and moved to her side for a better look. Alis gently slid the artifact from the hybrid's grasp.

Dayn sucked in a tense breath, waiting for something horrible to happen. This was Kor's temple, and the vengeful god's spirit would surely strike them down or visit some horrible curse upon them for touching the artifact. "We can't take that thing," he told her in a barely audible whisper.

"Just look at it," Alis said, lust glittering in her reptilian eyes as she held the gemstone near the light.

A chill ran up the orishadaon's spine and he glanced over his shoulder, half-expecting the annaru to rise from their resting places in protest of her actions. Disturbing an object of such power, especially one found in a place like this, was foolishness. Why couldn't she see that?

"It's too dangerous," Ryl warned.

"If it's as *dangerous* as you two say, we can't leave it here for the annaru to find," Alis countered.

"What good will that cursed thing do for you?" Dayn's shrill voice echoed off the walls of the chamber and carried down the temple's eroded halls.

"We have to take it with us." She absolutely refused to relent. Her amber eyes never left the shining ruby.

"What's wrong with ya? Put that back."

Dayn's skin prickled and he shuddered as the temperature seemed to plummet. Why was Alis so entranced by that awful thing? It didn't matter, because he wasn't about to invoke the wrath of Kor by letting her steal from the dead god's shrine.

Ryl reached for the gauntlet.

Alis quickly pulled it away from him. "It's mine, and we aren't leaving without it," she insisted, holding the gauntlet up for them to see.

"We have to go," Dayn said. "Now." A preternatural silence settled throughout the catacombs and his words came out louder than intended. A gust of wind whistled through the abandoned halls. The stony eyes of the statues were all fixed on Alis, attentively watching the scene unfold.

"Just listen to me for once," Dayn begged, spinning in a slow circle to face each of the six glowering statues that ringed the platform. They looked almost alive, guardians frozen in time to watch over this place and its relic. He reached for the gauntlet but Alis easily avoided him.

"What harm can it do?" she asked innocently. "Look, it even fits me." She slipped the gauntlet on.

"Alis, no!" Dayn cursed himself for allowing things to continue this long. "Get rid of the gauntlet now."

Her eyes lit up greedily as she stroked the ruby. "What are you both so worried about? It's just a dusty old gauntlet."

Dayn's patience was nearing its end.

Metal was unnatural, created using techniques stolen from the annaru long ago and lost hundreds of cycles before anyone alive in this chamber was born. It had the power to steal a tribesman's soul, unless that tribesman happened to be an orishadaon with the strength and willpower to protect himself against such a fate.

What Alis did was a sacrilege. Metal violated the natural world. If the Swift Claw tribe ever found out she had put the gauntlet on willingly they would execute her in a most painful way.

"It feels like it was made for me," she added absent-mindedly, turning her hand over and flexing her fingers.

Ryl threw up his hands in exasperation. "What are we gonna' do?"

"Damn it!" Dayn cried, fed up. "Get it off your arm now!"

Alis' faraway look vanished. "Oh, all right." She gripped the gauntlet. "I'll take it off, but I'm still bringing it back with me."

Dayn groaned.

She paid him no mind as she gave the gauntlet a slight tug. It didn't move. She tried again, but it remained stuck. "It won't come off." She pulled harder. Gripping the artifact around the wrist, she heaved with all her might. Muscles bulged and a vein in her forehead throbbed, yet she couldn't remove the thing. "It won't come off!"

Dayn moved to help her. "You must be doing it wrong."

Ryl laughed. "Whadda' ya mean 'doin' it wrong?' It's a gauntlet, there's only one way to take it off."

"This isn't funny!" Alis growled, trying again to remove the artifact.

"Let me see." Dayn took hold of her wrist and tried to work his fingers beneath the metal. The instant he touched the gauntlet his psychic alarm went wild.

"Behind ya!" Ryl called a late warning.

Alis suddenly yanked her hand from his grasp. He noticed Ryl and her looking past him with their mouths agape as the klaxon in his head continued to howl.

A tall silhouette appeared at the corner of Dayn's vision. Even as he lurched away from it, something hard and heavy slammed into him from behind, pitching him forward. He hit the ground hard, his world momentarily disappearing in flashes of light and pain.

"Dayn!" both his companions hollered as one.

All thoughts of the gauntlet forgotten, Alis was instantly at his side, frantically pulling on his arm. "Get up," she demanded, grabbing him around the waist and hoisting him to his feet.

"What hit me?" Dayn rasped through clenched teeth.

Ryl hefted his spear and jabbed at something beyond the orishadaon's line of sight. "Get him out," he said to Alis, ignoring the question.

Alis released her grip on Dayn's waist and pushed him towards the exit.

He stumbled forward on wobbly legs, shaking his head to clear the fog-shrouded thoughts from his mind. It was then that he saw his assailant for the first time, and froze in unblinking horror.

7.
RISE INSIDE

The corpse of the hybrid monstrosity was on its feet, alive and standing across from Ryl, deflecting jabs from the hunter's spear with the flat side of its curving blade. Dayn's mind failed to comprehend what his eyes saw. It refused to believe it.

Stiff vertebrae grated against one another as the aberration twisted its neck and fixed Dayn in its lifeless gaze. Dust wafted from long undisturbed bones as it pointed a desiccated arm in his direction. "You are not worthy of the gauntlet's power," it rasped, ignoring a stab from Ryl's spear that shattered one of its ribs.

Dayn's sensibilities wouldn't accept that the thing was truly alive. How could it be? He remained rooted to the spot, unable to move, staring in awe and horror. Points of light burning inside the monster's hollow eye sockets held him in place more firmly than any physical grip ever could.

A booming voice broke through his disbelief. "Move!" Ryl shoved him hard enough to snap Dayn out of his stupor.

His willpower returned, the orishadaon scrambled backwards, narrowly avoiding a blow from the monster's blade. Chips of shattered stone flew into the air as the heavy sword struck the spot where he had been standing only an eye blink before.

"We have to get out of here!" Dayn backpedaled, frantically ducking a vicious slash that ruffled his unkempt hair. The hybrid followed him step for step, wispy cords of smoke rising from its empty eyes as the sword rose for another strike. It lashed out again

44

and this time the blade bit into his forearm. Dayn pressed his hand against the wound, blood seeping between his fingers, and stumbled away on the verge of panic.

"Are ya goin' or not?" Ryl interposed himself between the two combatants, using his own considerable bulk to block the creature's advance. Big as he was, Ryl looked insignificant before the towering form of the hybrid.

Alis tore a flimsy bone dagger from its sheath near her foot and slipped behind the creature, looking for a weakness to exploit.

Dayn raised Agidyne to defend himself. "You two aren't dying for me."

"Let's hope it doesn't come to that," Ryl said as he jabbed at the monster's snarling face. It easily turned the blow aside and countered by striking him with a balled fist. That single hit drove Ryl to his knees, forcing the air from his lungs in a loud *whuff*. The undead thing stepped around the hunter and made straight for Dayn, whose sweat-slick palm tightened around Agidyne.

"Stay away from him!" Alis darted forward, swinging her dagger in a wide arc to keep the monster at bay.

"Alis, no!" Dayn screamed. He pointed his blade at the hybrid's face and reached deep within his soul, calling on reserves of orishadai he didn't know he possessed. Despite the fear in his heart, he held his ground long enough to draw out the necessary soul energy. The task proved incredibly difficult. Orishadai needed time to replenish itself naturally after each expenditure, time he didn't have.

Still gasping for breath, Ryl recovered his senses and jumped to his feet in time to take another wild stab at the gauntlet's guardian before it reached Dayn. This time the aberration caught the spear in its clawed hand and yanked it from Ryl's grasp, tossing the weapon aside with apparent disgust.

Seeing an opening, Alis shot forward and buried her dagger in the creature's knee, snapping the blade off in the process. The guardian hardly noticed as it raised its own weapon, ready to cut the orishadaon in half.

The blow never came.

Dayn went deep inside himself to dredge up enough orishadai for his purposes. "Out of the way, Ryl!" he warned, pulling Alis to his side.

All his raging soul energy focused itself into pure, destructive force. Miniature arcs of lightning danced across Agidyne as the air between his sword tip and the monster shimmered. A wave of blinding blue light ripped through the aberration with the force of a charging horn-face, eliciting an ear-splitting scream that reverberated throughout the temple as the thing's body blew apart.

It exploded in a hailstorm of shattered bone fragments. Dayn wrapped an arm around Alis and fell to the floor on top of her, using his own body to shield her from the worst of the skeletal shrapnel. A few stray shards nicked her arms and legs, though he fared much worse, with dozens of bone slivers embedding themselves in his exposed flesh.

When the dust eventually cleared, he looked down at Alis to see if she was alright.

"Thanks," she said gratefully.

"I'm an orishadaon. It's my duty to protect you."

She grinned when he didn't move. "Does your duty include letting me up?"

"Oh." He got to his feet and offered her a hand. "Sure."

She refused the hand and got up on her own, dusting off her Swift Claw tattoo while taking in the destruction. "I'm impressed."

"That was amazin'!" Ryl beamed, a wide grin splitting his face. He ran a hand over his bald head and yanked out a sliver of bone. "I never seen ya do nothin' like that before."

Blood dribbled from Dayn's nose and across his chin, a common occurrence after expending orishadai. "I think I'm going to be sick," he gagged, putting a hand over his mouth and another around his stomach. Heat coursed through his veins as he fought back the red tide seeping through cracks in his slowly dissolving mental barriers. Certain risks came with using his powers, and he had taken a great gamble just now.

"Ya gonna' be alright?"

Dayn breathed heavily, wiping sweat from his brow as he leaned against a statue for support. He couldn't keep doing this to himself, the harder he pushed the greater the toll his powers exacted from him.

"Dayn?" Alis implored when he didn't answer Ryl's question.

The orishadaon waved away their concern, too tired to speak.

A gust of warmth blew through the chamber, and Dayn felt

cheated by the lack of cool air. The wind picked up. It started as a gentle breeze, but before long a blistering gale blew through the catacombs, bringing the whispers of innumerable voices with it.

Ryl retrieved his spear while Dayn hunched near Alis, feeling utterly drained.

The shadows at the edge of Agidyne's dimming light grew thicker and darker, writhing like a living thing in agony. Dayn waved the sword left to right, momentarily driving the darkness away. Shadows soon returned, pressing against the edge of the light. He didn't have the orishadai to strengthen the weapon's glow.

"I think we should leave," Alis said, cautiously backing off the platform and towards the archway.

"For once I agree with ya." Ryl backed up beside her, warily eyeing the darkness to either side of the arches.

Shadows suddenly poured from every recess, a tidal wave of living, squirming blackness that spilled into the room, enveloping the annaru bones and their statues.

Dayn nearly tripped over his own feet in his hurry to escape the onrushing tide. The three of them turned in unison and ran.

8.
SACRIFICE

Dayn realized almost immediately that he was in trouble. Limping on his aching knee, he had already fallen behind by the time they reached the first corner, and as he stared down a new, seemingly endless hall, he came to understand that he had little chance of outrunning the shadows.

"Where are we? Which way?" Ryl frantically searched for anything that looked familiar.

Dayn urged him forward. "I don't know. Keep going."

Alis suddenly let out a cry of pain and gripped the gauntlet. She staggered into a wall, squeezing her wrist as if she meant to tear off her hand and the gauntlet with it. "It burns like fire," she hissed between clenched teeth as her face contorted into a mask of pain.

"Sorry, girl, but we can't slow down." Ryl pulled her along by the elbow. "Ya have to keep movin'." The darkness crept closer with every waster moment. "Which way?" he asked as the corridor ahead branched left and right.

Dayn grabbed Alis by the shoulders and looked her in the eyes. "You said you saw a way out. Which way?"

"Left?" Ryl asked uncertainly.

"Right," Alis corrected, still clawing at her wrist in desperation.

"I'll help her, you lead the way," Dayn said.

"I don't need your help," Alis said between sharp intakes of breath. She pushed herself away from him and took two steps before collapsing into his arms. "Well, maybe a little help," she admitted, grinning in spite of the pain.

Dayn slung an arm around Alis. "Hurry, Ryl."

The shadows coiled around one another, lashing out in anticipation as they squirmed down the corridor. Dayn felt like he was trapped in another nightmare as he dragged Alis' struggling form along the bleak passageway.

"My hand feels like it's on fire," she said through gritted teeth.

Dayn tried to remember what Sharna had told him when his ribs were broken by his brother during their duel. "Don't think about the pain," he recited. "Focus on something in front of you, push the pain to the back of your mind and—"

"This isn't one of your lessons," she cut him off, realizing what he was trying to do. Her voice sounded harsh, the words forced out with great difficulty. "I'm not an orishadaon, I can't will the pain away." Her arm shook violently, the gauntlet's ruby emanating a harsh red light that seemed to draw the shadows to it rather than drive them away.

"Ryl," Dayn called ahead, "we have to find that way out."

"Whadda ya think I'm tryin' to do?" the big man shouted back, turning his head from side to side at the next intersection.

Alis cried out and quickly pulled her free hand away from the gauntleted wrist. Dark red lines wriggled beneath her flesh like worms, spreading outward from the relic. At the sight of them, she let out an anguished wail.

"Just go right!" Dayn shouted in agitation, trying to stop the woman in his arms from tearing her hand off. "Think about the savanna Alis. You remember the blue sky and waving grass. Think about that," he instructed.

The red lines crawled all the way to her elbow and showed no signs of stopping there.

She's dying, Dayn thought to himself in horror as his knee began to buckle from the stress of carrying her.

The shadows at his back surged forward, pressing against Agidyne's weak light, threatening to drown it out.

With his knee sending spurts of fire up his leg, Dayn bit down hard on his lip to occupy his mind with another pain. Alis' flesh burned hotter than fiery coals as the marks made their way up her arm and across her shoulder, wasting no time before they invaded her neck and the side of her face.

Ryl rounded the next corner and let out an excited cry. "I think I found somethin'!"

"Fight it," Dayn whispered in Alis' ear. "Whatever it is, you can beat it."

"Hurry," the hunter called.

"We're coming!"

The heat of Alis' body seared his flesh, but he refused to let go. He would get her out of this place even if he had to die to make it happen.

Once around the corner Dayn found Ryl standing before a staircase much like the one they had used to get into the catacombs.

He tried to show it to Alis, but she did not respond. Her body was dead-weight in his arms. She could not stand under her own power, much less climb a flight of stairs, and he was in no condition to carry her. Ryl would have to take her, but he couldn't drag them both.

"Damn."

"What is it?" The hunter was busy trying to usher him onto the stairs.

"Take Alis and go. I can't make it with my knee and I'd just slow the two of you down."

Understanding dawned on Ryl's face as Dayn shrugged Alis' arm from his shoulder and handed her to him.

The hunter ran a nervous hand across his necklace of trinkets. "I guess this is it, then." He turned his back on Dayn and Alis, walked into the center of the corridor, and squared his shoulders. He flicked a speck of dust from the tip of his spear and glared defiantly at the tide of darkness breaking against the dim light.

"What in the Aether are you doing?!" Dayn grabbed his friend by the arm. "Get her out of here!"

Ryl grinned sadly and shook his head, causing the bones on his necklace to rattle together. "I'll give this thing a fight and buy ya some time."

"No," Dayn refused flatly. "It's not supposed to be like this, you have to go."

"I've chosen my fate." Ryl replaced Alis' arm around Dayn's shoulder. "Get her outta' here and be safe. Ya deserve each other."

Dayn remained at his friend's side. "You don't have to do this."

"Go on." Ryl nudged him in the chest with the butt of his spear. "And take this with ya, I won't be needin' it." He handed the orishadaon his belt, the vial of healing water sloshing around inside one of its many pouches.

"I'm supposed to protect *you*," Dayn's voice quivered.

"Protect her now, that's yer new duty."

"I can't do this," Dayn mumbled. The backs of his heels brushed against the lowest step. There had to be another way he told himself as his feet went up to the second. He had to do something, his mind screamed as he saw the darkness writhe at the edge of Agidyne's light. His feet were on the third step. Ryl raised his weapon and Dayn was on the fourth step. No, no, no! was all his weary mind thought as he turned and ran, casting a last glance at Ryl's back as his friend let out a roar and rushed beyond the reach of the light.

Dayn's head spun. His knee felt like it was going to explode. What was happening? He couldn't remember where he was. There was shouting from behind him, shouts of challenge from a deep and confident voice that Dayn recognized. It wasn't long before the confident shouts turned to bloodcurdling screams. Pain-filled, horrible, gurgling screams that tore at Dayn's heart and shredded his sanity. One thought eventually cut through his growing madness, embedding itself in the forefront of his mind with utmost clarity.

Ryl was dying.

Alis cried out in his arms as the gauntlet's probing tendrils sank into her flesh and slowly disappeared from view. She screamed the same terrible scream that echoed up the stairwell behind him. The pain-wracked cries surrounded him, enveloped him.

"Alis," he rasped. He had to get her out of here. Ryl's sacrifice would not be in vain. Resolve burned in his heart, lending strength to his weary body. He plodded drunkenly up the stairs, ignoring every bit of his own pain as he dragged Alis to safety.

What seemed like an eternity of agony later, he finally reached the top and came out in a narrow room, only to find the exit blocked by a massive slab of black obsidian.

"No!" Dayn furiously pounded the black rock. He beat his fist against it until his hand left bloody knuckle-prints against the stone, and still he pounded. Ryl wasn't supposed to die. *Whack*. Alis had to live. *Whack*. He wasn't supposed to fail them. *Crunch*. The bones in his hand gave out before the stone.

His shoulders sagged and he slumped to the floor, dragging Alis down with him.

"So close," he wheezed, laying his broken hand on her pale arm.

Dayn looked mournfully from Alis to the staircase. The thing that had murdered Ryl would be here soon, and he had no doubts about what it would do when it found them.

Was that the fate the ancestors had chosen for him, to be torn apart by a nightmarish horror? To the Aether with the ancestors then, he would make his own fate.

Dayn rose shakily, focusing on the stone slab that blocked his path. With one bloody hand against the obsidian, he pushed using all the strength he possessed.

Alis' head lolled to the side as the last bit of life left her body.

He let the sword fall from his grasp and placed his other hand on the slab, grunting with exertion as he heaved on the mighty block. It didn't move.

Agidyne's light faded, plunging him into darkness.

Determined to succeed, he pried into the depths of his soul, beyond his mental barriers to a dark and primal place he had only touched once before, to catastrophic effect.

He probed to the core of his being, the very center where his life-force dwelled, and opened the red tide's prison. It bubbled up to lend him strength, eagerly consuming part of his soul to fuel its efforts.

With the forbidden power swelling inside him he was stronger than before, stronger than any human. The full force of its fury coursed through him. Spidery cracks radiated across the obsidian surface from beneath his palms. His heart shuddered violently within his chest, skipping a beat when he felt the slab move. He planted his feet firmly against the ground and pushed again, allowing the tide to do irreparable damage to his soul in order to draw on more of its power. A sliver of moonlight spilled into the room.

Alis gasped.

Stone grated across stone as Dayn forced open a space between the slab and the wall just large enough to squeeze through. He gave the obsidian one final push and something in his leg popped.

Harsh whispers rose from the stairwell, their low, sinister sound reminding Dayn that he had to hurry. He tugged Alis towards the column of moonlight, pushing them both along with his one good leg.

Its hunger sated, at least for a while, the red tide receded, leaving him feeling cold and empty in its wake.

Shadowy tentacles rose out of the stairwell.

"No demon will ever take her from me," Dayn told them, and unceremoniously shoved Alis outside.

The shadows shot towards him instead.

With the tentacles lashing at his back, Dayn grasped Agidyne in one hand, Ryl's belt in the other, and rolled through the opening onto a patch of damp earth in a moonlit clearing.

The tentacles reached the edge of the darkness and froze, refusing to enter the moonlight. They writhed angrily for a time before withdrawing into the darkness, letting out a terrible roar that erupted from deep underground. The earth shaking cry faded to a dull echo that was quickly drowned out by the croaks of frogs and the chirps of insects.

Dayn was more than a little surprised to find himself lying outside the gaping mouth of the same blade-nose monument he had bumped into earlier that lunar.

Too weak to move, he lay still and stared up at the stars. They were pinpoints of light in the tapestry of the sky, each one the soul of a fallen ancestor. When he died, his soul would rise up into the night sky to be one with his tribesmen for all time, assuming there was anything left of his soul by then.

Two great orbs of light shared the sky with the stars, one white, the other bright emerald. These spheres were the remaining moons, and they shed their combined glow across the dreadful jungle.

A shimmering blue light traced its way over Dayn's inert form and he found his gaze drawn to an azure haze that split the heavens in two. This was Vernac, the former third moon, shattered by Kor long ago. The act, and the cataclysmic rain of skyfire that followed, nearly destroyed the human race. All that was left of Vernac now was a thin chain of blue dots spread amongst the stars in a long, broken line. Despite its destruction, the shattered moon still lit the night with its intensity.

Dayn slapped a handful of clinging mud across the bloody slice in his forearm and his throbbing forehead, then reached up to staunch the flow from his nose. "Alis?" he croaked.

She lay on her back a few paces away, open-eyed and unblinking.

"Alis, are you all right?"

Her blank expression was directed at the gauntlet.

"Alis," he called her name again. "Alis!"

She blinked as if she had just noticed him. "What?"

A crushing weight seemed to lift off Dayn's chest. He breathed a shuddering sigh of relief. "Are you well?"

She looked confused. "Well? Yes."

"What's wrong?"

"Wrong?" A wide grin split her face. "Nothing is wrong. I've never felt better."

9.
AN OATH ONCE TAKEN

He crawled towards her, pulling himself along with great difficulty using only his uninjured arm. As he neared the spot where she lay, the scout suddenly rose on steady legs and headed towards the edge of the clearing.

"Come," she said briskly, "we need to be away."

Dayn stared up at her in startled silence. A moment ago she was on the verge of death, but now she appeared perfectly fine.

Alis halted her determined stride to turn and glare at him. "I'm not waiting. If you wish to stay . . . ?" She let the question hang in the air. After a moment she shrugged and marched towards the tree line.

He couldn't believe what he heard. She was behaving like a completely different person. Was this really happening? She was actually going to leave him here! "I can't walk," he called after her.

She did not slow her step. "Keep up or get left behind."

"Wait," he pleaded, pushing himself off the ground. It took everything he had just to stand upright, yet he could not stop there. He managed a shuddering step forward. An explosion of pain from his knee caused spots of light to dance in front of his eyes.

"Ryl's dead," he told her, gasping. She must have known, though she seemed not to care.

Through the haze of pain he saw Alis stepping into the trees. In mid-stride she wrapped the fingers of her gauntlet around a thick tree branch and effortlessly snapped it off. Stopping again to stare at him, Alis leaned on the branch as if it were a cane and smirked cruelly. "Are you coming or not?"

Not even a word for Ryl? Nothing?

"I can barely walk!" Dayn cried in frustration.

"Like Sharna says, the pain is in your head." Her reply was as cold as her demeanor.

"That's strange, because it really feels like it's in my knee!" Dayn angrily gestured to the swollen flesh.

Alis rolled her eyes. "You've had worse. Here." She offered the makeshift cane to him. Dayn snatched it out of the air. "You've wasted enough time already," she chided. "Now, let's go."

He stared, shocked at how uncaring she had become. What was the gauntlet doing to her? "After you," he said bitterly, swallowing a less courteous reply.

After entering the dense wall of foliage that ringed the clearing, the orishadaon could scarcely see two paces past his face. Only by following the dark outline of the scout against the backdrop of undergrowth could he navigate through the gloom at all. Alis' annaru heritage blessed her with the ability to see as well in the dark as in the light, and she used this ability to full effect, paying no attention to his obvious struggles.

Dayn's mind wandered, filled with thoughts of Ryl, death, destiny and everything in between, eventually settling on tattoos. He carried the same one as Alis, the three red slashes that marked them as members of the Swift Claw tribe, but he also bore the twisting brand of an orishadaon. He had endured many hardships, not the least of which was a duel with his brother, to acquire those marks, all in an effort to make himself stronger for the tribe.

That strength had done Ryl little good; the hunter was dead because of Dayn's failure to protect him. The swirling lines etched into his flesh served as a permanent reminder of that.

He continued to brood throughout the night and into the following morning. Alis pressed onward without rest until the sun soared above the treetops and baked the jungle with oppressive heat, and by then Dayn was too tired to waste further energy on brooding. He settled into a state of numb, empty-mindedness that allowed him to keep going on sheer willpower.

"Where are we going?" he eventually asked.

"Away."

"Back to Nesthome?"

Waves of shimmering humidity rippled the already foggy air, casting the jungle in a surreal light. Alis rested a hand on her hip and peered into the distance. "Be quiet. You're making too much noise."

Dayn had had just about enough of her reprimands. He was not a child on his first hunt; she had no right to speak to him that way.

"I can still hear you breathing," she said, kicking irritably at a fallen chunk of bark. "Quiet yourself."

Dayn stared at her in bewilderment. This was not the same Alis who had accompanied him into the catacombs. "What's happening to you?" he whispered, hoping that she would hear him, if only so that he might receive an answer.

The orishadaon took a drink of warm water from a pool that had collected in the center of a wide cycad leaf. He could have drunk from any of the Tresslevale's murky streams, but this way he didn't have to worry about leeches, snakes or flesh eating fish.

The scout mumbled to herself and picked up the pace, stalking off into the underbrush. She slipped through the cluttered vegetation effortlessly while Dayn found himself getting caught on every vine and dangling branch.

A jolt shot up his leg as it brushed against a fallen log, sending him stumbling into the nearest tree. He grabbed his knee and instantly pulled his hand back when pain lanced through it again.

"You look like the Aether itself," Alis commented, a hint of concern creeping into her voice. For the first time since they'd left the tunnels, a bit of the old Alis emerged.

"What do you care?" Dayn snapped.

"I care."

He thought he saw sympathy in her pitiless eyes. The orishadaon frowned, confused by her sudden change. "I'll be fine," he said cautiously. "It's really not that bad." He put weight on the leg to prove it and grimaced as his knee buckled under the pressure.

"Yes, it certainly isn't that bad," she assured him in a mocking tone. "Which is good, because we aren't stopping." Just like that, Alis was gone again.

"I need a moment," Dayn begged.

She shrugged, unconcerned.

The orishadaon leveled a resentful glare at her back as she walked away. At this rate, fatigue would claim him before any jungle creature had the chance.

Shortly thereafter, they came upon the spot where Dayn and Ryl had fought the first wave of the annaru war-pack. Carrion eaters and opportunistic karda had picked at the corpses, leaving little for the insects. Even so, in less than a lunar thousands of maggots, blood worms, and other less-wholesome creatures had infested the carcasses.

Dayn put a trembling hand on Agidyne's handle and looked away from the gruesome remains. This was his doing; the loss of life was his fault. There were strict rules prohibiting an orishadaon from taking a life, and even though annaru were not included in those rules he still regretted his actions. He had sworn to protect life at all costs, and he meant to do just that from this lunar on.

"Never again," he swore to himself.

Alis looked up from one of the corpses. "What are you mumbling?"

"I'll never let anyone die again. I swear on the blood of my ancestors that no one else will die because of me."

Alis' fit of laughter caught him by surprise. It took some time before she calmed down enough to explain herself. "You shouldn't make promises you can't keep," the scout chuckled, shaking her head.

Her callous reaction caused his anger to bubble up, threatening to bring the red tide with it. He breathed in and out, forcing himself to remain calm. "What are you talking about?"

"You'll see when we get back," she laughed, though Dayn did not understand why. "Let's go, we don't have time for this."

The orishadaon grabbed her by the wrist before she could get away. "What's going on?" he demanded. "Why are you in such a hurry?"

Alis tore her arm from his grasp and brushed past him. "The blade-nose is after us," she said, as if it were obvious.

Dayn sucked in a sharp breath at the mention of the creature. "How do you know that?"

The scout offered him a wicked smile by way of response.

"Stay here and find out," she challenged.

There was no way to know if she spoke lies or the truth, but when Alis turned to leave, Dayn followed.

10.
REVEL IN LOSS

The Swift Claw scout set a brutal pace for their trek. She trudged on for another lunar, never stopping, never slowing, and showing no sign of weariness.

Dayn, however, barely managed to keep pace with her. He shuffled forward on bloody, lacerated feet, leaving a pair of shallow furrows in the carpet of moss and dead leaves. His body swayed with every step, and he stumbled constantly, crashing through the underbrush like a drunken thunder-foot. Any child on his first hunt could follow the trail he left behind.

Once, he thought he heard the blade-nose roaring in the distance. The jungle played tricks on his mind, distorting sound, making it echo in unnatural ways. It was impossible to tell how far away the creature might be. After that he kept glancing over his shoulder, expecting to see the beast. When he didn't, he let out a sigh of relief, and then a moment later tensed up and checked again. He repeated the process in an endless cycle until his nerves were so jangled that he jumped at every sound, too delirious to separate reality from the fictions of his own paranoid mind.

Now and again, he paused briefly in his endless march to flip over a rotting log and snatch up some of the multi-legged creatures that scurried away, plopping their squirming, segmented forms into his mouth and chewing before he had a chance to be nauseated. Eating them was necessary for survival, he told himself, ignoring the sensation of tiny legs scrambling about beneath his tongue as he bit a centipede in half and swallowed it. He gagged only once, when one of the insect's half-chewed bits caught in his throat, and then proceeded to climb back up into his mouth. Dayn vomited, then immediately went back to eating more insects to replace the ones he had spit up. He would need all his energy for the journey ahead, and he couldn't afford to waste a single meal, no matter how vile.

At least there was no need to worry about the insects being poisonous, orishadaons were immune to most poisons. His body was capable of fighting off almost any naturally occurring toxin, because Sharna had subjected him, throughout his many seasons of training, to almost every toxin found in the natural world.

He trudged onward, ever onward, instinct guiding his footfalls. His perception of the world narrowed to encompass nothing more than the next spot his foot would land. Anything more was impossibly far away and entirely too much effort to think about.

It began to rain just after sunrise the next lunar, dark clouds blotting out what little sunlight filtered through the thick canopy of vegetation overhead. A heavy cascade of raindrops slapped against the leathery leaves in a deafening pitter-patter chorus. It let up shortly after it began, only to start again before nightfall.

The journey went on seemingly forever, with him plodding through the rain behind Alis. Lunar after lunar went by in this way. No sleep, no rest, just one foot in front of the other in endless repetition.

He had long since forgotten how many lunars the two of them had been on the move when Alis' seemingly inexhaustible stamina began to wane. As another night descended upon the jungle, this one blissfully dry, she called a halt to their steady march, stopping Dayn with a simple gesture from her gauntleted hand.

"We'll rest here," she informed him.

Without saying a word, Dayn collapsed into the dense carpet of rotting leaves that littered the jungle floor. There wasn't enough strength left in his weary limbs to carry him another pace. It mattered not that the spot he had landed upon was terribly uncomfortable, a knot of roots pressing against his side like a fist driven up through the earth. He curled into a ball and shut his eyes, falling immediately into fitful slumber.

Sleep brought no rest for the orishadaon, nor respite from the horrible memories that plagued his waking moments. He saw Ryl again, spiraling down into a gaping chasm of nothingness, reaching out, calling for help as he plummeted into oblivion. Dayn reached after him in futile desperation, forced to watch his friend disappear beneath a grasping wave of shadow, gone forever.

All at once Dayn's conscience shrieked and screamed, pleading for release from its torment, crying out against the injustices of his life and taunting him for his failures.

In that dark place he heard Ryl's accusatory voice and so many others clamoring to be heard, all shouting over one another for his attention. They always said the same things.

It's all your fault. I took you in, helped you, and this is how I was rewarded, blamed one, a woman whose blackened, skeletal face he quickly drove from his thoughts for fear of the dreadful memories it would conjure. Memories of that place so long ago, and so very far away, when he had first lost control.

I'm dead because of you charged another, this one a Swift Claw hunter lost to a crocodile when he strayed near a river during a hunt.

Why didn't ya save me? Ryl's voice echoed louder than the others.

There were many more; too many.

Only his parents remained quiet. They were there, somewhere in the back, silent as all the restless ghosts of his mind should have been, but they never intruded. His mother and father merely watched, content to see him suffer, apparently finding it unnecessary to cause him more pain.

"I did as you asked," he moaned, begging for forgiveness. "I've looked out for the tribe and I kept him safe. I kept my brother safe. That's what you wanted, isn't it? Isn't it?!"

His mind slipped seamlessly from dream to memory. The figures that formed before him were hazy at their edges, cloaked in an obscuring mist that made them difficult to focus on. They were clear enough for him to recognize them for what they were. This was the moment when everything had changed.

"I don't want to see this," he told the apparitions taking shape before him, to no avail.

His parents coalesced out of the mist, rushing by in a panic, taking no notice of his presence.

Dayn recoiled in horror, already knowing what came next. He couldn't close his eyes to shut it out, for it was all taking place in his mind and there was nothing he could do to spare himself the mental anguish of reliving this moment.

An annaru grew out of the mist, its form appearing almost demonic after residing for so long in the bowels of his memory. It tore into his mother, killing her. Dayn's father ran towards his mate, only to be hacked down from behind by a pair of scaled one apparitions. His brother's form coalesced upon the ground nearby, a saurian wrist blade rammed into his back. His brother remained alive, though the injury should have killed him. The orishadaon screamed in frustration, the sound creating a gale that wiped away the foggy scene and deposited him back in the Tresslevale.

He woke up panting. Dead leaves plastered themselves across the side of his sweat-drenched face.

A fire blazed before him, driving back the night. His eyes squinted in the sudden brightness. Heat given off by the crackling flames warmed his pale, shivering flesh. Embers fluttered into the still air, scattering like stars in the night sky before winking out one by one. Each star an ancestor, each ember a star . . . disappearing. Was it a portent or merely the musings of his demented mind?

Alis sat cross-legged across from him, the fire rising up between them. "Troubling dreams?" she asked, slitted eyes gazing directly into his. Her eyes, normally so bright and full of life, seemed to drink in the darkness.

"I saw my parents," he replied between gasps, struggling, somewhat unsuccessfully, to bring his breathing under control.

"Definitely troubling," she remarked, still glaring at him.

Dayn wriggled closer to the fire, basking in its warmth. It helped sooth his growing tension, if only a little.

"What are you looking at?" he asked, feeling self-conscious. Before she could answer, he quickly brushed his face clean of the dried leaves sticking to it.

After a decidedly uncomfortable length of time, Alis redirected her gaze to the sky without uttering a word.

"Fine," Dayn grumbled, closing his eyes to lean against a nearby stump.

He heard a rustling from across the fire. When he opened his eyes, Alis was on her feet.

"We're going?" he asked, rising shakily, his good hand on the rotted stump for support.

She waved her metal appendage at the darkness before her. "There are mountains out there," Alis told him without explaining the significance of her words.

The orishadaon frowned at the vague statement. "It's a valley; there are mountains all around us," he said irritably, surprised by the vehemence in his hoarse voice.

She seemed not to notice.

"We may yet reach the savanna in time," Alis said, her eyes unfocused. After a quick blink she was on the move, once again threatening to leave him behind if he did not keep pace.

With a weary sigh, he set out after her.

11.
HER VOICE RESIDES

He tried to focus his attention on something besides the constant pitter-patter of rain against the thicket of thorns above his head. Biting wind tousled his hair. A bolt of lightning lit the storm-wracked scrubland and he anxiously ducked beneath the cover of diminished brushwood.

"Keep low, we can't let it see us," Alis warned.

An insect crawled across Dayn's face and he swatted at it irritably, cursing when he hit the curtain of branches and sent a shower of thick, dewy droplets cascading down on himself. "Perfect," he grumbled, and put his arms up over his head to deflect the rain.

The open savanna and its waving stalks of yellowed grass were only a short run away, on the opposite side of a stretch of thorny scrub. If the blade-nose didn't have them pinned down they would already be home.

The pair of weary travelers reached the savanna's outskirts a lunar ago, but the karda had arrived shortly thereafter, and there was no way to move across the open grasslands without it catching them.

Spindly thorn bushes flailed like barbed whips in the howling wind and Dayn huddled closer to the ground to escape their lashing. His legs sank into a shallow mud hole and he cursed, pulling them free of the sucking mud and trying without success to clean them off. Why he bothered, he didn't know. Dried mud,

grime, and blood clung to him like a second skin, covering every
bit of his body. More muck hardly made a difference.

BOOM!

Deafening thunder shook the earth and drowned out the
shrieking wind. The shriek of the wind, so much like Ryl's last
high-pitched screams rising out of the darkened tunnels, made
Dayn cringe with guilt. Had it happened four lunars ago, or was it
five? Ten? It might have been a hundred, for all he knew.
Everything after escaping the temple was a blur.

"How long do we have to wait here?" he moaned.

Another flash of lightning illuminated his surroundings and he
craned his neck for a better look. No sign of the blade-nose
amongst the swaying thorn bushes.

"As long as it takes," Alis answered evenly. She whispered
something under her breath and after a pause, nodded as if
someone had answered. Not one hint of emotion passed across her
mud-streaked face to give away how she might be feeling. It took
Dayn a moment to realize she was squeezing her gauntlet-locked
wrist so hard her knuckles had turned white.

"Are you hurting?"

She quickly let go of her wrist. "I'm fine."

"You sure?"

"I told you I was fine."

"I'm just worried."

"Don't be."

The gauntlet had changed her in the lunars since fleeing the
tunnels, that much was obvious. Her mind was elsewhere and she
barely spoke, except to herself. Dayn frequently reminded himself
that she had been that way since putting on the artifact, but he
could see no way of removing it. They had already tried everything
short of hacking off her arm.

"Are you staring at me again?" the scout asked without ever
looking in his direction.

Boom!

He averted his eyes with the next clap of thunder. Of course
she had noticed him glaring, scouts were trained to be utterly
aware of their surroundings.

"It makes me nervous." She shifted uncomfortably.

With a sigh, Dayn tilted his head towards the storm clouds

darkening the sky and let the cool rain splash his face. He opened his mouth and gulped down the water, clearing his throat when he finished.

"Alis?" he called tentatively.

No response.

"Why do you hate me?"

Her amber eyes turned to regard him coldly.

"That's not what I meant to say." Dayn shrunk beneath her stern gaze. "What I mean is, why are you so angry with me?"

She rolled her eyes and patted his shoulder reassuringly. A bolt of lightning caught the reflective sheen of the gauntlet, glinting off the crimson metal. "I don't hate you, I just think you're reckless."

"Reckless?"

"And stubborn."

"Stubborn?" he frowned. "What do you mean by that?"

Her gaze was intense. It felt like a predator was sizing him up for a meal. He shuddered.

"Do you want to die?" The question hit him like a punch to the gut, driving the air out of his lungs.

"I don't—"

"Why do you keep putting yourself in danger?"

"I'm only—"

"Sooner or later you're going to get killed."

"I'm just trying to keep you safe," he blurted.

"You're more important to the tribe than I am, you should worry about keeping yourself safe."

And you're more important to me than the rest of the tribe combined, Dayn thought to himself. Ryl had died to protect her from that demon, and Dayn was not about to waste the sacrifice. "It's my duty to protect the Swift Claw tribe, and you're a Swift Claw."

A gust of wind sent Alis' dark hair flailing in all directions, a tangled mane surrounding her amused grin. "Let no one say you lack courage or honor, Dayn. Sense maybe, but courage and honor you have."

"I've sense enough to know I don't want to die." Dayn ran a hand through his own sopping hair and sighed. "I didn't want Ryl to die either."

"I know he was your friend, but you can't blame yourself for what happened."

Dayn lowered his head shamefully. It was all too easy to blame himself for Ryl's death. He could still hear the screams. He rested a shaking hand against his forehead and squeezed his eyes shut as he relived his friend's last moments for the hundredth time.

"Dayn?" Alis put her arm around him.

"I couldn't save him," he sobbed, breathing raggedly as images of a shadowy monstrosity slithered into his head and silenced the screams. Tentacles wrapped around his friend while tears of helplessness and guilt welled up in Dayn's eyes. Ryl's grim and blood-spattered face flickered before him and Dayn bolted upright, skewering himself on the canopy of thorns.

Alis hurriedly yanked him back down. "By the blood of the ancestors!" She brushed a strand of dripping hair away from her eyes. "This is exactly what I'm talking about. What if the blade-nose saw you? It could be after us now."

Dayn ignored her and punched the ground with a battered fist, ignoring the pain that radiated through the broken bones of his hand. "I couldn't save him."

"Stop hurting yourself." Alis grabbed him by the wrist before he could repeat the act.

He looked at her in the next flash of lightning, truly looked at her. After so long in the Tresselevale, her tanned skin had faded to sickly white, making her numerous cuts and scrapes stand out all the more. Strands of unkempt hair sprawled across the patches of scales on her shoulders, sweeping down her back as well as over her breasts. Tiny, emerald scales covered her shins and forearms as well, marking her annaru heritage.

"You're all I have left," he whispered to her.

Alis' amber eyes glowed like bright embers. "You care too much about me. The tribe comes first." He tried to argue, but she silenced him with a hand against his lips. "You said it yourself, your duty is to the Swift Claw people. The tribe comes first."

She deserved better than him. He was not strong enough to protect Ryl, what made him think he would be able to do better for her? "This is all my fault. Ryl . . . that thing on your hand, I . . . it's all my fault. I wasn't there for either of you."

"There you go again, taking the blame when it's not your fault." She gave him another pat on the shoulder. "I put this thing on myself, it isn't your fault I did it."

Dayn closed his eyes but could not escape the horrible images or the gut-wrenching screams. More screams, there were always more screams.

Alis smiled half-heartedly. "Remember when we were young, how I always wanted to hold Agidyne but Sharna would never let me? Remember when I took it and ran away?"

Dayn stared at her blankly. Where was she going with this?

"You knew it was me, but when Sharna asked you where it was, you said you lost it."

The orishadaon smiled knowingly.

"If anyone found out I'd taken metal, much less the orishadaon's sword, the punishment would have been worse than I can guess. I think Sharna knew it was me, but you never said anything."

"I knew you'd give it back."

"Is that why you let my father whip you ten times for losing a holy artifact?"

Dayn shook his head. "No, I let him do it because if he found out what really happened he would have killed you."

"Exactly. You're always taking the blame to stop others from getting hurt. You took the blame for something so you could spare me pain."

"I wouldn't be much of an orishadaon if I didn't."

"Well, you don't have to protect me from guilt Dayn. I can handle my own burden."

"But it's my duty," he argued.

"It all comes down to duty with you. You'd give your life for me and you don't even know why. Well forget your duty." She ran the back of her hand across his cheek. "Just do your best. That's all anyone expects. I don't blame you for what happened and neither would Ryl. He gave his life so you could live, not so you could wallow in guilt."

Dayn wanted to argue, he wanted to further condemn himself for abandoning Ryl to the shadow beast and for not being there when Alis needed him, but he couldn't find the words. The entire conversation led back to Ryl as if she planned it that way all along.

He was too transparent; she knew his responses before asking the questions. She was good. She was also smirking at him right now because she knew exactly what he was thinking, and he was thinking she was right.

"How do you do that?" He was still shaking, but not as much, and the screams were quieter now.

She winked at him. "Wouldn't you like to know?"

He wrapped his arms around her and she rested her head on his shoulder. "Thank you," he whispered.

The embrace lasted but a moment before a terrifying howl cut through the air and they pulled apart.

Boom!

Any sense of comfort shattered as the blade-nose repeated its chilling call.

The joints on the gauntlet *clinked* together as Alis clenched and unclenched her fist. She grunted in discomfort. When Dayn checked to see what was wrong she was gripping her wrist again, trying to staunch the advance of the red lines radiating up her arm. The color in her amber eyes faded to a dull glow.

"No." Dayn shook his head at the sight. "Not again, this can't happen to you again." Another presence stared out from behind her eyes, one that gave off a malevolent aura that he had not felt since the annaru temple.

Alis wiped the thick sheen of sweat from her brow and stuttered, "I . . . can't . . . stop him. It's coming, he's calling it."

Dayn's heart pounded in his chest. "Please, not again," he begged the ancestors. "Don't let this happen again."

"You . . . have to . . . run." She could barely speak through the pain. Her fingers trembled ever-so-slightly. She gritted her teeth, but the thing Dayn noticed most was the fear in her ever-widening eyes. There was nothing either of them could do to stop the lines as they twisted up Alis' arm.

"What do I do, Alis?"

"Get away from me!" she growled in a deep and grating voice that was not her own. Her shoulders sagged from the effort of her mental struggles and she started to turn away, but spun back and lashed out at Dayn without warning. Her balled fist connected with his temple and the resounding crack of metal against bone echoed in his head long after he crumpled to the ground. He rubbed the side of his face and glared up at her.

Her flesh bulged as the red lines skittered through the veins in her neck. "He's . . . in . . . my head." She spoke in her own voice this time, but doing so was obviously a struggle. "Please . . . run."

"I don't know what's going on, but I'm not leaving you out here. You're too important."

"I'm not important to the tribe!" she wailed in consternation.

"You're important to me!" Dayn got up just in time to catch Alis as the marks spider-webbed across the side of her face and her knees buckled.

"Make him stop," she whimpered and clawed feebly at the gauntlet, pounding the vermilion ruby when it began to glow. She flashed Dayn a final look of desperation and shuddered before her eyes rolled back in her head.

"Alis?!" Dayn shook her gently. "No. Don't die. I can't do this by myself; I need you." Her soft breath on his cheek alerted him to the fact that she was still alive. Whatever the purpose of those marks, they were not meant to kill her. He held her comatose form close and stared through the storm towards the savanna.

As if to taunt him, a bolt of lightning lit the sky and illuminated a towering shape moving amongst the distant scrub brush.

He scooped Alis up and, with little concern for himself, desperately pushed his way through the tangle of thorns. He fumbled with his sword in the tight confines of the scrub and almost dropped Alis. His hands, slippery from mud and rain, finally managed to grip the sword's hilt and pull it free. Weapon in hand, Dayn rabidly hacked his way through the spiky branches.

Alis convulsed, clawing bloody gouges into her wrist. She let out a scream that rivaled Ryl's final, pain-wracked cry. The hairs on the back of Dayn's neck stood on end when the blade-nose answered the call with a mournful bellow of its own.

With a final swing from Agidyne, he stumbled out of the brush into an endless sea of waving grass dotted by rocky outcroppings every few hundred paces. "Damn," he remarked, scanning his surroundings from left to right. "Which way is Nesthome?"

There was nothing to do but guess. A voice in his head, or maybe a vague memory, told him to go left. Dayn offered up a prayer to the ancestors, asking them to spare Alis from whatever evil curse had befallen her, and stumbled out of the cover of the scrub and onto the open savanna, carrying her in his weary arms.

12.
THE STRENGTH TO GO ON

Stalks of grass blew wildly in the wind, rasping together like a hundred thousand hissing snakes. They groped his legs and clung to his rain-slicked skin, slowing his painful march. He turned his head to protect his eyes from the stinging rain and used his own body to shield Alis.

"Where's Nesthome?" He gazed about, flinching as heavy droplets pelted his face.

The next flash of lightning failed to illuminate his village, but it did silhouette the blade-nose.

"Damn," he cursed and pressed on. Moments later he bumped into a rocky outcropping and set Alis' shivering form atop it. He rested a hand over his wildly pounding heart and another against his knee. By the blood of the ancestors it hurt!

Alis' teeth chattered and she drew herself into a ball. The red marks pulsated beneath her flesh, radiating a dull crimson glow.

Icy drops pounded his face as he gazed over his shoulder at the karda's dark shape. He set his jaw resolutely. Orishadaons did not give in to pain, they were above it. Sharna said that to give in to pain was to show weakness. Pain was merely a fault in the person. "I'll keep going. I'll never give up." He would prove his worth to the tribe, and most importantly, to Alis.

A horrible howl rose above the sound of the storm. Deep and resonant, the karda's cry chilled Dayn's blood, but he fought down his growing fear. Fear was another weakness, and he could not afford to be weak. He had to be strong for her.

Alis reached out blindly with the gauntlet, grasping at the air in reaction to the karda's bellow. "I'm here," she seemed to call out to it. The marks on her arm burned bright as fiery coals.

"Shhh!" Dayn frantically pushed her arm down.

"Here," she continued to moan, forcing him to slap a hand across her mouth.

Too late! The next flash showed the karda moving towards them. Every moment he wasted resting against this boulder brought it closer.

"Not good," he said, scooping Alis into his arms. She was warm to the touch. Not warm like she had a fever, but warm like he was standing too close to a blazing fire. "Definitely not good."

He had barely taken three steps before the pressure on his knee brought him to a sudden halt. He gritted his teeth against the pain. "No weakness." He forced himself to take a step. "Show them all how strong you are." Another step, this one accompanied by a grunt of discomfort. "Don't let her down, not like Ryl."

Memories came flooding back, bursting through the thin walls he had built up in his mind. His body shook with frustration. He would protect Alis above all else, no memory would keep him from his duty.

Dayn took another step, and then another. Alis latched her hand onto his shoulder and squeezed with waning strength as her unconscious features contorted in terror. "He's coming," she murmured. "Almost here."

"You're going to be fine," he comforted her in his best soothing voice. "Let him come, I'll protect you." His knees shook, as much from his own unease as from the injury, or maybe more from unease. "I'll get us out of this, but I could use some help." At that, he glared angrily at the sky and the ancestors who were supposed to be watching over him.

Thunder shook the earth, followed closely by multiple streaks of lightning that lit the savanna as if it were midday. The blade-nose was no more than a hundred paces away, its water-slick scales shimmering magnificently in the bright flashes of light. Rivulets ran down the massive horn on its face and between its oddly expressive eyes, which narrowed menacingly as it caught sight of him.

Alis suddenly opened her eyes. "He's here!"

Dayn ran.

He ran faster than he thought he could. He flew across the savanna, the wet stalks of grass barely touching him as he left the blade-nose behind.

Pop! So loud was the noise that at first he thought it was more thunder. It was not until his leg went limp and the ground rushed up to meet him that he realized the sound had come from his knee. Superhuman reflexes took control. An eye blink before striking the earth his body twisted in midair so that, rather than falling on top of Alis, he landed on his back with the scout cradled safely in his arms.

The dead weight of her body came down on his chest, driving the air from his lungs. He gasped for breath, his throat emitting hideous wheezing sounds that churned his stomach with revulsion. He rolled onto his hands and knees, gagging as if about to vomit.

Whoosh! He drank in the air greedily, filling his lungs to near bursting. "Definitely not good," he coughed, holding his chest with one arm.

A shape loomed out of the darkness. The karda's nostrils flared as it glared down victoriously, savoring the orishadaon's fearful scent.

Dayn wiped rainwater out of his eyes. "You swore you'd protect her," he chastised himself. His hand inadvertently went to Agidyne and his fingers latched around the cold metal of the hilt.

Alis laid in the mud next to him, groaning in agony as she warred against whatever evil spirit resided within the gauntlet. She continued to fight, and would for as long as she had the strength to go on. That knowledge lent Dayn strength.

"Pain is weakness," he said, breath misting in the air. "Overcoming pain is strength." He could do this, he was an orishadaon. He kissed Alis' forehead. "I'll never let you down again, I swear on the blood of my ancestors."

He focused on the distant horizon as lightning lit the sky.

There! He spotted the collection of huts and a makeshift watchtower surrounded by a crumbling, stone wall. The rolling hills of the savanna had blocked it from his view until now. He grinned up at the sky maniacally. "You can't stop me now," he laughed. "Damn you and damn my fate! I will keep her alive and there's nothing you can do to stop me."

He pushed himself off the ground, rising shakily to his full height. All his weight settled upon his one good leg. Planting his foot in a muddy groove, he braced himself for the karda's eventual assault. His heart beat furiously as he listened in anticipation to the beast's heavy breathing, waiting for the intake of breath that would signal its lunge. He held its hateful gaze, not daring to move.

Lightning flashed and the karda breathed deeply. Dayn raised his sword above his head, screaming at the top of his lungs as he leaped towards the beast. The blade-nose's massive head snaked forward, mouth agape.

His mind went blank and he stopped screaming. All the world froze for a single, thrilling instant. The creature's cavernous mouth filled his vision, open wide enough to swallow him whole. Time flowed faster and faster until the blade-nose was upon him.

Dayn sidestepped the gaping maw. Not to be denied its prey, the blade-nose lashed out, slamming its head into his back. The tip of the karda's horn skidded across his shoulder while the end of its snout hit him with such astounding force that he was catapulted through the air. He screamed a long time before slamming down against the wet earth.

All he wanted to do was lie down and die in peace, but he could not rest with all the yelling. He wished whoever was making the noise would be quiet. It took Dayn a moment to realize the screams were his own. Barely able to remain conscious, the orishadaon tried to rise, only to collapse face first into the mud. At that moment he knew he was going to die, pummeled into the ground by the massive weight of the blade-nose or crushed between its jaws.

"I'm sorry." He reached out to Alis and his hand fell limply to his side. "I tried, I really tried." He let the rain wash over him, drowning all his thoughts and worries as he waited for a pair of massive jaws to close around him.

"Yer not givin' up are ya?"

Dayn's eyes widened in surprise.

A familiar figure stood above him, defiant as always with shoulders squared and jaw set. He glowed with courage, ignoring the pounding rain that seemed to pass through his radiant hide. "After what I did, yer just gonna' sit there and quit?"

"You . . . you died."

The karda glared through the ghostly form, nostrils flaring as it pried its jaws apart to reveal gleaming rows of jagged teeth.

"So will she if ya don't do somethin'."

The truth of those simple words cleared Dayn's clouded mind. It could not end like this, not so close to home. He would not allow it. Primal fury welled up within him and his powers took control. Despite the agony it caused, the orishadaon forced himself to move.

"No!" he shouted, taking a backhanded swing at the karda's snout as its massive head descended towards him. Orishadai surged through him, fueling his strength. His fist connected with the blade-nose's head, knocking it aside with sheer brute force. The karda stumbled backwards, shaking its head in discomfort.

Dayn staggered to his feet, shuddering as a crisp breeze blew across the exposed bone of his shoulder blade. Miraculously, he still held his sword.

The ghostly figure grinned proudly.

Dayn focused his thoughts and gathered his mental energies, drawing the symbol of the mind's eye in the air with his free hand. Pain and doubt warred for his attention and threatened to distract him, but he fought for control until, slowly, he began to win.

Spike was less than ten paces away and closed the distance with a single stride.

The spark of power grew within Dayn, pulsating as he fed it more and more of himself. Unstable energy threatened to pour out in a wave of catastrophic destruction that would consume him and everything nearby. The orishadai needed to be channeled and unleashed upon the karda.

"Now!" yelled the ghostly figure.

It began as a single point of agony inside his chest that quickly expanded to fill his entire body. Dayn fell to his knees as white-hot pain washed over him. He released his orishadai in a beam of blue energy that shot from his outstretched palm and into the face of the blade-nose, sending scales and chunks of blackened flesh flying in every direction. The karda writhed beneath the full force of Dayn's strike. It reared back, turning its head to the sky and roaring before toppling to the ground with a final, spasmodic jerk of its limbs.

Dayn smiled grimly. The flesh had been seared from the left

side of the karda's skull, burning away one of its eyes and leaving the bone exposed along its jaw where the lips had withered to nothing. In death, the blade-nose wore a hideous smile, as if it was laughing at him.

"Is it dead?" He took a hesitant step towards the quivering beast.

The shimmering form appeared at his side. "Ya aren't done yet."

Before Dayn could ask his friend what he meant, the karda wheezed, flecks of burnt meat and bloody spittle flying from its mouth. Another wheeze was followed by a deep throated, threatening snarl. Dayn stared in horror as the blade-nose twisted in the mud, trying to get its legs beneath it.

"That's impossible!" he shouted as if his words would convince the karda to die. He stared over his shoulder at Alis, remembering his oath to protect her. This entire battle might be nothing more than the ancestors testing the strength of that oath. "To the Aether with you then," Dayn growled. "I won't run like a coward."

The karda finally managed to stand, and it towered over him. Twin plumes of mist rose from its nostrils each time the giant carnivore took a labored breath. Dayn's fear and the nauseating stench of burnt meat twisted his stomach into a tight knot.

"This isn't over yet," the orishadaon said to himself, remembering that he still had Agidyne. He smiled in spite of the beast.

Right now all that mattered was getting Alis to the safety of Nesthome. He would not rest until that happened.

Dayn howled at the blade-nose, gripping his sword in both hands and raising it above his head as he charged. His muscles burned, his body protested every move, but at that moment strength of purpose pushed him beyond the pain. The karda's head came down, open jaws showering him with bits of spittle and red foam. The orishadaon threw himself towards those jaws in a blind fury.

"Die!" he cried, ramming the rusted blade straight up. It missed the open mouth, sinking instead into the karda's already useless, milky eye. Spike's jaws snapped shut. Its massive head jerked back alarmingly fast. Dayn had no time to let go of his sword before he was pulled from the ground. Moments later the creature's violent thrashing dislodged his blade from its eye socket and sent him careening wildly through the air.

His body soared for thirty paces and then came down with the force of a falling comet, splattering mud in its wake. The cool, soothing mud seeped into his shoulder and lessened the pain, although he did not care for the way it felt against the exposed bone.

Too much pain and anger. His mind had been all but lost for a brief moment. He failed Sharna by letting his rage take control yet again. His mentor would be ashamed and his ancestors must have been laughing at him. A soul could only take so many lapses in control before it gave in to bitterness and hate. When that happened, he would fall from the grace of the ancestors and become a creature of demonic lust and power, a shondaon.

The blade-nose shook its head, the motion sending droplets of blood raining down amongst the waving grass. It grunted in confusion and toppled over, finally giving in to the grievous wound. Its chest still rose and fell, but with the damage it had endured, the blade-nose would not survive much longer.

Their brutal conflict came to an end with Dayn alive, if not well. "I told you there was nothing you could do to stop me," he said to the sky.

"Ya can't stop yet," said the ghostly form, still hovering over him.

Dayn nodded knowingly in response. When he hobbled over to Alis she tentatively reached out to touch him, stopped, afraid the slightest contact would cause him more harm.

"It's all right," Dayn croaked, reaching down to push a strand of hair away from her eyes. "It's just a scratch."

It might have been the rain that caused the moisture welling up in the corners of her eyes, but Dayn preferred to think that she was happy to see him. "A scratch?" she grinned weakly and he nodded.

"I made you a promise." He slung his arm under hers and lifted her up.

"Dayn, your wounds," she protested.

"I'll be fine," he lied as blood gushed out of his shoulder and down his back. His own fate was unimportant so long as Alis made it back to Nesthome. He looked up at the angry clouds with a sneer. "You couldn't stop me."

"What was that?"

"Nothing." He shook his head. "Forget it." He limped towards the village with Alis helping him as much as he helped her, aware that his strength waned with every step. Even when he made it back, there was little they could do for him aside from binding his wounds and hoping his orishadaon-born toughness would do the rest. What really mattered was, could they do anything for Alis? As Dayn looked into her loving amber eyes, he desperately hoped they could.

PART II

WHEN IDEALS FAIL

13.
WAKE UP HATE

The unmistakable presence of the beast loomed over him as he traversed a surreal tangle of undergrowth. The undergrowth shifted, arranging itself into a maze full of grinning skulls and laughing voices. Thorns sprouted from the walls, which closed in around him, cutting off his retreat. With nowhere to run from the beast, and its presence drawing steadily closer, he dove headlong through the encircling spines.

The thorns gouged his naked flesh but he tore his way through until he finally tumbled out the other side to land on a patch of waving, dew-spattered grass. The green maze melted away, replaced by an endless horizon and bright blue sky.

His feet carried him quickly across the open ground, although he could not remember why he was running. It had something to do with being chased, but by what? He didn't know, and it didn't matter. His earlier terror drained away and he ran faster. For a brief moment he was at peace.

Then the sky turned black as hate and a raging inferno scorched the grassy field. Smoke blotted out the sky while the ground beneath his feet dissolved to ash. Shadowy figures snarled and hissed as they burrowed up through the blanket of ash, reaching for his soul with their clawed hands. The first demon grabbed at him . . .

. . . and his eyes snapped open.

He found himself lying on a pile of karda hides inside a dim and dreary hut. Beams of soft light streaked through cracks in the patchwork ceiling, encircling him in a protective halo of radiance. Dayn reached out to the light.

He grunted in discomfort and pulled his arm to his side, cradling it protectively as he bit down on his lip to stifle a cry. His shoulder ached immensely and he did not dare move again.

He slowly turned his head to inspect the hut and found little of interest. The mud brick walls were crumbling, the reed-woven roof sagged dangerously and the hovel was empty except for a bowl of water near his feet.

Water! His mind screamed as he licked his cracked lips. The inside of his throat felt as if he had swallowed a handful of sand. He desperately needed a drink, but the bowl was too far for his battered body to reach without disturbing his shoulder. By the blood of his ancestors, he wanted that water more than anything he had ever wanted before.

Dayn calmed himself and focused his attention on the bowl, imagining it floating through the air to his bedside so that he might take a drink of the cool, soothing liquid. Soon enough, the bowl began to rock gently back and forth, then lifted into the air.

Closer, Dayn thought, his body trembling as a dull throb built against his temples. He gritted his teeth against the pounding in his skull and clenched his hands into fists to stop them from shaking. Just a pace more. He reached out in desperation and instantly regretted it.

A hushed cry escaped the orishadaon's lips. He grabbed his shoulder, forgetting about the bowl long enough to let it fall to the ground. The fragile clay shattered on impact, spilling its sought after contents across the earthen floor.

"What's going on?" a voice asked groggily from the other side of his bed.

Still clutching his shoulder, Dayn rolled over.

Alis slouched against the wall next to him, bleary-eyed from her sudden awakening. Deep worry lines wrinkling her forehead, coupled with the dark circles around her eyes, told him she had not been sleeping well.

He forced a weak smile. "Sorry, I didn't mean to wake you."

"Dayn?" She rubbed the grit from the corners of her eyes. "You're awake!" She grabbed his hand and gave it a gentle squeeze, as if he might not be real and she needed to reassure herself that he was there. "Are you hurting? I'm so glad you woke up. I didn't know if you were ever going to wake up and Sharna said you might never come back," she rambled excitedly. "I thought the ancestors had taken you for sure."

The orishadaon massaged his temples with a hand swathed in bloody bandages, mindful of the pain in his swollen knuckles. "My head hurts," he rasped.

"Sharna said that would happen." Alis grabbed a dry rag and looked to where the bowl of water used to be. "Where's the—?"

"I broke it," Dayn said.

"How did you manage that? You haven't even gotten out of bed."

"I used orishadai," he answered, instantly regretting it when he saw the look of consternation on Alis' face.

"You were using your powers?" she chided him. "In your condition? Sharna said you should rest. It's the only way you're going to get better."

"I needed a drink," Dayn argued hoarsely, his throat feeling as rough as the bark on a scrub tree.

"And did mindlessly wasting your orishadai get it for you?" She motioned to the shattered pieces of clay scattered amidst the mud puddle on the floor. "You just hurt yourself more."

"It's not that bad. I'm . . ."

"Really?" she cut in. "Not that bad? Look at yourself Dayn, you almost died." A fire burned in her amber eyes, making him want to sink under his pile of hides and disappear. "Promise me right now you won't use your powers until you get better." She gave his hand another squeeze. "Sharna doesn't want you using them anyway."

"I don't care what Sharna wants!" Dayn snapped, pulling away. "She's the reason I'm like this. She sent me into that jungle to rot. Now Ryl is dead, you've got that gauntlet stuck to you, and I look like this." He waved a hand over himself. "So, tell me again why I should listen to Sharna?"

The scout glared at him angrily and he met her stare, too stubborn to look away. Just thinking about his mentor sending him into the jungle, "to find his destiny", caused the red tide to boil within him.

"You can be so stupid when you're like this," she said.

The anger drained from him in a weary sigh. He was about to apologize when she silenced him with a hand across his lips.

"Forget about Sharna then. Do it for me. Just promise *me* you won't use your powers until you get better."

Dayn sighed again. He could see that she truly cared about his safety, maybe even as much as he cared about hers. "Alright," he agreed. "I promise I won't use them . . . *unless* I absolutely have to."

"Stubborn." She rolled her eyes and smiled.

He smiled back and then shuddered, his face twisting into a grimace. "My head," he grunted between clenched teeth.

Alis reached into a pouch around her waist and pulled out a familiar vial of blue liquid. "It's yours now anyway, you might as well take it." She yanked the stopper off and handed it to him.

Dayn looked himself over, realizing for the first time just how close he had come to meeting the ancestors.

His skin, the sickly white color of chalk, was drawn tightly over his bones. Haphazardly wrapped bandages covered the worst wounds. Clay badges etched with warding runes stuck to the cloth strips, their holy markings there to keep evil spirits from infecting his wounds. Every bit of exposed flesh was criss-crossed with shallow cuts and bruises. His knee looked worse than ever, swollen and black as it was, and on top of all that he had his shoulder to worry about, too. Perfect.

Even though he wanted to be rid of the agony his wounds were causing him, he gently pushed the vial away. "Why do people keep trying to give me that? I'm not dying Alis, save it for someone who is."

"You need your strength," she insisted.

"I'll heal. Just tell me how long I was unconscious."

She took her time replacing the stopper in the vial, purposefully avoiding his gaze.

"How long?" he repeated.

"Eight lunars," she responded sorrowfully.

His mouth fell open in surprise.

The scout set the artifact down next to Agidyne, which stood propped against the far wall. "A lot has happened since we left the tribe to search out your destiny, and most of it isn't good."

"What do you mean? What's happened?"

"Well," she hesitated. The joints of the gauntlet *clinked* as she involuntarily squeezed her hand into a fist.

Dayn endured the pain in his shoulder so he could lay a reassuring hand on her arm. "Don't worry. I'm sure the ancestors will show Sharna how to get the artifact off."

After a mournful glance at the gauntlet her glinting eyes narrowed. She gave a derisive snort and pulled her arm from Dayn's grasp. "Who says I want to take it off?" She stood up, towering over him and holding out her arm so he could see the crimson gauntlet. "Ever since I put it on I feel stronger. I'm more powerful now than I ever was before finding it."

The gemstone began to glow. Dayn shrank back as a vicious sneer spread across Alis' face. She laughed to herself while the gemstone glowed ever brighter.

The orishadaon clutched his shoulder and sat up straight. She was not the kind of person prone to sudden fits of rage. That was his domain. This was the work of whatever evil spirit lay imprisoned within the gauntlet.

He forced himself to lock eyes with Alis. Recognition softened her features.

The gauntlet's light faded, ending the outburst as suddenly as it had begun. "I'm sorry." Her shoulders sagged and her arms fell to her sides. "I don't know why I did that."

Dayn let out the breath he had been holding and relaxed. "It's the gauntlet," he said. "The sooner it comes off the better."

"I'm so sorry," she apologized again.

"I'm going to find Sharna right now." Dayn tried to stand but his body refused to obey. He fell back into the hides, head spinning as white spots of light exploded before his eyes.

"She can't take it off!" Alis blurted as he lay there.

"What?" he asked through the haze of pain.

"Sharna can't take off the gauntlet!"

Dayn's shock kept him from responding. Sharna did not have the power to remove the cursed artifact? In her time she was the most powerful orishadaon the savanna tribes had ever seen. Age and many long seasons of relying on orishadai had taken its toll on the elder, but her knowledge of the world was absolute. If she did not know a way to rid Alis of the gauntlet and its evil prisoner there was no hope.

"You're sure there's nothing she can do?"

Moisture welled up in the corners of Alis' eyes. "Sharna says there's a demon inside me and the only way to save my soul is to kill me before it takes hold."

The words drove an iron fist into Dayn's chest and crushed his heart between icy fingers.

"Toran was holding off on the cleansing ceremony until you awoke because Sharna insisted you be there. Now that you're awake they . . . they can . . ." The stress of it was too much for her and she broke down in a fit of tearful crying. The doomed woman put her head down beside him. Not knowing what else to do, Dayn wrapped his arms around her. She shuddered violently, the motion sending fire racing through his shoulder, but it was nowhere near as intense as the fire that burned inside him.

They were going to cleanse her. Dayn had seen Sharna perform the ritual only twice in his lifetime. It was a brutal and barbaric thing akin to torture, with death as the victim's only release.

He witnessed his first cleansing from afar; the second time Sharna forced him to take part. The ill-fated tribesman, whose name Dayn chose not to recall for it brought back too many awful memories, lasted two whole lunars before the cleansing ended his life and freed his soul.

How could his mentor expect him to put Alis through that same nightmarish experience?

"I won't let it happen," Dayn vowed.

"You must not stop it," she objected between sobs. "It's the only way to save my soul. I don't want the demon to take me."

"There has to be a better way." Dayn tried once more, without success, to get up. Before he could make another attempt someone outside started to yell.

"You two, come with me," the angry voice ordered. "I know she's in here." The flap covering the tent's entrance flew aside and a pale, lean man, with jet-black hair and piercing blue eyes, strode in.

Two spear-wielding tribesmen, Toma and Gorm, walked in behind the younger man, glaring at Alis from across the hut with a mixture of revulsion and fear.

Dayn groaned at the intrusion, addressing the leader of the trio in a wearied tone. "Kind of you to visit me, Merek."

Merek ran his piercing blue eyes over the orishadaon and let out a derisive snort. "Kindness has nothing to do with my visit."

Alis hastily wiped the tears from her eyes. "Come on you two, not now." The slightest quiver in her voice alerted Merek to her grief.

"Oh, you've made the half-blood cry," he remarked with mock-sincerity. His eyes lit up with malicious glee at the discomfort his presence brought to the pair. "Shon-touched as she is, it doesn't really matter."

"What do you want?" Dayn growled.

"It doesn't concern you, *orishadaon*." The young man forced the last word through barred teeth. "I'm here for the half-blood." He delivered the message as if it were a death sentence, which, for Alis, it was.

"Don't call me half-blood," she snarled, narrowing her saurian eyes.

Toma, taller than Dayn by half a head and doubly as broad, took a step forward and pointed his spear at Alis' stomach, while Gorm, slighter of stature than his hunting companion, propped his weapon against the wall and produced a coil of rope.

Toma had always been a brute, one who enjoyed flaunting his skill over those he perceived as weaker than himself, which naturally included everyone. Unfortunately for the rest of the tribe, he was a skilled hunter and a veritable wall of bone and muscle, giving him the size and ability to back up his threatening demeanor.

Gorm, on the other hand, had been an honorable man until his mate was taken by the Black Tooth tribe during one of their frequent raids. He blamed Dayn for the loss, claiming that the orishadaon had failed to protect her.

"That's close enough," Alis warned, swatting Toma's spear aside with the flat of her hand. Before she could pull her dagger from its sheath near her ankle, Toma brought his spear back around in a flash of movement and rested its tip against her throat.

"Don't." The muscle-bound hunter shook his tattooed head in warning.

"What are you going to do?" Merek sneered at Alis. "Do you really think you're fast enough? Toma is the best with a spear in the entire tribe, next to Ryl of course, but he's dead now."

Dayn bristled with rage at the last remark. His fury was enough to block out the pain as he rose to his feet.

"Dayn!" Alis gasped.

"Stop. This. Now." The orishadaon purposefully over-enunciated every word. He channeled a tiny bit of orishadai and sent an invisible tendril of it to Toma's spear haft. By clenching his hand into a fist he tightened the tendril, snapping off the end of the spear.

Alis' hand shot out and caught the sharp tip before it hit the ground, turning it on Toma in an eye-blink.

Dayn silently apologized to the scout for breaking his promise, but he needed his powers now more than ever if he wanted to protect her.

Gorm dropped the coil of rope and grabbed his weapon, preparing to hurl it at Alis despite the tight confines of the hut.

Merek held up a hand, halting the inevitable combat. "Our gardaon ordered this." The young man shook his head at the futility of Dayn and Alis' actions. "If you don't like it, talk to Toran."

Dayn's entire body trembled with barely suppressed rage. The red tide demanded release. "I like him even less than I like you," he hissed.

Merek calmly flicked his wrist.

Dayn immediately felt a heavy blow across the side of his face, the force of it nearly driving him to his knees. His eyes bulged as he pointed an accusing finger at Merek. "Never use your powers on a fellow tribesman!" he fumed. Dayn instinctively reached to his side for Agidyne, cursing himself for a sun-baked fool when he remembered that it was leaning against the opposite wall.

"Enough of this madness," Alis cut in. She stopped threatening Toma with the spear-head and tossed it away. It was clear she was trying to placate the two orishadai users before the situation got out of control. "Merek, tell me why my father sent you here."

"Toran thinks you should be isolated from the rest of the tribe until the cleansing," he responded without ever taking his eyes off Dayn.

His eyes, while chillingly ruthless, were eerily similar to the orishadaon's.

Dayn glowered at Merek. "Toran's her father, how can he do that to her?"

Merek shrugged. "He's waiting in his tent, go ahead and ask him."

"I'm asking you."

A tense moment of silence passed as the two orishadai users attempted to stare each other down.

"I'll go," Alis eventually interjected.

"No," Dayn refused, unwilling to accept that death was the only way to preserve her soul. "I'll get that gauntlet off you. We'll find a way to banish the demon."

Merek appeared on the verge of laughter. He limited himself to a soft chuckle. "She's already dead. It's just a matter of time now that you're awake."

"Get out!" Dayn waved him away, doubling over from the pain of moving his arm. A clay badge plastered across his shoulder cracked and tumbled away, exposing the angry red flesh underneath.

"Dayn!" Alis turned to him but was quickly blocked off by Gorm and his weapon.

"You are so pathetic." Merek let fly with his laughter. He stopped abruptly to spit with disgust at the orishadaon's feet. "Some *orishadaon*, lying in bed like a cripple."

"Get out!" Alis screamed, but her tone failed to wipe the smug look off Merek's face.

Gorm handed his spear to Toma and retrieved the rope. "Give me your hands," he ordered Alis as Toma prepared to skewer her if she refused. She did not refuse, and Gorm expertly bound her wrists with the coarse rope, shoving her towards the exit when he finished.

"I'm leaving now." Merek pushed aside the door-flap and paused with his back to Dayn. "Oh, and welcome back, *brother*."

"The ancestors damn you!" Dayn shouted, rousing more laughter from his younger sibling.

"Bring her," Merek ordered, letting the flap fall down behind him.

"Go," Toma grunted, jabbing Alis between the shoulder-blades with the butt of his spear.

"Don't hurt her!" Dayn called after them in desperation.

Then they were gone. He slumped against the wall, staring blankly at the streams of light pouring through cracks in the woven branches above his head.

He could hear Merek and the other tribesmen taunting Alis. The scout was barely clinging to sanity; if they set her off there was no telling what she, or the demon inside, might do in retaliation.

Dayn probed the flesh around his shoulder and grimaced. The bone no longer protruded, but it wouldn't take much to split open the scab of unhealed scar-tissue. Toran would look for signs of weakness, and as an orishadaon he could not afford to show any.

One overconfident step in the direction of the exit was all it took for his knees to buckle. Dayn was on the ground before he realized what had happened.

It required a tremendous amount of concentration, as well as a generous application of stubborn persistence, to get back up. With one hand gripping the wall to steady himself, he managed to rise by his own power, although a gentle breeze at that moment would have blown his feet out from under him.

"The tribe doesn't care about your injuries," he berated himself. "Nothing matters to them, especially not your pain. Nothing matters to you but saving Alis. Don't let them stop you from saving her. Don't let anything stop you."

14.
PORTRAIT OF AUTHORITY

He made it to the door and, with one quivering hand, weakly pushed aside a karda hide flap blocking the exit. Dazzling rays of sunlight stabbed his eyes like radiant spears, forcing him to look away. After so many lunars in the dismal Tresslevale, he had forgotten how intense the light of the ancestors could be.

When his eyes adjusted to the natural brightness, Dayn set his watchful gaze to inspecting his home, as any good orishadaon would.

From where he stood, the sound of crackling flame was plain to hear. The sound's source, a roaring blaze in Nesthome's central fire pit, sent a thick plume of oily smoke and the scent of cooking meat into the air.

On the far side of the village, a crowd of excited children chased a hopper lizard between mud brick huts, laughing and carrying on as they batted at it with sturdy clubs.

Blurry forms milled about in the distance. As he focused on them, willing his vision to clear, they solidified into the shapes of women toiling in the morayth groves. From those fields came the intoxicating smell of freshly harvested morayth.

He turned his attention skyward, instantly throwing up a hand to shield his eyes from the sun's glare. Far to the west, dark storm-clouds churned across the horizon while bolts of lightning arced to the ground amidst muffled claps of rumbling thunder. He quietly cursed his ancestors for the ill omen such a storm represented.

At that moment a trio of hunters passed by carrying the body of a fleet-foot, no doubt taking it to be cooked at the fire along with whatever else had been caught that lunar.

He did not intend to eavesdrop on the hunter's thoughts, but in his weakened condition Dayn's unstable powers forced him to glimpse into their minds, and he cringed at their unspoken words.

We should keep away from him, worried one wiry hunter.

Pathetic, thought a second.

The largest of the trio, Mord, had only one word in his mind: *shon-touched.*

The word made Dayn tremble with suppressed anger. Shon was the ancient word for demon. Shon-touched was the same as saying a demon possessed him. Mord's thoughts, no matter how private, were unforgivable. He glared at the hunter, who calmly met his gaze and nodded, a token show of respect.

"I am not shon-touched," Dayn hissed between bared teeth, causing Mord to arch an eyebrow. "Do you hear me?" He raised his voice. "I am not shon-touched!"

Confused and more than a little frightened, Mord quickly ushered his hunters and their catch away from the orishadaon.

Dayn cursed them all as they moved off. He had dedicated his life to defending their village, what right did they have to think such things of him?

"You pretend respect, but you can't hide your true thoughts from me." A mirthless grin split his face. "You hear me Mord! You can't hide your thoughts from me!"

One of the other hunters, the wiry one, turned around, holding a simple bone dagger in his hand. Before he could take so much as a step towards the orishadaon, Mord slapped the weapon from his grasp and pulled the furious tribesman back.

"Damned fool," Mord snarled at the hunter, loud enough for Dayn to hear. "That one is worse than his brother. Are you trying to get yourself killed?"

Dayn scowled while Mord attempted to subdue the irate hunter. After a brief struggle, Mord won out, dragging the smaller man away. When they were gone Dayn's shoulders slumped and he let out a dejected moan. His tribesmen were full of fear and revulsion, yet he sought to inspire neither emotion in those around him. All he wanted was to help them, why couldn't they see that?

By the time he made it to Toran's hut he was in poor shape, physically as well as mentally. His chest heaved with each breath and his legs wobbled from the simple effort of supporting his emaciated form. Bandages over his shoulders and across his back had come loose, revealing numerous unhealed wounds.

"I can't show weakness." He straightened his back, at the same time willing his knees to stop knocking together. This was it, time to see if he could spare Alis from her fate. He took a deep breath and pushed aside the flap covering the entrance to the gardaon's hut.

The heady aroma of sweat and morayth wine assailed his nostrils as he stepped into the gloomy interior. His skin felt sticky in the damp, humid air, causing tiny bumps to rise along the exposed flesh of his arms. He took a final breath of fresh, savanna air and let the flap fall down behind him.

Torches driven into the bare earth illuminated the tent's murk, their flickering light dancing across hundreds of cycles worth of accumulated relics. There were weapons like Agidyne—the sword Dayn just now realized he had neglected to bring—pieces of armor, equipment, and even more bizarre objects that no living tribesman could identify, all resting in scattered piles across the floor.

He shuffled past heaps of cursed metal that glistened magnificently in the fire-light, stopping exactly ten paces away from a grisly chair built from the gardaon's many hunting trophies. Skulls from both annaru and karda adorned the makeshift throne, each one taken from a particularly skilled or dangerous opponent. At the very top, resting directly above Toran's head, lay the skull of the previous gardaon.

Every bit as grizzled as his throne, Toran lounged atop his chair, greedily sucking morayth wine from a well-used bowl. Unlike his daughter, who showed few signs of her annaru heritage, Toran was a hideous blend of human and saurian anatomy. Taller than Ryl by at least a hand-span, the gardaon's bulging, muscular form threatened to crush the throne beneath its weight. Toran offered Dayn a cruel smile full of jagged teeth and leaned forward, revealing rows of gleaming, emerald scales along his back and forearms.

He swallowed a mouthful of morayth wine to clear his throat before thoughtlessly tossing the drinking bowl aside. It landed on top of a pile of relics, spilling sticky juice across a bronze shield older than the Swift Claw tribe. "Our orishadaon wishes to grace us with his presence." The gardaon's deep voice rumbled forth like an avalanche, commanding the attention of all those present.

Half-shrouded in shadow, Gorm leaned on the haft of his spear by the far wall, watching Dayn through hate-filled eyes. Meanwhile, Toma crouched on the opposite side of the tent. He flashed his orishadaon a predatory grin and wiped a hand across the front of his chipped and blackened teeth. Merek stood at Toran's right, while Sharna waited on his left, leaning on her cane, back bent under the weight of many long seasons of life.

Merek looked petulant as ever, while his old mentor's weathered features were scrunched into an unreadable mask. Age lines creased the corners of her rheumy eyes and the edges of her narrow mouth, giving the impression of a frail old madwoman at the end of her life.

Dayn knew better than anyone how false such a judgment was. Sharna's elderly features were a result of overusing her powers; she was not yet past her fortieth season. Much orishadai rested within her tiny frame, and her advanced aging had done nothing to weaken her control or her volatility.

He shuddered, wishing he had his sword.

The decrepit woman stepped in front of Toran, making a show of fluttering her drab green robes as she reached inside them. "You have come to beg on behalf of the gardaon's daughter," she said with typical foresight. "She is possessed by a demon and must die, the ancestors have shown me." She waved a hand before her, scattering several tiny bones across the floor. "You see?" She leaned forward, her hunched back creaking like the boughs of an ancient tree, and motioned for those nearby to look closely. "They are always the same." The woman gathered up her bones and tossed them again. Her weather-beaten face relaxed into an expression of deep thought. "Always the same." She wrung her hands and nodded to herself.

Dayn watched the position of the bones during each toss and saw no pattern in their placement. "Which demon possesses her?" he asked, doing his best to hide the pain he felt, though it was difficult with everyone watching him so intently. Unfortunately for him, Toran was an astute warrior, used to discerning weakness in his foes. It did not take the gardaon long to realize Dayn's wounds still troubled him.

"Still hurting from your little fight with the blade-nose?" Toran leaned back, reaching for a bundle of uncooked meat at his feet. "Not much of a fight though, the beast seems to have gotten the best of you, and worse, it survived." He bit down on a mouthful of the meat, causing a stream of animal blood to spurt across his chin.

The blade-nose survived? Dayn staggered backwards in disbelief. No creature on all of Urth could survive having two paces of steel embedded in its face.

Regaining his composure, Dayn turned his full attention to Sharna while refusing to look at Toran, a grave and intentional insult. "Which demon?" he repeated his question.

"The ancestors do not see fit to show me," Sharna answered in a scratchy voice.

Dayn kneeled before the old woman. "Then how can you know she's possessed?"

"She is possessed," Sharna assured, collecting her fortune bones and tucking them away inside her robes. "Her destiny has already been decided, but it is not the ancestors that guide her, just as it is not the ancestors that guide you." She placed a gnarled hand atop his head. "I sent you to the Tresslevale to find your destiny, but it seems your destiny has found Alis instead."

Dayn looked up into her cold gray eyes. "I don't have time for riddles, Sharna. I found nothing but death in that jungle."

"Death was supposed to find you!" Her stern words jolted him into alertness.

"Me?" He glared at her without comprehending.

The old woman shook her head in disappointment. "I foresaw your end in that place. You should not be here." Her calm reply sent him reeling.

"You . . . you sent me to die?"

"Fate was to take you from this world," Sharna confirmed. She took her hand off his head to scratch her narrow chin.

He staggered back, glaring at her as if she were some demon out of his nightmares. One question forced its way out amidst his confusion. "Ryl? Did you know Ryl was going to die?"

She nodded.

His senses dulled. Her simple gesture closed off the light of his mind. His mouth gaped open, struggling to form the words to describe how utterly betrayed he felt. Lips moved at a frantic pace, unable to settle on a clear set of words.

"I . . . don't . . . understand," was all he could finally manage.

His mentor watched him carefully as she explained. "Your fate and Ryl's were intertwined, neither of you should have lived. Only Alis was meant to return," she finished, clearly vexed by the error in her precognitive powers.

"I, I don't understand." Dayn dropped to his knees.

"Neither do I." She stroked her chin. "My visions have never been wrong."

Dayn's world fell apart around him, leaving him alone atop a precipice in the midst of a gaping void. "You killed Ryl," he whispered to himself, taking a moment to let it sink in. New purpose filled the emptiness. "You." He turned his steely gaze to the old woman. Raising his voice, he repeated it. "You killed Ryl!"

Sharna shrugged off the accusation. "I merely introduced him to his destiny."

"You sent us to die!"

"Such was your fate," she said matter-of-factly.

Dayn's face burned red with fury.

"Enough," Toran barked, cutting off a less than civil response from the orishadaon. "Sharna, leave."

The old woman offered a slight bow to the gardaon, brushed past Dayn, and exited the tent without another word. It all happened so fast he did not have time to react.

"You still walk with a limp," Merek called from across the tent after she had gone.

"Did my daughter not offer you the healing waters?" Toran asked accusingly. Gorm and Toma flanked Dayn, their eyes filling with malicious intent as they gripped their spears tighter in anticipation.

Dayn was unable to answer. The shock of his encounter with Sharna proved too much for his mind, and he needed time for rational thought to return.

"You will answer!" the gardaon roared, taking Dayn's silence for defiance.

Dayn blinked his way through hazy thoughts. Sharna's words were meant to unsettle him. He needed to collect his wits if he wanted to save Alis. It would not help his cause to anger the gardaon any further. "She did," he finally replied.

Toma and Gorm watched his every move, and Dayn felt like a cornered horn-face hunted by a pack of claw-toes.

"See what disrespect he shows the tribe," Toran snarled. "We generously offer the healing waters to him and he refuses our gift."

Merek shook his head in disapproval.

"No," Dayn quickly objected. "I thought it would be better to save it for someone who really needs it."

"You thought!" Toran bellowed back. "You don't think. I think for the tribe, not you."

Toma and Gorm snickered behind him and it took all of his willpower not to turn around. He sucked in deep breath after deep breath, concentrating above all else on keeping the red tide from rising within his soul.

When next he spoke, it was in a steady voice. "'A true orishadaon is a master of his body'," he quoted Sharna. "We heal faster than normal tribesmen. I don't need the healing waters."

Toran silenced him with a wave of his hand. "Enough of this!"

Dayn gulped, looking towards the exit, his only escape route.

"What happened to Ryl?" The gardaon leaned forward, his amber eyes narrowing.

"Did Alis not tell you?"

"You tell me!" Toran snapped.

"He was killed by the same creature that cursed Alis," Dayn quickly explained.

"How was he killed?" Merek asked. "Ryl was twice the hunter you are. How did he die while you still live?"

Dayn closed his eyes as the darkness welled up inside him. "He died to save me," was his only answer. No amount of prodding could get him to reveal more. A gurgling scream echoed in his thoughts. The horrible memory resurfaced, playing through his mind for the thousandth time.

Toran spit on the ground disgustedly, oblivious to Dayn's internal conflict. "Did you see your tribesmen fall?"

A shriek cut to the depths of his soul. "I heard his screams."

Toran glared at him. "Did you see him fall?"

After a moment of silence, Dayn simply said, "No."

"So you left him to die?" was Merek's shocked reply. "What kind of an *orishadaon* would leave someone behind like that?"

Toran waited for an answer.

Dayn ignored the question. "What are you going to do with Alis?"

"She is cursed, a danger to the tribe," Merek said. "When the sun rises tomorrow you'll cleanse her yourself."

"You will purge the evil from her," added the gardaon.

Dayn shook his head. "I won't do it."

Toma and Gorm gasped at his defiance.

No one had ever dared to openly refuse Toran's orders; the entire tribe was too terrified of him.

The gardaon looked to be on the verge of a violent outburst.

"Then I'll do it myself," Merek cut in before Toran went berserk. Even Merek feared his wrath.

Dayn swallowed the lump in his throat as he stared down two hunters and his brother, all three more than willing to kill him if their gardaon gave the word, though Toran was likely to do the killing himself if such a need arose. "You can't make me do this," he pressed his point. No sense holding back now, he'd already angered them all.

"You do not tell me what I can do." Toran rose up off his throne and stalked towards the orishadaon, who took a hesitant step back and froze as the half-blood gardaon bore down on him. Toran pulled his arm back and Dayn clenched his jaw, waiting for the blow. It came an eye blink later, in the form of a might fist against his skull.

Dayn managed to avoid crashing into any of the tribe's artifacts as he fell, which would only have made things worse. Unfortunately, the blow itself jarred his senses, and in his moment of weakness the red tide swelled upward and burst through the cracks in his mental barriers. It burned through him like a brush fire, feeding upon his anger.

He squeezed his hand into a fist and pounded it against the earth, beating the ground as if it was the source of his pain. Struggling to suppress the tide in his state pushed him to the brink.

A whirling cloud of dust whipped up around him. He gripped

his skull as images flashed before his eyes. There were annaru and screaming tribesmen. Flames burned everything, rising up into the sky and washing over his village like a tidal wave. In the center of it all stood Alis, strangely unaffected by the chaos around her. A massive shadow loomed over the battlefield and, to Dayn's surprise, instead of raising a weapon she offered the thing her hand.

A shockwave that sent sacred objects flying in all directions cut through the air, with Dayn at its center. Toma and Gorm were thrown to the ground by its violent force, while Merek ducked and covered his head. Toran raised a trunk-like arm to guard his face, but otherwise remained motionless.

The dust cloud settled around Dayn as he regained control. He swayed back and forth, a trickle of drool running across his chin as blood dripped freely from his nose. He glared at Toran with a hateful, unblinking stare that made even the Swift Claw tribe's gardaon step back in fear.

"Enough," Toran growled uneasily. He waved Dayn away. "Get out of my hut."

"I won't let you kill Alis," Dayn stated.

"If you speak against me one more time I'll cut you down myself!" Toran roared, raising a fist to strike him again.

Dayn hastily backed away, fearing another blow would shatter the tenuous hold he possessed over the red tide. He turned his back on the gardaon and limped angrily out of the tent.

"Damn it," he cursed the instant he was outside. A strong breeze tossed his unkempt hair in every direction and brought the sound of buzzing insects to his ears. In the distance a horn-face bellowed.

"Do you enjoy pain, child, or did you hope to accomplish something by provoking him?" Sharna asked in a belittling tone. The decrepit old woman had appeared at his side without his noticing, and it bothered him that she could do that so easily.

"Provoking him?" Dayn shouted indignantly, spittle flying from his lips. "He hits me, and *I'm* provoking him?!"

The orishadaon let out a frustrated scream and at the same instant a nearby hut collapsed, torn apart by the chaotic storm of orishadai released by his overburdened mind. He watched the pieces of mud-brick and sticks scatter in the wind and fell to his knees when it was over, burying his head in his hands.

"Damn you to the Aether," he sobbed shamefully. Another lapse in control! He would never be able to contain his powers if things kept up the way they were. "I need to go." He struggled back to his feet. "I need Agidyne."

Dayn tried to shuffle away but Sharna wrapped her bony fingers around his injured shoulder and gave it a squeeze. His teeth clamped down, nearly taking off the end of his tongue, and he sank back to his knees.

His mentor's eyes flashed dangerously. "You *will* listen to me, child."

"To the Aether with you," he snarled, inviting another squeeze of his shoulder.

"Do not throw your petty curses at me, *child*!" Sharna snapped, her domineering tone further infuriating the orishadaon.

"Don't call me a child!" He squirmed in her grasp, causing wave after wave of agony to roll forth from his shoulder. Like a cornered animal, he clamped his teeth around her knobby knuckles and bit down, hard. When blood dribbled over his chin, Sharna merely shook her head in disappointment and tossed him away, oblivious to her wounded hand.

Dayn spit the blood from his lips in disgust. "Don't ever touch me again," he warned.

"You are mine, child," she continued to deliberately insult him. "I'll do what I like with you."

Dayn's nostrils flared. "This is all your fault! You brought this misery into my life."

"It is a shame you are so weak. I thought I trained you better."

He turned his back to walk away.

"Know something, Dayn." His mentor's calm voice forced him to stop and take notice. "Fate has seen fit to trade Alis' soul for yours. She is going to die in your place."

Dayn whirled around. "No one will take Alis from me! Not you, not Toran and not that demon inside her. No one!"

"Have you finished your little tantrum?" Her calmness grated on his nerves.

"When I find my sword, I'm going to show this ungrateful tribe just how bad my tantrums can be."

Sharna laughed at his boast and waved him away.

He hobbled towards his hut, knowing that if he looked back he would break down right there and give in to the rising tide within him.

15.
REMINDED

He gripped his throbbing chest with a hand that shook uncontrollably, teeth bared against the red-hot tendrils squeezing his heart. His grip tightened as the discomfort increased, until it became difficult to breathe. Each labored inhalation came as a gasp, accompanied by jolts of pain from behind his ribs and a furious shuddering throughout his entire body.

"What . . . do . . . I . . . do?" he panted, stumbling blindly away from Sharna and her cackling laughter.

He had only made it a few dozen paces when the stress of all that had happened finally caught up with him. A flare of agony shot through his knee, his only warning before the limb went numb, then limp, depositing him in the mud.

He wiped at his grime-splattered bandages with clumsy swipes, tearing away the few that remained.

Sitting under the light of the ancestors, covered in muck and criss-crossed with countless wounds, Dayn chuckled at the absurdity of his plight.

The chuckle abruptly turned into a bout of roaring laughter, his voice rising in volume until it reached a fevered pitch. He ran a shaking hand through his hair, smudging mud across half his face. The laughs quickly became sobs.

"Help me," he pleaded, turning his woeful gaze to the sky. "Please, for Alis. Help me."

"Dayn?" implored a hushed, inquisitive voice from around the corner of a sloping wall.

Embarrassed, he threw a hand in front of his face to hide the moisture gathering at the corners of his eyes.

A young girl, only six seasons old, with long, braided hair and wide, searching eyes, poked her head around the wall. "Are ya hurtin'?" she asked tentatively.

The peculiar accent struck his mental defenses a devastating blow. Images of Ryl's blood-spattered face flickered inside the orishadaon's mind while the hunter's dying screams rang in his ears.

Dayn swallowed the lump in his throat and forced a weak smile for the child. "I'm fine, Kala," he lied.

"Ya look like yer hurtin'," she insisted.

The memories conjured by her voice made it hard for him to concentrate. He tried to meet her wide-eyed stare, found it impossible. Guilt gnawed at his guts as she passed her inspecting gaze over him. He decided to change the subject.

"Have the ancestors been kind to you while I was gone?"

"Yes," Kala replied with a bright smile, absently twisting a stray braid around her finger. She showed no fear of him, unlike the other children. It helped that he had been close friends with her brother.

He swallowed again. "I'm glad to hear that."

Kala's gaze seemed to pierce to the core of his very soul. "Are ya sure yer not hurtin'? Ya look sick."

"I feel like I'm going to be," he muttered, pushing off the ground and flinging mud from his trembling hands.

She giggled upon seeing him toss the muck away. "Are ya playin'?" She immediately scooped up a handful and patted it into a ball. A playful grin crossed her face and Dayn did not have to read her mind to know what was coming next.

"Kala, wait." He held up his hands in submission. She hurled the mud ball at him anyway. As it splattered across his chest and knocked him over, she giggled mischievously, thinking he was going along with her game.

In reality, he was so weak that the mud ball had taken him off his feet.

He landed with a grunt on his backside.

"Brought down by a child with a fistful of mud," he groaned.

Kala kneeled at his side. "That was fun!" Her ever-present smile never wavered, nor did her piercing stare.

By the blood of his ancestors, why did she keep looking at him like that?

He patted the top of her head with a muddy hand and her delighted shriek brought the slightest hint of a grin to his face.

"No fair," she giggled.

"You started it." He took a deep breath and wiped the sweat from his forehead.

Kala suddenly became serious. "Did ya hear about Alis?"

His smile instantly disappeared.

"Is she really possessed?"

"There's nothing to worry about!" he blurted.

Kala kicked at a loose stone, her brow furrowed with concern. "Alis is different since she came back," the little girl told him with her eyes aimed at the ground.

It was strange that the child would be so concerned about Alis. From what Dayn knew, the two had never spoken more than a few words to each other. The scout was no friend of Ryl's family and made it a point to stay away from them whenever possible.

"Alis is just tired." He did not want to upset Kala with the truth. Her young mind would be filled with enough worries when she found out her brother, like both her parents, was dead.

Perhaps that was why he could not meet her gaze. He was responsible for the death of her only sibling and too terrified to admit it.

"Where's Ryl?"

Her question stole the breath from his lungs and he quickly turned away before she could see the guilt reflected in his eyes. He opened his mouth to speak, but could not find the words.

Dayn knew he had to tell her, she deserved that much. No matter how hard he tried, however, he could not force himself to speak of Ryl's fate.

"He's still in the Tresslevale," Dayn finally whispered when it became apparent that the child would stand there waiting all lunar for an answer. It wasn't exactly a lie, but neither was it the awful truth in its entirety.

At that instant he was willing to tell her anything, if only she would stop glaring at him.

The inquisitive child brightened at the mention of the jungle, never doubting the truth of Dayn's words. "What was it like there?" she asked in wide-eyed curiosity.

Images of the blade-nose and its gaping maw flooded his mind. He grimaced, squeezing his head between his hands when he recalled the memory of the shadow beast and what it must have done to Ryl. It was impossible to shut out the grisly images.

"Dayn?" Kala tugged on his bandages expectantly.

Screams echoed through his thoughts and he whimpered pitifully. "Ask me again sometime," he told her in a shaky voice.

The little girl frowned. "Is Alis goin' to be alright?"

Again, she did not ask about her brother. Kala had no reason to, Dayn supposed. Ryl always came back to her alive and well. Entire hunting seasons had gone by without incident, yet one trip into the jungle with an orishadaon had been enough to cut her brother's life short.

"She needs help, I have to see her," Dayn answered at length.

Kala gasped, glancing around furtively. She leaned in close and whispered, "Ya can't see her. Merek took her to the pits and no one's allowed to go there."

Dayn sighed wearily. "An orishadaon can go wherever he wants."

"The others say she's shon-touched." The girl shivered, twirling another braid of hair around her finger. "They say I should stay away from her."

The afternoon sun baked the muck to his body, sizzling him inside a muddy shell. The heat did nothing to help his temperament. "Everyone else is wrong!" he snarled. "Alis isn't possessed, she just needs help."

"Possessed?" Kala's brown eyes opened in terror. She shook her head and backed away. "Ya shouldn't help a shon-touched, Toran would be mad."

To the Aether with Toran, he thought. "Shhh, we can't let anyone know about what I'm going to do." He reached out to comfort the girl. To his surprise, and dismay, Kala recoiled from his touch. It was the first time she had ever shown fear of him.

"No, Dayn." The girl turned and ran away.

"Wait!" Dayn's shoulders sagged as she disappeared from sight around the corner of a hut. He slumped against a crumbling wall.

Alis was going to die, it was his fault, and there was nothing he could do about it.

Before he fell completely into self-pity, Dayn felt a tingle race up his spine, telling him another orishadai user was nearby.

"Do you want the half-blood that much, *orishadaon*?"

He could not help but cringe upon hearing his brother's all too familiar voice. "How long have you been skulking there?"

Merek strolled forward, grinning down at him. "Long enough. You should take better care of yourself. You're in no shape to be breeding with her like that."

"The ancestors damn you," Dayn cursed.

His brother pulled three small stones out of a pouch on his belt and arranged them purposefully in the palm of his hand. He sent one flying into the air with a thought, and levitated another shortly thereafter. The two stones wove a figure-eight until they were joined by the third pebble in a phenomenally complex dance.

"You may have beaten me during the Succession, but that didn't stop me from improving my powers. You should have killed me when you had the chance, I'm stronger than you, now," Merek bragged shamelessly.

Dayn watched in silence while his younger sibling displayed his newfound abilities.

"Nothing to say to me, brother?"

The anger in Dayn's heart gave way to profound sadness. Everything he cared for was being stripped away: his friend, his love, even his family. The ancestors would not be satisfied until he was a broken, empty shell.

"Why in the Aether would I kill you?" he finally replied, exhaustion creeping into his voice. "I promised our parents I'd watch out for you."

"Is that what you were doing during the Succession?" Merek snapped angrily.

"*You* almost killed *me*!" Dayn snapped back. "How many of my ribs did you break with that last attack of yours?"

Merek looked away. "It doesn't matter."

"It doesn't matter that the fight was over when you hit me?" Dayn questioned in a biting tone. "And I suppose you don't care that I let you live even though you were the one who challenged me?"

"You *let* me live?" There was a dangerous edge to his brother's voice, one that threatened violence if Dayn didn't choose his next words carefully.

"I was protecting you," the orishadaon responded.

"You destroyed my life when you beat me!" Merek drew himself up to his full height. The stones spun faster above his palm. "I should have won that fight! I'll never be anything as long as you're alive."

Dayn shook his head. "You'll be nothing as long as you care more about yourself than protecting your people."

Merek trembled with rage. The stones swirled at a dizzying speed.

Dayn hung his head, knowing there was nothing he could say to placate his brother's fury. Since they were children Merek had been envious of him and his status within the tribe.

"You're afraid I'll become more powerful than you," Merek accused.

"Yes," Dayn freely admitted.

"I knew it!" his sibling whooped victoriously.

Dayn waited for his brother to finish gloating. "I'm only afraid because I know what you'll do with that power when you have it," he said in his calmest voice. "There can be no hatred in your heart or you'll fall to the demons and become a shondaon."

Merek stopped grinning. "Don't repeat Sharna's lessons to me, I've learned them as well as you have."

"Then listen to them!" Dayn leaned forward, concentrating on a large stone amongst the rubble at his back. The stone shot forward and smashed Merek's pebbles out of the air. Before his own stone fell back to the earth, Dayn had slouched against the nearest wall, a wet trickle running from his nose and across his lips. Even small expenditures of power were too much for him at the moment.

Merek spit into the mud. Malice burned in his eyes. He pulled a bone-bladed dagger from his belt and pressed the tip against Dayn's cheek.

Dayn glared back at Merek with an unblinking stare of his own. A bead of redness blossomed around the dagger's tip. "Strike true," the orishadaon said calmly.

Merek hesitated.

"Well, are you going to do it or not?"

The younger man's hand went rigid, cutting a shallow groove across his brother's cheek. Merek breathed heavily, almost panting. "No." He shook his head. Slowly, he retracted the knife.

Dayn found it impossible to keep the shock from his face.

"Don't look so surprised." Merek tucked the knife into its sheath.

Dayn frowned. "You aren't known for your compassion." He wiped at the blood on his face and held it up for his brother to see.

"I have no compassion for you," his sibling replied. "If I killed my own brother now, I'd be banished. If I wait until after you free the half-blood, Toran will gladly let me do it just to be rid of you." He grinned his typical, self-assured grin. "So go ahead and drag her out of the pit I threw her in, I'll be waiting when you do."

Dayn's nostrils flared. In a show of disrespect, he turned his back on the younger man.

Merek only laughed at the empty gesture.

Rage boiled up inside Dayn once again. It seeped into the corners of his mind, clouding his judgment. Maybe he should turn around and show Merek why it wasn't wise to threaten an orishadaon.

No! He shook his head to banish the dark thoughts that had crept into his mind along with the red tide, berating himself for allowing such ideas to enter his head. He was an orishadaon; it was his duty to protect the tribe, every single member. Preserve life, never take it.

With his brother still laughing behind him, Dayn left to retrieve Agidyne from his hut. Merek chased after him, uttering more taunts, until Dayn flashed a look of warning that sent his younger sibling scurrying away to Toran's tent.

A few moments later Dayn stepped out of the heat and into his own shady hut.

It only took him a moment to gather up his sword and the vial of bright blue liquid lying next to it. The vial disappeared into one of his pouches before he pulled Agidyne's rusty blade from its sheath and tossed the tanned karda hide aside. The sword's notched blade was longer than his forearm, a little too long for him to swing without it being awkward. Strange symbols that supposedly spoke of the wielder's fate were etched along its entire, rust splotched surface. Too bad he didn't know what they meant.

This was it, he realized, the last time he would ever see Nesthome or any of his fellow tribesmen. Once he walked out of the hut he would no longer be one of them. He would be set on a course of action that would see him killed if he failed, and, possibly, if he succeeded.

"Protect her now, that's yer new duty." Ryl's last words would be his motivation. Of all the words Dayn had spoken and heard this lunar, those were the only ones that mattered anymore. Alis had been sentenced to death. If freeing her brought about his own demise he would consider it a fair trade.

He recalled Alis saying he would give his life for hers, and that he didn't even know why. She was only half right. He would most certainly die for her, but in spite of what she might think, he knew the reason. It was because he loved her more than anything else on all Urth.

Dayn picked up a handful of dirt and squeezed it in his palm. It was the dirt of his home; it had sustained him for many long seasons. He breathed in its scent, committed it to memory. Opening his hand, he let the dirt fall away, carrying his loyalty to the tribe with it.

After a deep breath, he raised Agidyne and carved the Swift Claw tattoo off his chest, damaging part of his orishadaon brand in the process. He almost passed out from the pain, but he kept cutting until there was nothing of the tribe's symbol left. These people had turned their backs on him, and now he had done the same to them. They would most certainly kill him for his transgression, that much was clear, but before he died he would ensure Alis' safety by removing the gauntlet, and the ancestors help anyone who got in his way.

16.
ALL THESE GOOD INTENTIONS

Agidyne in hand, Dayn approached a dilapidated hut encircled by a cloud of buzzing black flies. The hut was a rickety thing, little more than some karda hide walls and a sagging ceiling strung up between four bent corner posts.

As he drew closer his nose scrunched up at the reek of body odor and offal hanging thick in the air around the structure.

An acute, persistent pain clung to his chest where he had slashed it up; one more ache to add to his growing collection.

Two men sat outside the hut's only entrance, their spears resting within easy reach against the building's side. The first, a tall, gangly hunter with nervous eyes, gave the cloud of insects around him a perfunctory swat and picked six stones out of the dirt. One side of each stone was painted black, while the other was white. He grinned mischievously as he tossed them into the air, revealing rows of sharp, filed teeth.

The second man—also a hunter, if his bald head was any indication—tried guessing how many rocks would land facing up. A series of jagged scars covered his scalp, the side of his face, his lower jaw and his neck.

"Three white," the scarred one called out in anticipation.

Both men watched with growing excitement as the stones fell to the ground. When the last one landed, exactly three white sides lay facing up.

"Ha!" Scar threw up his hands triumphantly.

Tooth grunted. "You must be cheating," he grumbled.

Scar ignored the remark and pointed at the chiseled karda tooth strapped to the other man's waist. "I'll take that new dagger of yours," he decided.

Before Tooth could remove the article, both guards noticed the orishadaon, and their eyes went simultaneously to the sword in his hand.

Scar leaped to his feet and grabbed his spear. "Stop right there. Don't come any further."

Tooth took up his own weapon and stood just behind his partner.

"I'm here to free Alis," Dayn said without breaking his stride.

He envisioned Alis in the hut, lying at the bottom of a pit surrounded by the tribe's waste, and the revolting image strengthened his resolve. He squared his jaw and marched on.

"Did you hear me?" Scar growled, waving his spear before him.

"Be careful," Tooth said, eyeing Agidyne with obvious distress.

"I'm here to free Alis," Dayn repeated as he halted a few paces in front of Scar, making a point to keep Agidyne's tip aimed at the ground. There was still hope that he could save Alis without violence, so long as he did not push the already stressed guards too far.

Tooth poked his head out from behind Scar. "No one is allowed to see the shon-touched," he informed Dayn in a shaky voice.

"Then I'll just close my eyes while you let her go," Dayn replied drolly. He stepped forward and Tooth jumped back, bumping into one of the hut's corner posts in his hurry.

Scar stood his ground. "It was her own father that ordered her put down there," he said icily, letting his eyes wander over Agidyne and the fresh wound upon the orishadaon's chest.

It seemed both guards had a healthy fear of the metal artifact, as well they should. Those who were slain by an artifact like Agidyne would never be with their ancestors, would have no afterlife at all. Dayn could steal their souls with a single swipe and they knew it.

"I have as much authority as your gardaon," Dayn told the pair, making sure to say *your* gardaon, not *our* gardaon. He took another step towards the disquieted guards. "You're not worried about this are you?"

When he held up the sword, Tooth let out a soft whimper.

Swallowing the lump in his throat, the furtive guard glanced around as if he hoped to spot more tribesmen to put between the orishadaon and himself.

Scar, however, kept his feet firmly planted and did not budge a pace. The sweat beading on his brow belied his unease, but he hid his fear well. He tapped the point of his spear against Dayn's chest, just missing the wound there, and shook his head.

"Stay back."

The orishadaon narrowed his eyes and a steely edge crept unintentionally into his voice. "I'm telling you to let her go."

He sized up the two guards. The skittish Tooth would surely flee at the first sign of trouble. Scar, on the other hand, was loyal to Toran, and would not neglect his duty.

"Go get the gardaon," Scar commanded his cringing partner. "Or Sharna. Just find someone."

Dayn turned towards the unnaturally quiet pathway behind him. There were no karda calls, no women yelling to one another in the fields, no conversations or children laughing throughout Nesthome. The entire world had gone silent, drawing a deep breath of anticipation as it waited for him to act.

"You saw my Succession," Dayn said evenly. "You know what I can do."

"I saw Merek smash your chest in with a thought," Scar replied haughtily. "What's to stop me from running you through?" He motioned with a nod to the spear point tapping Dayn's chest. When Dayn refused to move, Scar said to his partner, "Go get Toran."

Tooth needed no further coaxing. He bolted away, calling out the gardaon's name as he rushed towards the distant tent.

The time for subtlety had ended. Dayn couldn't afford to reign in his powers any longer. The whole of the Swift Claw tribe would soon be there to stop him, and if that happened there was no telling how much destruction might be caused.

He focused his thoughts on Scar's right hand, the one with the tightest grip on the spear. He saw through the tribesman's flesh to the tendons running through each finger.

The orishadaon's next move required finesse, one mistake and Scar would never use his hand again.

Tendrils of orishadai wrapped around each tendon and slowly dragged them loose, forcing the hunter to release his grip. Scar sensed what was happening and struggled against it, but he was too late and his spear fell from limp fingers.

Dayn brought Agidyne up and gently tapped its tip against Scar's exposed chest. "Now, what's to stop me from running *you* through?"

The guard gulped. "You'll never get out of Nesthome alive."

"It's not my life I'm worried about." Dayn lowered his sword and pushed past the sweating guard.

He waited until he heard the sound of Scar's fleeing footsteps before making his way inside the dingy hut. It took a moment for his eyes to adjust to the gloom. The stink inside was so bad that he hardly believed it possible.

Dank, filthy pits, each at least twenty paces deep, dotted the earthen floor. The holes were only a few paces wide, not enough to lie down or sit in. Prisoners were forced to stand for the duration of their sentence, which could last as long as five lunars for a severe offense. Those in the hole were fed nothing, and would occasionally be showered with whatever awful waste the guards decided to dump on them.

Dayn knew from personal experience that the holes were too deep and dark to see out of, so he shouted Alis' name and waited for a response.

"What do you want?" an angry female voice shouted back.

Dayn smiled upon hearing her defiant tone. She had not given up.

He rushed to the edge of the hole her voice had come from and leaned over, instantly pulling his head back when the rankest odor he had ever smelled wafted out of the pit.

"If you have something else to toss down here then get on with it."

She must have mistaken him for one of the guards.

"There'll be no more of that," he yelled into the darkness.

"Dayn?"

"Who else?" He hurriedly tore strips of karda hide from the walls of the hut and tied them together to form a length of rope. When he finished he looped one end around his waist for leverage and lowered the other down to Alis.

"Grab it and climb out," he instructed.

"Are you sun-baked?" she asked incredulously.

"We don't have much time." Dayn braced himself on the edge of the hole.

"Toran will kill you!" she objected.

The orishadaon frowned. "Climb up!"

"Just get out of here."

Dayn cursed under his breath. "Alis, listen to me. . ." He paused, thinking he heard a noise outside. When all remained silent, he continued. "Alis, I swore I'd protect you. If you die next lunar I'd be breaking that oath, and I've let enough people die already. So," he took a deep breath, "you're coming with me now if I have to jump into that pit and drag you out myself."

After a moment of silent contemplation, Dayn felt a tug on the rope as Alis began to climb. The strain on his wobbly legs was great, but luckily did not last long. After a few moments she appeared out of the blackness and Dayn heaved on the rope, accelerating her climb. She grabbed the lip of the pit and crawled out, covered in a foul gunk he could not identify.

His bleeding chest was the first thing she noticed. "What happened to you?" the scout asked worriedly, reaching out to touch the mass of lacerated flesh.

"I made a choice," he answered, backing away.

She dropped her hand to her side. "What are you planning to do?"

"Whatever I have to."

"You shouldn't be doing this, what about my soul?"

Dayn snorted disdainfully. "If you want to be free of the demon you have to get rid of the gauntlet. Dying won't save your soul." He grabbed her by the wrist and led her outside.

They exited the hut to find a mob of tribesmen waiting for them, the gardaon and Sharna at the head of the crowd, accompanied by Toma, Gorm, Scar and the rest of the tribe's hunters. The entire rabble was armed, and looked ready to take action against their wayward tribal protector. Merek was conspicuously absent.

Sharna leaned on her twisted cane for support and hobbled forward, accompanied by Toran. "You have tied your fates together," she said to Dayn, disappointment clouding her watery eyes. A fit of coughing overcame the old crone and she spat a wad of red-tinged phlegm into her palm before wiping it on her robe. When she spoke again her voice was as rough as the bark on a scrub tree. "Orishadaon's are forbidden to breed with those of annaru blood, Dayn. You know this."

So, they completely misunderstood his intentions.

"Get away from the orishadaon," Toran said to his daughter, hefting a heavy wooden club the size of an uprooted tree. Alis' eyes went wide with fright as her father stomped towards her. She tried to back away, but Toran grabbed her gauntlet-locked wrist and yanked her closer. "So your loyalties are with him and not the tribe?" He scowled. "The ancestors will surely banish your soul to the Aether for this."

With a look of terror on her face she tried to claw his hand away from the gauntlet. "Let go of me, you don't know what he'll do."

Toran's grip tightened, threatening to snap her wrist. "There is nothing the orishadaon can do for you now."

"Not him," Alis corrected between teeth clenched in pain.

"Let go of her," Dayn growled, ready to lash out with Agidyne if the gardaon did not comply.

Toran snarled at him, his bestial annaru nature coming to the fore. With a casual flick of his wrist he hurled his daughter through the air. The scout landed with a grunt of discomfort and rolled to her feet at the head of the mob. Toma grinned down at her savagely. Tooth licked his lips.

"Take her alive," Toran ordered the gathered tribesmen. "The shon-touched will be cleansed in the morning. And you," he directed his attention to Dayn. "You can die with her. My daughter has been possessed by a demon and forsaken the ancestors," Toran addressed the Swift Claw tribe in a booming voice. "Her curse will fall upon us unless she is cleansed."

The crowd cheered, happy to see blood spilled as long as it was not their own.

Toma swung his spear like a club, catching Alis in the side.

The scout shuddered but did not fall.

"Keep the orishadaon alive," Toran told his hunters. "We will sacrifice him as well." He threw out his arms and a great cheer went up.

"Enough," Dayn said under his breath, anger building in his soul as the tribe continued to scream their adulation.

"Sacrifice, sacrifice, sacrifice," they chanted.

Dayn clenched a trembling hand into a fist.

"Sacrifice, sacrifice, sacrifice."

"No more death." He found it impossible to raise his voice over the roar of the crowd.

Sharna turned her gaze in his direction, sensed the weakening of his mental barriers.

"Sacrifice, sacrifice, sacrifice."

"You must be quiet!" his mentor warned the tribe, to no avail.

"Sacrifice, sacrifice, sacrifice."

A howl of fury erupted from Dayn's lips, accompanied by a shockwave that ripped through the crowd, knocking many tribesmen to the ground and casting dust dozens of paces into the air.

For an eye blink the gathered members of the Swift Claw tribe fell completely silent. They stared at him in open-mouthed shock, unable to respond to what they had just seen.

Then chaos erupted throughout Nesthome.

Screams of terror went through the crowd when Dayn turned on them like a cornered karda, eyes blazing with fury as he prepared to throw himself at whoever crossed him first.

Toma and Gorm were the first to recover from their initial shock; having already witnessed one of the orishadaon's outbursts earlier that lunar, they were ready for the effects of this one.

Before Alis could take advantage of the confusion and flee, Gorm swept her off her feet with a blow to the back of the knee. An instant after she hit the ground Toma slammed the butt of his spear into her forehead. A grunt escaped her lips and she went limp, eyes rolling into the back of her head as a gasp of air escaped her lips.

Dayn roared in rage and dashed towards the fallen scout.

His mental alarm told him someone was approaching from behind. He instinctively dropped to all fours, narrowly avoiding a sweeping blow from Toran's club. Before Dayn could scramble away, the gardaon reversed his attack mid-swing, smashing the heavy wooden cudgel into the orishadaon's spine.

The blow hurled Dayn against the ground, all the breath escaping his lungs in a shuddering hiss.

"This is it for you," the gardaon said, raising his leg over the orishadaon's exposed back and slamming it down in one quick motion.

Dayn sensed a brief flash of pain before he lost all feeling below his waist. A sharp kick to his hand forced him to release Agidyne. As soon as the sword was out of reach, Toran gripped Dayn by the back of the throat and hoisted him up.

"Bring my daughter," the gardaon called, carrying his catch towards the pits with one hand.

Toma and Gorm moved hastily, each hooking an arm around Alis to drag her unconscious form behind them.

"I smell your fear," the gardaon said after sniffing Dayn. The orishadaon dangled close enough to see Toran's pointed tongue flick out of his open mouth.

Dayn reached up and wrapped the fingers of his bandaged hand around Toran's throat, but could not muster the strength to squeeze.

The gardaon laughed at such a pathetic attempt on his life. He did not even bother to swat Dayn's hand away. "Bring Alis here." He motioned to a hole in the center of the hut, the same one from which Dayn had pulled her. Toran took her unconscious form in his other hand and suspended the two captives above the dark pit.

"You want to be with my daughter? Then share a hole with her," he said, releasing his grip on both of them.

17.
PERFECTLY BROKEN LIFE TO LIFELESS

While he hurried after a distant murmur, *It* ceaselessly hunted him through the twisting pathways of a nightmare jungle. His nameless pursuer shortened the distance between them and he knew it would never give up, not until he was caught in its cage-like jaws and unable to break free.

A distant voice echoed through the trees, calling him closer.

He stumbled through the darkness as a chaotic array of images shot past all around, too quickly for him to focus on any particular one. There were brief glimpses, though: terrible carnage, bloody catastrophe, and most disturbing of all, his own dead body impaled upon Agidyne.

He could not stop for a closer look, he had to keep going or the unknown thing snapping at his heels would catch him.

A needle-point of light pierced the suffocating veil of darkness that surrounded him. Some irresistible force tugged him towards that point, guiding him unerringly towards its warm embrace.

The world turned on its side and suddenly he was tumbling downward. He felt sick as he plummeted past the light into an endless sea of black, where he floated in limbo, allowing the calm emptiness to envelope him.

Then, without warning, *It* was there, writhing in the darkness and shattering his brief moment of serenity. He lashed out at his pursuer, fighting against its iron grip with all his strength as shadowy tendrils coiled around him. He groped blindly, reaching for anything solid as he struggled against the unseen foe.

"Dayn," he heard the name, his name.

Recognition sharpened his senses. "Alis?" he squinted into the void.

"Who else would be down here with you?"

Dayn's eyes snapped open, revealing a pitch black curtain of darkness on all sides. "No!" he screamed into the emptiness, battering the tentacles with a flurry of steadily weakening blows. Strength waning and mind afire, he knew not where he was or what was happening.

Unable to escape his perpetual nightmare, he cried out hysterically and continued to pound the unseen limbs that ensnared him.

Two sturdy tentacles quickly wrapped their way around his chest and anchored him to the spot with a vice-like grip he was powerless to break.

"Quit struggling." Alis' pleading voice sounded deceptively close, as if she were lost in the void along with him. That could not be. It was his prison, his and his alone.

"Get away!" He lashed out with renewed vigor, hoping to drive away the darkness and its false Alis.

"You're hurting me," protested the illusionary Alis with alarming sincerity. The instant she spoke the tentacles squeezed tighter, pinning his arms to his sides.

He fought on, refusing to give in to the hopelessness welling up within him.

"Damn it, Dayn, stop!"

Her sharp, biting tone drove back the dreamlike haze fogging his thoughts. It had to be her, no demon could so perfectly mimic that reproving voice. Dayn stopped flailing, and in response the tentacles loosened their hold on him. His sluggish mind came to realize that there were no tentacles, only Alis trying to keep him from thrashing about in the tight confines of their shared prison.

His body pressed against hers, their chests touching in a way that let him feel both their throbbing heartbeats at once, pounding in perfect unison. Together in all things, he thought with a grim smile he knew she wouldn't see.

He let out a sighing breath, allowing his body to go limp in her arms. His head lolled across her shoulder, a mat of Alis' tangled hair dangling atop his cheek as he breathed in her familiar scent along with a mixture of other foul odors he did not care to identify.

"Are you all right?" she asked when he had finally settled down.

An icy chill spread through the orishadaon's body, numbing everything below his waist. His legs dangled uselessly beneath him; if not for Alis holding him up he would be lying in a crumpled ball amidst whatever filth filled the bottom of the pit. Only her tight hold and the warmth of her body kept him from shivering.

He focused his attention on the circle of light some twenty paces above his lolling head. It looked so far away, like the souls of his ancestors shining beyond his reach in the night sky. He wanted so badly to touch the light, to let its warmth wash over him and drive away the chill.

"Sure, I'm fine," came his belated response.

The chill continued spreading through his body, the worst of it centered around his spine. It moved outward from there, creeping into his chest and up his shoulders, a frigid shadow across his soul. Odd that he felt no pain; his back should be in agony where Toran had stomped it. Instead there was only numbness.

"All for nothing," he croaked weakly, thinking of how his trusted mentor had set things in motion by sending him into the jungle to die. What had she meant when she said Alis was supposed to live, and that she had taken his destiny from him? "Damn you Sharna."

He felt the scout sling her arm under his own, the better to keep him from slipping out of her grasp. "Don't be so harsh," she chastised while propping him up between the mud-brick wall of the pit and her back. She wormed her way around behind him so that she could hook her arms under his to hold him up more easily.

A scream of agony bubbled up into his throat as the motion jarred his shoulder, but he bit down on his tongue, refusing to trouble Alis with his pain.

She was shaking her head, he could tell by the way her hair brushed back and forth across his face. "Sharna didn't do this to us," the scout objected. "She had your welfare in mind, why can't you see that?"

His choking laughter echoed against the walls. Of course Alis didn't know the real reason he was sent to the Tresslevale; apparently Sharna had not told her the truth. "Everything I am, I am because of her." He grinned at his own private joke.

She almost dropped him as he shuddered with even more scornful laughter.

"What's wrong with that?" Alis' question was part confusion, part frustration. She looked up to Sharna with a certain degree of respect, and it obviously bothered her to hear him speak of the decrepit orishadai user in such a demeaning way.

"Look at me!" his voice came out barely a whimper, but the tone carried such bitterness that it was impossible to ignore. "I'm a cripple and a failure. I couldn't even save you," he berated himself.

A moment of silent thought from Alis, and then, "I don't see a cripple and a failure."

Dayn raised his head off her shoulder. "What do you see, then?"

"A stubborn idiot."

"This is no time for jokes," he said, with more rancor than he had intended.

"Did I sound like I was joking?" she countered harshly. "You got yourself into this. I told you Toran would kill you if he caught you."

He hung his head shamefully. She had warned him, he could not argue that point. He opened his mouth to tell her he was sorry, but she cut him off before he had the chance to speak.

"Save your apologies Dayn, they don't do either of us any good." She knew him too well, could anticipate his responses before he had a chance to say anything at all. Alis was the only person who could truly claim to understand him.

The chill spread past his shoulders into his neck. Each passing moment sapped more of his strength. He fought to remain conscious. His head drooped across the scout's shoulder again. "I'm sorry for everything," he whispered into her ear.

"I told you I don't want to hear any more apologies."

"Please," he begged pitifully. "I need to say this before . . . before . . ," he trailed off mid-sentence. Before they kill us both at sunrise, he was about to say.

Alis remained tensely silent.

He cleared his throat, praying his mind would remain focused long enough for him to finish what he had to say. "I never wanted to cause so much . . . trouble," he began hesitantly. It took all his mental strength to speak in a clear, steady voice. "Not just for you and Ryl in the jungle, for the whole tribe."

He heard her disapproving sigh, could imagine her rolling her eyes. "People die," she said flatly. "It happens. Accept it and move on."

"Ryl shouldn't have died!" After the sudden outburst he broke down into a fit of rasping coughs.

"Easy," she crooned in a soothing voice while rubbing his back. "You're not well. Calm down."

How could he calm down when they were both about to die? For that matter, how could she be so calm? Just thinking about the agony Alis would have to endure during her cleansing ritual filled Dayn with righteous fury. It made him even angrier to know that there was nothing he could do about it.

"I've seen enough death," he lamented.

"Sounds like you're giving up," Alis observed.

"Maybe," he replied.

"Dayn." She put a hand on his chin, turning his head to face the sound of her voice. Her eyes flashed bright amber in the darkness, drawing his undivided attention. "You can't change fate. You just have to accept that."

"I can't." Dayn's teeth chattered as he spoke.

"When are you going to stop?" She gave him a shake. "When will it be enough guilt? You can't accept responsibility for every act of destiny that befalls the tribe."

"It's an orishadaon's responsibility."

"Some things are meant to happen whether you want them to or not." Her tone spoke of desperation, the words made all the more relevant by their current plight. "The only thing you need to apologize for is being too stubborn to realize that."

"No!" Dayn's wheeze was barely audible. "If all destiny has in store for us is death, why should we accept it so willingly?"

"Because you can't fight fate," she told him resolutely.

"Why not? Why can't I create destiny?" He asked the question which no tribesmen, not even Sharna, had an answer for. It was a question that had been in the forefront of his thoughts all his life.

Most believed fate to be a trap, ensnaring every individual at birth, forcing them to travel down a single, predetermined path.

He felt that destiny was a maze of infinite pathways, all with the same destination. One at least had the freedom to decide which path they would travel, even if they all led to the same, inevitable conclusion.

"You really believe you can fight the will of the ancestors?"

He nodded wearily. "I have to."

He could picture the look of consternation on her face. Envisioning it brought a smile to his lips.

"That's why I love you." She pressed her forehead against his. "Forget all that, let's just hold each other a while." Alis placed a tender hand on his aching shoulder and though he could not see it, he felt the brightness of her smile.

He noted his pain fading almost instantly. In fact, none of his wounds, not even his chest, bothered him anymore. His consciousness slowly receded into the lonely depths of his mind. It was very peaceful. He let his worries drain out of him as the tips of his fingers went numb.

Wait. Numb? That seemed wrong.

Alis stroked his hair, brushing a hand across his cheek as tears welled up in her eyes, reflecting their amber glow.

"I'm sorry," she whispered, sobbing softly. "We'll be together again soon."

"No," he mumbled, the word too slurred to understand. Dayn clung to what remained of his faded orishadai. "Please, no," he whimpered.

"I'm sorry." Tears rolled down her cheeks and splattered across his face. She continued to stroke his hair as the darkness pulled him away.

He tried to tell her he loved her, but only managed to croak out a strangled cry of desperation. He had to fight it. There was something he had to say, someone he had to help. An obscuring haze drifted across his thoughts. He had to save her . . . yet he could not remember who she was. What did he have to do? He was . . .

. . . an orishadaon.

Wild hair, blowing in the wind.

He had his duty.

A bright smile, just for him.

A destiny.
Amber eyes, filled with tears.
An inescapable fate.

18.
BECOMING THE CATALYST

He awoke to the sound of a distant horn-call. His eyes rolled out of the back of his head, memories flooding into his reawakened mind as if commanded to do so by the low, mournful blaring of the horn. Once again, darkness greeted his return to awareness.

His first conscious thoughts were not for himself.

"Alis?" he groaned, reaching out with a bandaged hand that brushed against the cold stone wall of the pit. She was gone, taken while he slept.

No, that was wrong, he had not been sleeping. He remembered the emptiness laying claim to his soul, dragging him against his will to the afterlife. The wounds he suffered during his fight with Toran were too much for his frail earthly shell, he should be amongst the ancestors.

Dayn shoved the torrent of confused thoughts to the back of his mind, focusing on more immediate concerns as he had been taught. Concentrate on the present, Sharna had instructed him. Be mindful of the immediate moment in time. Allow your abilities to deal with the future and your willpower to overcome the past.

He grinned ruefully, realizing there was no escape from Sharna's teachings, no matter how much he wanted to be free of their burden.

The first thing to do was find out what kind of shape his body was in. A few moments of cautious movement told him he was fine, except for a bit of stiffness.

Not only had the spreading numbness left his body, but he felt no pain from his numerous injuries. Even the fresh cuts on his chest seemed to have healed shut. Curiously, he ran the formerly broken fingers of his hand over his back and found the debilitating shoulder wound had healed itself too.

Not even orishadaon healing could knit flesh back together so fast, something else was at work here.

"Alis, you didn't."

He shoved his hands into the numerous pouches strapped around his waist, anxiously rooting through them until his newly healed fingers brushed against a familiar glass tube. He pulled the vial out, noticing immediately that the relic felt lighter. When he held it next to his ear and gave it a shake, no sound of sloshing liquid accompanied the motion.

"Alis," he moaned, squeezing the empty holy relic into his palm. Her last act had saved his life, while condemning him to live the rest of it without her. He pressed a fist against his heart, honoring her memory.

Watery eyes turned to the halo of light above his head. Tears streaked down his face, splashing amidst the filthy water lapping at his knees. "You should have saved it for someone who deserved it!" he cried. "I was supposed to die with you!"

Another of the signal horn's eerie wails cut through the air, interrupting his mourning.

The orishadaon went rigid, his grip on the vial tightening reflexively. It shattered inside his clenched fist, lacerating the flesh with countless glass slivers. He hardly noticed the pain.

The horn's summons meant a cleansing was about to come to an end. If he was still down in the pit, it must have been for Alis. She was alive!

He beat his fists against the stone walls in desperate fury. "Let me out of this damned hole!" he bellowed at the halo of light.

As expected, no one came to his aid.

A long bout of shouting at his overseers and thrashing against the confines of his prison left him weak and gasping for breath. After a final scream of despondency, he slumped against the wall, panting heavily.

It was no use. No one listened to his cries for freedom and climbing out was impossible. Or was it?

Remembering the morayth berries in the jungle, and how he had levitated one, gave Dayn an idea. If he could make other objects float, surely he could do the same with his own body. Rather than direct the flow of orishadai outward into the berry, he would instead channel it into himself.

That was it!

He pushed off the wall and stood in the center of the hole. Eyes closed and hands held at his sides, he concentrated on blocking out all external distractions (particularly easy since he was at the bottom of a pit built for isolation). The orishadaon traced the symbol of the mind's eye along the wall with a bloody palm, humming to himself in a low tone to keep his focus. When he was ready he envisioned an invisible hand lifting him out of the pit.

Nothing happened.

"No!" he raged. He had so little orishadai left, barely enough to keep the red tide in check, and certainly not enough to spare for what he wanted to do. Apparently, dying was bad for the soul.

Despair weakened his mental barriers, letting the tide's influence creep into the boundaries of his mind. A precise combination of powerful orishadai and steadfast mental control was necessary for halting the tide's advance, and at the moment, Dayn possessed neither.

He slammed his bloody palm against the wall in frustration, driving the glass shards deeper. Pain flared through his hand, causing the tide to surge. Not really knowing why, he concentrated on the pain and the effect it had on the red tide, committing the sensation to memory. He used that memory, building on its intensity, sharpening it to acute focus.

A dull spark of power ignited in the empty vacuum of his soul.

He slammed his palm against the wall again. The spark burned more brilliantly than before.

"I need more," he growled, driving himself into a maddened frenzy by repeatedly bashing his hand on the wall. The red tide fed on the rage, filling his embittered soul anew with furious energy that came from somewhere he could not describe, somewhere dark and full of hate. He did not care if it came straight from the Aether itself, so long as it helped him escape the pit.

As the tide pressed against the boundaries of his reason, the orishadaon let out a wild, animalistic scream. Arcs of white lightning crackled across his flesh, illuminating the dank hole as the spark inside him erupted into a roaring flame.

He almost allowed the tide to take control. How easy it would be to give himself up to its endless rage. With his defenses weakening, the tide pushed farther beyond his barriers than he would have permitted, were he in his normal state of mind. At that moment, however, all he could think about was freeing Alis from her fate, no matter the cost.

A column of invisible force pushed against the bottoms of his feet, thrusting him upward. Moments later he floated a few paces above the pit's dark rim, tiny bolts of lightning arcing about the air around him as he hovered towards the exit.

His nose rankled at the smell of himself; human waste mixed with burning ozone.

He kicked the grime from his floating feet and allowed himself to touch down, feeling the cool earth squish between his toes. Electricity sprang into the mud beneath his footfalls, baking it into a hardened crust.

Such incredible power coursed through him! It was not orishadai; he could feel a vacuum within himself that used to be full of soul energy, but no more. Something else surged through his body in white-hot waves.

Sharna had never mentioned anything like this in her teachings. The old witch must have been keeping the knowledge from him. He felt deceived. No, worse than that. He felt betrayed, and the raw emotions fed the red tide further. It was so near to the surface, so very close to overwhelming him, yet a small part of his reason fought the onrushing tide, refusing to let it take over completely. As long as he remained in control he could draw on this limitless new power and use it to rescue Alis.

With a glowing fist, he swiped aside the hut's door-flap, leaving it waving in the breeze behind him. His squinting eyes slowly adjusted to the savanna's brightness, and as they did he surveyed the village of Nesthome.

It was just after sunrise, the light of the ancestors sluggishly crawling into the sky from its place of slumber beyond the horizon.

A ramshackle watchtower with its sole occupant kept silent vigil over the waking village. The watcher, high in his post, remained blissfully ignorant of the orishadaon's presence, eyes turned as they were towards the savanna, scanning for signs of danger.

Danger meant many things on the savanna: a herd of horn-faces grazing too close to the village, an annaru war-pack on the move, or even an approaching storm. Odd, Dayn thought in a whimsical sort of way, that this lunar the danger came not from the savanna, but from within the relative safety of the village.

A multitude of disharmonious bellows erupted from the center of Nesthome, startling the orishadaon from his musings while immediately drawing his attention. A crowd of overzealous tribesmen gathered at the main fire pit, all hollering their individual war chants, filling the air with a deafening cacophony in an effort to draw the attention of the ancestors to Nesthome.

The tribe's capable hunters pressed together in a tightly packed circle, flailing their limbs in every direction, mercilessly bashing those around them with wild abandon.

Their glazed eyes, ceaseless shouting, and particularly vicious behavior all led Dayn to a single conclusion; Sharna drugged the men, as she had during both previous cleansings.

The women and the young milled about at the edge of the savage gathering, some cursing the ancient demons for taking one of their own, others calling upon the mercy of the ancestors to see Alis through safely to the afterlife. Still more encouraged the riotous hunters to greater outbursts of violence.

It looked to Dayn as though they had been at it for a while. All of the hunters bore fresh scars, mostly bruises and scrapes, although a few unconscious forms lay strewn about, forgotten amidst the chaos.

One woman suddenly dropped to her knees and, overcome with grief, wept as she begged the ancestors to take pity on Alis.

"My daughter weakens!" Toran's booming voice rose above the din of screaming tribesmen.

The women and children were the first to react, harsh whispers spreading through their ranks. The restless hunters caught on to the gardaon's meaning more slowly. Only a few stopped their frenzied dance, and they were quickly smashed to the ground and trampled by those who had not heard the message. The rest continued unabated, completely oblivious to Toran's call.

"Stop!" the gardaon bellowed in a voice that stilled the world with its intensity.

The hunters fortunate enough to be both conscious and upright immediately dropped to their knees and bowed before their leader, touching their foreheads against the muddy earth out of respect for his position. Their undivided attention turned to the naked figure standing at the gardaon's side.

Alis stumbled drunkenly through the kneeling crowd, feet hobbled by a wooden pillory that kept her from taking anything more than half-steps. A stone twice as large as a man's head was tethered to her wrists with a short length of rope that would have pulled her to the ground if she dropped it.

The stone represented the weight of her guilt, and she had to carry it openly before the tribe. If it fell from her grasp it would mean she was too weak to accept responsibility for her crimes, which in turn would mean her unclean soul was not fit to be with the ancestors. She would be banished to the Aether for all time as punishment.

Warding runes, tattooed across every spare bit of flesh on her naked body, were meant to strengthen her soul against the depravations of demons that would come to claim her at the end of the cleansing. The markings were somewhat similar to Dayn's orishadaon brand, except they were made up of tiny squiggles that Sharna called "writing."

It was clear from Alis' unfocused expression and stumbling gait that she was no longer aware of her surroundings. Ugly bruises created a patchwork of discoloration across every visible part of her. Only sheer determination kept her on her feet, and Dayn could tell that she would soon falter, regardless. The revelers had been pounding her into exhaustion for the better part of the morning, possibly longer. A body simply could not take that kind of punishment. It was a wonder she had lasted this long.

Toran, despite having walked at her side during the entire ordeal, did not have a single scratch anywhere on his body. Not even during the drug-induced hysteria of a cleansing ritual would one of the tribesmen consider striking him, for fear of his deadly reprisal.

"She has suffered enough," he said to Sharna in a voice that allowed no argument. "Let the ancestors pass their judgment on my daughter now."

It could have been a trick of the wind blowing over the distance between them, but it sounded to Dayn like the gardaon felt a hint of pity for his daughter!

Without lifting their foreheads from the mud, every tribesman turned to face Sharna, who, along with Dayn's brother, stood apart from the gathering.

Merek waited in silence, watching the proceedings with a tight-lipped sneer. The young orishadai user cast his contemptuous glare across the gathered masses, frowning at how they debased themselves before the uncaring ancestors.

"We can't end the cleansing without the orishadaon," the persistent old woman's voice creaked like the boughs of an ancient tree.

"We have an orishadaon!" Toran responded with the harshness of a thunder clap, and pointed a thick finger at Merek.

Dayn's brother grinned in satisfaction.

Sharna coughed and leaned heavily on her cane. "Merek is not the tribe's orishadaon. He failed his Succession and is not fit to protect the Swift Claw as long as his brother still lives."

All satisfaction wiped away, the terrible scowl her comment brought to Merek's face would have sent most tribesmen running for their lives, if they weren't high on a drug so powerful that too much could wipe a person's mind blank.

"Merek is the orishadaon now, and you *will* show him respect," the gardaon growled.

"He does not deserve my respect," Sharna said and reached inside her fluttering green robes to pull out the fortune bones. She cast them into the dirt and kneeled down for a closer inspection. "I see much death." She pointed at one of the bones, a particularly old and rotten one. "But not your daughter's."

Toran waved off the prediction. "Superstitious nonsense."

Merek stomped a foot on the fortune bones before Sharna could retrieve them. "If the tribe is in danger, why haven't I foreseen it?" He seethed at her earlier comment.

"Because you lack foresight," came Sharna's brusque reply. Without sparing the young man a single glance, she turned to Toran, adding, "We must have Dayn here, it is the tribe's way."

At his far off vantage point, Dayn rubbed a dirty hand over his face, for the first time noticing the tiny bolts of lightning that danced across his flesh. A slight smile tugged at the corners of his mouth. The red tide rose in a great swell, only to be pushed back by a supreme effort from that tiny part of himself that continued to resist.

19.
WAKING THE DEMON

Rage guided his steps as he approached the pack of drugged hunters. He was still a long way from the central fire pit when the tower's watchman cried out a warning. Dayn's breath caught in his throat. He froze mid-stride, gripped by apprehension as he waited for the man in the tower to draw the tribe's attention.

"Annaru!" the watcher yelled unexpectedly from his post. "Annaru!"

The orishadaon blinked in disbelief. "Wait." His eyes widened in surprise. "Annaru?" He whirled to face the savanna.

Beyond the crumbling ring of stone surrounding Nesthome, an unknown number of shadowy figures moved amongst the waist-high stalks of billowing grass, loping towards the village on all fours like a pack of hunting beasts.

"By the blood of the ancestors!" Dayn gasped.

Toran squinted up at the watcher. "Annaru?"

"All around the village!" The man pointed frantically.

"How many?"

"They're everywhere!" responded the watcher, too terrified to form an accurate estimate.

"Death comes for us all!" Sharna exclaimed in utter terror, lower jaw sagging until her mouth formed a wide O. The elder's weak frame trembled so violently that her walking stick fell from her grasp, forcing Merek to retrieve it. When he tried to hand it back she dropped it again, oblivious to everything besides the words of the screaming watcher.

Presently, Toran pointed at Toma, then at Gorm. The two hunters nodded in understanding of some predetermined message and rose to their feet, carrying their spears. "All of you, get your weapons. To the walls!" Toran demanded of the others.

The hunters responded slowly to his order, finding it increasingly difficult to coordinate themselves with the drug haze clouding their minds.

Dayn almost felt sorry for them. The drugs were powerful, and the poor wretches who took them probably could not remember their own names, much less how to wield a weapon to defend themselves. The annaru had picked a perfect moment to attack, almost too perfect.

While the hunters slowly rose to do Toran's bidding, Toma and Gorm shoved through the crowd, making their way towards Alis. Both of them looked perfectly fine, suffering none of the ill effects of Sharna's drug. Toran must have made sure they did not take it.

Once the pair reached Alis, it only took Toma a moment to live up to his malicious reputation. He swatted the back of her leg with the haft of his spear, forcing her to her knees. She grunted in discomfort, but did not let go of the guilt stone.

Gorm shot his fellow hunter a disapproving scowl.

"Don't move," Toma ordered, shoving Alis' shoulder with his foot, oblivious to Gorm's icy stare.

Alis ignored the order, or in her delirious state, did not understand it. She rose on shaking legs, turning her unfocussed stare from left to right. While gazing out over the savanna, the scout's eyes suddenly flashed with deadly clarity. As if by some miracle, she regained her senses, and gave Toma a look of unbridled hatred.

"You'll pay for damaging my vessel," she told him in the same gravelly voice she spoke in whenever the gauntlet's prisoner overtook her mind.

Her sudden change in demeanor startled Toma. He froze, confusion written all over his weathered face. It took him a few moments to regain his composure. Once he did, the hunter pulled his spear back and swung at the side of her knee.

"Stop!" Gorm cried. Too slow, he reached out a hand to catch the weapon and missed it.

The heavy blow connected as intended, sweeping Alis off her feet. As she fell sideways, her hands went down to soften the landing, and the massive rock landed on top of them with a bone-shattering *crunch*. To her credit, only a single cry escaped her lips before she bit down on her tongue to silence any further moans of pain.

"I will kill you, human!" the horrible voice sprang, once again, from Alis' lips. The gauntlet saved her right hand, but every bone in the left was smashed beneath the stone's weight. Beads of sweat cascaded across her temples and down her brightly flushed cheeks. She writhed in agony, trying to pull her hand from under the rock's crushing embrace.

Bearing witness to her agonized struggles proved too much for Dayn. There was an eruption of fury within his soul and the strange new energy he had discovered filled his body with unbelievable strength. The red tide flooded in along with the energy, drowning his mental defenses in an ocean of rage that colored his vision crimson. He stormed forward, daring anyone or anything to bar his way.

The slowly dispersing crowd took notice of him only after he plowed headlong into its midst, eliciting shouts of surprise from those who were not quick enough to scatter before his wrath. The ones who failed to get out of the way, or were shoved into his path to divert his attention, found themselves sprawled across the ground, writhing in agony as miniature bolts of lightning sizzled their skin.

It was not until he pushed away the last stumbling hunter and cleared a space around her that Alis finally noticed him.

"The healing waters worked!" she exclaimed, her own voice forcing its way through the demon's control.

The familiar tone of the scout's voice calmed him enough to momentarily halt the tide's progress. It receded, scraping away a layer of his soul as it went. The blinding crimson haze evaporated, granting him a semblance of control. It seemed that each time he called upon his newfound power the red tide grew stronger. In the future he would have to use it more carefully.

Dayn found himself in the middle of a riot, twitching tribesmen lying in the mud all around him while others fled for their lives in every direction.

Toma and Gorm gaped at him, their surprised expressions almost comical considering the circumstances. The two hunters continued to stare, transfixed by the sight of him rolling the guilt stone off Alis' hand.

Without the stone's pressure on her ruined fingers, fresh blood spurted out of them, dribbling down her forearm. She made no move to staunch the vermilion cascade, instead grabbing the guilt rock with the gauntlet and slamming it down atop her ankle pillory. The wood came apart with a splintering *crack*.

The instant she was free a terrible change overcame her. Few would have noticed the difference, but Dayn recognized it immediately. Her stance, bearing and demeanor altered drastically, from an impression of subtle strength and grace to a more regal pose of haughty arrogance. The thing standing before him might have been Alis once, but no more.

"Gardaon!" it rumbled contemptuously, the sound altogether inhuman.

Toran turned away from giving orders to a glassy-eyed tribesman, irritated by such an untimely distraction. When he saw who had interrupted him, his scowl turned to a tight-lipped stare, betraying his surprise. He quickly overcame the shock of his daughter's sudden transformation, and the even greater shock of seeing the orishadaon with her.

"Kill them both!" he demanded without another moment's hesitation.

Toma grinned and moved forward while Gorm looked torn between his duty to his gardaon and some inner conflict of conscience.

"Annaru are attacking!" The man in the watchtower continued to shout his warning until a barbed javelin streaked through the air and struck him between the shoulder blades, silencing him for good. His body toppled out of the tower, dead before it hit the ground.

Oblivious to the horde of scaled ones battling all along Nesthome's outer wall, Alis hefted her blood-smeared guilt stone in one hand, ready to crush Toma when he came too close. She held her ground before his predatory advance, waiting patiently as he circled over and over again. To Dayn, the scout appeared bored.

Toma, believing her disinterest to be a sign of weakness, lashed out with a spear thrust aimed at Alis' midsection. His first mistake was missing. The scout's body became a blur as she twirled gracefully away from the spear's deadly tip. His second mistake was not getting out of the way when she knocked his weapon aside and lunged forward with supernatural speed, bringing the guilt stone down upon his head.

Dayn's stomach lurched and he turned away, the horrible image of Toma's collapsing skull imprinted forever in his mind. Rational thought warred with the red tide, struggling to reinforce its tenuous grip on his sanity. Every spilled drop of blood strengthened the tide, added to its growing momentum and increased the pressure placed on him to stay in control.

"The tribe will fall! Death comes for us all!" Sharna professed, much to the amusement of Merek, who stood beside her, smirking. He did not seem to care that Alis had gone insane and started killing tribesmen.

"Kill those two!" Toran screeched, a web-work of veins bulging against the scaly flesh of his neck as he pointed a thick finger in Dayn and Alis' direction. "Kill everything that threatens the Swift Claw tribe!" he added as Toma's crumpled body hit the ground.

Gorm rushed to his fellow hunter's side, though there was little he could do. When it became clear that Toma was beyond help, he slowly raised his eyes to Alis' back. "Face me, demon," he challenged the thing.

Purposefully ignoring him, Alis casually tossed the guilt stone aside, wiped a stray drop of Toma's blood from her cheek and flicked it away. A devilish crimson hue surrounded the gauntlet's ruby.

"Face me!" Gorm shouted in a final attempt to draw the demon into an honorable confrontation. When Alis did not move, the hunter jumped over Toma's corpse and stabbed his spear at her back.

The scout turned and her gauntleted hand shot out. She clasped Gorm's spear, shattering it. Thrown off balance by her unexpected maneuver and robbed of his weapon, Gorm tried to retreat. Alis slipped in close, meeting the hunter's fearful gaze for one brief instant. Then she slammed her fistful of jagged splinters into his bulging eyes, permanently blinding him. He let out a loud, lingering scream, until the scout wrapped her metal-encased fingers around his throat and squeezed. Gorm reached up with both hands and pounded ineffectually on her wrists. Alis clenched her hand into a fist, crushing the hunter's throat in a shower of bloody foam that erupted from his gaping mouth.

She dumped his limp body next to Toma's and turned towards her father, who had watched without moving while she sent the tribe's two best hunters to meet the ancestors.

Merek, too, observed the grisly display of martial skill, content to watch, rather than take part in the battle.

With no one left to fight for him, Toran was forced to confront his possessed daughter.

The demon snarled and kneeled down to slip a bone-bladed dagger from a sheath around Gorm's waist. It ran a thumb across the edge, opening a shallow cut which it quickly licked clean. "No one harms my vessel," the thing said.

Weapon at the ready, Alis barreled towards her father without sparing another word, catching Toran in the midsection with a brutal shoulder tackle that swept both of them off their feet. They went down in a ball of punching fists and thrashing legs, Alis jabbing repeatedly at her father's exposed side, intent on a fatal strike to the kidney. The gardaon was no stranger to combat, however, and he turned aside each blow before it landed using his scaly forearms as shields. Curses rose from the lips of father and daughter alike as they struggled to pry themselves free of one another.

Dayn, caught in the throes of a mental duel with the red tide, could only watch in stunned silence. The demon had taken hold of Alis once again, and this time she might not be able to break free of its influence. "Do something," he commanded himself.

Indifferent to the chaos around him, Merek casually strolled through the screaming mob, eyeing the panicked tribesmen and his raving mentor with equal parts amusement and disgust. "I have to do everything," he sighed.

The sounds of annaru slaughter rang throughout Nesthome. A nightmarish chorus of saurian shrieks and howls filled the crisp morning air, met by the dying cries of tribesmen who had been mortally wounded but had not yet passed on to the afterlife.

Dayn pounded his leaden legs, willing them to move so that he might do something, anything, to help Alis. "Damn it all to the Aether! Move!"

"Trying to run away?" The question came from Merek. "You really should. Coming back for the half-blood was a mistake." He shook his head regrettably and thrust out his hand. A column of seething red light burst from his palm and streaked towards the orishadaon.

Dayn clenched his fist and a shimmering wall appeared before him, deflecting Merek's bolt into the air. Pain lanced through his skull as blood trickled from his nose in a steady stream. At that exact moment, the tide launched another assault against his senses, attempting to drown him in a sea of endless rage. It would continue to gain strength each time he used the power, and here he was, facing an orishadai user.

Don't think about that now, he told himself. Think about saving Alis. Focus on the present. "Why are you doing this?" he cried in frustration. "The tribe is dying and you want to fight now?"

"Hmph," Merek snorted with disinterest. His body trembled as he built up a surplus of orishadai. He let out a soft groan that quickly turned to a shout of fury as his muscles swelled with coalescing power. The younger orishadai user screamed his battle cry and charged, intent on beating Dayn to death with his bare fists.

Dayn ducked under the first awkward swing to grab hold of Merek's extended arm. Firmly gripping the limb, Dayn brought his elbow down on top of it as hard as he could. The arm did not break, but the chords of muscle within it strained against the pressure put on them.

Though in intense pain, Merek made a fist of his free hand and slammed it repeatedly into his brother's side, causing Dayn to suck in a ragged gasp. The younger orishadai user followed through with a blow to the stomach that forced the breath from Dayn's lungs in a loud *whoosh* of air.

Wheezing as he slumped forward, Dayn sent his elbow in a cartwheel spin and brought it down on top of Merek's head. His younger brother let out a grunt as the elbow connected with his skull. He fell forward, bleary-eyed and flailing mindlessly. It looked as if he would go down, but Merek caught himself with one arm and pushed himself back onto his feet. "That hurt," he muttered to himself, shaking his head. He took another moment to catch his breath before rushing forward again, swinging his fists in a bewildering flurry of blows that Dayn could not hope to block.

Instead, the orishadaon weathered the assault, protecting his face from the worst of it while pressing forward through the hail of fists, reducing the force behind each one by giving his sibling no room to swing. His brother pulled back a fist for the powerful strike that would end the fight, leaving himself momentarily exposed. Dayn took advantage of the opening and jerked his head forward, delivering a merciless head-butt. Merek's nose exploded in a shower of red that splattered across both their faces.

Dayn immediately kneed his wailing brother in the stomach, dropping him to the ground. When Merek tried to rise, Dayn, aided by a swell of the tide's fury, delivered a vicious kick to the back of his brother's skull. The younger orishadai user collapsed with a groan and lay still.

The brief moment of respite gave Dayn a chance to check on Alis. She and Toran had untangled themselves and were walking in slow circles around one another, each looking for an opening to exploit, neither finding one.

Toran's arms bore numerous superficial cuts from his daughter's dagger, nothing that would slow him down or give him trouble.

Alis, on the other hand, was unwell to begin with, and Dayn could not tell the difference between her fresh scars and the ones inflicted by the drugged revelers.

Merek uttered a pitiful moan from his place on the ground. Dayn guessed that his brother would regain his senses soon, and decided to use what little time he had before that happened to help the scout.

"Stay back," the demon inside her snarled at his approach, never once taking its slitted eyes off Toran. "This one dies by my hand." The gauntlet's crimson aura glowed brighter when Alis lunged forward. Blinded by the demon's rage, she stabbed at Toran's heart.

The blade only grazed his chest, skillfully knocked aside at the last moment by a deft swipe of his forearm. He responded with a devastating backhand that twisted his daughter's head around so far that her chin glanced off her shoulder.

Alis lurched violently, caught completely off guard by the blow. Somehow she managed to stay on her feet. Barely conscious now, with nothing but the demon's hatred to keep her going, Alis gripped the dagger's blade between her thumb and forefinger and hurled it at her father.

The dagger flew unerringly, embedding itself in Toran's throat before he had time to react. His eyes, so full of self-assurance only moments before, opened wide in disbelief. He wrapped a hand around the handle protruding from his neck, a hideous gurgle bubbling from his lips as he tried to wrench it free. With a stiff grip on the dagger, the tribe's gardaon let out a final, strangled breath and pitched forward into the mud.

20.
WHAT DWELLS WITHIN

"The tribe will fall! Death comes for the Swift Claw this lunar!" Sharna shrieked in horror, spouting one dire prophecy after another at such a frantic rate that her insights blurred into an indecipherable stream of mindless gibberish.

The demon inside Alis stared at the dagger jutting from Toran's lifeless body. In one quick motion it leaned down, yanked the weapon free, and rose to its full height, curiously inspecting it.

Dayn had a flash of memory. He saw himself back in the Tresslevale, surrounded by annaru corpses as their fresh blood dripped from Agidyne's rusty blade. Did the scaled ones view him the way he viewed the demon—as a mindless killer possessed by inhuman power?

A resentful fire burned behind Alis' eyes. For a brief instant her face twisted into a mask of anguish, then the demon took hold again, banishing all traces of emotion from the scout's haggard features.

Dayn closed his eyes to Nesthome's horror, only to be assaulted by the sounds of dying wails and saurian howls. The agonized screams weighed heavily on his conscience, crushing him beneath their tremendous sorrow. "This can't be real. This can't be real," he chanted hopelessly.

"Denial will not stop this," intoned the demon in its deep, guttural voice.

Dayn stared at it. "This is all your fault!"

It regarded him coldly from behind Alis' amber eyes. "You brought me this vessel. The fault is your own," it rumbled.

"You called the annaru here," he said. "You brought them here to stop the cleansing."

The demon remained impassive. "Believe what you want." It held up its arm to show him the gauntlet. "I have my vessel now, and before the sun sets your beliefs will be as dead as your tribe."

Not my tribe anymore, Dayn thought to himself, one hand straying to the blank patch of skin on his chest.

Sharna continued her apocalyptic rant throughout the brief exchange. Unfortunately for her, the demon grew tired of listening. For all her foresight, Dayn's former mentor realized what was about to happen too late to stop it. The demon raised its bloodstained dagger and slammed it into the old woman's chest, violently jerking it free to stab her again and again.

"Sharna!" Dayn cried out.

The old woman stared in open-mouthed shock at the dark smear spreading across the front of her robes. Suddenly alert, she thrust an open palm against her attacker's chest. An invisible orishadai battering ram slammed into the demon, lifting it off its feet and knocking it through the wall of an adjacent hut. With what little remained of her strength, Sharna held out her hands and slapped the palms together, toppling the rest of the hut. She toppled along with it.

Before the building had completely fallen, Dayn tore his eyes away from the demon wearing Alis' body and slid to his mentor's side, cradling her head in his arms. He wanted to curse her for all that she had done to him, to blame her for ruining his life and sending him to die, but he could not.

The old woman reached up, gripped his shoulder with a claw-like hand and pulled him close. "You are needed elsewhere," she rasped, her voice a harsh whisper.

"Don't speak." Dayn held her close, watching her life pump out through the gaping holes in her chest.

She should have been dead. It was a testament to her power that she could cling to life while so gravely injured. Only the conditioning of an orishadaon, coupled with a supreme force of will, kept Sharna alive.

"Your destiny has found Alis," she choked, red spittle flying from her cracked lips. "Take it back, or all that you are dies with her." A final hiss of breath rattled her fragile form. She shuddered violently and her hand fell limply from Dayn's shoulder.

"How?" He shook Sharna's lifeless body in frustration. "Damn it, how do I take it back?" As he let his mentor slip out of his grasp, searing red light erupted from the wreckage burying the demon. When it pushed itself free of the rubble, Dayn rose to face it.

"Worry not." It tossed aside a hunk of rock and brushed the dust off its bare chest. "You will join her soon."

"What in the Aether are you?"

"More than you can imagine."

"Demon."

The terrible thing chuckled. "So much more," it answered vaguely.

Dayn knew he had to do something. Alis' life would be forfeit if the thing inside her had its way. He stalled for time. "Why that body? Why did you have to take her?"

It watched with disinterest as villagers scrambled about aimlessly, men and women alike rushing to defend Nesthome against the scaled one invaders. "She is annaru. It is in her blood," it answered without taking its eyes off the surrounding chaos.

Dayn stepped cautiously towards the demon. It paid him no heed. For hundreds of cycles of the seasons, the gauntlet had been its prison. If he could force it back inside then perhaps Alis could take control of her body again. He would need help though; to distract the demon long enough to get inside its mind, and only Merek was left to lend him the aid he required.

"What are you?" he asked again while stealing a glance at his brother.

The demon finally turned to face him and Dayn shrank back before its unflinching glare.

"Do you not recognize me, human? I was only gone three centuries." When Dayn did not respond, it shrugged and turned its attention elsewhere. "A bit before your time," it remarked.

Three centuries? Three hundred cycles. That was about the time that . . .

No. Dayn refused to believe it. He cautiously made his way

towards Merek, moving slowly to avoid notice. The demon couldn't be what he suspected, it just couldn't. His brother remained motionless, and now the demon was only a few paces away from him. It had killed Toma, Gorm, Toran and Sharna without hesitation, and would certainly do the same to Merek given the chance. Dayn needed to get his brother out of harm's way before attempting anything.

The orishadaon waited for the demon's attention to be drawn to another part of the village before reaching out to his sibling's mind. For all Merek's boasting he was still the weaker orishadai user, and Dayn easily forced aside his sibling's mental barriers.

Merek? You're not safe. You have to get away from Alis.

Dayn? His brother's thoughts were clouded by pain. *What are you doing in my mind? Get out! Get out or I'll kill you!*

Be still! There isn't much time. I need your help.

You'll get no help from me.

If you don't, we both die.

"You seem preoccupied." The demon arched an eyebrow questioningly. "What draws your attention more than me?"

If it realized what he was doing, Merek would be exposed. Dayn swallowed the lump in his throat. Sweat beaded on his brow from the effort of holding a mental link while staying aware of his surroundings. The tide swelled within him. "You can't be here," his voice quivered with the strain of speaking. "You're dead. My ancestors killed you."

The demon smiled, a cruel, mirthless gesture. "Your ancestors were weak. They failed."

Who is that?

It's the thing inside Alis. We have to force it out before it kills anyone else.

Merek's mind went silent. *I'm listening.*

Dayn quickly told him of his plan to drive the demon back inside its prison, and for the briefest instant, his eyes went to his brother's unmoving form.

The demon followed his gaze. "So that is what you have been doing." It reached towards the back of Merek's throat.

"Look out!" Dayn yelled, aloud and inside his brother's mind at once.

The young orishadai user needed no such warning. With the

demon's hand hovering half a pace above him, he rolled over, blood from his nose splattered across a hateful grimace, and rammed a dagger—the same one used to kill Toran and Sharna—into Alis' thigh.

Both Dayn and the demon let out an angry cry.

"Alis!" the orishadaon shouted.

His concern for her safety was unnecessary. The demon's hand came to rest on the dagger and its cry turned to mocking laughter. "This is the best you can do?" It slowly drew the weapon out of the wound and tossed it away. The torn flesh writhed and stretched, tendons and muscles reconnecting as the puncture knitted shut before the orishadaon's startled eyes.

"This is nothing compared to the agony of the Aether," the demon told them. "It will take more than that to stop me." To further prove its point, the demon showed both brothers its mangled hand, which proceeded to piece itself back together. Dislocated bones clicked into place, tendons stretched anew and a fresh layer of skin covered it all. After barely a moment the crippling wound was fully healed.

"This is madness," Merek said. He then grinned deviously. "Should be a good fight."

"Be wary," Dayn warned.

"Worry about yourself. Once I kill the half-blood I'm going to finish you."

The demon flexed its gauntleted fingers eagerly.

Merek stretched out his arm, splayed his fingers. Coils of black orishadai pressed through the flesh of his open palm, their color mirroring the shade of his own darkened soul. The coils wound around one another, forming a massive tentacle that lashed the air like a maddened beast. It shot forward, wrapping itself around the demon's neck.

The demon reached up and calmly poked the tentacle with a finger. The shadowy appendage melted away faster than it had appeared. "My turn." It made a fist and Merek fell to the ground, clutching his chest. He gasped for breath as if he were suffocating, reaching out to his brother in desperation.

"Let him go," Dayn said firmly, stepping forward.

Merek's eyes bulged as his lips turned blue.

The demon did not release him. Instead, it watched Dayn's reaction, perplexed. "The vessel's memories show me you and this one are at odds. Why do you defend him?"

When Merek opened his mouth to speak only drool and a wet gurgle came out. The demon tightened its fist, causing the young orishadai user's eyes to roll up into their sockets.

Dayn interposed himself between the demon and Merek. "Let my brother go!"

The demon shrugged, giving its wrist a casual flick.

Merek gasped, finally able to draw breath into his crushed lungs.

All at once, Dayn's chest tightened with suffocating pressure. He dropped to his knees, sweat pouring down the sides of his face. Before he could even think of defending himself the breath left his lungs. Veins in his neck bulged outward, threatening to burst.

"Dayn!" Merek's voice floated through his muddled thoughts.

He had to fight back. More than his life was at stake. The demon couldn't be allowed to win like this. He envisioned a thick wall of the new power encircling his heart, blocking it off from whatever evil force the demon had summoned against him. The pressure lessened enough for him to suck in a few gasps of air. Not much longer now, and the red tide would have him. "You . . . can do . . . better," he panted, taunting his attacker with a forced smile. "I thought . . . gods were supposed to be . . . powerful."

The creature watched in fascination as Dayn rose to his feet. "Impressive," it said.

"What . . . do you mean . . . 'god'?" Merek wheezed between breaths. He licked his blue lips and wiped the sweat from his ashen face. One of his hands clutched his chest and the other was pointed palm first at the demon.

So much for the plan, Dayn thought to himself. It was all he and his brother could do to survive against the thing inside Alis, let alone defeat it.

The demon shook its head. "The young human does not know who stands before him? Introduce us, orishadaon."

"What in the Aether is the half-blood talking about?"

"Go ahead," it said to Dayn. "Tell him."

Dayn gulped. "Be away from here, Merek. Run while you have the chance."

"I'm not going anywhere until I know what's going on."

"I already told you, that's not Alis anymore." Dayn had difficulty believing it himself, but it was becoming more and more obvious that the woman he loved was gone, replaced by something so horrible that he did not want to give it power by saying its name aloud.

"Then what is she?" his brother demanded.

Dayn hesitated. "You wouldn't believe me if I told you."

Merek flashed him a look of irritation. "Get out of my way you sun-baked idiot." He pushed Dayn aside, about to unleash a blast of orishadai when a pair of massive, muscle-bound annaru rushed towards him from around the corner of the nearest hut.

The scaled ones wore metal plates decorated with intricate designs upon their shins, forearms and shoulders that added to their bulk and made them appear more menacing. Crude markings, drawn in blood, covered their scaly hides, markings that looked remarkably similar to those branded on Dayn's own flesh. Strapped to the creatures' wrists were giant blades carved from fire-hardened karda bones, and they swung them about excitedly as they bounded towards the two humans.

Dayn stepped forward to confront the pair and spotted a third scaled one lurking inside the doorway of another hut. It was only a few paces away from Merek, who hadn't yet noticed it.

"Behind you!" the orishadaon warned before facing the first two attackers.

With his hands clasped together, he made a chopping motion in the direction of the annaru and abruptly pulled his palms apart. At the same time, both scaled ones, in spite of their great mass, were simultaneously lifted from the ground and hurled in opposite directions. One slammed headlong into the annaru sneaking up on Merek, and they slashed each other to pieces attempting to untangle themselves. The other crashed through the thatched roof of a burning hut and leaped out the door an instant later, narrowing its eyes at Dayn as its singed tail went rigid with rage.

Dayn paused to catch his breath and fight back the tide. He clenched his trembling hands into fists, willing himself to remain in control just a while longer.

The annaru came straight at him. He prepared to defend himself, but shouldn't have bothered. To the scaled one's misfortune, Merek chose that moment to enter the battle.

The younger orishadai user swept it off its feet with a focused blast of orishadai and pinned it against the ground using an invisible barrier. "You should not have come here," he said, glowering at it contemptuously. With a thought, Merek twisted the annaru's knee sideways at an impossible angle. The sound of snapping bone accompanied the scaled one's dreadful, high-pitched shriek. "You have to pay for what you did to our tribe." He snapped its other knee.

Dayn shuddered at his brother's sadistic display. He turned to see what Alis had been doing during all this and his eyes opened in alarm. "Hey!" he cried out. "Where did she go?"

Merek pulled a heavy section of stone wall from the remnants of a collapsed hut and dropped it on top of the annaru's skull, finishing his grisly business. He wiped the blood from his nose with the back of a hand. "The half-blood ran off, did she?" He squinted into the smoky haze drifting throughout Nesthome. Flames licked at the sky, engulfing everything in a maelstrom of heat and ash. "Oh well." He shrugged, unconcerned with the destruction. "I have something to do first. Go find her, I'll catch up."

"What could possibly be more important than this?"

Merek refused to meet his gaze. "You'll see soon enough. Now go. Just make sure not to get yourself killed."

Dayn arched an eyebrow. "Since when do you care?"

"I can't kill you later if she gets you now," he replied without a hint of sarcasm.

21.
SET THE WORLD ABLAZE

Dayn watched Merek until a cloud of smoke obscured his receding form, then ducked into an alcove between two mud-brick huts. He rounded the buildings, ending up on a cluttered lane that led past the gardaon's hut.

A handful of frantic tribesmen battled against the annaru war-pack along the congested path. Their cries of pain and despair cut through the smoke-filled air, adding to the din of crackling flames and the moans of the dying.

Where Toran's hut once stood, a blazing inferno now raged, engulfing the tribe's artifacts along with the structure and wiping away hundreds of cycles of carefully collected human history as if it had never existed.

The scaled ones would pay.

Off to Dayn's right, a snarling annaru bore a drugged hunter to the ground beneath its immense bulk. It fell upon the barely coherent man, tearing hunks of meat off his flanks with its toothy jaws, devouring him alive as if he were a common beast. Further down the path, another scaled one dragged a struggling woman into an empty hut, for what purpose he dared not dwell on. Beyond that, a third annaru rammed both its wrist-blades through a hunter's back, killing him instantly.

Something besides tribesmen and annaru moved amidst the swirling clouds of smoke and ash. Shadowy forms, bigger than any scaled one, slithered through the haze, allowing the orishadaon only brief glimpses of their sinister forms. What little he saw of the creatures' obscure silhouettes convinced him that demons from the Aether stalked his village, leaving fire and death in their wake.

"Merek!" he shouted above the deafening clamor. Soul energy saturated the entire area, making it impossible to pinpoint his younger brother's location by detecting his orishadai. "Merek!" he called again, though he knew it to be pointless. His brother couldn't hear him. No one could. They were all dead.

Something fell against his back and sent him stumbling. He spun around expecting an annaru or the shadowy form of a demon, but instead gazed into the glassy eyes of a young woman. Her lifeless body slumped into the dirt, revealing a deep slash from the back of her neck to the base of her spine.

He reached out to touch her, stopped short, covering his mouth with a trembling hand as he forcefully wrenched his eyes from the dead girl. These people, his people, were dying. They were dying because he allowed Alis to put on that damned gauntlet and because, in his arrogance, he had forsaken them. They were dying because he was weak. All this needless death might have been prevented if only he had done something to stop it. If only he had used his orishadai to defend the tribe as he was taught.

An annaru stalked out of the billowing smoke behind the woman, one wrist-blade streaked with fresh blood. Its tail went rigid at the sight of more prey.

The girl had inadvertently saved his life by alerting him to the annaru's presence before it could sneak up on him. His mental alarm had been blaring constantly since he first encountered Alis, and he'd been forced to ignore its distracting call until now, a mistake that could have proved fatal.

Weaponless, drained of orishadai and unable to use his newly discovered power without inviting the red tide into his soul, Dayn was no match for the scaled one in single combat. For some reason, that didn't seem to matter.

"Damn you to the Aether!" he cursed, not knowing whether he meant the words for himself or the invader. It did not matter. He refused to run. He would stand and fight and die, if it came to that.

The creature clacked its wrist-blades together impatiently and hissed between pointed teeth. Its upper lip curled into a cruel sneer as it advanced, swishing its stiff tale back and forth behind it.

Dayn launched himself at the annaru. It sidestepped his reckless charge and lashed out with a backhand swing that would have taken his head off his shoulders if he had not fallen onto his belly to avoid the blow. Before he could regain his footing, the scaled one splayed a three-toed foot across his back and shoved him down. He squirmed desperately, unable to escape from beneath it. He instinctively called upon the power, bringing the tide along with it.

A wrist-blade's sharpened tip pressed against the base of his skull, giving him pause. Was this it, then? Would it end here, all his efforts for nothing? He felt the creature's foot tense as it prepared to thrust the blade into his brain. "I'm sorry, Alis," he whispered.

To his surprise, the weight on his back mysteriously disappeared. Dayn glanced over his shoulder, not knowing what to expect. It certainly wasn't the sight of the annaru, lying on its stomach fifteen paces away, writhing against an invisible weight that pressed it into the dirt. Without warning, the scaled one shot straight up into the air, then came crashing back down. The sound of its ribs snapping like branches made Dayn wince. This happened again and again, the creature's struggles becoming weaker with each successive strike against the earth, until it stopped moving altogether. It lay there, breathing shallowly, limbs bent awkwardly, blood seeping from between its broken jaws. Shards of splintered bone poked through its scaly chest.

Something landed in the dirt beside Dayn and he lurched away, only to stop when he saw Agidyne lying there. Merek appeared out of the surrounding smoke, arms crossed, managing to look smug even with blood running from both his nostrils.

He nodded towards the artifact. "Take it," he said, ignoring Dayn's wide-eyed glare. "Go on, don't just lie there."

The orishadaon hastily retrieved his weapon, turning it over in his hands to inspect the notched surface. He had committed every dent, scratch and flake of rust to memory. The sword appeared to be in the same condition as the last time he had seen it. Once Agidyne was back in his hand, Dayn felt strong again. It was comforting to hold the familiar weapon once more. "I thought I'd never see it again," he muttered, as much to himself as to his brother.

Merek laughed at the remark as he strolled towards the dying scaled one. "Weapons make you weak," he called back. "I don't need a weapon, my powers are enough." He leaned over the annaru, resting a foot victoriously upon its chest as he stretched one hand over its skull. The young orishadai user leaned closer, as if to whisper a secret into its ear. "My brother is mine," he said pitilessly and sent a bolt of glowing orishadai through the creature's head.

Dayn opened his mouth to comment, but his words were cut off by the hissing of another annaru that stumbled out of the surrounding firestorm. Steam rose off its blistered hide. It snarled painfully, tearing at its scales, madly flailing its wrist-blades back and forth. It seemed oblivious to its surroundings as it rushed towards Dayn, shrieking.

He deflected its first undisciplined strike using Agidyne, shattering the saurian's brittle weapon in the process. The annaru gnashed its jaws, sending thick strands of drool spilling across its blackened lips.

Dayn barreled shoulder first into the scaled one with the intent of knocking it to the ground. Instead, he rebounded off it, feeling as though he had run headlong into a solid wall. It lashed out at his face with its remaining wrist-blade, forcing Dayn to bat the weapon aside using Agidyne.

He realized too late that his clumsy block had left him wide open to a counterstrike. The scaled one slashed at him with its broken blade, carving a jagged line across his bare chest. As he backpedaled away from a second swipe, the annaru bent low and lunged forward. It slammed into him with enough force to lift him off his feet and hurl him backwards.

He bounced off the karda-skin wall of a tent and pitched forward, rolling onto his back as the annaru leaped on top of him. He brought Agidyne around at the last instant, and the scaled one impaled itself on his blade. It kept flailing at him, too stubborn to accept death until the ancient sword pushed through its ribcage and out its back. Even then, it continued to twitch.

Dayn uttered a disgusted grunt as he rolled out from under the twitching body, pulling Agidyne along with him. Once on his feet, he turned to his brother furiously. "Were you just going to stand there while it tore me apart?"

Merek shrugged. "You have your sword, what do you need me for?"

"Damn it, Merek! I could have been killed!"

The young orishadai user shrugged again.

"Merek," Dayn hissed between barred teeth.

His brother wasn't listening. He was busy searching their surroundings for signs of Alis.

Sounds of the tribe's declining resistance filled the air, along with thick plumes of smoke. Flames rose towards the home of the ancestors, leaving nothing but burnt timber and flurries of gray ash in their wake.

Merek closed his eyes, concentrating. "I can feel the half-blood's energy. She's close. This way." He set off towards the source of the unique sensation caused by the thing that inhabited her body.

They passed numerous corpses along the way, many with bizarre injuries caused by no weapon Dayn had ever seen. He knew of nothing that could cause a man to curl into a fetal ball, blood oozing from his eyes, nostrils and mouth.

"You think it was her?" Dayn asked.

"It was the half-blood," Merek replied assuredly, increasing his pace.

Dayn neglected to mention the demons he had seen earlier and tried not to dwell on what such creatures might be capable of if they chose to fight.

"Is anyone still alive?" he shouted over the crackle of flames. Acrid smoke scraped his throat raw and caused him to cough violently. He wiped at the sweat matting his forehead, sprinkling the layer of grey ash at his feet with tiny droplets. His chest ached a bit, but not enough to be a distraction. He had suffered much worse, after all. "Anybody?!"

No answer came, unless one considered the sound of his world burning away to nothingness an answer, which, in a way, it was.

"Come on," Merek urged. "She's close."

22.
HEROES AND MARTYRS

They tracked Alis easily enough by following the path of wreckage and twisted bodies she left in her wake. The siblings found her resting against the side of a hut, while nearby, Mord struggled to knock an arrow into his bow.

The lone hunter gritted his teeth in determination as his blood-slicked fingers slipped across the bowstring. His labored breathing, interrupted every few moments by an angry curse, could be heard all the way from where Dayn stood.

The demon—no, Dayn now knew that the thing within Alis was no demon, but rather a fallen god—looked more amused than concerned, if its relaxed posture and crossed arms were any indication. It didn't bother seeking cover. It just leaned calmly against the hut, waiting.

Dark shapes moved through the surrounding haze. Dayn spotted three distinct forms in the smoke, all but their outlines obscured behind a shifting wall of wind-blown ash.

The orishadaon cast wary glances at each of the three skulking silhouettes. "Leave Alis to us," he called, waving Mord back.

"Let him try," Merek interjected, oblivious to the presence of the unearthly creatures. "Maybe he can weaken the half-blood for us."

"You . . . you'd let him die on the chance he might hurt Alis?" Dayn sputtered in disbelief.

His brother's silence was answer enough.

The god within Alis paid little attention to the orishadai users, instead focusing on the hunter.

"I'll put this arrow between your eyes," Mord threatened, his obvious unease causing the words to ring with false confidence. Normally stern and commanding, Mord now sagged from the pain of having barbed javelins embedded in his shoulder and stomach as he trembled in barely repressed terror. Not that he could be faulted for being afraid. Mord was gravely injured, facing an opponent he failed to understand. It was a credit to his courage that he stood and fought while the rest of his tribe ran away or lay dead.

Dayn looked between the god and Agidyne, guessing the distance. Twenty-five paces at most. Could he get to the creature and hack it down before it noticed him or attacked Mord?

As he considered his options, it occurred to him that he was thinking about killing Alis, not just the monster inside her. A fallen god might be in control of her body, but when it was forced out she would need the body back. If slaying the thing meant sending Alis' soul to meet the ancestors, he could not bring himself to do it.

Merek broke the silence with a sudden cry. "Shoot it!"

"I'm trying!" the hunter yelled back irritably.

"Try harder!"

"Don't do it!" Dayn pleaded.

Mord finally managed to place the arrow against the string. He raised his bow and aimed directly at Alis' face, ignoring the orishadaon's plaintive cry. The god stared down the length of the shaft into Mord's eyes, its stolen face an unreadable mask.

Its calm acceptance of the situation unsettled Dayn. He knew the god would never intentionally put itself in harm's way. If Mord's weapon posed any threat it would have killed the hunter instead of toying with him.

Before Dayn could warn the hunter, Mord released the arrow.

Alis' head jerked backwards alarmingly fast, a wooden shaft protruding from her cheek. Turning back to Mord, she reached up and tugged the arrow out as if plucking a pesky thorn from her flesh. The hole in her face healed shut within moments.

"Pathetic," the god chided in its gravelly voice.

Mord backed up a pace as it stalked towards him, then abruptly halted. Honor kept him from retreating, so he faced his doom with as much poise as Dayn had ever seen from a man about to meet his ancestors.

The god slammed the stony tip of the arrow into the waiting hunter's forehead.

"Oh!" Mord sounded more shocked than hurt. His eyes rolled up, trying to get a better look at the shaft protruding from his head, and continued to roll up until only the whites showed. The hunter collapsed.

"No more!" Dayn cried. His body jolted into motion before he realized what he was doing. Light engulfed his arm, flowing through his fingers into Agidyne. He screamed a curse at the thing inside Alis and charged, holding his sword aloft.

The god hastily raised its gauntleted fist to deflect the blow. Dayn hacked at the upheld arm, Agidyne glowing magnificently as it cut through the air. The two artifacts connected in an explosion of sparks and sizzling bolts of electricity. As Dayn turned away from the blinding sight, the gemstone affixed to the gauntlet's back flashed once and burst, ruby shards flying in every direction.

The instant it happened, a trio of demonic wails tore through the orishadaon's thoughts; one of anguish, another of rage, and one so terrible that it was beyond comprehension.

Alis let out her own agonized cry and stumbled backwards, protectively cradling her arm against her tattooed chest. The warding runes etched into her bruised flesh glowed faint blue upon contact with the gauntlet and she quickly yanked her arm away. "Why?" she asked in her own, distressed voice. "Why did you do that?"

Dayn, whose mind was slowly disappearing beneath the weight of the tide, took a step towards her, only to have Merek shove him aside violently.

The younger orishadai user gripped Alis by the throat, a look of madness passing across his flushed face. Squeezing hard, he declared: "If orishadai won't work, I'll strangle the life out of you with my bare hands!"

The ruined gauntlet gave off a harsh glow. Crimson marks quivered beneath Alis' warded flesh, pressing hard against the protective markings meant to keep such things at bay. A steadily brightening vermilion light shone from the artifact, bathing the ruins of Nesthome in an unholy afterglow.

Dayn's psychic alarm rang so loudly in his mind that he had trouble hearing anything else. Even the crashing of the tide against his senses was dull in comparison.

Alis calmly pried Merek's hands away from her throat, overpowering the hysterical orishadai user without struggle. "He's coming back," she choked out the warning. "Dayn, he's coming back for you!"

A tremendous burst of raw power exploded from the gauntlet, hurling Merek through more than thirty paces of open air. He landed awkwardly, his head rebounding off the firmly packed earth. The shockwave struck Dayn next, battering him to the ground with invisible fists as hard as solid stone.

Fierce gusts of superheated wind tore through the village, kicking up clouds of scorching embers. Flurries of burning debris whipped up and down pathways forcing annaru and the few surviving villagers to take cover wherever they could. Flames spread to every hut, engulfing them like a hungry beast. Of all the screams Dayn had heard that lunar, nothing quite matched the shrill, throat shredding wails of the people being consumed by the flames.

Red-hot coals rained down on his naked flesh, forcing him to cover his face with both arms. A trio of demonic shapes loped through the smoke, converging on Alis. The last he saw of the scout was three shadowy forms falling upon her.

A pillar of ash careened past him, tearing off the roof of a hut and sending a dazzling umbrella of burning grass stalks into the air above his head. Cinders alighted on his back and he gritted his teeth, pushing each new discomfort to the back of his mind as he focused on erecting a barrier to protect himself from further injury. Normally, he would use orishadai for the task, but he didn't have any to spare at the moment. The new power would have to suffice.

Dayn concentrated on forming the protective barrier, fighting against the conflicting energies within himself as increasingly powerful waves of force spewed forth from the gauntlet and increasingly volatile waves of the red tide washed over his mind. He gritted his teeth in determination, holding his mind together with thoughts of Alis. He could do this. He could save her and himself, too. The tide didn't have him yet. Stay in control just a little while longer, he thought desperately.

Dayn traced the symbol of the mind's eye in the dirt beside his head, watching it blow away before he could finish it. "Fine," he snapped at the injustice of it all. Damn the ancestors and their watchful gaze, he would do it himself, as always. The orishadaon stood up and accepted the full force of the storm against his body.

He became a focal point for the storm's fury. Wind lashed him like one of Toran's whips. Debris pummeled him like the fists of his irate mentor when he was young. Fire seared his body as it had all those seasons ago. Pain had summoned the power before, and pain would summon it again. Precious agony wracked his weary form, setting his nerves ablaze. It scuttled over his flesh, stabbing, stinging, throbbing and burning a path across his entire body. The tide fed well. The power came as expected, predictable, dependable. If not for its link to the tide, it would be perfect.

It started in his stomach, the sensation of teeth gnawing at his guts. The feeling spread steadily outwards into his chest, through his limbs, beyond him, bursting through his flesh and into the air around him. A shimmering, membranous film encircled Dayn, driving back the storm of fire and ashes.

Once he had a temporary refuge from the destructive force unleashed by the god's gauntlet, Dayn hastily scanned his surroundings. Alis and the demonic trio were nowhere to be seen, lost within a whirling miasma of flames. Merek remained where he had fallen, completely exposed to the harsh effects of the all-consuming fire.

"To me!" Dayn waved at his disoriented brother. His newfound power could serve as a natural barrier against almost anything, but the gauntlet's energy would tear Merek into tiny bits if he did not get inside a barrier.

Dayn's self-control waged a silent battle with the encroaching tide. He needed the power, not the accompanying waves of fury, but there was no way to separate the two. Until now, he had managed to keep them in a precarious state of balance, but that was changing quickly. Things were about to shift in favor of the tide. He could sense the transformation within himself and despaired for what he would become if he continued to draw on the power.

The orishadaon cursed himself for a sun-baked idiot and pressed his lacerated left hand through the protective cocoon, giving up more of his mind to the tide's depravations so that he could form a separate shield around Merek by channeling energy through his exposed arm.

BOOM!

A second shield encircled his brother moments before the world disappeared in a flash of light. The thunderous sound signaled an apocalyptic eruption of power from the gauntlet. That power crashed against both barriers, rippling across their surfaces in wave after endless wave of destructive force.

Despite terrible pain, Dayn refused to pull his arm out of the firestorm, determined to save Merek, if not himself. The outer layer of his skin blistered from the intense heat as he struggled to keep his brother safe.

An ocean of fire washed over the world. He heard a steady, deafening roar as energy battered his shield, saw nothing but swirling red emptiness, and felt agony as the skin of his forearm shriveled away. He knew he was on the verge of blacking out; keeping two barriers up at once was taxing his strength. The pain from his hand, the surging of the red tide or the massive effort required to control his own fury would have been enough to drag his mind into darkness, but under the pressure of all three, he would soon succumb.

The gauntlet seemed to possess a limitless supply of destructive power within its shattered ruby. His new power seemed limitless as well, but using it came with a price, one he could scarcely afford to pay much longer. Any more punishment from the gauntlet and his self-control would snap, the shield would drop and he would burn away as the rest of his life was burning away around him.

"My arm," he moaned and bit down on his lip. The feeling in his fingers had long since gone away, yet a fierce pain continued to radiate up and down his forearm. He reminded himself that without the barrier, his entire body would be consumed by such agony, though it was a preferable fate to letting the tide take over.

All around him, fire raged across what was once his home. An indistinct shape moved through the maelstrom, making itself visible for only a moment before disappearing back into the swirling inferno.

He recalled the memory of yet another of his dead mentor's lessons through the haze of pain clouding his mind. "Keep your thoughts focused on the present," he recited between clenched teeth. "Concentrate on what you are doing. Push everything else to the back of your mind. Ignore the pain. Pain is a distraction for the weak." If that reasoning held any truth, he felt exceptionally weak and distracted.

A gap in the fierce winds beyond the barrier showed Merek clawing his way through a hellish landscape of ash, then vanishing behind a wave of consuming flame.

The surface of the barrier rippled around Dayn, bulging inward from the pressure of the firestorm on the other side. His control weakened. The closer the tide came to his mind, the more of his mind disappeared beneath its rage. The tide would not kill him; it would fill him and corrupt him, turning him into a murderous beast unlike anything the savanna tribes had ever seen.

He slapped his free hand against the largest bulge in the barrier and pushed with all his waning strength, holding it in place.

The tide wormed its way through his mental defenses, touching upon the inner workings of his mind. The wall of mental force flickered momentarily and he thought for certain that he was about to meet his ancestors. "I . . . I can keep this shield up," he said between teeth clenched together so forcefully they threatened to shatter. More bulges appeared along the inside of the barrier.

Merek stumbled out of the firestorm and collapsed at the edge the barrier. Dayn severed the flow of power to his sibling's shield and pulled the young orishadai user inside using his withered limb. Instantly the sickly sweet odor of charred meat assailed his nostrils.

No longer forced to keep both barriers up, he was able to pour the entirety of his new power into the one shield necessary to keep both of them alive. The barrier's surface flared with newfound vitality, reforming itself by pushing back the bulges. The orishadaon let himself feel a glimmer of hope.

The gauntlet's blinding light dimmed a moment later, seemingly giving up now that it had no chance of destroying him. The raging storm outside abated, allowing Dayn a clearer view of his surroundings. He spotted hunks of rock, roof thatching and body parts amidst the rain of falling debris that pelted his barrier with the force of falling comets.

When the deadly rain ended, leaving nothing but a field of

charnel waste sprawling amidst scattered wisps of red-tinged smokiness, Dayn severed his connection with the power, leaving the red tide clinging to the limits of his mind. It could go no further so long as he never touched on the power again, but if he ever did . . .

The barrier fell away. A wave of hot, stinging air hit him like a slap in the face. When he saw what remained of his hand he quickly looked away. A shudder ran through his entire body and his wobbling knees gave out. An instant later he vomited into a pile of ash.

"Ugh!" Merek rolled away from the mess to lie on his back, staring up at the inky clouds dotting the sky.

The destruction was far reaching. Nesthome's walls had scattered to the wind. The morayth fields were pits of burnt muck and the surrounding savanna a wasteland of ash. It was as if the ancestors themselves had come down from the heavens and swept the village off the edge of Urth. The entire place and all its inhabitants, even the invading annaru, were utterly, entirely gone.

Curls of smoke rose from Dayn's body; the last traces of his summoned power evaporating into nothingness. He choked back a cough, struggling in vain to wipe the taste of bile from his lips and stop the blood from pouring out his nostrils. He felt faint. His head swam in a sea of confusion. Liquid fire burned in his veins, offsetting the unnatural chill that lingered in his flesh. He had never been without orishadai before and he did not like the unbearable feeling of emptiness forming in its absence.

"Still alive, I see," a deep and grating voice interrupted his anguish. Dayn weakly raised his head, disbelief turning to panic as he saw the god gazing over the remnants of Nesthome.

Hands planted firmly on hips, Kor proudly admired his handiwork. "Sometimes I impress even myself." He grinned through Alis' teeth. "I never thought you would have the courage to sacrifice your village just to draw out my power. You humans have developed some courage while I was gone. Good for you."

Merek gazed up hatefully at the lone woman standing amidst the destruction she had wrought, too weak to do anything after enduring all that he had.

Dayn gaped at the god, his lips moving at a frantic pace, emitting no words, no sound at all. Questions tore through his confused mind. Kor was alive again? How did Alis' body survive that apocalypse? Did anyone else escape? Kor was alive?

"How did. . . you can't . . . I don't . . ." he stuttered, nothing sticking in his brain for more than a fleeting instant.

The reborn god motioned, and three sinister shapes rose up behind him, hidden amidst drifting banks of acrid smoke. Their presence filled Dayn with dread, sent him shrinking back before the awesome terror that they inspired.

"My sword." His horrified mind finally latched onto a coherent thought.

"It's right here." Kor bent down and brushed away the flaky gray powder at his feet to reveal Agidyne's handle. "An impressive weapon, if only you knew how to use it." He lifted it up and tossed it into the dirt beside the orishadaon. "In your condition, it will do you no good, unless you plan to kill yourself with it."

Dayn tried lifting the sword off the ground, tugging on it without success. His muscles refused to obey him.

"It is pointless, orishadaon. As long as I remain inside this vessel, no weapons can hurt it." Upon seeing Dayn's shocked expression, the god moved closer and elaborated. "Yes, nothing will hurt precious Alis. She is still in here." Kor gestured towards the melted remnants of the gauntlet. "She keeps me company. 'I'll tear out my own throat to stop you,' she says. 'You'll pay for what you did to my village,' and on and on she goes. Full of stubborn determination that one. You two have much in common."

Dayn bristled with anger. The tide simmered within his empty soul, unable to break free and consume him. Its lurking presence frightened him almost as much as the reborn god standing before him. He tried to raise Agidyne again but even that small effort was too much for him.

"Kill it, Dayn!" Merek tried to push himself into a sitting position, falling back down after rising less than a pace.

Kor laughed. "If only you two could see yourselves. You look like the Aether, and I should know." The god shook his head sadly. "An interesting battle, but you lost. It is time to end this." Alis' fingers gripped Dayn by the throat, hefting him up until his feet dangled a full pace off the ground.

Dayn groped awkwardly at the inhumanly strong grip, failing to free himself. The god's thumb pressed into the hollow of his throat, cutting off his air. His sword arm hung uselessly at his side. He had no will to wield it against the woman choking the life out of him.

The god grinned knowingly. "Worry not, orishadaon, this will be mercifully quick."

"Stop, half-blood." Merek managed to prop himself up on one elbow, only to collapse within moments.

So much for a rescue. Dayn waited for the twist of the god's wrist that would snap his neck, or the quick squeeze that would crush his throat, but it never came.

Kor's hand shook, his iron grip loosening as a troubled look passed across his stolen face. His fingers twitched in a vain attempt to finish the job they had started. He dropped Dayn.

Alis' voice broke through the god's control. "Leave him alone."

"Alis?" Dayn asked tentatively.

"Be silent!" Kor growled, thrashing blindly as he stumbled away against his will.

"I won't let you kill him!" Alis strained to assert herself, the scout's features a complex mix of Kor's anger and her own desperation.

"Stop fighting. This is my body now!" the god raged. His three shadows watched impassively from inside a drifting cloud of smoke.

Alis showed no signs of giving up the power struggle.

Kor shuffled backwards in a halting, jerky gait, a fight for control ensuing before each new step. When he was far enough away that he no longer posed an immediate threat to Dayn, Alis gave up her body to the god once more.

Kor twisted his neck left to right, cracking bones numerous times as he worked out a kink. "Ah," he grunted. "Better." The god circled the pair of orishadai users, careful not to get any closer. He kicked up a cloud of ash in his wake. He hissed and growled annaru noises at the gauntlet, finally relenting after what sounded like an argument. "It seems the vessel wants you alive." Kor made no attempt to hide his displeasure. "Because of you, I do not have the energy to resist her." He shook his head regrettably. "I must be going, then. I have to ascend to godhood again, and there is a strict schedule for such matters. You know how these things are, it is all about timing."

Dayn's already confused mind failed to grasp the significance of the god's words.

"That is all for now, orishadaon. We will meet each other again, I am sure of that, and perhaps next time we can finish this." Kor wandered off into a bank of hovering fog, the three shadows trailing obediently after him.

Dayn watched with a vacant expression as the four of them disappeared amidst a cloud of swirling smoke. Was he dreaming? It felt like a dream. "You can't leave," he mumbled confoundedly. "You can't leave like that."

"You're letting the half-blood get away?" Merek's voice was full of condemnation. A cloud of ash fluttered off his shoulders as he leaned forward, only to sink back down an instant later. "This is all your fault," he grumbled.

23.
HAUNTED BY THE ASHES

Dayn traced an intricate series of symbols in the air by moving both hands in tandem, weaving an invisible tapestry that only the souls of the deceased could see. He hummed to himself at a frantic rate, desperate to keep the pace of his seemingly random gesticulations. Before now he had only done this once, for the tribe's previous gardaon, and at that time both his hands had been intact.

Toran was not always ruler of the Swift Claws. One lunar he just appeared, his young daughter trailing behind him, and challenged the previous gardaon to a fight for leadership of the tribe. The old gardaon readily agreed to the challenge. Not long after he was with the ancestors. They burned his body the next lunar and Sharna made sure Dayn personally performed the last rites.

There were exactly one hundred very specific motions involved in the last rites ceremony. It was essential that they be woven in exactly the order Sharna's teachings specified, or else the body would not release its hold on the soul, and the tribesman would be trapped between the world of the living and the land of the dead.

Dayn completed the hundredth motion and opened his eyes to the glowing symbol of the mind's eye hovering in the air before him. With a deep exhalation of breath, he scattered the glittering sigil to the wind, releasing his mentor's soul.

It was fitting that Sharna, whose duty it had been to watch over the tribe, was the final Swift Claw to receive the last rites. In a way, freeing her soul from its earthly prison released her from her earthly duties, passing on the burden in death as it had been passed to her. With the aged woman's soul set free, Dayn knew his mentor's responsibilities fell to him.

The lower half of the sun dipped below the horizon, darkening the sky and plunging the savanna into twilight shadow. Somewhere far away a horn-face wailed. Another horn-face mimicked the sound, and another, until an entire herd of karda bellowed their baritone frustration.

There was so much to be said for his people that Dayn did not know where to begin. *I'm sorry*, might have been a good start, if the angry spirits of the Swift Claw tribe would accept such a modest apology. Maybe, *I wish you were all still alive*, would placate their bitter souls? *I know I failed to protect you, but I tried my best*, might satisfy them. No, he knew his deceased tribesmen did not want words, they wanted blood. Blood was the only way to repay such a grave misdeed as failing to protect those under his care. Still, it seemed wrong for him to say nothing.

From behind him came Merek's contemptuous grunt. "Is that it? Nothing to add?"

Dayn stared at his ash-coated hands with detached calm, one limb whole, the other a tightly clenched ball of blackened flesh held against his chest in honor of those who had departed. A gentle breeze kicked up clouds of soot that stung his eyes, causing them to water. He wiped at the moisture but the ash on his hands only made it worse.

"Well?" Merek expected him to continue. Only the ancestors knew what was going on in the young orishadai user's mind. He seemed to be holding up well, considering everyone he knew was dead.

Dayn remained silent, shaken to his core by the events of the past lunar, unable to form his most rudimentary thoughts into coherent words. Encroaching darkness slithered into his soul, taking the place of his lost orishadai. It held him within its oppressive embrace, waiting for the red tide's prison to be unlocked. When that happened the tide would flood into him, replacing his soul and turning him into a demonic minion of the

Aether, fueled by undying hatred and endless agony.

"Nothing?" Merek asked a final time. After waiting impatiently for a response, he shrugged. "Oh well, they were weak. Weaklings deserve nothing." He ran a hand over his haggard features. "I heard what they used to say about you, and I know they thought worse of me. I'm happy to be rid of them." He lifted a waterskin to his parched lips and took a long drink.

Dayn did not move, staring blankly at wisps of ash blown free from an embankment. Images formed in the twirling dust, cruelly grinning faces of those who had given themselves over to the afterlife. Their piercing eyes promised retribution.

"They held us down, kept us from our real power," Merek continued his monologue. "Now there's nothing to keep me from using everything I have. Every last bit," he added in a whisper.

Dayn blinked, dissolving the condemning, wind-blown faces.

"It's getting dark," Merek pointed out. "Find some wood and start a fire. I'll see if I can find anything we can use in all this mess." He threw out his hand to indicate the scattered remnants of Nesthome.

The orishadaon considered his brother's words. A few scrub trees had survived at the edge of the destruction, there might be some wood there. He trudged off in that direction.

"Wait," Merek called after him.

Dayn slowed to a stop but did not turn around.

"You're going after the half-blood right?"

The orishadaon had no response.

"You know we have to kill her." A cool breeze blew another cloud of ashen faces into the air. Merek shielded himself, fanning away the soot without noticing the faces within. The sneering visages scattered, falling back to the earth with silent screams.

Dayn walked away, wanting to be alone with his thoughts.

Everything he touched died. First his friend, then his village. With Kor possessing Alis' body she was beyond physical death, but the god could easily extinguish her soul. All Dayn had left was the faint hope of saving her, and even that was corroded by doubt.

The orishadaon gathered firewood in the state of a solemn, mind-numbed zombie and shuffled back to the ruins of his home when he was done. He dumped the kindling next to what used to be the tribe's central fire pit and slumped down dejectedly beside it. It did not take long to get the fire started. Once he had it going, he poked a stick into the base of the flames, sending a shower of glowing embers into the air.

Dayn warmed his hands, consciously ignoring the one burned beyond repair. Shortly after the damage had been done, he clenched the hand into a fist and now the brittle fingers remained stuck that way. It was unfortunate that Alis had already given him the healing waters, for he had need of them now.

The crackling flames captivated him, emptying his mind of bitter thoughts almost as if they were being dumped into the fire to be burned away. For a time he watched the mesmeric, dancing tendrils of flame as they waved back and forth, casting a tiny circle of light across the graveyard of his village. He basked in their warmth and marveled at their subtle power. To think that such a small and insignificant thing could grow into a mighty blaze capable of burning away everything he knew.

"Dayn," said a voice from out of the darkness behind him. Snapped out of his trance by the voice, he whirled around to face his assailant. When he saw no one he rose, putting his back to the flames. Fire licked at his legs as he put every bit of space he could between the enigmatic speaker and himself. Unable to see more than a few paces beyond the fire's revealing light, he suddenly realized just how exposed he was.

"Ya always were too twitchy." A ghostly figure walked out of the shadows. The fire's light passed straight through its waxy, translucent skin, leaving it swathed in shadow even while it stood in full light. Its black eyes glittered dully, but held none of their former luster.

"You're dead!" Dayn hissed, gazing around to see if his brother was nearby.

"Is that any way to talk to a friend?"

Dayn glared at the spirit.

It rubbed the back of its neck bashfully.

"Spirits don't come back from the afterlife."

The ghost offered him a mirthless grin. "They do if ya don't perform the last rites."

"This can't be happening."

"I wish it wasn't."

Cold sweat beaded across Dayn's exposed back, from the closeness of the fire he told himself. If he could stop himself from trembling he might have been able to believe it. This was all too much for him. His mind refused to grasp the idea that his deceased friend was standing here talking to him. The fight with Kor must have shattered what remained of his tenuous hold on sanity. Yes, that had to be it.

The spirit came towards him, jolting him back to reality. "Yer hurtin', I can see that, but don't damn my soul just 'cause yer havin' a bad lunar. Ya have to go back and save me."

"You're already dead, you're beyond saving," Dayn responded without looking directly at it.

"My soul, not my body ya sun-baked idiot." It reached out to swat Dayn across the back of the head and its hand passed straight through. The ghost looked at its lucent arm and frowned. "I keep forgettin' about that."

"I don't even know why I'm listening to you." Dayn slumped down beside the fire and turned his back to the ghost. "You're not real."

It pointed an accusation at Dayn's swirling tattoos. "Those aren't just decorations. Ya took an oath to protect yer people from harm no matter what the cost. That includes the dead ones."

"Leave me alone."

"Dammit Dayn! I don't want to live like this anymore."

"Live?" Dayn laughed bitterly. What a joke!

"Quit actin' like a karda's ass," the ghost snapped.

"I'm not going back there, Ry. . .," Dayn stopped short of calling the apparition by its name, or else he would have had to admit that it was truly there, or that he had gone completely mad.

"What about me? How many times did I save ya? How many times did I defend ya against the tribe? I'm not askin' fer much, Dayn."

"You're asking me to go back to the worst place I've ever been. You're asking me to risk my life."

The spirit rolled its eyes. "Like I said, I'm not askin' fer much."

It was just like his friend to crack a joke in a situation like this. Dayn could not help but laugh, a harsh chuckle filled with more bitterness than one his age should know.

"Ya have to go back to the temple to save her anyway," the spirit was pleading now. "Just make a quick stop fer me."

"What makes you think Kor is heading back there?"

The apparition glared at him as if he had asked the most foolish question of his life. "Where else would he go?"

Dayn laughed again, less bitter, more natural. It felt good to laugh, and the spirit had a point. If Kor was going to ascend to godhood again, then the annaru city was the most likely place for it to happen.

"See, it's all startin' to make sense now. We just had to get that ol' brain of yers workin' again." The ghost grinned.

Dayn could not suppress a half-smile of his own. "You never did take anything seriously."

"How could I? Someone had to lighten yer mood, might as well have been me."

"Right now it almost feels like it did before . . ." He did not bother finishing the sentence.

"Speak for yourself." The ghost pushed a hand through itself and wiggled its fingers. "I don't remember ever bein' like this."

"*Orishadaon!*" Merek's harsh voice cut through the brisk night air, and Dayn turned towards his brother as he walked into the fire's light. "Who in the Aether are you talking to?"

"I was . . ." He turned back and the ghost was gone. Dayn hung his head and cursed under his breath. "I was just thinking out loud."

"About the half-blood?" Merek sat down by the fire and made himself comfortable.

"About how to find her," he replied.

"And how to kill her?"

"No," Dayn said, laying down and closing his eyes. "We're going to kill Kor."

PART III

ALL THAT REMAINS

24.
ONE MORE TIME

"I don't understand," Merek griped, not for the first time. He squashed an incessant mosquito against the back of his swollen neck, grimacing at the wet smear it left behind. "Now you want to kill the half-blood?"

Dayn shoved aside a heavy curtain of vines with his uninjured hand. "No," he corrected, grunting from the effort of pushing the unwieldy foliage. "I want to kill Kor." The orishadaon protectively clutched his left hand against his chest to keep it from rubbing against anything, which would have sent tremors of pain through his entire arm.

"What made you change your mind?"

Dayn shrugged, giving the slippery vines a final tug.

"This isn't like you." His brother's words were strained by lunars of unrelenting tension. The nerve-wracked young man continually scanned the jungle with unblinking eyes, prepared for the danger he was sure lurked behind every tree. One wide-open eye watched his surroundings while the other seemed to remain permanently fixed on Dayn. Merek never allowed his brother to get more than a few paces from his side.

"I have to do this, that's all that matters," Dayn responded eventually.

Merek grunted his dissatisfaction. "You still haven't answered my question."

Dayn crawled to the top of a muddy incline and waited,

catching his breath while the younger orishadai user caught up. "What . . . question?" he huffed.

Neither of them had slept in lunars. Even Dayn, who was used to the jungle by now, had been unable to rest. Exhaustion was taking its toll after half a dozen lunars of stumbling about aimlessly.

Dayn's paling flesh was drawn tight over skeletal features; dark circles ringing his sunken eyes added to the deathly appearance. His gut rumbled, but he could not find so much as a single morayth berry to sate his hunger. Aside from the fistful of bitter-tasting grubs he pried out of a rotting, hollow log the lunar before, he had not eaten in quite some time.

Merek fared worse. Every bit as haggard and hungry as his brother, his pride had also been dealt a devastating blow. His shattered nose was healing crookedly as a result of Dayn's head-butt, and he sometimes complained about his ribs hurting, probably from being battered by the shockwave released by the gauntlet. He hovered on the edge of madness, calm one moment before flying into an accusatory rage the next.

"Tell me why you decided to kill the half-blood," Merek demanded.

Dayn sighed. "I'm not killing Alis. I'm going to get rid of Kor."

"There is no Kor."

"Yes there is."

Merek shook his head, perturbed by his brother's insistence. "Maybe there was a long time ago, but this idea of him possessing the half-blood is just some delusion your mind created to justify what you have to do."

"Kor is real," Dayn assured. "You heard the voice, saw Alis' wounds heal up as fast as they did."

"The work of the demon she brought back from this place," Merek argued.

Dayn ignored him. "Kor needs to be stopped. I won't let him hurt any more innocent tribesmen."

"How many innocents were harmed in Nesthome?" Merek said venomously as he clambered to the top of the slope.

"Quiet yourself."

"Don't tell me to quiet myself!" Merek shouted, interrupting the jungle's cacophony with his sudden outburst. He pressed his face close to his brother's. "I am an orishadai user of the Swift Claw tribe. You do not speak to me like that!"

Not even the animals were intimidated by the young man; they continued their chirps and howls, almost drowning out the sound of Merek's irritated voice—almost.

Dayn rolled his eyes, knowing all-too-well where the present situation would lead. "The tribe is dead," he said evenly, struggling to keep the strain out of his voice. "Orishadaons have no authority any more. Our existence is pointless. *Your* existence is pointless."

Merek's lower jaw quivered with rage but he clamped his mouth shut, remaining perfectly still except for a single twitching cheek muscle. He allowed the slightest hint of a grin to curve the corners of his lips.

Dayn instantly recognized the look.

Long ago, when Merek had only seen twelve seasons, he single-handedly killed three annaru with his orishadai, an unheard of feat amongst the secluded Swift Claw tribe. Ambushed outside the village, the callous young boy made short work of the unlucky scaled ones; twelve seasons old and already an efficient murderer. When the sun dipped below the horizon and he returned to Nesthome, the only indications that anything had happened were the bloody spatters on his face, which he refused to let his mother wipe away, and his strange look of mayhem—the same look he was giving his brother, now.

"We should keep moving," Dayn suggested tactfully.

Merek held his ground, as well as his glare.

"I know what you're doing. It's not going to happen." Dayn laid a comforting hand on his brother's shoulder. "Save your energy for when we find Alis."

Merek eyed him dangerously. When he spoke, his voice was uncharacteristically calm. "Get that hand off me or it'll look worse than the other one when I'm done with it."

Dayn did not doubt that his brother meant it. He gave the charred remains of his left hand a worrisome look. "I'm not going to fight you."

"Why not?!" Merek shoved him angrily.

Dayn caught himself on a slanting tree. "Because we have to

work together! Mother and father taught us that blood takes care of blood. Do you remember that?"

"I told you before never to speak of them!" The young man's rage bubbled to the surface, threatening to take control.

It was Dayn's turn to press his face close to Merek's. "Does thinking about them make you feel guilty for all the horrible things you've done?"

"I don't feel anything," his brother snarled.

"You should feel guilty."

Merek's eyes bugged with barely contained hatred. "*You* should feel guilty! You're the one who killed them!" he spat vehemently.

For an instant, Dayn's shoulders sagged as the crushing burden of his own guilt pressed down on him. Then he bristled with anger of his own. "You were there too, why didn't you save them?" It was not so much a question as an accusation.

"I tried!" Spittle flew from Merek's quivering lips. "Six annaru, Dayn. I killed six by myself. Do you know how much that took from me? Don't blame me for your mistakes. Sharna pushed me too hard with her damned training, I couldn't do any more."

"She pushed me just the same." Dayn slapped his chest to emphasize his next point. "And I was out there fighting the annaru with the rest of the tribe."

"Liar! You were protecting that damned half-blood instead of your own family!"

Dayn's nostrils flared.

Merek might have been the smaller of the two, but he was also furious, and fury counted for a lot when the person involved wielded orishadai.

"Which one of us are you trying to convince?" Dayn questioned sharply.

The younger man squeezed his hands into tight fists, and Dayn thought for sure that Merek would attack him. If it happened, there was little he could do to defend himself without orishadai. Surprisingly, his brother took out his aggression on the nearest tree instead, pounding his fists against it until they left bloody dents in the gnarled wood.

When the outburst ended, Dayn simply said, "Let's go."

Argument settled, for the time being at least, he turned to

leave, and was caught in the throes of a powerful vision that dropped him to his knees. Images of gnashing teeth and green-skinned hunters hurtled through his mind. Water! A tremendous amount of water crashed against him. He was falling, plummeting into a dark abyss! No. Wake up. Wake up!

He opened his eyes to find himself on his back, staring up at a small patch of sky visible through a break in the canopy. A tiny halo of light surrounded his prostrate form. He wiped the cold sweat from his face, blinking away the salty droplets that stung his eyes. A convulsive shudder ran through him.

"Merek?" he rasped.

His brother was curled into a tight ball a few paces away, moaning pitifully with his eyes squeezed shut and his face twisted into a hideous grimace.

Dayn realized he, too, had curled into a ball, knees braced against his chin. He uncoiled himself and crawled to his brother's side.

"Merek?" He gave his sibling a gentle shake.

As soon as he touched him, his brother lashed out, landing a back-handed swing just above Dayn's eye. The blow caught him completely unawares. His world blurred into a kaleidoscopic flurry of greens and browns, slowly returning to normal as he regained his senses.

"Merek!" He slapped the young orishadai user across the cheek as hard as he could.

His brother screamed and bolted upright, eyes open and wide with fright. He spun around, staring at his surroundings in confusion. "What happened?"

"A vision," Dayn answered, standing up. He realized his nose was bleeding and wiped it clean.

"A vision?" Merek reached up to staunch the flow from his own nostrils.

Merek never had visions. He lacked foresight, as Sharna so straightforwardly explained, shortly before Kor sent her spirit to meet the ancestors.

"You must have got caught in mine." Dayn tried to rationalize what might have happened. "My visions are so strong that sometimes others get drawn into them." When his brother nodded, Dayn took it as his cue to continue the explanation. "Sharna used to say I had too much orishadai, more than anyone could control. I think she was right."

Merek took in a great gulp of air and breathed it out in a loud *whoosh*. "I . . . I don't even know what I saw," he stammered.

Dayn smiled sympathetically. "It's happened to me a hundred times and I never understand them." He patted his brother on the shoulder. "Come on, when I have one it usually means something bad is about to happen. We should be away."

Merek weakly pushed Dayn's hand off his shoulder, but nodded in agreement.

The tangled underbrush kept them from making any appreciable progress. It wasn't as if there was a path they could take, or a trail for them to follow. Dayn and his brother might have been the first tribesmen to ever travel that part of the jungle, which would mean they had lost Alis' trail. He was no hunter, that had always been Ryl's talent, so all Dayn could do was pick a random direction and hope.

When the sound of a gurgling river reached his ears he recalled the vision and its sensation of water crashing against him.

"Water." His brother perked up. "I could use a fresh drink." He jiggled his empty waterskin.

Dayn was noticeably wary. Predators made a home around the Tresslevale's rivers and streams, patiently waiting for their prey to come to them. Those who strayed too close might be eaten by any number of nasty beasts, from claw-toes to snap-mouths. He was about to warn Merek of the danger, only to have his voice drowned out by a sudden, earth-shaking roar.

His brother instinctively dove for cover behind the nearest patch of foliage, fearfully poking his head out to gaze around. Sweat beaded across his forehead as he scanned the jungle for signs of karda.

The bestial roar was followed by a chorus of excited shouts and whistles from at least three different beings.

At first, Dayn could not understand a word that was being said. It took him a few moments to realize that whoever was out there was speaking his language, in a thickly accented tone that made it difficult to decipher.

Two sharp whistles. "Be getting behind it! Behind it!" cried an unknown speaker.

"Not be going that way!" shouted a different one.

Another whistle, then a piercing scream rang out, along with the alarmed cries of the previous two voices.

Merek looked to Dayn, who started creeping in the direction of the noise. "What are you doing?" the young orishadai user hissed, tentatively sliding out of his hiding place.

"Whoever it is might need our help," Dayn said, intent on discovering who was out there.

Merek scowled. "It's not our problem. We have enough trouble."

"We still have our duty."

"My duty was to the tribe. Whoever is out there isn't a Swift Claw."

Dayn could not deny his instincts. Training with Sharna had conditioned him to ignore his own well-being for the sake of others, promising pain if he refused to help. His entire life had been a constant exercise in suffering and tolerance. Even with his tribe gone and his mentor dead, the lessons he learned were etched into his mind as surely as the orishadaon brand was etched into his flesh. There was no ignoring his duty.

"I'm going," he stated flatly. "Do what you want."

Merek frowned at his brother's stubbornness. Rather than argue, he chose to follow along in silence.

The undergrowth grew thicker at the water's edge. Foregoing the element of surprise, Dayn drew Agidyne and hacked at the tangles of brush with desperate fervor. After many clumsy swings he managed to clear a path to the riverbank.

Before he stepped onto the muddy shore, the orishadaon heard the sound of a karda's labored breathing; one titanic intake of breathe, followed by a reverberating exhalation. The beast sounded hurt, or at the very least, tired. It also sounded big.

He batted his way through thick creepers dangling over the river's dark surface. Curtains of moss obstructed his view, but he could still see enough to be surprised by what was happening along the opposite bank.

Downstream, near the point where the river surged over the edge of a cliff and plummeted an unknown distance to the valley below, three green-skinned creatures fought a blade-nose. Not just any blade-nose, *the* blade-nose. The same one he had fought outside Nesthome, the same one that had almost killed him twice.

All that remained of the right side of the beast's face was a mass of charred and bleeding meat, the result of his orishadai striking it during their second confrontation. Had his blast gone a bit deeper it would have burned a hole through the karda's brain. Too bad he had not been more accurate.

Across the way, a muddy beach separated the inky water from the solid green of the jungle. Two . . . creatures—he could think of no other way to describe the humanoids—ran around the blade-nose, jabbing at its sides and underbelly with javelins. The dismembered pieces of a third creature sprawled across the mud.

"What are those?" Merek pointed to the odd-looking hunters.

Their bodies were vaguely humanoid, with gangly arms and legs, slender torsos, and bark-like skin that varied in shade from dark green or brown on their backs to bright emerald or faded yellow on their chests. Leaves or tangles of vines crowned their heads instead of hair, and their fingers were tipped by jagged talons that belonged more on the foot of a claw-toe.

The blade-nose lunged forward, snapping at a vine-headed huntress who dodged to the side and buried her (it looked like a female to Dayn, although he couldn't be sure) javelin in the beast's snout. With a snarl, the karda reared back, taking the hunter's javelin with it. The green-skinned warrior immediately picked up one of her fallen comrade's javelins and hurled it into the karda's chest.

The blade-nose twisted its head down and snapped the shaft off between its teeth, spitting out the wooden shards in disgust. Dayn knew it would take more than a few sharpened sticks to drop such a beast.

"Stay here," he instructed his brother, wading towards the far shore with Agidyne in hand.

"Are you sun-baked?" Merek gasped, giving the water lapping at his ankles a wary look. "Why are you going over there?"

"We have to help!" Dayn insisted loudly. "What do you want to do?"

"Nothing," Merek replied in typical, self-serving fashion.

Dayn's eyes opened wide as he watched the leaf-headed hunter dash forward to jab the karda in the back of its knee. The beast bellowed in frustration as the barb struck home and lashed out with its foot, catching the unfortunate hunter in the chest and hurling him (once again, Dayn couldn't be sure, but he thought the hunter looked like a male) against one of the trees lining the riverbank.

That left the vine-headed huntress to face the karda, alone. All that remained of her third companion, the one whose scream had alerted Dayn to the conflict, was a torso and a few other unrecognizable bits lying in the muck. Translucent orange sap drenched the beach for twenty paces in both directions, and only now did he understand what the substance truly was: the hunter's blood.

"I've got to help," Dayn repeated.

"Then why not just blast the karda from here?" Merek practically shouted in frustration. "If we both hit it, the thing has to go down, and I won't have to worry about being torn apart by its teeth."

His brother's words held a strange sort of wisdom. Dayn had a hard time accepting this.

"What if we hit one of the hunters?"

Merek thrust out his palm in the direction of the blade-nose. "Who cares, the plant things are as good as dead anyway."

"You're *worse* than Kor, you know that?"

Merek only grinned.

Without another word, Dayn hesitantly pointed his hand at the blade-nose, though the gesture was only for show. He could no longer draw on orishadai and calling the power was out of the question.

Merek, however, was more than capable of tapping into his soul's energy. Dayn could sense the build-up of power in his brother as the young man funneled orishadai through his arm and into his palm.

Dayn let out a desperate moan and dropped his arm, accepting that his reserves of orishadai were drained. It was up to Merek to bring the karda down.

"Don't miss," he whispered, along with a silent prayer to the ancestors.

His brother finished channeling the necessary orishadai and let out a wild scream, sending a blood-red bolt of energy sizzling over the river's surface. It cut through the air fast as a lightning bolt, streaking directly towards the karda's charred face.

25.
THE UNSTABLE AND THE UNSTOPPABLE

The vine-headed huntress and the karda both turned towards Merek upon hearing his scream. The huntress' jaw fell open at the sight of the two siblings standing upon the opposite riverbank.

The blade-nose narrowed its remaining eye at Dayn. Half a heartbeat before Merek's bolt of orishadai slammed into the center of its forehead, the blade-nose swiveled its head out of the way. Its muscular neck snaked downwards, ducking beneath the searing blast. A coppice of trees at the beast's rear exploded amidst roiling soul energy.

Merek automatically backed towards the cover of the jungle, a worried look on his normally dour face.

The blade-nose lifted its head to glare at the pair of orishadai users.

"What is it waiting for?" Dayn asked, edging towards the jungle.

"It's hurt," Merek observed, slipping one foot into the twisted cover of foliage at his back. "Maybe it's afraid?"

After a brief moment of indecision, the blade-nose charged the newcomers, rather than continue its duel with the huntress.

"Maybe not!" the young orishadai user corrected himself as he scrambled backwards through clusters of draping vines.

Dayn put himself directly in the charging karda's path. He fought down his terror, knowing full well what the blade-nose was capable of and how much of a chance he stood against it.

At the sight of his brother standing firm, Merek halted his retreat, if only to prove to Dayn that he was not afraid. "I'm no coward," he hissed. "I won't run from a fight."

Dayn scooped a rock out of the mud at his feet as the karda bore down on him. "Running now doesn't mean you're a coward. Be away from here!"

The blade-nose bared its yellow teeth and snorted, coils of mist rising from its nostrils with each troubled breath. It stomped towards Dayn, kicking water into the air and driving a small wave ahead of its massive form. In less time than it took to blink, the karda approached to dangerous closeness, yet neither Merek nor Dayn moved.

"RUN!" Dayn pushed his brother into the jungle. The blade-nose turned its head to follow him, and Dayn hurled his rock at the beast's snout. The missile bounced harmlessly off its thick hide, but served its purpose nonetheless. The karda turned back, fixing its full attention on the elder sibling.

The orishadaon involuntarily backed up a pace, his chest tightening with fear. Nausea twisted his stomach into a knot and made bile rise into his throat.

The karda continued to plow forward, its charge slowed by the strong current and churning muck along the river bottom.

"I will not fear my enemy," Dayn chanted. "I will not fear my enemy. I will not fear my enemy." Even if he tried to flee, the karda would quickly overtake him. Since running away was impossible, he was left with only one completely insane option.

He charged the blade-nose.

The two rushed towards one another. At the last moment Dayn ducked the beast's snapping jaws and wove between its trunk-like legs. The karda almost caught him with a slash of its tail but he hurled himself face-first into the water to avoid the blow.

Sometimes insane worked.

The karda spun on the spot, threatening to flatten him beneath a flurry of stomping feet. It kicked up a wave that crashed against the orishadaon and washed him out from under it.

Without looking back, he paddled to the bank on the far shore. Fighting the karda in the open was folly; he had to put the jungle at his back so the beast could only come at him from one direction.

By the time the blade-nose realized where he was, Dayn had

reached the other side.

Bare-chested and half-drowned, he stood with nothing but his sword to defend himself against a furious mountain of muscle and teeth.

When the blade-nose came at him again he lashed out with Agidyne, dragging the rusted blade across the wounded flesh around the karda's eye. This enraged the beast to no end, and Dayn was driven back by its fury.

With his peripheral vision he scanned the area for anything that he might put between the incensed karda and himself. There was nothing but the river and some large tree trunks that had washed up on shore. He arched an eyebrow as an idea entered his mind.

Dayn ducked another bite and ran for the nearest log, one that he noticed was hollow. He wasted no time as he crawled inside. The blade-nose shoved its snout in right behind him, trying without success to force its oversized head into the tiny space. The horn on its snout caught on the edge of the wood, keeping the deadly jaws at bay. It growled menacingly and pulled its head free, snorting and snarling as it paced around the log.

Dayn dragged himself into the middle and waited. The karda continued to circle, confused by the sudden turn of events.

For a moment the jungle became silent, and Dayn allowed a tiny sliver of hope to enter his thoughts. In the midst of offering thanks to any ancestors who would listen, a two-pace-long horn crashed through the far end of the tree, shattering his hope as well as a large chunk of the log. The horn smashed through again, closer this time. Dayn pulled himself towards the opposite end as the horn made a third hole that barely missed his feet.

He stared out of the end of the log. The jungle's edge was a long way off, too far for him to safely reach the protective wall of trees and cycads.

A startled shout escaped his lips as the karda suddenly bit into the log, its jagged teeth piercing the trunk on either side of his body. Dust and pieces of bark rained down on him. Light fell across the orishadaon when the karda's tiny, three-fingered hands stripped away what remained of the tree, leaving him completely exposed. His heart froze in his chest as the karda opened its jaws to deliver the killing blow.

He heard a loud whistle. "Being afraid to fight a real warrior, karda?" someone taunted from nearby. The whistle and strange accent told him it was the huntress. Dayn had completely forgotten about her.

A javelin sprouted from the karda's neck. A second javelin pierced its scaly hide a moment later, causing the blade-nose to hesitate in its attempt to swallow him. Taking advantage of the distraction, Dayn worked the arm holding Agidyne free and stood up on the karda's blind side, dangerously close to its gaping mouth.

His muscles bulged as he gripped the rusted handle of his sword with both hands. The pain in his blackened fingers went beyond intense, but Dayn struggled through it all the same. Orishadaon conditioning was powerful indeed.

With a guttural scream, more bestial than human, he side-stepped around its head and drove his blade into the creature's remaining eye. Agidyne slipped in all the way to the hilt, blinding the beast.

The karda let out a wild howl and thrashed its head from side to side, refusing to die even though it had an arm's length of metal embedded in its brain. It tried to yank the blade out, but its pitiful forearms were too short to reach.

Dayn, remembering his mistake during the second fight with the karda, had already let go of the sword and jumped clear of the log. He scrambled down the beach, his feet flinging mud into the air behind him as the roar of the karda and the waterfall rang in his ears.

The blade-nose whirled in the direction of his fleeing form, sending a shower of crimson droplets splattering across the river's tumultuous surface. It sniffed the air and stalked after him.

No! Dayn's mind screamed in disbelief. Impossible! The blade-nose was half-dead and blind, it could not still be chasing him.

With a thick wall of green to his right and the burbling river on his left, he ran the only way he could, down the beach straight towards the waterfall.

The karda increased its lumbering pace, stumbling after him drunkenly.

The lip of the waterfall loomed before him. Below the cliff

spread a rocky pool of water surrounded by waving, emerald tree-tops. A winding river snaked away from the pool towards the shimmering horizon.

Another completely insane idea came to him. "Sometimes insane works," he reminded himself.

As he waded out into the river the rushing water rose to his knees, pulling at him with such fantastic force that he thought it would yank him off his feet and sweep him over the falls. He dug his heels into the muddy river bottom in a desperate attempt to stop himself, coming to a halt barely five paces from the drop-off.

The blade-nose angled its head in his direction, still trying to pull Agidyne out of its eye with a tiny forearm. It sniffed the air and emitted a low growl.

"Come on, karda, I'm right here. Come and kill me!" he yelled.

The muscles in the karda's legs went taught, bulging against azure scales. Its pace increased.

"Dayn!" Merek shouted at him from the far bank.

"Be getting away from there!" the huntress warned, waving him towards the jungle with a shrill whistle.

Dayn continued to shout at the steadily approaching karda, refusing to move from his position. It would die or he would, there could be no other outcome.

"You want me, beast? I'm right here!"

Its cavernous chest heaved with the effort of drawing breath, but the blade-nose was too enraged to give in to its pain.

"Here, damn you!"

One, two, three steps and it was running as fast as he had ever seen it move.

"That's right, come on!"

Four, five, six steps and it was almost on top of him.

Dayn held his ground until the last possible moment before lunging to the side.

The blind karda trampled the muddy river bottom where he had been only a moment before as it stampeded over the edge, bellowing in surprise as the ground beneath its feet suddenly fell away and it plunged towards the rocky pool below.

In the wake of its passage, Dayn found himself swept up by the current. Despite his efforts, he could not get a foothold on the muddy river bottom.

"Oh no," he moaned knowingly.

The current pitched him over the edge right behind the karda. There was nothing he could do to save himself, no way to stop the impending descent. He was forced to watch, stomach lurching with every plummeted pace, as the rock wall of the cliff flew by and the pool's surface rushed up to meet him.

Far below, the falling blade-nose struck a jagged stone pillar rising out of the pool and came to a lethal halt upon the spire. Despite its horrendous wound, the karda feebly kicked at the air, wasting what little remained of its life trying to pull itself off the rock.

The orishadaon hurtled towards the grisly scene, watching with grim satisfaction as the blade-nose twitched a final time before he plunged through the surface of the churning pool.

26.
SLUMBER WITH EYES WIDE SHUT

His head swam in a sea of inky darkness as enveloping tendrils dragged him into their drowning embrace. Lungs flooding with liquid calm, he barely struggled while sinking weightlessly to the bottom of his nightmare, coming to rest on a patch of soft earth. A cloud of silt sprayed into the air around him and . . . no, wait . . . there was no air.

Water flooded his lungs! He clamped his mouth shut, putting a hand over his nostrils to keep from breathing in any more. The orishadaon kicked off the bottom of the pool, propelling himself towards the light. His head broke the surface and he drew a desperate breath, sucking in equal parts water and air.

He blinked the algae from his eyes and searched for the shore, finding it far to his right. Sputtering on water already in his lungs, he paddled awkwardly towards the reed-choked bank.

When he finally flopped onto dry land he lay there, caught between clarity and unconsciousness, too weak to drag himself any further. To the Aether with the danger of lying in the open, all that mattered was the much needed rest he was about to take. The orishadaon lay his head in the mud and closed his heavy-lidded eyes.

"Dayn!" came a distressed call.

"Huh?" he groaned, slowly peeling his mud-caked face off the ground.

"Dayn, are you down there?" shouted a far off voice.

"Yes," he murmured.

"Dayn!"

He recognized the frustrated voice as that of his brother. "Here," Dayn croaked, waving a hand to signal that he was still alive. He tried calling out again, but his throat squeezed itself shut and the words came out too garbled to be heard over the roar of the cascading waterfall.

He rolled over, turning his gaze to the sparkling cliff-face at the top of the falls. A trio of silhouettes perched precariously at the edge, glaring down at him from a height of two hundred paces.

One silhouette was much taller than the rest. It held up another shadow that looked to be slouching. The third, and smallest silhouette waved.

"I can't believe you survived that fall!" Merek yelled down to him, sounding slightly disappointed. "Stay there and we'll come to you."

Dayn gave his brother another wave and lay back down.

Creatures in the jungle squawked their disapproval of his presence, carrying on like the maddened beasts they were. The waterfall's spray cooled the air, making the grove's temperature almost bearable. Unfortunately, the cool air did not save him from the clouds of insects that gnawed voraciously on his exposed flesh.

A long time passed without anything to break up the monotony of his wait, and he was thankful for the peaceful respite, regardless of its duration. It was his first conscious rest since setting out for the Tresslevale with Ryl and Alis.

A winged karda circled overhead, shrieked mournfully, and landed on a rocky spire in the center of the pool. It turned its hollow-crested head in the orishadaon's direction, glaring at him with a pair of intense gray eyes. An ugly scar marred its pointed beak.

The beast hopped from its spire onto the blade-nose's carcass, waddling towards the massive, horned head bobbing gently atop the water's surface. It stopped its awkward tottering next to the rusty sword hilt protruding from the karda's eyeball.

"Nice sword, isn't it," Dayn said conversationally when the winged karda glared at him.

The karda poked at the eyeball with its scarred beak.

"Get away from that," Dayn called out hoarsely.

It stabbed the eye again.

Angry at being disturbed, Dayn rolled onto his stomach and crawled back into the water.

Blood clouded the murky pond, scenting the water with its coppery tang. Churning water at the base of the falls spread the crimson mess about the pool, forcing Dayn to swim through it on his way to the ravaged karda's body.

He grabbed the blade-nose's hind leg, holding on as a wave of exhaustion threatened to pull him under. "Get away from my sword," he wheezed at the winged karda, which continued to pick at its meal.

He paddled along the blade-nose's stomach, holding himself aloft by clinging to its rough underbelly scales. While making his way past a forearm, the feasting winged karda gave a quick twist of its beak, wrenching the eyeball free along with his sword. Both Dayn and the karda watched Agidyne splash down and sink beneath the water's surface.

Dayn cried out in horror. He sucked in a deep breath and dove after it, kicking madly towards where he had last seen the sword. He would not loose Agidyne, it was too important to him. After being passed down to each succeeding orishadaon for an untold number of seasons, he would be damned, literally, if the sacred relic was lost.

Dayn swam through the gloom to the bottom of the pool and rooted around in darkness, finding nothing but rocks and mud. He shot upwards, bursting through the surface to suck in another gulp of air. As soon as he had it he dove again, burrowing his hands into the clinging muck and swishing them around.

Where is it!? Please let me find it, he begged, churning up a cloud of silt which mixed with the karda's blood to turn the water a rusty brown. His lungs burned for air, but he refused to surface until he found it. He could sense the ancient relic's presence, close enough to touch.

There!

His hand brushed against something that sliced open his palm. He ignored the sharp pain, tightening his grip around the blade before propelling himself to the surface with sword in tow. He came up beside the blade-nose's gaping jaws and, wrapping the crook of his elbow around its horn to anchor himself, lifted the sword out of the water to make sure it was all right. Despite its plunge, Agidyne appeared fine, and why shouldn't it be? Relics of the ancient times were sturdy enough to handle a little water.

After taking a moment to catch his breath he swam back to shore, careful not to lose the sword again. Dayn flopped onto the bank, spitting out a mouthful of disgusting water.

"What are you staring at?" he snarled at the winged karda still perched atop the bobbing head of the blade-nose.

It continued its unblinking observation of him for a brief period, then spread its wings and flapped itself into the air and out of sight.

"Stupid karda," he cursed absently, gazing at a white cloud drifting far overhead.

After lying still for long enough, the local wildlife forgot about him. Frogs croaked loudly, insects buzzed through the air, and snakes slithered amongst the reeds, all while Dayn sat there watching the tree tops sway in the wind. The perpetual, calming roar of the waterfall crashing against the rocks below eventually lulled him to sleep.

27.
NOT ALONE

He awoke to find Merek gripping him by the shoulders, shaking him frantically. Dayn cracked open his eyes, but otherwise did not react to his brother's touch.

Merek quit shaking him. "Oh, so you are still alive."

Dayn closed his eyes and rolled over with a groan.

"Get up you sun-baked idiot. We can't stay here."

He did not bother with a response.

There came a loud whistle. "Orishadaon?" The feminine voice rustled like leaves in the wind.

Dayn rolled back to find both surviving plant creatures, the leaf-headed one and the vine-headed huntress, standing over him. The vine-haired huntress who had saved him from death at the jaws of the blade-nose appeared unharmed, while the other could not walk under his own power and had to be helped along.

"I be calling myself Janeli, my hunter be calling himself Exil," the huntress said, indicating the sagging figure in her arms. Janeli was tall and slender, well suited for life in the jungle. Her skin was a mottled greenish-brown with rough, bark-like patches on her shins and forearms. Thin, ropy vines hung from her head in place of hair.

Exil had the same chiseled features and lanky body as Janeli, with a beak-like nose, a thicker brow, and a crown of rustling leaves rather than dangling vines. Neither of them wore any sort of clothing.

"How . . . how did you know I was an orishadaon?" Dayn stuttered in confusion.

Exil weakly raised his hand to point a clawed finger at Dayn's tattoos.

"And you be carrying metal," Janeli added, shifting her weight to better support her slouching companion. "How you be calling yourself?"

He looked around, wondering if he was still dreaming. "Dayn," he answered cautiously.

"Dayn," she repeated in his cautious tone, making it sound like a question. "And you, warrior," she turned to Merek. "How you be calling yourself?"

The young orishadai user eyed the plant creature skeptically.

"Go on," Dayn urged.

"Merek," his brother responded hesitantly.

"Dayn and Merek be saving our lives and defeating the karda," Janeli intoned. "I be giving thanks."

"I be giving thanks," Exil mimed.

Janeli extended a clawed hand towards Dayn, causing him to tense up. When her arm was stretched all the way out she opened her palm and splayed her fingers. It was obvious from her expectant expression that she wanted him to do something.

The bewildered orishadaon sat up and looked closely at the strange plant creatures. From a distance, either one of them might appear vaguely human, but up close the differences were all too apparent. Janeli's features were too angular, as if someone had hewn her high cheek bones, dainty chin, and flawless skin from the bark of a tree. She had the features of a young woman, but who could tell when dealing with nature spirits?

"I was just doing my duty." Dayn rubbed the back of his neck bashfully. "Besides, if it wasn't for you tossing your javelins when you did, I'd be dead, so I should be thanking you."

Janeli waited silently, still holding her arm towards him.

Not knowing what else to do, Dayn mimicked the motion and stretched his own arm towards her. The nature spirit clasped his palm in hers and squeezed. Her grip nearly crushed his hand.

"My life be given to you," she said, gazing into his eyes.

Dayn looked from his pulsing palm to the nature spirit's claws and back again, confusion evident on his creased brow.

Janeli ignored his odd expression. "What you be doing in the jungle?" she asked curiously.

"We're lost," Dayn answered with a rueful grin.

Merek stepped up beside the two and cleared his throat. "Do you know where to find the annaru city?" he asked the huntress.

She nodded and released Dayn's hand. "I be knowing."

"Can you take us there?"

Dayn arched an eyebrow at his brother's insistence. Merek obviously wanted to find and kill Alis, but his urgency bordered on obsession. "I'm looking for a friend," he told the huntress tentatively.

Janeli whistled. "I not be seeing any friends here," she stated flatly.

Dayn's heart fluttered. "Oh."

"What your friend be doing here?" Exil rasped, his voice rough as tree bark.

Janeli set the plant man against a tree where light breaking through the canopy fell across his inert form.

"She was forced to come," Dayn explained. "By Kor."

Both plant creatures recoiled as if struck, immediately slapping their clawed hands across their ears. Janeli let out a threatening hiss while Exil moaned, his green skin fading to a sickly greenish-white.

The vine-headed huntress turned to Dayn with murder in her eyes. "Do not be speaking the Betrayer's name aloud!" she snarled, clacking her claws together.

Exil shuddered at the mention of the fallen god.

"To the Aether with this." Merek turned to leave. "I'm not listening to their superstitious foolishness."

The huntress took exception to the remark and, fast as a gust of wind, sidestepped Exil, brushed past Dayn and landed a solid punch against Merek's jaw. The orishadai user stumbled into a nearby tree, saving himself from falling over by slinging an arm across a low-hanging branch.

"Be silent." Janeli's voice, normally like the melodic rustling of leaves, was now more akin to the strained and angry groan of an ancient tree about to topple.

"No more of that." Dayn took a step towards her. She shot him a cold glare, drawing back her clawed hand to tear out his throat in a single swipe.

Dayn swallowed a lump of fear. "Wait!" He put up his hands, realizing too late that he was holding Agidyne and the move would be perceived as threatening.

A strangled gasp from Exil stopped the huntress mid-swipe. "Be stopping!" the leaf-headed man coughed, his entire body shuddering with each breath. Jagged amber lines sliced across his chest, a memento of the karda's kick. Wooden spurs, soaked in amber sap, jutted through his quaking chest, remnants of what could only be his ribcage. "The Betrayer's return be written on the Urth Mother's roots," he said with a whistle that sounded more like a wheeze.

The huntress shook her head. "The Betrayer is being dead."

"He's alive inside Alis," Dayn cut in.

"You be doubting my words?" Janeli snapped harshly. "I not be dishonoring myself by lying to you."

Dayn shook his head, causing the world to spin uncontrollably. He was weaker than he thought after battling the karda. "I don't know what to doubt or what to believe anymore." He put a hand against his forehead and closed his eyes. "All I want is to find Alis and be away from this place."

"Please be forgiving Janeli, she not yet be mastering her anger," Exil choked on the words, a trickle of amber sap dribbling out the corner of his mouth and down his chin.

Janeli's irate expression melted away, replaced by a sympathetic glare. She knelt down and tenderly wiped the sap away from Exil's lips with the back of a claw. When next she spoke, it was in a softer tone, full of concern for her companion. "If you are being right, we must be taking them to the Urth Mother," she whispered.

"I'm not going anywhere with them." Merek hiked a thumb in Exil and Janeli's direction. The young orishadai user rubbed his jaw and glared rancorously at the plant woman out of the corner of his eye. A slight smile turned the corners of his lips.

Dayn knew that look. "Don't start anything, Merek," he warned.

Exil shook his head, rustling the leaves growing there. "There is being no time. The Betrayer be too close to his tomb. If he be reaching that place . . ." his sentence trailed off as another fit of coughing overcame him.

Janeli nervously paced back and forth in front of her wounded companion.

It was unclear to Dayn exactly which one of the plant creatures was the leader, although it appeared that Janeli held the decision-making power. It was also apparent that she readily deferred to the wisdom of Exil.

Eventually, Janeli came to a stop in front of the injured warrior, lines of worry creasing the faded green bark on her brow. "What we be doing then?" she asked in frustration.

Exil took a deep, wheezing breath that caused his entire body to shudder. "Be sending for help," the plant man instructed. He had to stop and collect himself before continuing. His wounds must have been grievous indeed. "You." He pointed a clawed hand at Janeli. "Be taking the orishadaon to the temple."

The look that passed across Janeli's face said more than words could: she did not like Exil's plan. Nevertheless, she did as he asked.

The huntress produced a small wooden flute, from where Dayn could not say, and put it to her lips. She blew into the instrument, but no sound came out. Contentedly, she returned the flute to its hiding place and stared up at the sky, peeking through the tangled greenery.

"What did you do?" Dayn asked curiously.

"The music will be calling Lirex," she said, as if the simple explanation was all he required.

"What music?" Merek scratched his head in confusion.

"What's a Lirex?" Dayn followed her gaze to the sky. "And why do we need one?"

"You will be seeing soon enough."

The perplexed orishadaon did not have to wait long. The sound of flapping, leathery wings soon rose above the crash of the waterfall. A dark shadow appeared across the water's surface, heralding the arrival of a giant winged karda moments before it dropped into view. The animal landed in the shallows of the pond, digging its talons into the muck for purchase. It waddled to Janeli's side on its wing tips and crooned to the huntress, who dutifully stroked the underside of its neck with the backs of her claws.

"This," she smiled, "be Lirex."

Dayn looked from his sword to the ugly scar on the karda's beak and frowned. "I think we've met."

Janeli whispered something to the beast, then whistled loudly and pointed a claw into the air. "Be telling them," she instructed.

The winged karda squawked an answer while rapidly bobbing its head.

"Be hurrying," urged the huntress.

Lirex dutifully waddled to the water's edge, spread its massive wings to catch a current of warm air blowing off the falls, and launched itself into the air. Leathery wings snapped taut, and the karda rose in steady circles until it reached the top of the cliff and soared out of sight. Janeli continued to monitor the karda's progress long after it disappeared beyond the falls.

It all happened so fast that Dayn had little time to question anything until after the karda was gone.

"Where is it going?" he asked.

"We be having many allies," Janeli replied, still gazing after the karda.

Merek spit in irritation. "More, like you," he growled.

"We are being too few," the huntress told him evenly. Obviously, she had not noticed the scorn in the young orishadai user's voice, or else she took no offense to it. "There are being more humans than you, and I be sending for their help."

Both siblings found themselves taken aback by the idea.

"What do you mean ... you're saying . . . more people?" Merek sputtered.

Dayn looked to Janeli for an answer to his brother's stuttered question.

"The Fire Wing tribe be my people's allies since the time of the Betrayer," she told them both in a calm, quiet tone, as if such information was common knowledge, which to her, it probably was. "Their leader be Agar, their orishadaon, Brun. They be strong men. Trustworthy men."

Dayn felt sun-baked, and, swaying, put a hand against the nearest tree to steady himself. "Oh," he moaned, almost toppling. "Another tribe, allied with you?"

Merek looked caught between rage and disbelief. "Another . . . orishadaon?"

Janeli knew more about Kor than she was saying, more it

seemed, than Dayn's people had ever known. He needed her to reveal everything.

The huntress ignored their odd stares and moved to help Exil to his feet.

"You must be hurrying," he rasped, wiping more sap from his mouth as she hauled him up.

"Only when you are being joined with Emara Ekara," she told him forcefully. Janeli half-carried the plant man to the nearest sunlit clearing at the edge of the pond. When his strength gave out and he collapsed into her arms, she dragged him the rest of the way, his claw-tipped feet digging furrows in the soft mud. The huntress stood her warrior up in the center of the clearing and stepped back.

"Be going with the swiftness of Auxia," he said, eyes glazed and unfocused.

"Emara Ekara be granting you her strength," she whistled her reply.

Swaying back and forth, the injured warrior spread his arms and raised his face to the sun, basking in its warm glow. Slowly, hesitantly, he opened his mouth and began to sing, or so it sounded, though Dayn had never heard such a mournful wail before.

Exil emitted a hollow groan, utterly inhuman in its chilling incongruity. The closest approximation Dayn's mind could make was that of wind howling through a canyon, yet that in no way accurately described the sound echoing forth from Exil's open mouth.

When Janeli added her 'voice' to Exil's, Dayn jumped in alarm. Air whistled up from her throat and past her lips, loud and menacing, like a hurricane of rustling leaves and scraping tree bark. The eerie chorus rose in volume, drowning out the sound of the nearby falls.

Dayn watched, enraptured by what happened next.

The earth at Exil's feet began to churn. A riot of tendrils and vines burst out of the muck, coiling around his ankles. The squirming foliage constricted his legs, working its way steadily up his chest. It climbed his singing form, invading every orifice until his entire body was encased in a shell of living armor and he was lost beneath its wriggling surface.

"By the blood of the ancestors!" Merek gasped.

When the hunter's song was choked off by vines forcing their way down his throat, and Janeli could no longer see her companion beneath the greenery, she ceased her keening and turned to face the orishadai users. "We be having little time," she told them.

Dayn pointed a trembling finger at the squirming mass of tendrils enveloping the plant warrior. "What in the Aether is happening to him?!" he cried in revulsion.

"Emara Ekara be healing him," she said calmly.

"But, the jungle is killing him," Dayn blurted.

"Emara Ekara is being the Urth Mother, and Exil is being one of her children. Emara Ekara not be killing her children," the huntress tried to explain.

Dayn stared at Exil's writhing shell, saying nothing more.

"I don't trust her," Merek stated matter-of-factly.

Where the orishadai users came from, such a statement was a grave insult. For members of an isolated tribe, trust was vital to survival. If a tribesman could not be trusted he served no purpose. Exile or death were the only outcomes.

The huntress did not react as expected to the remark. If anything, Merek's words seemed to amuse her. "The Betrayer not be caring about your *trust*," she told him, punctuating the last word with a shrill whistle.

Merek kicked at the earth. "What do you think?" he asked his brother.

Dayn remained silent, his gaze fixed on Exil.

"Dayn!" Merek swatted him across the shoulder.

Dayn blinked away his confusion. "What is it?" he focused on Merek, who eyed him suspiciously.

"Should we go with the plant thing?"

"I don't know." Dayn kept casting glances at Exil's prison of foliage.

Merek scratched the back of his head and looked around the jungle with indifference. "I hate this place." He spit at a cycad, much to Janeli's irritation, judging by the stern glare she gave him afterward. "But I hate the half-blood even more. If going with this *thing*," he indicated the huntress, "means a chance to get even with her, I say we do it."

Bringing Merek along for the next part of the journey was a

terrible idea, Dayn was absolutely sure of that. Even if his brother managed to restrain himself, which was unlikely, Dayn would still end up wasting precious time and energy trying to keep his sibling from inflicting any permanent damage on Alis.

There was also the very real possibility that Merek might be killed. Dayn had enough blood on his hands already, without being responsible for the death of his only surviving family. "You're sure you want to do this? You could die."

Merek laughed.

The odd response made Dayn uncomfortable. He stepped away from his brother and turned to Janeli. "Will Exil be all right if we leave him here?"

"Yes."

"Oh. Okay."

"We must be hurrying," Janeli said after a moment of awkward silence.

Dayn waved her forward, indicating that she should lead. She was the only one who knew the way, after all. He couldn't help taking one last look at the squirming mass encasing Exil's injured body before he left. The sight simultaneously intrigued and revolted him.

These creatures were so alien in everything that they did. Dayn had encountered something like them once, many seasons ago when Sharna had sent him in search of the healing waters, but the memory of that time was locked away, never to be relived. In any event, the creatures in his memories were not the ones standing before him now. Still, he wasn't sure if he should trust Janeli, though he followed her anyway, hoping that she might be able to lead him to Alis, and to Kor.

28.
BEFORE WE DIE

The musty odor of decay hung heavy in the cloying, mist-shrouded air.

Untold numbers of annaru stalked through the fog, their scaly forms slipping from shadow to shadow like ghosts, impossibly silent and all but invisible. Only their eyes could be seen, glowing dimly amidst the dark underbrush as they skulked about. They were no doubt searching for Dayn and his companions. Kor obviously expected the orishadaon to attempt some sort of rescue and had taken precautions to stop him. What the god could not have expected, though, was that Dayn would have someone as skilled as Janeli to guide him past the horde of scaled ones.

The huntresses' eyesight, hearing and scent were all superior to the orishadaon's, honed to inhuman perfection by a life of struggle in the Tresslevale. When annaru patrols drew near, Janeli's senses detected them and steered Dayn and Merek away, averting disaster on more than one occasion.

While the light of the ancestors still soared high above their heads, the trio reached the outskirts of the crumbling city they sought, only to find its streets infested with more scaled ones than Dayn could count.

"Annaru," Janeli warned her companions, ducking behind a low stone wall as three of the saurian creatures wandered into her line of sight.

After finding cover, Merek poked his head over the wall to see for himself. "Bah," he scoffed. "Only three. I can take three myself."

"What about the ones that show up after that, and the ones after that?" Dayn countered.

"I'll kill as many as it takes to get to the half-blood," the young orishadai user boasted.

"They'd swarm you before you got ten of them," Dayn said frankly, then thought better of it. Merek would kill a hundred annaru, just to prove him wrong. "And it doesn't matter," he quickly added before his brother could argue further.

Janeli kept watch while the two siblings bickered. "What we be doing?" she asked, shifting uneasily when more annaru came into view from a different direction than the previous three. "We are being surrounded, here."

Dayn leaned against the sagging wall, thinking. There was no way to press further into the city without being spotted, and they could not afford to let Kor know they were coming. Dayn was counting on the element of surprise to help him rescue Alis' mind from the god. If walking through the city was impossible, what else could they try?

Flying was out of the question. Even if that damned karda, Lirex, could get them in, Kor's minions would see them and raise the alarm. So, they couldn't fly and they couldn't travel overland. What about underground? There was a way, but . . .

A lump suddenly formed in his throat, and he swallowed it down. "I know how we can get in," he told his companions. "It's over that way."

Janeli pointed a claw in the indicated direction, and Dayn nodded. "Be staying close," the huntress whispered, and moved off into the undergrowth. Both siblings quickly followed.

Shortly thereafter, Dayn parted a tangle of vegetation to reveal a small clearing, in which sat a massive stone obelisk carved in the shape of a blade-nose.

"I told you it would be here," he said to his brother, who stared open-mouthed at the great carving.

Janeli peered through the brush, sharp eyes darting back and forth to take in the clearing. The structure itself was the most threatening thing to be found, although that would change quickly if more annaru arrived. "And it be leading all the way to the center of the city? It be looking too obvious."

Dayn shuddered at the thought of what lurked inside. "There's no reason to hide the entrance," he said, dredging up awful memories he had hoped to leave buried.

The obelisk's looming form made him recall Ryl's death, and the unnatural thing that had caused it. With such a fearsome guardian in the under-tunnels there was no need to defend them, or so Kor apparently thought, as he had posted no guards. Or perhaps the god believed Dayn would not be sun-baked enough to try that route after already encountering what lurked in its depths.

Dayn didn't want to go back into the catacombs, but it was the only way to get past the multitudes of annaru that had gathered in the ancient city to witness the ascension of their fallen god. This was his only chance to gain access to the temple and save Alis.

Still, he had doubts, most of them regarding his sanity. Only a complete fool, or a man driven to the brink, would even consider what he was about to do.

Janeli, however, had no knowledge of the guardian and shared none of his apprehension. "Be coming." She waved the two orishadai users forward with a clawed hand. "When darkness be falling and the moons rising, we are being too late." She crouched low and darted across the clearing before Dayn could protest.

He ran to catch up, hoping to warn her of what was waiting below.

"Wait for me!" Merek hurried after them.

The obelisk's gaping jaws hung open, its dark chasm of a throat leading deep into the earth where it eventually connected with a series of dank, abandoned tunnels. Dayn vividly recalled his last time in those unholy places far beneath the earth. Visions of Ryl's final moments flashed before his eyes every time he closed them.

"What you be waiting for?" Janeli pressed when he did not immediately enter the open mouth.

"Well? Lead on." Merek nudged him towards the back of the throat.

"I'm trying to remember the way," Dayn stalled, wiping cold sweat from his brow with the back of a trembling hand. This might be his plan, but that didn't mean he had to like it. He delayed further, causing his companions to grow restless.

Janeli urged him onward. "Be hurrying, orishadaon, we must be stopping the Betrayer before the moons rise to their apex."

Merek rolled his eyes at his brother's unease. "You aren't afraid, are you?" he taunted. "Don't worry, if the half-blood tries anything, I'll protect you."

It was not Alis, or even Kor, that he feared. Merek simply did not understand. Dayn hung his head despondently. He had to tell them. "Before we go in, there's something you both need to do," he began, staring at the mud clinging to his bare feet. "I want you to think about the most horrible thing you can. Whatever it is you're most afraid of, picture it in your mind."

"I not be understanding."

"What in the Aether is this about?"

"Just trust me," he insisted. "Think of the most terrifying thing you can."

Both his brother and the huntress hesitantly closed their eyes and concentrated.

Merek wore a deep frown. "Now what?"

"Now imagine something infinitely worse, because that's what's waiting for us down there."

Merek opened his eyes to glare at him. "Was that supposed to be funny?"

"I'm not laughing," Dayn replied, not meeting his gaze.

Janeli's face remained scrunched up in concentration as she diligently tried to imagine something worse than her worst fear. Somehow, Dayn doubted she would come up with anything as horrible as the shadow beast.

"The ancestors watch over us," he prayed before stepping through the darkened entrance.

Merek paused to wait for the huntress. "You coming?" he asked, causing her to forget Dayn's instructions and open her eyes.

The pair moved in behind the orishadaon.

Nearly everything was as Dayn left it, from his footprints in the dust to the spidery cracks along the surface of the obsidian door, created when he forced it open. The only exception was an inky black stain on the flagstones that began at the entrance and disappeared into the darkness of the stairwell. He knew without doubt that the stain had not been there before.

Dayn moved to the back of the statue's throat, taking care to avoid contact with the substance. He pulled Agidyne out and considered willing the blade to glow as he had his first time in the tunnels, then decided against it. Even a small use of the new power might be enough to let the red tide in. He would not risk it, not when they were so close to Alis.

Merek, understanding the need for illumination, pulled a fist-sized hunk of rock from one of the pouches on his belt. A surge of orishadai crackled across the stone's surface before sinking into it. A moment later the stone glowed bright as any torch, driving back the shadows.

"You lead the way," Merek said, pushing his brother towards the pitch-black stairwell. "It's time to kill the half-blood."

Dayn squared his shoulders. "I told you before, I'm not going to—"

"I know, I know, you aren't going to kill her." Merek rolled his eyes. "That's what I'm here for."

Dayn thought about arguing, realized it would be pointless, and decided not to bother. He took a deep breath and began the descent.

Cool air wafted up from the depths, bringing with it the morbid scent of death. Its heady aroma was overwhelming, unbearable. It invaded his lungs, making him gag.

"Don't let me find it," he begged the ancestors and anyone else who might be listening. "Please don't let me see the body."

Once in the catacombs, he froze. Down the corridor, at the very edge of the light cast by Merek's globe, a dark shape sprawled amidst a darker stain of black. Dayn crept closer, heart beating hard against his ribs. Despite his mounting tension, he edged towards the skeletal remains, fighting the urge to turn and flee.

Light fell across a desiccated figure, revealing a skinless form, completely devoid of innards. All that remained were bones covered in a crust of dark ooze.

The body was impossible to identify in its current state, but Dayn knew who it belonged to. He knew whose bones they were and the ultimate sacrifice their owner had made for him. He pressed his burnt fist against his heart in honor of his deceased friend.

Merek placed a hand over his nostrils. The odor emanating from the dark muck was indescribably rank.

Dayn kneeled beside the body and covered his face in shame. "You died to save me," he said to the remains. "You shouldn't have died, not for me."

His brother looked on with growing impatience. "What are you babbling?"

Dayn prayed that Ryl's ancestors would see the virtue of his actions and admit him into the afterlife. "I swear, when this is done I'll burn you myself and send your soul to the sky. I swear it on the blood of my mother and father."

He desperately wanted to speak with his friend's spirit one last time. That did not happen. Either Ryl could not or did not want to appear.

"What in the Aether is that mess?" Merek backed away, stifling a gag.

Dayn ignored him.

Janeli watched in silence, seeming to understand the orishadaon's need for a moment alone with his thoughts.

After a time, Dayn rose up and gave Ryl's remains a curt nod.

Merek looked between his brother and the thing on the ground, throwing his hands up in exasperation. "Fine, don't tell me anything."

Without another word, Dayn left the body where it lay and continued down the hall.

29.
WHEN DARKNESS FALLS ON THE SHADOW OF A MAN

The tunnel stretched out before him, a forlorn and seemingly endless length of dank stone that magnified every sound; footsteps sounded like thunderclaps, each breath rumbled like an earthquake. This place acted as a perfect mirror for his soul: swathed in darkness and empty of all but the sinister force lurking deep within.

A subtle tingle in the back of his mind stopped him before he got more than half a dozen paces. Shivers of fearful recognition rippled the flesh along his spine. Something was coming.

Ryl's pain-wracked screams rang in his ears anew, as real and loud as the first time he had heard them. His terror distorted the chilling screams into something far, far worse. Only in the deepest pits of the Aether would Dayn have expected to hear the sounds that plagued his grief-stricken mind. He gritted his teeth and hoped the throat-strangling shrieks would fade away before they drove him mad.

Merek cupped his hands over his ears and cried out in pain.

Janeli, who did not possess the ability to tap into her soul energy, was unaffected by the shadow beast's mental howl. As such, she still had her wits about her when the thing approached; a living wall of blackness slithering towards the trio. "What is that being?" She pointed to a cluster of shadows coiling together at the edge of Merek's weak light.

Dayn raised the tip of his blade towards the demonic thing. He had no orishadai to protect himself, leaving the ancient sword as his only defense against an opponent that could not be harmed by mortal weapons.

"I need your help," he said to his brother, who was slow to recover from the initial mental assault. Merek spit on the rough stone at his feet, eyes flashing dangerously as they locked with Dayn's.

Swirling shadows crashed against the light, diverting Dayn's attention. He forced himself to stand his ground before the demon's onslaught. "This is going to be over quick if we don't work together," he told him.

Merek gritted his teeth in frustration. "All right," he said begrudgingly. "What do you need?"

Dayn hastily outlined a plan. "Put up a shield around all three of us. We're going to run through that monster."

"Through it?!" his two companions blurted as one.

"Yes, through it!" Dayn insisted. "We can't kill it, we can't even hurt it. Our only chance is to get away from it."

"I . . . I do not run from fights like a coward," Merek said, trying to sound confident.

"Then you'll die," came Dayn's blunt reply. "You can't do anything against it. That *thing* was never meant to exist in this world, only in nightmares and the Aether. Now make the shield!"

"Do it yourself if it's so important," the young orishadai user said petulantly.

Dayn hung his head in shame. "I . . . can't," he confessed. "I haven't been able to draw out orishadai since we left Nesthome."

Merek looked to the shadows pushing against the light, and of all the possible reactions, he sighed. "I have to do everything myself." His entire body went rigid, the hands at his sides clenching firmly into fists. The air around him shimmered and became a crimson haze, expanding to take both Dayn and Janeli into its confines. "I can't hold it up for long," he cautioned between clenched teeth. "If you're going to do something, it better be now."

"Run straight at it," Dayn instructed. "The orishadai should drive it back."

Merek snapped his head around to glare at him. "*Should*?"

"Do you think I fight demons every lunar? I've never tried this before!"

"Then why are we trying it now!"

"We be doing what after getting past it?" Janeli cut in before an argument could break out between the brothers.

"We keep running," Dayn said.

"That is being your plan?" she scoffed.

"Not enough time to think up something better," he admitted. "Keep close, Janeli, you're only safe inside the shield."

And they ran, straight towards the demon.

The darkness exploded in a swirl of writhing shadows and black, smoky tentacles. It rolled backwards like a reverse tidal wave and disappeared beyond the light, exactly as Dayn predicted. He could sense it fleeing down a side passage, and knew it would not go far.

"Save your strength, drop the shield," Dayn shouted over the demon's terrible wails.

The air around the trio ceased its rippling and all signs of the shield faded away.

"Now what?" Merek cast a wary glance over his shoulder as he ran.

"Pray to the ancestors I remember where to go." Dayn dug deep into his memories, searching for the ones that would guide him through the tunnels. Hopefully, he could use his gifted orishadaon memory to get the others and himself through the maze safely. All he had to do was recall the way.

"You dragged me down here with that thing and you don't even know how to get out?" his brother huffed.

Dayn ignored the question. "Turn here." He indicated a tunnel that looked no different than the rest. More twists and turns down similar corridors brought them to an archway leading into the room where the gauntlet and its guardian used to rest.

The same forbidding piles of skulls were stacked against either side of the entryway, their fleshless faces locked in hideous, toothy grins. Dayn led his group onward without pause, confident that he could find the way out.

The demonic guardian picked up their trail at that point. It stayed beyond the range of the light, always there, yet seldom seen.

A haunting specter of death if ever there was one, waiting patiently for them to make a mistake as it shadowed their every move.

Now and again Dayn would look back and catch a quick glimpse of the squirming darkness, but only for an instant before it pulled itself out of sight.

The next thing he recognized was the room with the obsidian table where he had smashed the annaru skeleton to pieces.

As soon as they were past the room a callous hissing, like the rasp of metal on stone, echoed through the tunnels.

He kept a wary eye on the shadows both ahead and behind. The pounding of his heart grew so loud it almost drowned out the screams that filled his mind.

Something about all this felt . . . odd. He couldn't tell exactly what. Wait! He had it. Another presence intruded on his thoughts! Wicked laughter rang inside his head as he realized what was happening.

An overpowering darkness crashed against his mind's defenses and sent tendrils of agony writhing into his every nerve. Wild muscle spasms arched his spine, then snapped it forward, hurling him face first to the ground. He landed in a crumpled ball, face skidding across the rough stone, leaving a bloody smear in its wake. At some point during the fall his fingers sprang open, releasing their hold on Agidyne.

Merek ran on a few paces before the *clang* of the sword striking stone alerted him to his brother's predicament.

Dayn found himself at the edge of the light, his body half draped in shadow. The fact that his awkward tumble had left a ragged scrape across the better part of his jaw barely registered as he fumbled desperately through the gloom for the hilt of his weapon.

He got a hand on the sword and scrambled to his feet as Merek came rushing back towards him, driving away the darkness with his glowing hunk of rock. A head-splitting screech rang out as the black tentacles that had been about to envelop Dayn pulled back. Madly thrashing shadow limbs cracked the tunnel walls in their hurry to escape the searing light.

With one hand on the fractured stone wall to steady himself, Dayn rose to his feet and ushered his companions onward.

"I'm fine," he said to the huntress, who looked at his ruined face with concern. Only then did he realize the extent of the damage, and how much it hurt.

"Clumsy, sun-baked idiot," Merek said furiously, unaware that his brother had just weathered a mental attack of immense power.

The shadow beast forced a continuous stream of wails into Dayn's mind. He tried covering his ears to muffle the sound, but it did nothing. Each scream was driven directly into his thoughts, and without orishadai there was no way to fend off the demon's torturous attacks.

A tiny bit of orishadai would be enough to erect a mental wall capable of warding off the assault, yet it was beyond his ability to muster even that much in his own defense. He had to do something. If things continued as they were his sanity would soon collapse beneath the weight of the shadow beast's onslaught.

He followed his memory further into the tombs and twisting corridors of the under-tunnels. The place was infinitely immense. Without the benefit of his orishadaon memory, he would have been hopelessly lost.

More familiar landmarks drew his attention: a stretch of corridor he remembered, a room with a carving of Kor, a collection of fungal growths. Each one connected another puzzle piece inside the seemingly endless maze of his memory.

It felt like he had been underground for lunars. Without the sun or moons to watch he had no way of knowing how much time had passed beyond the timeless void of the catacombs.

The shadow beast's endless keening wore away his reason, pushing him to move faster, which caused his body to grow wearier. Every instant he spent listening to the unearthly howls filling his mind brought him that much closer to running Agidyne's blade through his own heart to end his misery. He was playing into the demon's trap, wasting his strength long before he had a chance to confront it. Not that it would do any good to fight.

In the back of his thoughts, something stirred. A vague memory told him he was almost free. The tunnels did not go on forever, a way out would soon appear.

"Orishadaon?" Janeli slowed her tireless pace to a comfortable jog, allowing him to catch up. "Your brother be looking unwell," she observed. "You be looking worse."

"I'm fine," Merek huffed from a few paces ahead.

Dayn's lungs burned with every gulp of air, and his legs strained from the effort of each stride. He offered the huntress a weak smile—all he could manage—and nothing more.

The wailing in his head intensified, causing a grunt of discomfort to escape his lips. Something sticky and wet pooled inside his right ear. His staggering gait caused the substance to spill out and run down the side of his jaw. He quickly wiped it away, smearing his already scarred face with more blood.

Merek too, found himself affected by the newly intensified screeching. His legs wobbled and he was forced to put a hand against the wall for support.

The shadows behind the trio grew thicker and darker, if such a thing was possible in a place where darkness already ruled.

"We're almost out," Dayn reassured his brother. Of the two, Dayn looked worse by far, and felt worse, too, but he was nonetheless worried about Merek. His younger sibling might hate him, but they were still brothers. Blood took care of blood.

"Worry about yourself, orishadaon," came his sibling's reply. It was the first time he had ever referred to him as "orishadaon" without scorn in his voice.

Dayn pointed to an open archway at the end of the corridor. "In there." Neither he nor Merek were in much shape to climb the stairs he knew to be on the other side of that archway, but they would have to if they wanted to survive.

Dayn gritted his teeth against the pain in his pounding temples and gave his head a quick shake to clear his ear of sloshing blood.

The stairs were beyond the door, exactly as he remembered. Up the trio went, and up and up. The stairs wound ever upward, taking an eternity to climb. After a while Dayn felt dizzy. This led to a bout of nausea that, combined with the unending wails in his mind, sent him reeling.

A misplaced foot nearly cost him his life. He managed to save himself by grabbing hold of a crease in the stone wall, and fell to his knees rather than pitching backwards. In all regards a better outcome, albeit a painful one.

He was trailing behind his two companions already, and could not afford to drop back any more. Dayn forced himself to rise and stumble forward, hurrying after the safety of Merek's light.

He found himself at the very edge of that light as he regained his footing. The shadows drew closer than he would have liked. One wispy tentacle whipped through the darkness at his back. Another dared to enter the light and immediately burned away, leaving a cloud of glowing embers in its wake. If it was willing to risk damaging itself to get at him, his demonic pursuer must be growing restless.

Merek half crawled, half stumbled up the stairs with one hand on the steps to steady himself as he hurried along. "How far . . . does this thing go?" he wheezed, wiping sweat off the sides of his face.

Dayn pulled his ankle out of the way in time to avoid another swipe from a roiling bit of darkness. "It didn't feel . . . this far . . . the first time," he panted.

The stairs seemed endless. Any higher and he was sure they would come out amidst the clouds in the kingdom of the ancestors.

Dayn doubted anything besides the direct intervention of the ancestors could put a stop to the shadow beast at his back, but he vowed to try. The thing had to pay for what it did to Ryl.

Light hurt it, that much he knew. When he reached the top of the stairs he would flush the thing out of the tunnels and into the glaring light of the ancestors.

"I be seeing the top," Janeli called from above.

"Merek!" Dayn shouted.

The younger orishadai user slowed his pace by a half-step. "What?"

With Merek only a few paces ahead, Dayn was completely bathed in protective light. He no longer had to worry about shadowy tentacles clawing at his ankles and dragging him down into the black abyss. "I . . . plan . . . kill demon," he wheezed.

His brother stumbled in surprise. Dayn caught him before he could fall and pushed him onward.

"To the Aether . . . with that," the younger orishadai user scoffed. "I'm getting out . . . you stay . . . fight it by yourself . . . if you want."

"Be hurrying," Janeli called back, sounding further away.

Dayn redoubled his speed, or would have if he could muster any more strength from his straining legs.

"We can kill it," Dayn insisted in one quick breath.

"How?" Curiosity crept into his brother's strained voice. The young orishadai user hated to retreat from a fight, so the idea of getting back at the demon must have appealed to him.

Once Dayn had his brother's full attention he began to lay out his simple plan. "At the top," he paused, gasping. "Hide . . . your light," he finished after a moment.

"What?"

"It'll make the demon feel safe," Dayn explained carefully. "When it crawls all the way out of the staircase," he paused for another gasp of air, "make the light shine as bright as you can. There's only one tunnel above us and it leads straight outside into the light," he sputtered, on the verge of collapsing from the effort of so much talk.

Merek tossed the plan around in his mind, weighing its viability against the odds of his survival. It was not until he came into the circular room at the top of the stairs, and saw for himself that there was only one way out, that he agreed to help.

"This is insane, but I'll do it," he said with a grin.

"What be happening?" Janeli asked from her place at the top of the stairs. She had no idea what they were planning.

Dayn gave his brother a nod of thanks. "Everyone against the wall, as far away from the stairs as you can get." He ushered them back from the opening. "Hide the light!" he cried when he had his back pressed against the stone.

"Are you being insane?!" Janeli shrieked.

The room disappeared into darkness, all except for a tiny speck of sunlight shining at the far end of the exit tunnel. That same tunnel would take them to a creature far worse than the demon they were about to face.

One impossible challenge at a time, Dayn told himself without humor.

As the shadow beast closed in, the screams inside his mind grew unbearable. He clapped his hands over his ears, crying out in frustration when it did nothing. His heart pounded faster and faster, threatening to burst in his chest.

The raspy, whispering sound that the demon often made grew louder as well.

"It's close!" Merek yelled.

Dayn held Agidyne, shielding his mind with the calming memories conjured by the blade. He focused on recalling memories of his father. The man had been a hero to the Swift Claw tribe. On more than one occasion he had saved fellow hunters from certain death at the claws of annaru and the jaws of karda. If not for Dayn's failure that fateful lunar, the tribe's hero would never have died.

"It's here!" The shout interrupted his train of thought before he could descend into self-pity.

Dayn felt the demon's presence the instant his brother shouted the warning. "Light, now!" he yelled in alarm.

Merek's glowing stone burst to life, much brighter than before.

In response, the shadow beast's howl shook the temple to its foundation, causing dust and hunks of stone to rain down from the ceiling. Dayn's knees buckled and he went down at the same time, only to be caught mid-fall by Janeli.

A wicked smirk spread across Merek's face and he ran towards the demon, screaming a war cry as his light pushed it away from the stairs before it could escape back into the safety of smothering darkness. Bright red cinders exploded in all directions as the light burned the demon's shadowy flesh to ash. It had no choice but to retreat down the tunnel, exactly as planned. Merek raced after it, holding the light before him.

"Follow him," Dayn rasped, shivering uncontrollably after the final, devastating blow to his mind. Janeli set him against the wall for support, gave his ragged form a concerned look, and ran after the other orishadai user.

Merek's maniacal laughter echoed down the corridor, louder than the demon's dying wails.

Dayn stole a moment to collect himself before hobbling after his brother, using Agidyne as a makeshift cane. As he struggled towards the light at the end of the tunnel he noticed a familiar set of hieroglyphics on the wall by his head. He recognized the picture, that of a single figure surrounded by annaru, Kor hovering in the air above.

He cringed as an infernal whine filled the air, loud enough to be heard from one end of the ancient city's ruins to the other.

He was greeted at the end of the tunnel by his smiling brother, a stunned plant woman, and a cloud of glowing ashes that fluttered to the stone at his feet and evaporated into nothingness.

Merek clapped him across the shoulder and let out a laugh equally as loud as the demon's death scream. "It worked." He wiped flakes of red ash off his face and his grin broadened.

"I never be seeing such a thing," Janeli gasped. She hid beneath the legs of a giant annaru statue, careful not to let any of the strange ash touch her flesh. She pulled a hand back as if bitten when one fluttering flake brushed against her wrist.

Dayn, too, was wary of coming into contact with the demon's 'remains.'

His brother, however, had no such qualms.

Merek sniffed the air. His grin broadened further, threatening to split his face in two. He pointed down the stairs towards the base of the great temple and dug his heels into the stone, bracing himself for battle. "Annaru," the young man said gleefully.

30.
A (PER)VERSION OF TRUTH

Six scaled ones rushed up the temple stairs towards them. Many more gathered at the base of the great monument, snarling amongst themselves while pointing at the pair of humans and the plant woman. Sooner or later the entire population, hundreds of annaru, would arrive, and then there would be no chance of saving Alis.

Janeli moved further up the stairs, towards the second tier and its bloodstained altar of bone and iron. "What is being your plan?" she asked, eyeing the pack of scaled ones scrambling towards them with a mixture of loathing and fear.

Between the three of them, their only weapon was Agidyne. They had little chance of success if they chose to stand and fight.

Merek stepped to the front of the platform and waited patiently for the first annaru to reach him. "Go on." He waved his brother away. "I'll handle these, and any more that come."

As the first scaled one neared the top of the stairs Merek thrust his hand out, palm first. The creature let out a surprised howl as orishadai took control of its body. Its three-toed feet clawed for purchase on the stone, found none, and then lifted into the air. The creature's long tail thrashed back and forth angrily, but there was nothing it could do to save itself.

Merek flicked his wrist and the scaled one was hurled from the temple. Dayn looked away before it hit the paving stones far below. The sickening wet slap of impact alerted him to the creature's final fate.

The scaled one's abrupt end caused the other five annaru to hesitate. In the time it took for them to renew their charge, Merek used the distraction to dispatch another one by the same method as the first. Once again, Dayn averted his eyes.

"I told you I can handle this," the young orishadai user insisted. His voice carried with it a bitter edge, one that spoke of mayhem and revenge. He never took his cold, unforgiving eyes off the four remaining scaled ones.

Dayn retreated to Janeli's side, watching in twisted fascination as one annaru doubled over, grasping its stomach in agony. Its legs went out from under it and it fell against the stairs, only to have its skull caved in an instant later by one of Merek's crushing mental attacks.

Three annaru left.

"Stay with him," Dayn instructed the huntress.

Janeli switched her fearful glare from the saurians to the young orishadai user. "He be doing such awful things," she said, repulsed.

Dayn shrugged. "He's always had a talent for murder."

The plant woman grasped him by the arm. "What you want I be doing?"

He shrugged again. "I don't know, make sure he doesn't get himself killed."

"I want to be going with *you*," she blurted, sounding afraid of Merek, rather than worried for Dayn's safety.

Another annaru let out a howl of pain. One more down, and the final two were unlikely to reach the first tier before Merek dealt with them. A second, larger group of scaled ones gathered at the bottom of the steps, donning sets of deadly looking wrist-blades before they too charged the young man's position.

Dayn waited patiently for Janeli to release his arm. "You won't stand a chance against what's up there, and I can't protect you," he said. "Stay here and don't get in Merek's way. I'll get Alis and then we'll all escape back through the tunnels. Just hold this spot until I get back."

Janeli clasped his shoulder. She pried her eyes off Merek for the first time since the battle began and fixed Dayn with an intense gaze. "May you be fighting with the strength of Emara Ekara, the swiftness of Auxia, and the cunning of Malar," she said, giving his shoulder a final, reassuring squeeze.

He offered her a faint smile. "Just try not to get yourself killed."

With that he turned and faced his destination, the top of the ancient, moss covered structure. Kor was waiting for him at the summit, waiting for the moons to rise so that he could regain his lost power and start his war against humanity all over again. All that stood between the human race and extinction was a very tired orishadaon with one ruined hand and no orishadai.

He stalked up the steps, ignoring the horrible noises that reached his ears from Merek's place on the first tier.

Dayn made sure to spit disrespectfully into the bloodstained altar on the second tier, once for himself and a second time for Ryl, before moving on.

In short order, he reached the top tier and stood staring into the rune carved archway before him. He ran his charred hand over the markings, feeling the rough stone grate across his blackened fingertips. Something about the odd runes made the hair on the nape of his neck stand on end. Maybe he sensed their meaning, or maybe it was the closeness of his people's greatest nemesis; either way, the place made him uncomfortable.

In the span of an eye blink, his connection to reality snapped and a collage of images blossomed inside his mind. A huge chamber filled with flickering light. An impenetrably deep shadow. Agidyne lying on the ground. Despair, overwhelming despair.

Dayn grasped his wrist and yanked the hand away from the stones, reeling from the mental backlash. He put a hand against his sweaty forehead, composing himself with a series of deep breaths.

"No time to think about it now," he told himself regarding the vision. He had enough to worry about without wasting thoughts on incomprehensible hallucinations.

The sun hung low in the sky, its bottom brushing across the jagged peaks ringing the valley. As soon as it dipped below those mountainous peaks the moons would rise and, if Janeli's warning was accurate, it would be too late to stop Kor.

"Alis," he whispered her name reverently. Then his features turned grim. "Kor!" the orishadaon bellowed into the dark opening before him. He stepped through the archway into a vast chamber.

Hundreds of burning torches illuminated the orishadaon's surroundings with their writhing orange glow. The far reaches of the room disappeared beyond the range of the light, remaining dark as the catacombs beneath the temple. Any number of Kor's minions, or Kor himself, could have hidden within that darkness and Dayn would never know.

Huge columns, half as big around as he was tall and decorated in bizarre swirling patterns that matched his tattoos, rose more than fifty paces before disappearing into shadow. He ran a hand over the nearest column's smooth surface, marveling at the intricacy of its design. Each and every one of the thousands of decorative markings must have taken tremendous skill to carve, as the identical symbols etched on his own body had.

"Kor," he said, taking his hand away from the pillar. "Come out and face me, you coward!" He hoped petty insults would goad the proud god into revealing himself. It worked, to a degree.

"Dayn?" replied a woman's voice from out of the darkness.

The orishadaon's heart fluttered with recognition. The sound of approaching footsteps reached his ears and he quickly ducked out of sight behind the pillar.

"Where are you, Dayn? I can't see you." It sounded like Alis. It really sounded like Alis.

"Nice try, Kor," he whispered to himself, peeking around the side of the column. The god was luring him out, using her as bait.

Alis' voice cracked when next she spoke. "Please, Dayn," she sobbed. "Please help me."

Her sorrow broke his heart, and it was all he could do to keep from running to her. She stepped out of the shadows and the orishadaon quickly pulled his head back behind the pillar. The erratic pounding of his heart would surely give him away if he could not quiet it. Each beat came louder than the last. He put a hand over his chest to muffle the sound. Not even the closeness of Agidyne calmed his frayed nerves.

"Help me," she begged, falling to her hands and knees. The metal gauntlet scraped against the rough stone, its ruby emitting a soft flash of light each time one of Alis' tears struck it. If this was an act, it was certainly a good one.

Dayn felt as cruel as he ever had for leaving Alis out there alone.

"It wasn't me that attacked you," Kor, or maybe Alis, tried to convince him. "Kor did it. I can't control him. Please, Dayn, I need your help to get him out of my head."

"No, you are mine," the god's gravelly voice spilled from Alis' lips. "Stop resisting me, you will damage yourself."

"Leave me alone," she wailed.

Kor laughed at her desperation.

The whole situation was too much for Dayn. He could not sit idly by while Alis was in such obvious pain. The orishadaon slipped out from behind the pillar and called to her.

She whirled around, cheeks stained with tears. "Dayn!" She threw her arms out and ran to him. He caught her and pulled her close, happy to feel the warmth of her body against his own. "I knew you'd come." She buried her head against his shoulder, trembling as each bout of sobs wracked her body.

"I couldn't leave you to your fate." Dayn nearly choked on the words as his emotions got the best of him. He could not remember a time when he had felt so overjoyed, and yet so incredibly wretched at the same time. Kor's presence was still buried within her, and the god would surely assert control at the first sign of weakness. If Dayn let his guard down, even for an instant . . .

Alis' lips twisted into a pained snarl. She slammed the gauntlet into his unprotected jaw, sending him tumbling backwards. The orishadaon landed on the hard stone to the sound of a dead god's jeers.

"You cannot have her, she is mine," Kor gloated, parading Alis' body around to prove his point. "Did you really think I would give her up so easily?"

Dayn rubbed his jaw, feeling a fragment of tooth shake loose. He spit it out and wiped his lips clean with the back of his hand. "If you need a body, why not take mine?"

"It is in the blood," Kor said cryptically.

"What's in my blood?"

"Not yours." Kor shook his head, refusing to say more.

The god was talking in riddles. What was so special about Alis' blood? Then it occurred to him. She was part annaru, and Kor was their god. Was it possible that he could only exert his influence over those who possessed the blood of his chosen servants?

That was why, when they were in the tunnels, no one could hear the god's whispered words but her. The annaru blood in her veins allowed Alis to hear Kor's mental call.

The god nodded as if reading his thoughts. "Now you understand." As he said this, Dayn suddenly became aware of an otherworldly presence, or presences, as it turned out. Kor's shadow minions, the same ones that had been in Nesthome, emerged from the deeper darkness to surround the orishadaon, their features hidden by the gloom that seemed to hover permanently about them.

The weight of his revelation and the nearness of the demonic trio nearly crushed Dayn's spirit. No wonder Alis had insisted so strongly on accompanying him into the Tresslevale, it was her destiny to find the gauntlet resting in the catacombs bellow this very temple. She had been right all along, fighting fate was impossible. No one could escape it.

He tried to ignore the demons and focus instead on the god.

"What do you want?" asked the embittered orishadaon.

Kor leaned casually against a pillar, running his eyes over the odd runes carved into the stone. He completely ignored Dayn's question.

"Damn it, Kor! Why did you take Alis from me?"

The god sighed, reluctantly tearing his eyes away from the odd markings. "I came back to stop your kind from ruining the world," he said.

"To stop the humans," Dayn scoffed. "The only danger to the world comes from you," he countered angrily.

"What I did was necessary!" Kor bellowed after the accusation. "Humans were calling creatures of the Aether, they had to be stopped."

"Liar!"

"It is no lie," the god said with such conviction that it was difficult to doubt him. "Vernac's fall should have wiped your kind away, but others intervened on your behalf."

"I don't believe you." Dayn waved Agidyne at the god.

Kor held up a hand, imploring him to listen.

Dayn stayed his sword thrust, but kept the weapon at the ready.

"Your belief does nothing to change the truth," Kor said sadly, his head hanging low and his shoulders sagging wearily. "I did not want to destroy your people," he admonished, "but I could see no other way to defend Urth against humanity. The gift of orishadai was not enough for your ancestors, so they sought deals with demons and other, more horrible, things. They turned away from their gods, from me, as I always knew they would.

"I sacrificed everything. I lost my powers, my body, even my place in this world was taken away. I traveled to the Aether inside a mortal to fight the demons. I killed their lord, and found myself imprisoned in their nightmare realm for my troubles."

Kor stopped his story, as if the mere thought of the Aether troubled his divine mind with unspeakable memories. "I cannot go back," he muttered to himself. "I will never go back there. That is why I need this body. One soul is such a small reward for all that I have sacrificed, do you not agree?"

Dayn spit on the stones at Kor's feet. "You can't have Alis. I want her back. You're more a monster than the demons." His grip on Agidyne tightened until his knuckles turned white.

"Do not be stupid, boy, you have only survived this long because I allowed it."

The tip of the sword trembled, as did Dayn's arm. "Lying again, Kor? You already tried to kill me, but Alis stopped you."

"Back in that hovel where we first met?" The god shook his head as if listening to the prattling of an ignorant child. "I wanted you dead, then; my anger outweighed my better judgment."

Dayn took a threatening step towards Kor.

The god made no move to stop him, secure in his invulnerability. "That was then, orishadaon, things change."

Dayn did not lower his blade, but neither did he step forward to use it.

Kor continued. "This vessel is . . . well, it is weak. Human bodies are so fragile, but orishadaons," he grinned, "orishadaons have so much more to offer."

"You said you couldn't take my body." Dayn drew his arm back to swing.

The god never flinched. He even leaned forward, daring, taunting Dayn to hack him down. "I am not after you," he whispered in his sinister tone. "I am after your child."

31.
REGRET NOT THE FALL FOR SALVATION

Kor's words struck him harder than a physical blow. Dayn found himself torn between open-mouthed shock and total disbelief. "My . . . child?"

The god took a step forward, driving the flustered orishadaon back towards the entrance. "Yes, boy. If you and this woman have a child it will have your power as well as the annaru blood I need to take control. The perfect vessel."

"*If* we have one?" Dayn came to his senses. He dug in his heels and planted Agidyne's tip against the god's exposed throat. His good hand shook with the effort of holding the sword steady. He hated Kor, wanted the god dead more than anything, but he could not harm him without also harming Alis. He was not willing to trade her blood for the god's.

Despite the sword at his throat, Kor pressed forward, running the blade across the side of Alis' neck.

Hissing from the three shadow minions filled the air, a rough and grating noise that made the orishadaon flinch.

Dayn quickly pulled Agidyne away before it could do any more damage.

Kor grinned knowingly. "You cannot kill me. You know as well as I do that you will never hurt the woman. Touching really, but pathetic."

"Shut up!" Dayn waved Agidyne's bloody tip at him.

The god ignored his outburst and casually brushed the sword

aside with the back of his hand. "Can we end this now? You will not resist if it means hurting the woman. You have already lost."

Dayn edged his way towards the exit, one step ahead of the approaching god. "You destroyed my tribe, you killed my friend," he growled, casting a quick glance over his shoulder. "I'll never help you."

Kor sighed. "You have no choice. This has all been planned. Destroying Vernac ensured that the lunar conjunction would occur much sooner. If not for that, it would have taken thousands of years for the three moons to align, but with only two . . ." He let the sentence hang.

"Damn you," said the orishadaon. He hurriedly backed away, putting more and more distance between the god and himself.

"Willing subjects are so much more preferable." Kor grinned at Dayn's obvious discomfort, then abruptly cocked his head to one side, listening to something only he could hear. After a moment he nodded to himself and his sanguine smile broadened. "Your companions are not doing well."

Dayn's eyes narrowed. The god might be trying to distract him. Not much further to the entrance, and he would be able to see what was happening outside.

Kor rested his back against a pillar and crossed his arms over the warding tattoos on his vessel's chest. "Go ahead and look, I can wait."

Wary of a trick, Dayn kept one eye on the god as he stepped into the waning sunlight. Kor made no attempt to do anything, content to let the orishadaon see for himself.

Dayn shot a glance down the side of the temple. What he saw made his heart catch in his throat.

Blood covered Merek from his hair to his feet. Whether it was his, or that of the annaru he had slaughtered, was impossible to tell. At least a dozen saurian corpses lay heaped around him, their tainted lifeblood cascading down the side of the temple in a grisly waterfall. Double that number circled the exhausted orishadai user, waiting for him to drop his guard so they could strike him down.

Janeli stood with her back pressed against Merek's, a crude annaru wrist-claw strapped to her forearm. She lashed out at any saurian foolish enough to get close, although it was obvious to Dayn that she would soon be overwhelmed.

As he watched, the annaru grew bolder in their attacks. A scaled one darted in and swiped at Janeli's stomach, forcing her to block the attack and leave herself open to another creature on her right.

Dayn called out a warning, pointless since she would never hear him over the snarling war-pack surrounding her. Luckily, Merek deflected the new threat by summoning a shield with his drained orishadai, succeeding in sparing Janeli's life while leaving himself weak and defenseless in the process. When another annaru attempted to take advantage of his brother's infirmity, Janeli spun on her heels, forcing the saurian's claws down before they could pierce Merek's heaving chest. And so it went, his brother and the plant woman struggling on against insurmountable odds. It was only a matter of time before one of them made a fatal mistake, and then both warriors would be torn limb from limb by the ferocious annaru.

"Do as I say and I will spare them," said a voice into his ear.

Dayn whirled around, nearly cutting Kor in half with a wild swing from Agidyne. The god proved quicker than the orishadaon's arm, however, and caught the blade with gauntleted fingers.

Dayn tried without success to pull his weapon free of the god's grasp. Kor chuckled at the feeble attempt and grabbed Dayn's wrist with his other hand, bending back, forcing Dayn to grit his teeth in order to keep from crying out. "I'll kill you, Kor," he hissed.

"Do as I say and I will let them live," the god offered again, applying more pressure on the wrist.

Dayn couldn't help himself. He screamed.

"Is that a yes?"

Dayn shook his head furiously. He kicked at the god's shins while shockwaves of pain surged up his arm. Kor continued to push back on the wrist until the orishadaon's knuckles brushed against his forearm. Dayn's legs went limp. The god held tightly onto his wrist, refusing to let him fall. "Do as I say or I will tear out their throats and eat their hearts while you watch," Kor said icily.

It was hard to think through the pain. Darkness clung to the edges of his vision, threatening to expand and blind him with unconsciousness. He forced himself to weather the god's torture, using all the willpower he possessed to drive the darkness back. Orishadaon conditioning had trained him for moments like this; he would not let that training—Sharna's legacy—go to waste.

His companion's lives were in danger, that much he understood even through the haze of pain. If Dayn gave up his life to the god, Merek and Janeli would live, if not, they would die. Perhaps giving up was the right choice. If Alis was carrying Kor's vessel, she would be safe. The god could not kill her for fear of killing the vessel.

Kor applied yet more pressure to his wrist. "Let go of the sword, orishadaon."

Dayn whimpered pitifully.

"Let go of the sword," Kor repeated more forcefully.

His life for those of Alis, Merek and Janeli. One life for three. It seemed a worthwhile trade.

With great regret, he released his grip on Agidyne.

"How noble of you," the god commented as he calmly seized the weapon, letting go of the orishadaon's wrist in the process.

Dayn protectively clutched the wounded limb to his chest. Black and purple bruises marred the already swollen flesh. It was not broken, but holding anything would definitely hurt. He reminded himself that there were other, more important, things to worry about. "You said you'd let them live." H waved his burnt hand in the direction of the fighting on the first tier.

Kor ignored him, caught up in his inspection of the sword. He turned Agidyne over in his hands, mumbling something to himself as he read the runes etched along the length of the blade. A stray hand went to the wound on his neck, which, curiously, had yet to heal. Usually the god's wounds knitted themselves shut instantly.

"They're going to die!" Dayn yelled in the god's face. "You promised to let them live!"

Kor pushed him away. "Amusing," he said absently, speaking more to himself than to Dayn, who had nearly been flung off the top tier by the force of the push. "I doubt you know the significance of it. How very amusing."

Without sword or orishadai to defend himself, Dayn was at the god's mercy, a trait Kor was not at all known to display. "Help my brother!" he shouted, pointing at Merek as another annaru was reduced to a crumpled heap by the half-crazed orishadai user. The number of scaled ones gathering around the young man and Janeli had increased dramatically.

Kor lowered the sword and marched to the edge of the tier. He surveyed the scene before him with self-assured arrogance, obviously enjoying the fight. Eventually he held up his hand.

"Stop!" his voice rumbled over the gathered annaru. Each and every one of the scaled ones froze immediately, some in mid-strike, and turned their amber eyes towards the god.

"You!" Merek pointed at Kor. "I'll kill you right now."

Kor rolled his eyes and flicked his wrist in the direction of the orishadai user. An annaru stepped up behind Dayn's brother and brought the flat edge of its wrist-blade down on top of his head. Merek crumpled to the ground.

From where he stood, Dayn could not tell if his brother was still breathing or if the blow had killed him. "Damn you, Kor!"

"He is alive," assured the god. He turned to his followers. The annaru were so hushed that even a whisper would have reached them. "Bring them, and do not kill them yet."

The scaled ones surrounded Janeli, and without Merek's help she was quickly overwhelmed. To her credit, she managed to drop another one, tearing out its throat with a quick swipe of her 'borrowed' wrist-blade before a tight press of reptilian bodies forced her down. The annaru beat her senseless with a storm of vicious blows that would have killed a human.

Dayn gritted his teeth as the scene unfolded, wishing for a tiny spark of orishadai so that he could do something, anything, to defend her. Janeli and his brother might be alive, but there was no telling for how long, or what the god might do with them now that they were subdued. Kor could order them both killed as soon as he had his vessel.

"Are you happy, boy? They are alive, as I promised."

"To the Aether with you," Dayn spat.

"You forget, I have already been there." Kor left his place overlooking the battle and approached the orishadaon. "Now, human, you and this woman are going to make me a new vessel, or I will have that pathetic brother of yours devoured in front of you."

What other choice did he have but to obey? Either he did as he was told and the ones he cared about might die later, or he resisted and they were guaranteed to die now. Neither option was to his liking.

His shoulders sagged with despair.

The god, recognizing a defeated opponent when he saw one, shoved Dayn into the great chamber. "There." He pointed towards the back of the room, an area completely shrouded in darkness. "This will not take long."

32.
WALKING TALL

When it was over, three shadowy forms disengaged themselves from the surrounding darkness and moved towards the gasping orishadaon. Uncaring hands hauled his beaten form off the cooling stone and out of the god's sight.

"That will be all for now," Kor called after him, grinning slyly. "You may go to them, if you wish."

The shadows were not the demons he suspected, yet they were unquestionably demonic. They were also annaru, but at the same time, they were not annaru. Wispy fragments of darkness clung to them as they passed, shrouding them in an obscuring layer of gloom. Their ebony scales did not reflect the torchlight, but rather absorbed it, giving the impression that they were little more than walking silhouettes. All three stared out at him through the empty eye sockets of claw-toe skulls that covered their faces, eyes blazing an uncharacteristic crimson in the dim torchlight. Spiked metal plates covered their shins, forearms and shoulders, adding to their menacing appearance.

Two of the creatures held him up, while a third led the way. The one to his right had a deep scar across the front of its snout that split its upper lip in half. The lower lip looked as if it had been chewed away, leaving a hideous grimace of bared teeth fixed permanently on its reptilian face.

The creature to his left was missing both its eyes. Much of the damage was hidden beneath the bone helm, but Dayn could see that only lidless sockets remained, in which rested a pair of gleaming red gemstones.

The body of the lead creature (he could not bring himself to think of them as annaru) was a criss-crossed patchwork of scars, both old and new. The end of its swishing tail had been lopped off, along with two of the fingers on its left hand.

The orishadaon let out a soft groan of dismay as they dragged him away, towards where, he did not know or care.

Every bit of his body ached. He had resisted—it was an orishadaon's nature to fight on against all odds, to ignore pain and struggle through any ordeal. Unfortunately, the god proved to be a stronger opponent than even his stubbornness could hope to defeat, and he had received the most violent beating of his life as reward for his effort. Worse still, his desperate struggle had not stopped the god from conceiving a new vessel.

One of Dayn's eyes was swollen shut and crusted with blood. He cracked open the other to gaze about the poorly illuminated chamber. The torches were slowly being snuffed out, as hope had been during his brief struggle with the god, and he could scarcely see anything in the resulting dimness.

At the far end of the temple, outside the chamber's only entrance, the faintest glow of light radiated behind distant mountain peaks. The sun had fallen past the jagged mountaintops ringing the valley, smearing the sky shades of red and purple in its wake. Soon, Kor would have his godly powers back. Dayn had failed.

A throng of annaru emerged from hiding places amongst the gargantuan pillars, crowding around to watch him pass, landing more blows against his battered body. The two creatures carrying Dayn did nothing to dissuade the scaled ones from assaulting him, and he supposed they had no reason to. Annaru hated humans as much as humans hated annaru.

One creature slapped him across the face with its tail, opening a cut above his good eye. He barely noticed. With the innumerable scrapes, bruises, and welts already marring his face, one more hardly made a difference. He spit a gob of reddish phlegm in the direction of the offending annaru and allowed himself to be dragged deeper into the immense structure.

His feet bounced across coarse stone as his bearers carried him to a place at the rear of the chamber. All was blackness around him. Even his bearers melted into the unyielding dark, leaving Dayn with the odd sensation of floating through perpetual emptiness.

Then a light appeared out of that emptiness. Scribed upon the floor ahead was a ring of glowing runes that matched his own markings as well as those on the great pillars.

The instant his gaze fell upon the circle his heart rate increased tenfold. An overwhelming sense of dread flooded into him. Sweat beaded across his entire body, as if all the water in him were desperate to push itself through his skin. For the first time since they picked him up, Dayn attempted to struggle free of his captors. Their hold on him tightened as he thrashed in vain, his bare feet skidding wildly in all directions as they struggled for purchase on the uneven stone. The closer they got, the harder he fought, though he had precious little fight left in him. The orishadaon's mind screamed in abject terror. The runes conjured within him a primal fear he was unable to explain, and the thought of being enclosed within their eerie light frightened him more than anything.

His captors brought him forward with obvious intent, giving him a view of the two indistinct shapes already inside the ring.

"By the blood of the ancestors, Dayn!" he heard one of the shapes shout, or, he thought he heard it. To be truthful, he was none too sure of himself at the moment.

His demonic escort lugged him to the side of the runic circle and hurled his kicking bulk in without pause. He landed unceremoniously on his stomach, fighting the urge to scream. His every muscle protested the rough treatment and rougher landing. The klaxon call of his mental alarm went berserk the instant he crossed the runes.

The demons quickly disappeared back into the shadows.

Almost as soon as he struck the floor, a pair of hands gripped him around the waist and hoisted him into a sitting position.

"Don't touch me!" he hissed, pushing feebly at the assailant. He tried through sheer force of will to silence his mental alarm, found it impossible. Muscles tensed, and his entire body went rigid.

"Being quiet now." Janeli's expressionless face appeared

above him. "Be saving your strength for later." Despite the pain it caused him, he allowed her to clutch his trembling form against hers. It was better than lying face first on the floor, and it put a lot less pressure on his ribs, which hurt more with every rasping breath. It also helped bring his trembling under control.

The plant woman inspected his numerous wounds as he watched her through his one good eye. "What are you doing?" he croaked, barely recognizing his own hoarse voice. Was it desperation that he sensed in his tone?

She gently traced a clawed finger over a series of bruises on his chest, causing him to flinch. "Being sure you will not die," she answered flatly.

Her response caught him off guard. He did not want to die. Were his wounds really that bad? Without orishadai to bolster his natural healing he supposed they might be. Before he could pose her the question of whether or not he was going to live, he was interrupted by a call from his brother.

"Dayn?" The young man came forward tentatively. "You look terrible. Why in the Aether did you come back here?"

"Merek," he coughed. The young orishadai user looked awful himself. His bloodshot eyes darted back and forth at a manic rate, never resting on one place for more than half an instant. He was pale as a cloud and sweating profusely. A dried cake of blood smattered the back of his head where the annaru had struck him. "How's your head?" Dayn asked.

His brother poked the crust on the back of his skull and frowned. "Fine. No thanks to you. If you hadn't made a deal with the half-blood—"

"The annaru would be killing us both," Janeli finished, shooting Merek a warning glare.

Dayn looked around groggily. Something caught in his throat, more bloody phlegm, and he started to cough. "Oh," he moaned. "Why can't the ancestors let me die in peace?"

Merek snorted disdainfully. "Because you're too damned stubborn to die," he said with a fleeting grin. "Who do you think I learned it from?"

The remark made Dayn chuckle, though it hurt his ribs to do so.

"Being still, orishadaon, you be making your injuries worse," Janeli chided, forcing him to remain motionless with a surprisingly tender hand. She was especially careful not to injure him with her clawed fingertips.

"He said he was fine," Merek told her, attempting to brush her hand away. She easily avoided him and continued her inspection.

Dayn closed his eyes. With great effort, he released the tension in his muscles, allowing himself to sag against the plant woman. "Tired," he muttered under his breath.

"You must not be sleeping." Janeli's stern voice brought him back from the brink of unconsciousness.

"He's tired, let him rest," Merek said, in an oddly protective way.

"If he be sleeping now, he will not be waking up," Janeli replied, a hint of concern entering her rustling voice. "Your people's bodies be soft. I be surprised he still lives."

Dayn suddenly recalled the beating she had received earlier, when the scaled ones took her prisoner. He could see no outward signs of injury on her, despite the viciousness of the attack. Plant people were truly tough-skinned. "I'm fine." He choked down another coughing fit. "The annaru did worse to you."

"I am also being fine," she said dully. The huntress brushed away a few vines that were dangling in front of her eyes, the gesture reminding Dayn of Alis. Sorrow overcame him, and his heartbeat increased. He would trade anything to be with her again.

Dayn weakly raised his head, which Janeli pushed back down.

"You have to be away," he told the pair. "The god has what he wants, neither of you are safe, now."

His brother and the plant woman exchanged glances. Merek broke their shared silence with an awkward laugh. "And leave you here all by yourself? Like this? That would make me some kind of coward, now, wouldn't it." He shook his head at the foolish suggestion.

"Stop," Dayn croaked. "Don't argue. Kor will kill you. Janeli," he turned to the plant woman, "please, get my brother out of here."

"No!" Merek stomped his foot. "I'm not running away."

Dayn opened his mouth to speak, only to have a fit of coughing wrack his weakened body. He pounded his chest in frustration when the fit took an inordinate amount of time to pass. Eventually, he managed to clear his throat enough to speak. "Stop. Stop being so stubborn," he wheezed, inwardly chastising himself for being hypocritical. If it wasn't for his own stubborn behavior, they might not be in this situation at all. "We're the last of the tribe, Merek. We can't let the bloodline die with us."

"You're right, we can't." His brother nodded, then wrapped an arm around Dayn and hoisted him to his feet, eliciting a pained gasp from the orishadaon.

"What you be doing?!" Janeli cried out. She quickly reached for the battered orishadaon, but Merek yanked him away from her.

"We have to preserve the bloodline, like my brother said, so he's coming with us whether he wants to or not."

Dayn concentrated on pushing the pain to the darkest recesses of his mind, where it would not bother him until he allowed it to resurface. With so many agonies vying for his attention, the task proved impossible. It was all he could do to ignore the less serious wounds, there was nothing to be done about the rest. It was an odd sensation for an orishadaon, to be distracted by pain.

"We're going after the half-blood," Merek told his brother while gazing beyond the runes.

"There are being too many annaru," Janeli interjected, trying again to get Dayn back.

Merek laughed and retreated beyond the plant woman's reach. "No cage can hold me," he told her.

Dayn groaned, slinging an arm across his brother's shoulder for support. Being jostled about hurt his ribs and made it difficult to breathe. He needed to steady himself or he was going to pass out from the pain.

"I am not understanding how that be helping us." Janeli looked to Merek questioningly.

"It does not," a voice answered her from out of the darkness.

33.
SANCTITY OF BLOOD BROTHERS

Merek drew back from the edge of the runes, hauling Dayn along with him.

Janeli leapt before the back-peddling pair, claws splayed, guarding them from whatever might appear. It was a valiant gesture, every bit as brave as it was foolhardy.

Dayn, knowing Merek would be hindered by supporting him, unlatched himself from the younger orishadai user, and the trio formed a triangle, backs touching.

Merek gave him a supportive nod. "You're tougher than you look," he muttered so quietly that Dayn wasn't sure he had heard correctly. It was the closest his brother had ever come to complimenting him.

"I guess we both are," Dayn said.

Merek smirked at the remark. He put up a good facade, but it was obvious that the strain had begun to wear him down. His haggard features, sweaty face, and wild eyes were all signs of a man on the edge. He had nearly reached the limit of his abilities, and when he crossed over, the consequences would be disastrous.

"Be wary," Dayn warned, casting worrisome glances in all directions. The god could appear from anywhere.

"Wary of what?" Merek's eyes scanned the darkness beyond the runic circle, looking for any sign of the unseen speaker.

Wary of your waning control, Dayn wanted to say. "Wary of whatever the god has waiting for us," he answered, instead.

"I can take care of myself," Merek huffed, showing the first signs of fatigue since he started throwing around blasts of spirit energy as if his soul was a limitless reserve of power. As Dayn knew all too well, and his brother would soon discover, a soul's power was never limitless, no matter how stubborn or furious the owner.

"I've noticed," Dayn said in a hushed voice.

. In the next instant, his breath caught in his throat as the darkness at the edge of the runes melted away to reveal Kor.

The god strutted leisurely into the circle, suffering none of the mental torment Dayn had when he crossed it only a short time before. Kor bore himself in a regal manner while staring straight through the orishadaon with glazed, unfocused eyes. His gauntleted hand waved towards the faintly glowing symbols he had just stepped across. "They are drawn with blood. Do you know I personally killed every human that was used to write them?"

The words were devoid of emotion, a simple statement of fact without purpose.

Merek broke away from his two companions and stalked towards the god, intent on striking him down. Dayn grasped feebly at his brother's arm, desperate to hold him back, but Merek pulled free and marched on.

"No, you did not know that," Kor continued, ignoring the approaching orishadai user. He seemed to be unaware of Merek's presence, speaking in slow, practiced tones, reciting for an imagined audience. "Oh, I have killed many humans, hundreds, but these are the very best of them," the god droned. "They were all great warriors. One was a friend of the last creature I took as a vessel. He followed me all the way to the Aether before I killed him."

Another pace and Merek would be within striking distance. Sweat slicked the palms of Dayn's clenched fists, his fear for his brother's safety impossible to suppress.

The god's mood turned suddenly dark. "Now they will see my real power!" he roared with a detached expression upon his face. "Humans never deserved the life that was given to them! Humans are a blight on this world I only suffered to let live because of my damned siblings and their—"

A shimmering red haze engulfed Merek's clenched fist and he rammed it straight through the god's chest, cutting Kor off in mid-rant. The young orishadai user twisted his gore-spattered forearm, causing the god to cry out in pain for the first time since his rebirth.

"Damn you, half-blood." Merek spun his fist in a slow circle, eliciting another howl from the reborn god.

Still bellowing in pain, Kor gripped Merek's arm with both hands and dragged it out of himself, much to the surprise of the wide-eyed orishadai user. After that the god lurched forward, plowing into the young man before he could get out of the way. The two tumbled onto the runes, lashing out at one another madly as they rolled across the mystical markings.

Surprised by the sudden turn of fortune, Dayn could only stare as Kor landed blow after merciless blow on Merek's stomach. As soon as the young orishadai user made a move to protect himself Kor changed tactics and began striking him in the face.

"Stop!" Dayn yelled, staggering to his brother.

The god abruptly leapt to his feet, grinding a heel into Merek's gut as he faced the orishadaon.

The hole in Alis' chest was large enough that Dayn could see right through her. The wound should have killed any normal creature instantly, yet Kor stood without the slightest hint of concern for the gaping cavity in his chest. Gone was the god's blank expression, replaced by an intense, and fully lucid, glare.

Janeli shouldered past Dayn, clawed hands held defensively before her, preparing to intervene on the orishadaon's behalf.

"Stay back, Janeli." He waved the huntress aside. She was no match for the god without orishadai to protect herself, although, neither, he supposed, was he.

"Orishadaon?" she shot him a questioning glare.

"Let me deal with him," he told her, wishing she would get herself away from this place before it was too late. The battle was going badly and he doubted that any of them would survive if it continued much longer.

Kor watched the exchange with intense interest while his wound repaired itself. Newly grown flesh stretched over the hole, closing it in moments.

Rather than listen to Dayn's vague warning, Janeli darted

forward, swift as the wind, and buried her claws in the god's sides. Kor reacted immediately, shooting out an elbow that caught her in the jaw. The plant woman's head whipped around, tendrils of hair slapping against the sides of her face and then against the floor as she struck it. She remained still after hitting the ground, a thin stream of amber sap trickling from her open mouth.

Kor whisked forward and grabbed Dayn by the shoulders before he could react, pulling him close for a face-to-face confrontation.

"Why do you resist me?" asked the god as he tightened his grip, threatening to shatter the orishadaon's collar bone. "You cannot win. You cannot kill me. I am a god! No matter how much damage you do to this vessel, I will not die." Throughout his diatribe the god had slowly been dragging Dayn closer to the edge of the circle. "You, however, are only human," he said with distressing finality, then lifted the orishadaon off his feet and thrust him out over the grisly markings.

Dayn writhed like a man possessed. In spite of his oath to never harm Alis, he kicked her repeatedly in the chest and face, desperate to be free of her grip and the maddening effect of the runes.

"How do you feel?" Kor asked his struggling prey, shrugging off every one of Dayn's blows. "I will not kill you right away. That would be too kind a fate." The god paused a moment, thinking up a proper punishment, no doubt. "Ah, yes, I have it. I know of your tolerance for physical pain, boy, but how will you respond when I force you to watch me tear this vessel apart, only to heal it and start again. You will watch until the agony breaks your mind, and then you will have the honor of dying. What do you think of that?"

Dayn's face scrunched into a tormented scowl, foam bubbling through the corners of his tight-lipped grimace.

Kor mistook the look for one of fear, and he grinned cruelly. "Orishadaon," he called, his deep voice piercing through Dayn's agony like a knife thrust into his mind. "I am impressed, orishadaon, I thought the shon in the tunnels was enough to kill you. It seems I underestimated you. Luckily, I get to correct that oversight."

Dayn's bulging eyes flickered to his sword, which was strapped to the god's side. "Let Alis go." He choked out the words through gritted teeth.

"*Let Alis go*," Kor mocked him. "Why would I want to do that? In a few moments the moons will rise to the top of the sky and I will have my power back. If you manage to survive long enough you might even see it happen." Dayn struggled to remain in control, determined not to give up. "Your efforts are admirable, boy, but in the end they amount to nothing. You cannot stop me," the god gloated.

Dayn stared down at Kor with a contemptuous glare that could only come from one who knew he was about to die.

The god responded with a knowing nod. "I think I would rather kill you now and be done with it," he decided. "You have suffered enough."

Kor opened his mouth and prepared to bite into the orishadaon's exposed throat; a killing strike worthy of a creature whose true form was that of a colossal blade-nose.

As the god's warm breath caressed his neck, Dayn spotted something moving nearby. Merek, having been completely forgotten by Kor, rose up behind the god on unsteady legs. He gave his older brother a look that meant get down and stay out of the way. Dayn only wished he could do something other than dangle uselessly in the god's grasp as he felt the build-up of spirit energy within Merek.

Kor must have sensed it, too, for he cast the orishadaon aside and lunged after Merek.

Once again, blind terror filled Dayn as his airborne body crossed the runes. The feeling passed quickly, replaced by the stomach churning sensation of freefall. He landed outside the ring, rolling to a stop beside one of the massive pillars that held up the ceiling.

Back in the circle, Kor picked up Merek before he had a chance to unleash his orishadai and hurled him across the runes too. However, whereas Dayn struck the ground and rolled to a stop near the pillar, Merek slammed into the enormous column directly. The sound of his ribs shattering was drowned out by his screams.

Merek's cries rose in pitch and volume as he tried to sit up. The effort caused him too much pain and he fell back, momentarily defeated. "Can't . . . breathe," he hissed, wrapping his arms around his chest. The slightest touch against his ribs made him cry out in agony and he quickly removed his hands, lying prostrate on the cold stone.

Dayn was at his side in moments. As the orishadaon kneeled down, Merek wrapped a claw-like hand around his shoulder and pulled himself into a sitting position, emitting screams of pain all the while. "That . . . was . . . stupid," he said with a great deal of effort. "Help me . . . and I'll . . . kill the half-blood right, this time."

Dayn took pride in his sibling's tenacity. Against impossible odds, Merek would not give up, no matter how much he might be forced to endure. Dayn absently wondered if all orishadai users possessed such stubborn determination, or if it was just the two of them.

He hooked an arm around his brother's shoulder and, as gently as he could, lifted him up. Merek screamed again.

"Sorry," Dayn apologized.

"Save . . . your . . . apologies," Merek sputtered, coughing up a mouthful of blood. He removed his arm from Dayn's shoulder to stand proudly, if somewhat awkwardly, on his own. Possessing all the strength and stubborn determination of his brother, Merek insisted on being the first to take on the god, his injuries be damned.

Kor stood by, waiting patiently. "Are you ready to die, now?" he asked earnestly.

"Not before . . . I kill . . . you," Merek replied, aiming his outstretched palm at the god.

Kor disappeared in a blur of motion. He reappeared an eye blink later, standing an arm's length from the pair with Agidyne in his hand.

A single swipe of the ancient relic opened a deep gash across Merek's throat. The young man clutched desperately at the wound, gouts of blood spurting through his fingers as he wheezed something incomprehensible.

Kor grasped the orishadai user's forehead in his gauntleted hand. A harsh red glow emanated from beneath his palm, and then he hurled Merek against the same pillar he had struck only moments before. Merek hit the stone edifice with his shoulder and collapsed against it a second time, babbling nonsense about demons and a "horrible red sky." Crimson tears poured freely from his bloodshot eyes.

"What did you do to him?!" Dayn shouted at the god.

Kor remained silent.

Merek let out a hideous gurgle. Red froth erupted from his lips.

Dayn fell to his knees beside his brother, turning his back on the god. He grabbed Merek by the shoulders and gave him a shake. "Don't let him win!" he yelled in frustration. "Don't die!"

It was obvious that Merek could no longer hear him. His breathing was impossibly shallow, as if he was in a meditative trance, but he was not in a meditative trance, and his breathing grew shallower with each intake of air.

Dayn tried communicating directly with his brother's mind. To his dismay, he found Merek's thoughts isolated by a wall of fiery suffering that he was powerless to penetrate.

"Let me in, damn it," Dayn cursed, throwing his own mind against the wall of agony, only to be repulsed when the pain grew more terrible than he could bear. All the while, Merek's tortured mind was slowly being consumed.

Without warning, the younger man reached up and grabbed Dayn's hand.

"Merek?" Dayn trembled. His brother's body convulsed in his arms, making it difficult to hold onto him.

You'll have to do the rest yourself, he heard Merek's voice in his mind. It had to be in his mind, his brother was far beyond the ability to speak.

"No!" Dayn shook his head furiously. "You have to live." He grimaced at the blood leaking from his brother's ears and eyes, as well as the fatal wound on his throat. "What would mother think of me if I let you die like this?"

She probably wouldn't care, said the voice inside his head. Flecks of red spittle dribbled over his dying brother's chin.

"That's not true," Dayn objected. "They would have wanted both of us to make it home."

Merek's body choked on its own laughter. *Sorry I couldn't help you save the half-blood. You'll have to kill her now if you want to win.*

"I—"

Can't do this? Merek knowingly finished for him.

"Not alone." Dayn shook his head.

You never gave up before. Don't start now, Merek chastised.

"You aren't going to die." Dayn shook him again, his words ringing with false truth.

I didn't think it would hurt so much.

"Damn you, Merek, hold on!"

I deserve worse. I just wish I could tell the demons I did something worthwhile.

"You aren't going to see any demons because you aren't going to die!"

Dayn closed his eyes to the sight of his brother and focused on driving his mind into the soul weave. The barrier between this world and the weave was a thin one, and it was possible for an orishadaon to force his way through it without orishadai, provided he had the mental strength to do so.

Most found it impossible, but Dayn thought not of possibility, only necessity. From the weave he could lend his strength to that of his brother's waning soul and keep Merek from crossing over to the land of the ancestors.

His mind drove into the fabric shrouding the soul weave with all the force of will he could muster. At first the weave repelled him, but he would not be denied. He redoubled his efforts and slammed himself into the weave again. By concentrating every bit of himself on a tiny point no greater than the end of a hair, he managed to tear a hole in the fabric and slip his mind through.

As he caught sight of Merek's soul, the shock almost knocked him back into his body. The sphere that rose up before him was a churning mass of blackness, seething with those emotions that Sharna had trained the two brothers to suppress.

Dayn's own soul was a faded ball of blue and white luminescence surrounding a core of pure red. At one time, his soul had been a radiant beacon, shining across the weave to brighten everything around it. Long seasons of agony, hatred and struggle, had seen to the diminishing of his light.

He was not here because of the condition of his own soul, however, and from it he sent forth a single column of shimmering light. The column extended towards his brother's soul, and the blackness shuddered.

Stay away, Merek warned.

Dayn persisted, driving his soul towards his brother's cringing shadow. Before he could make a connection, the shadow pulled away, refusing Dayn's help.

Let me die, his brother insisted.

No.

I don't want your help. I failed, now let me die.

No.

Despite repeated attempts, Merek remained beyond his reach. His brother's soul shriveled as the chase continued, shrinking in upon itself as the body slowly died and its connection to the physical world weakened.

I won't let you die, Dayn said. *Too many have died because of me.*

I'm not one of the many.

I brought you here, Dayn lamented.

No one leads me, Merek said, defiant to the end. *I came because I wanted to. I fought the half-blood because I wanted to. Now I'll die because I want to. My destiny is my own, brother, it is not such a bad thing.*

The chase went on for a short while longer, Dayn loath to give in to his brother's final wish to be let free. Merek's soul was so small and fragile by then that bringing it back to the body and keeping it alive would have been impossible, yet Dayn could not bring himself to let go.

A spasmodic rippling overcame Merek's soul as the spark of life faded from it.

Goodbye, Dayn said, not knowing what else to do.

Die well, came Merek's whispered reply.

Dayn grudgingly gave up the chase. The coil of darkness enveloped itself and disappeared, leaving behind an empty hollow of oblivion where the soul of a proud, courageous warrior once rested, bringing to an end the short and brutal life of another Swift Claw.

34.
WASHED AWAY BY THE TIDE

Dayn found himself thrust out of the soul weave and back into his body by the sensation of a balled fist striking him across the temple. His sudden emergence from the weave left him weak and disoriented, while the ferocity of the attack drove him to his hands and knees, where he remained as the god battered him with another flurry of blows.

It was all the last remaining orishadai user could do to clumsily fend off the attacks with an arm that felt more like cold, heavy steel than flesh and bone. Kor easily hammered past Dayn's uncoordinated blocks and landed another solid blow against his skull.

Dayn grunted as he sprawled across the floor.

There was no one left, they were all gone. Every single person he knew had been taken away, leaving him alone to defeat a creature as old as the world itself, and worse, his only chance for victory required him to do the one thing he could not.

Another kick to his already aching chest curled him into a protective ball while driving the air out of his lungs in a ragged scream.

Kor's muffled voice reached out to him from impossibly far away. "Orishadaons are resilient," he said, "but you are nothing against *my* power."

The reality of his desperate situation stretched Dayn's physical and mental endurance to the limit. His body was bruised, his mind was broken. He had nothing left to give.

The god kicked him again and again, each blow crushing a little more of Dayn's self-awareness until his mind retreated inward to escape the pain. He lost himself amidst disorienting emptiness, plunging into a hopeless state that snapped his tenuous grip on sanity. Madness worsened the situation, dragging his consciousness towards a dark recess of despair where the taunting faces of his failures waited. He fled from their accusations, straight through the tempestuous sea of anger resting at the fringes of his being. Blinding red rage boiled his thoughts, flooded his senses. *Your* power? he thought about the god's last comment. I'll show him power. Inwardly, he laughed a maniacal, disparaging laugh and opened himself up to the tide. It crashed against his failing mental barriers and drove through them in a single, devastating push. Finally free of its eternal cage, and without his willpower to hold it back, the red tide surged into his soul, igniting a spark of demonic power that sent him down the shondaon's path.

Terrible, invigorating power, shondai, straight from the Aether itself, coursed through his body. Shondai was hatred, pure hatred born of the hellish demon realm, an emotion made manifest as devastating energy. It was a force so powerful, so all-consuming that it would burn out a normal human soul in mere moments. Dayn was no normal human; to the contrary, in his present state he could scarcely be called human at all.

Memories were swept from his mind, smothered beneath the onrushing tide. Alis disappeared from his thoughts, replaced by an all-consuming hatred for Kor. The woman standing before him ceased to be someone he loved and would die for. She became his enemy, one he meant to destroy. Emotional uprisings were quelled: pride, doubt, fear and love all beaten back until only rage remained. At that instant he ceased to be an orishadaon of the Swift Claw tribe, becoming instead an instrument of the fiendish shon and a prisoner within his own mind. He became a shondaon.

When Dayn put up a hand to block the next punch, Kor's fist stopped dead against his open palm. In fury, the god swung again, and that blow was swatted aside effortlessly as well. Stony-faced, Dayn rose and shoved his foe backwards.

"You cannot stop me, boy," the god growled in an inhuman tone, frustration showing on his face. After his next attack was deflected as easily as the previous two, he called out in an incomprehensible language.

In response, three silhouettes bled out of the surrounding darkness, congealing into solid forms as the final word of the invocation left Kor's lips.

The largest and most fearsome of the summoned guardians, the one missing fingers and the end of its tail, motioned to its eyeless brethren with a barely perceptible nod. The slighter, but no less deadly, creature moved forward to confront the shondaon, gliding soundlessly over the intervening flagstones.

Dayn saw it only as an unwelcome intrusion upon his vengeance. Before it could get any closer, an invisible wall of demon energy, shondai, struck the creature, ripping it apart in a flurry of dissolving shadow. Glowing embers fluttered in the air where it had stood, then flickered into nothingness.

Upon seeing this, the god immediately fled through the entryway, leaving Dayn inside the temple with an unmoving plant creature, a corpse, and the two remaining guardians. As he turned his rage against the foe's minions, both of them shrank back into the shadows and disappeared.

The shondaon swept his gaze through the temple's interior, searching for something to vent his frustrations upon. He recognized a pair of figures: one, a strange plant being, the other, a very dead human; he could not recall who they were or what they meant to him. Such memories were incapable of penetrating the bloodlust clouding his mind.

He stared blankly at the ravaged body leaning against a pillar, feeling nothing. The red tide immediately drowned any emotions he might have experienced at the sight, and though he felt he should know the person, he did not.

The young man with jet black hair staring up at him through glassy, unfocused eyes was one more failure in a long line of failures, that much he knew. An image of a faraway village appeared in his thoughts—a simple collection of huts surrounded by a low wall, with a tower standing above it all. Rage quickly swallowed up the memory, leaving in its place an emptiness he was at a loss to describe. Without memory, all he had left was a soul swelling with hatred, hatred centered upon the fleeing god solely because there was no one else to hate.

The shondaon clenched his one good hand into a fist, sending arcs of red lightning crackling up his arm. Without so much as a backwards glance at the corpse or the plant woman, he plodded towards the entryway, footfalls igniting clouds of sparks against the stone. The shondaon stepped outside and stared.

A pair of moons rested in the starry sky. The faint glow of the green moon fell across the jungle, mingling with light from its pale white counterpart. Vernac's debris shined dimly azure. All three moons were aligning—white overlapped by green with shattered pieces of blue floating before both the others.

Far below the moons, an army of scaled ones massed around the temple's base. Hundreds of them surrounded the ancient structure, casting their reverent gazes towards the lone figure standing at the temple's summit.

Looking up, Dayn spotted his foe.

The god, flanked on either side by a massive statue, one in the form of an annaru and the other carved to resemble a blade-nose, stood atop the roof of the temple, more than fifty paces above the shondaon's head. There were no handholds on the wall, or any other visible means of scaling its sheer surface. Kor smirked at him before disappearing from view.

Dayn put both of his hands on the wall and sucked in a great gulp of air. When he expelled the breath, dozens of tiny explosions wracked the structure's exterior, leaving numerous holes in their wake. He endured a discomforting hail of debris, his face contorting into a deepening scowl as each rock struck his flesh. When the bits of stone finished raining down, he gripped the newly formed handholds and hauled himself up the wall, letting loose a bestial howl as he went. Not surprisingly, there was no response from the foe to his sudden outburst. It only took a few moments to ascend to the top of the temple and pull himself onto its roof.

He ducked instinctively, barely avoiding a statue as tall as himself that careened through the air. It flew overhead, missing him by less than a finger width on its way towards the temple's lowest tier, where it crashed amongst the watching annaru. The crowd scattered for a brief instant before reforming around the crushed bodies of those saurians who had not moved quickly enough to get out of the way.

The shondaon siphoned demonic power from the Aether into his blackened soul. That power pressed outward, prickling his skin as it burst from his body to enshroud him in a semi-transparent, crimson bubble. Shield in place, he stood defiantly in the face of his foe's new onslaught.

A second, slightly larger, statue crashed against the barrier, nearly dislodging him from his perch by the sheer force with which it struck. He steadied himself and walked towards the god, intent on destroying him.

Over a hundred paces away, Kor tore a massive block out of the temple with his bare hands and hurled it as if it were a pebble.

The slab of rock hit Dayn's barrier and bounced off, plummeting towards the noisome crowd below. He ignored the distraction, increasing his pace as he headed straight for the god.

"Come, orishadaon, is deflecting rocks your only trick?" Kor taunted as he approached.

This time, his foe ripped out two blocks at once and threw them both. Each one collided with the demonically empowered shield, cracking the barrier down the center. The halves fell away, dissolving into nothingness.

It would have been a simple matter for Dayn to siphon the red tide's rage into the barrier and keep it whole, but he let it go, concentrating his power on the fifteen pace tall carving of an annaru standing next to the god. An invisible tendril of shondai sprang from his palm and snaked around the statue, tearing it loose with less effort than he expected.

The stone annaru toppled. In an eye blink the foe was gone from its path, moving with inhuman speed. The statue crashed down, shaking the entire temple with the force of its landing. A storm of billowing dust escaped from between cracks in the ancient building, filling the air with a choking, chalky white haze. The god's silhouette appeared amidst the obscuring cloud.

"You must be capable of something better," Kor called to him, obviously disappointed. After the last of the statue's broken pieces clattered to a halt, he added helpfully; "Here, let me show you something."

He put his gauntleted hand on the closest statue and gave it a casual shove. It toppled off its dais, colliding with another statue and knocking that one down as well. Those two hit another, creating an avalanche of stone that came straight towards Dayn.

Unconcerned, the shondaon remained perfectly still. Flashes of future sight told him where each effigy would strike, and he trusted that knowledge to help him avoid harm. Duck, sidestep, duck again and roll forward. With that he was beyond the reach of the falling statuary.

He did not rise immediately, choosing instead to remain hidden behind a pile of rubble that once resembled a ferocious blade-nose.

His foe waited impassively. "It would make things easier for me if you would hurry up and die," he called out.

Dayn crept towards him, hidden by interposing piles of rubble and clouds of wafting dust so thick they clogged his nostrils and made it hard to breathe.

"Why do you persist?" asked the foe, slashing an ancient, rusted sword through the air, one, two, three times. "Why do you care so much about this female? There are plenty more, you could have gotten another."

Dayn did not understand the meaning behind the words. He did not want the female. He cared nothing for her, seeking only to wipe the foe from the world. Without a word, he rose up a few dozen paces from the god, a lone shadow amidst the swirling dust.

"Ah." Kor turned to face him. "There you are. Do you care that much for my vessel, boy? Do you care enough to die for her? The moons have risen. I can feel my power returning. You have lost."

Two diametrically opposed emotions warred within the shondaon: hatred born of the red tide against something buried deep, half-forgotten beneath the rage. He recognized the foe, knew him (or was it her?) from a time when there was more than hatred within himself. An instant later the red tide washed away his awareness and once again he knew only the single-minded desire to destroy.

Dayn charged forward through heaps of dust-choked wreckage, snarling like a wild animal.

The god's leg muscles tensed and he leaped across the intervening destruction in a single bound. While in midair, he swung his sword in a devastating overhead arc, intending to split the shondaon in half.

Dayn saved himself by lunging inside the weapon's arc to catch the foe's elbow across his shoulder. Before Kor could pull back for another strike, Dayn wrapped both hands around the god's forearm and yanked down with all his might, tearing muscle and tendons while simultaneously popping the elbow loose from its socket. The arm went limp and the sword fell away, clattering loudly against the temple top. Kor seemed not to notice the loss of his weapon or his arm, plowing his other fist into Dayn's ribs.

Dayn coughed and staggered backwards. Another blow to the chest sent him careening towards the edge of the roof. He caught himself before going over and charged the god, burying an elbow in his throat.

Kor let out a startled gurgle and dropped to one knee while clutching his ravaged neck. Dayn knocked him prone with a solid kick to the face and then stomped a heel against his forehead to keep him there.

The ferocity of his last strike made him pause. Somewhere inside himself, he felt a twinge of forgotten emotion, but the madness of the tide had completely taken hold and he was no longer in control of his actions. What remained of his mind was merely a passenger of the red tide's fury.

Dayn pointed an outstretched palm at the momentarily defenseless foe and stepped back.

In response, Kor spit up a mouthful of blood and tried to choke out a few words. His crushed throat prevented him from saying anything coherent.

Dayn's palm glowed purest red, without a hint of its former blue radiance.

What was left of his rational mind screamed for him to stop. He heard the echoing cry of his conscience fade away, muffled by the crashing of the tide against his senses. He forgot rationality and gave in to hatred.

"Forgive me," he growled at the woman.

The incredible effort with which it took to speak those simple words should have been too much for anyone caught in the throes of shondai induced hatred. Shondaons were beyond caring and compassion, they were beyond the simplest expression of emotion. Yet, not even the red tide could extinguish his feelings for what this woman had once been to him, though his feelings only made what came next all the more difficult to bear.

35.
A BLACK HEART NOW REIGNS

Shondai erupted from his palm, its hellish glow illuminating the night sky in a flash of fiery red. The sudden burst of energy completely engulfed the god, peeling back patches of his skin, revealing the raw tissue and chords of wet muscle beneath. Kor let out a chorus of pain-wracked screams, each yell rising steadily in pitch until they became inaudible and he could no longer be heard above the sound of his own sizzling flesh.

Under the control of the red tide, Dayn released a second blast of shondai, watching his foe with unflinching apathy as bunches of musculature curled into tight, spiraling balls before burning up altogether. As more of the god's flesh disintegrated, fragments of the foe's gleaming white bones became visible across the ruin of his body.

Dayn channeled more shondai out of his soul and into a third beam, drawing on all the hatred within himself in an effort to exact vengeance on the god for reasons he could not remember.

Kor continued to shriek in unknowable pain as the stone beneath him grew red-hot, cracked under the intense heat of a fourth blast, bubbled after a fifth and dissolved altogether when Dayn let loose the sixth. The foe's shriveled body sank into a deepening depression until, finally, the seventh beam of shondai cut straight through to the underlying chamber. Kor plummeted through the hole, landing with a wet *slap* some fifty paces below.

The sky's color returned to normal as the last ray of demon

energy faded, leaving Dayn's palm singed and smoking. His nostrils filled with the scent of burnt meat, and a vague recollection flickered through his thoughts. He glanced at his left hand, trying to remember how it had come to look the way it did.

Alis was dead, the outlandish thought imposed itself upon his awareness. Alis? The name seemed familiar. Who did it belong to? It did not matter. Her memory was unwelcome in his mind, the pain of her remembrance unwanted. Untrue! He wanted to know her. He had to know her. Rage clouded his thoughts, blinding him to the answer. No! Fight it, fight hard! He had to remember her, he had to . . .

She was gone in an eye blink, disappearing behind an impenetrable veil of hatred. Only the foe remained and he could not rest until the god was destroyed.

Dayn moved to the hole his shondai had created and, with mechanical stiffness, stepped over its glowing edge into the void. He envisioned himself sinking weightlessly towards the floor and his body responded.

The red tide filled him, controlled him. It was no longer a part of him, it was all of him, but this time something was different. Images rode upon the tide's fury, images of a woman. He saw her at different times, in different places, none of it making any sense inside his jumbled mind.

The slow descent into the temple's dark interior gave him time to dwell on his elusive memories of her. He tried recalling her name, but it had already fled from his mind. Who was the mysterious girl that had intruded upon his vengeful thoughts?

Throughout the rest of his lengthy drop to the temple floor, Dayn battled against his own mind, fighting the red tide for control of the knowledge locked deep within his consciousness. He clawed the air, grasping at ghostly images, all of them slipping between his fingers before he could grab hold. Dayn gnashed his teeth in frustration, scattering the froth that had accumulated in the corners of his mouth.

The act broke his concentration and he fell, crashing down upon the unyielding stone of the temple floor. He rolled about, thrashing uncontrollably, his limbs reacting to the violent mental struggle taking place within his soul.

Kill her!

The woman's smile, warm and friendly.

Tear her apart, bathe in her cursed blood!

A reassuring hand placed upon his shoulder.

Destroy her! Destroy everything!

A tender embrace full of love shared between the two of them.

Love? What was love when compared to hate? Love was enough to give him pause, enough to clear the rage from his mind and give him a glimpse of what he had been before, if only for a moment.

He felt as if his mind were being pulled in countless directions, ripped apart by the ferocity of his own repressed sentiments. The experience was too much for him, and he let out a mournful wail that cut through the unnatural stillness of the dark chamber, bouncing off the walls and returning to him in a twisted, mocking fashion. All the world was laughing at his loss.

He kicked and screamed his way across the temple floor, battling an invisible foe.

Visions of the woman's flesh withering to blackened flecks filled his mind. The red tide and all its hatred surged over the image, engulfing it and drowning everything he was fighting to reclaim. He battered the rising wave of hatred back with thoughts of the woman, clinging to her memory as the only thing standing between oblivion and himself. The tide had swept away all that he was; his mind, his personality, his memory. Now only she remained, keeping him partially afloat above the swell of endless rage because he refused to release his hold on her.

Dayn pushed himself onto his feet and stumbled deeper into the temple's dark interior. Finding her was the key to beating back the tide and releasing his mind from its torment. She was something more than an enemy, this foe of his—something else entirely.

At any moment, he expected to find a mess of remains lying upon the temple floor. Not even orishadaon healing could mend the damage inflicted by his shondai, and the fall would have exacerbated the woman's already extensive injuries. Nothing could survive his rage.

His foot brushed against something in the gloom. A puddle of sticky wetness marred the flagstones. A bloody path led off into shadow with no sign of a body to be found anywhere.

"Im . . . imposs . . . ible," he stuttered, struggling to form each syllable using a voice good for little more than expressions of raw hatred. It felt good to speak, he decided, and vowed to try it again soon.

He followed the bloodstains, struggling with every step to control the actions of his own body. Each time he imposed his will upon the tide it became easier, though his efforts left him physically drained. After a few paces he slumped against a pillar to catch his breath and fend off the latest of the red tide's swells. It attempted to force its way through his crumbling self-awareness, trying to steal the woman's memory from his mind.

With an immense display of willpower, he continued on, limping alongside the bloodstained pathway while his mind ripped itself apart. He clung to a vision of the woman standing alone amidst tall stalks of golden grass, her look one of contemplation. Dayn focused on that image as he sought out her body.

But, why did he care? He barely remembered who she was, much less what she meant to him. What was he supposed to do when he found her?

He peered into the encircling wall of darkness and, in spite of his nagging doubts, took another step. Dayn moved on, knowing he had to locate the woman in his thoughts without understanding why. His apprehension grew each time he took a step and did not find her.

"I . . . find . . . you," he said, speaking aloud because it reminded him of a time before the tide, when he had been more than the . . . monster that he was now. Words reminded him of his lost humanity. "I . . . will," he added.

"Are you so eager to die?" came a strangled reply from somewhere ahead.

She still lived!

Dayn stumbled after the sound of raspy breathing, tracing it towards the back of the temple, where a glowing circle of runes waited. Somehow, he knew it was important to keep the foe from reaching that spot. If he (she?) made it there, something terrible would happen.

The shondaon increased his pace.

He reached the blackened remains of a woman who should

have been dead. Roasted meat covered the few parts of her body that hadn't burned down to the bone and rank smoke wafted off her in nauseating waves, its stink so strong that it turned Dayn's stomach. She was alive, though, struggling to pull herself along using one charred, skeletal hand and an equally charred gauntlet. When she realized she was being followed, the foe rolled onto her back and sat waiting.

The woman's face was particularly gruesome. Her hair was gone, as was her scalp and eyes, giving her a ghastly, skeletal appearance.

Dayn watched with morbid fascination, unable to look away from the grisly scene of her flesh slowly knitting itself back together. Tiny red strands crawled back and forth across her entire body, collecting themselves into layers of steaming muscle or patches of quivering, hairless skin. Her eyes were reforming as well. At present, they were no more than tiny white pearls resting at the back of her otherwise empty eye sockets.

She turned her sightless features in his direction. Smoldering lips pulled back to reveal blackened teeth. "What is wrong, *orishadaon*?" She spoke the word with a vehemence that made Dayn think of the dark-haired youth whose body rested against a nearby pillar. "Is this form no longer attractive to you?" The foe ran her scorched tongue over the blackened stubs of her teeth in what should have been an erotic gesture.

Dayn remained unmoved by the sight, deciding whether he should obliterate the foe while she was weak or offer to help the girl whose memory lurked in the forefront of his thoughts.

His hesitation allowed the woman time to heal. The tendons in her legs stretched and reconnected while layers of glistening muscles spread like an undulating red carpet from her hips to her feet. The muscles thickened, then tightened, and she made her first awkward attempt at standing. It took several more attempts, but she finally managed to rise on her half-formed legs. As soon as she was able, the woman hobbled off in the direction of the runic circle.

Dayn paused, unsure what to do next. His destructive instincts told him he should slay the woman immediately. A voice in the back of his mind—his conscience, perhaps—insisted that he let her live. What should he do? He needed to think this through carefully, but the chaos within his mind prevented any attempt at prolonged, coherent thought.

"Wait." He beckoned to the woman, reaching out to her with his blackened hand.

She turned slowly to face him, her ruined features giving away nothing, her eyeless gaze centered upon him as if she possessed some other means of sight. They stared at one another for long moments, saying nothing.

A cautious tension filled the space between them. The emptiness felt heavier, more solid, as if it were pressing against him; a suffocating, distracting sensation, like drowning in air. A disconcerting sound began in his mind, a quiet whisper that quickly grew to a deafening warning call.

The woman suddenly lurched forward, slower than she had been on the roof of the temple, but still impossibly fast, swinging her gauntleted fist straight for his face.

Dayn's instincts took control, propelling him backwards beyond the range of the foe's strike. She missed, barely, and only because she was slowed by her injuries. That gave him an advantage. She no longer moved as a blur, he could see her coming.

The woman didn't seem to care. She pressed the attack with a series of savage punches aimed at his head and stomach. Dayn avoided them all, but not as easily as the first. Before long he was off balance and retreating, forced into a purely defense role. He covered his gut and stepped back, knocking an oncoming fist away from his face. He stepped back, protecting his jaw from a hit before stepping back again and again, always moving away from his foe instead of taking the fight to her as he should have done.

"You cannot run forever," she told him in a practical sort of way.

Dayn protected his lower body from a two-fisted attack and once again stepped back, this time into the massive form of a pillar. His back pressed flat against the cool, unyielding stone that blocked his retreat. There was nowhere to run as the next fist flew towards his forehead. He hastily blocked and ducked at the same instant, managing to deflect the woman's oncoming fist into the pillar. Hairline fractures radiated outward from beneath the balled fingers of her gauntlet, spreading up the length of the column's decorated surface.

Bits of stone fell free, clattering against the floor at Dayn's feet as he hurried past the column. His gaze met that of the woman as he backed into the open. Her skeletal features twisted into a perverse grin and, still staring at him through sightless eyes, she put all her strength into heaving against the massive pillar. The spot she pushed against buckled, bringing down the entire column in one quick rush of stone and dust.

Dayn stumbled over his own feet in his hurry to get out of the way. He almost didn't see the woman coming towards him through the haze. He caught sight of her at the last instant, as she vaulted over the fallen rubble. Her lithe frame came down right beside him, lashing out with more punches before she even hit the ground.

Her smile was gone, replaced by a blank, yet somehow unsettling expression as she changed tactics, pressing her mangled body against his to deliver an elbow to his chest.

Dayn lifted an arm to block, only to have the limb easily batted aside by the foe's inhuman strength. Her blow connected as intended. Rather than resist, he allowed his body to roll with the force of the strike—which he drastically underestimated—and was thrown into the air.

His foe came at him the instant he hit the ground and Dayn rolled aside to avoid having his skull caved in by her stomping foot.

A thick carpet of dust fluttered from his sweaty hair as he scrambled back to his feet.

She stalked after him, waving a hand in front of her face to scatter the dust away from her newly grown amber eyes.

Both combatants circled each other warily.

"Why bother fighting? You can only lose," said the woman. She lunged forward, then pulled back before striking. Dayn jumped away, to her amusement. "You smell of fear, boy," she taunted.

Fear? Fear was good. It meant he could feel something again. His emotions were resurfacing through the veil of hatred that had been pulled over them.

The woman lunged a second time, her outstretched hands

eagerly reaching for his throat.

Dayn broke away, dashing behind a nearby pillar.

She followed, punching a fist-sized hole through the column before tearing her arm free with a fury that brought the pillar down.

Like a wounded beast, the ceiling shuddered and emitted a deep groan. The huge stones that made it up grated against one another as they shifted for the first time since their placement hundreds, even thousands of seasons ago.

As Dayn backed out of the thickening dust cloud, the woman followed.

She was almost whole again. Newly grown skin covered most of her body, with only a few raw, red scars visible, and they were quickly healing shut. Her face had knitted itself back together too, although her scalp was now as hairless as a hunter's. When the woman noticed him staring, she offered him a gracious nod. "Thank you, boy. I am enjoying our little game," she said earnestly.

Dayn immediately headed towards the nearest pillar, only to be intercepted by the woman, who hastily knocked it down with a backhanded swing.

How could she be so strong? he wondered. Her power was unbelievable. The columns were half as big around as he was tall, and yet she tore them apart with a single swing of her gauntleted fist!

He dived away from the falling debris. The entire ceiling, shrouded in darkness far above, trembled beneath its own immense weight.

The woman paid no attention to the worrying sounds. She closed in, flexing her metal fingers in anticipation of the coming kill.

Dayn hurriedly withdrew, intentionally putting his back against yet another pillar. All the other nearby supports had been knocked down, leaving the one behind him to hold up a huge section of ceiling all by itself. The stone blocks above him continued to groan their discomfort as dust spilled from widening cracks in their surfaces.

The woman pulled her fist back to strike.

As she attacked, time seemed to slow down around the two

combatants. Dayn could clearly see the fist coming towards his face, creeping forward as if it was pushing through water. He felt the rise of his chest as he sucked in a deep breath, the tensing of every one of his leg muscles, the coolness of the stone beneath his feet and against his back. It all went through his mind in a single instant.

The woman's fist burst through the time bubble and erupted towards him. Reacting on pure instinct, Dayn ducked the blow and sprang aside. As expected, she leveled the pillar in a single swipe.

Before she realized what she had done, hundreds of immense stone blocks were dropping on top of her head.

36.
THIS IS WHO WE ARE

Dayn channeled his limitless reserves of demonic energy into a shield. The power built up more slowly now that the red tide's control was no longer absolute, but it built up all the same. Stones crashed against the expanding, transparent membrane, burying him beneath a tidal wave of falling rock. He stood tall in the face of the merciless barrage, knowing that his life would be forfeit if his concentration wavered for even an instant.

A few paces away, his foe was attempting to dodge between the blocks as they fell using her superhuman speed and reflexes. For a few startling moments, she actually succeeded in avoiding harm, until a massive boulder crushed her legs, pinning her in place while more debris rained down. A wall of collapsing rock obscured Dayn's view of the woman at that time, and left him to guess at her fate.

When the final stone broke free from the ceiling, and the echo of its crashing faded from his ears, he released the flow of shondai that kept his shield in place.

By the blood of his ancestors, he felt tired. Much too tired to keep the rage within himself fed. He dropped to his knees, breathing heavily, ignoring the blood that poured from his nostrils and down his chin.

While his strength waned and his body surrendered to the strain of all it had endured since he transformed into a shondaon, the tide gradually receded from his thoughts, pulling back its influence, scraping away layer after layer of his soul as it released its hold.

An undeniable weakness settled into every bit of his body, sapping him of his resolve. It weighed him down, holding him firm so he couldn't move, couldn't think, could barely breathe. Without hatred to fuel his weary limbs and focus his thoughts, Dayn was reduced to a hollow shell housing the brutalized remnants of his wasted soul.

He could not live without the rage. It had been more than a part of him. It had been all of him and without it there was not enough soul left to keep his body alive. The tide was killing him even as it gave him back his mind. And how gloriously horrible the return of his mind was.

His entire life came back to him, moment by moment, scene by scene. It began as a trickle of images—Ryl, Sharna, his parents—that turned into a deluge of memory threatening to drown him beneath its immensity as surely as the red tide's rage had drowned him only a short time ago. Pictures blurred together into whole sequences. Sequences lined up in his mind. The gaps filled themselves in. He relived every instant of his life in a single, explosive eye blink.

It wasn't just the recollection of his life that returned. Without the tide to hold them back, all of his repressed emotions came rushing in, too; confusion, doubt, sadness, guilt and hope all rode in the wake of his memories.

The experience overloaded his senses, pushing his mind to the breaking point and beyond. For one perfect instant he saw his whole life arranged before him, every moment flashing with beautiful, crystal clarity before fading into the depths of his memory.

He remembered everyone. He remembered why he had originally come to this forsaken place. He recalled Merek's death, the loss of the Swift Claw tribe and Ryl's demise. Kor's possession of Alis remained at the forefront of his thoughts. A lifetime of painful memories, all relived in that one horrible, glorious instant, and she was all he could think about. She was everything to him, his reason for living, his only purpose for existing.

He hurt so much. Every part, mind as well as body pained

him. The list of agonies was too great to consider any one in particular. He had no orishadai, no way to divert the pain or block it from his mind, but if he did, he would still be left to endure the pain of his failure. All the death and destruction, the needless loss of life, and Alis was still dead. She was dead and he might as well be. No one had ever succumbed to the red tide and survived.

A faint blue glow caught his attention, forcing his senses to focus on the present. Awareness came slowly, crawling, clawing its way free of the empty void left behind by the tide. Concentrating on his immediate surroundings proved to be one of the most taxing experiences of his life as he forced his eyes to concentrate on the source of the odd, blue light. It couldn't be a torch, and he hadn't noticed any pieces of Vernac falling in the past few moments. It took all his strength to turn and face the glow, and when he did, his eyes refused to focus on the indistinct shape that hovered at his side.

"Come on, ya aren't done yet," said a familiar voice.

Dayn groaned at the intrusion, squeezing his eyes shut, then prying them open, willing them to see the apparition for what it must have been—a delusion, a construct of his fractured mind. "Go away," he whined, not caring if the ghostly figure he spoke to was real or not. There was no one left to hear him and judge his sanity.

"She's not dead yet," said the apparition, causing him to sit up, in spite of the agony it caused him. "That's right, she's alive. Ya can still save her."

Dayn's head drooped groggily to one side. He quickly shook himself awake and glanced around, seeing only destruction.

"She's close," the hazy figure informed him, pointing.

With a mighty expenditure of effort, Dayn forced himself to move. He crawled, scraping palms and banging knees, to the top of an encircling mound of collapsed debris. His deceased friend hovered effortlessly at his side as he surveyed the totality of the devastation.

Half the chamber was awash in a sea of rubble. Great heaps of stone rose up like arthritic fingers pointing accusingly towards the remnants of the ceiling which no longer supported them. Dust filled the air, obscuring everything behind a ponderously churning cloud of gray. His own body was so covered in the stuff that he could have passed for a statue if he stood still.

The moons and stars shone through a gaping chasm above his head, their light dimmed and barely visible through the haze.

From far away, the bellows, hisses and growls of furious annaru reached his ears. Adding to the din were the crackling flames of the torches scattered throughout the chamber, which all guttered and died as gusts of wind howled through the newly opened hole in the ceiling.

"That way." The apparition indicated an area a few dozen paces away.

Dayn hurriedly clambered down the opposite side of the mound, leaving the ghost behind.

He had been given one last chance to release Alis from the god's possession and he would not waste it.

He slowed briefly, putting a hand against his head as if doing so might stop the world from spinning out of control. The transition between the tide's all-consuming bloodlust and sudden, rational thought was a difficult one to make. Unfortunately, he did not have time to spare clearing his thoughts.

Dayn forced himself to stand and, with all the subtlety of a thunder-foot, blundered through the ruins of the temple. "Alis? Wh . . . where are yo . . . you?" he asked the dusty air. He called out her name over and over again, pausing only once to regain his balance after tripping over some jutting bit of stone.

"So, you survived, too," said a struggling voice from behind a heap of boulders, disappointment evident in every word.

Dayn carefully picked his way over the heap and stared down at Kor. The god lay on his back, legs crushed and pinned underneath a huge rock. Cuts, welts, and bruises covered every bit of his exposed flesh.

"You win, boy," the god rasped when he noticed he was being watched. "I have had enough of this."

While Dayn doubted the sincerity of the god's words, he hoped they were true. If Kor surrendered it would certainly make things easier. His curiosity got the better of him, and he crept closer. "After all th . . . this, you're gi . . . giving up?"

"There is nothing I can do if you stubbornly refuse to die," Kor admitted, gripping the column of stone on top of his legs with a white-knuckled fist. He pushed with all his might but the column refused to budge. "It might just be easier to wait until you are dead and dust before I return to this world."

"You're never coming back," Dayn said bluntly, too weary to argue the point further.

Kor whispered a response and Dayn moved closer. "The longer this world has to wait for me to kill your kind, the more demons slip through the Aether's barrier. By the time another picks up the gauntlet it will already be too late to fix all the damage."

"The world doesn't need you. Orishadaons will stop the demons in their own way," Dayn said resolutely, his passion giving him the ability to speak clearly.

The god gave up trying to free himself and dropped his hands to his sides in frustration. "Orishadaons like you are the source of the problem!" he boomed, his voice deafening in the near silence.

Dayn was too tired to flinch at the sudden noise. "That's a lie," he said, shaking his head at the futility of it all. Damn it, it was so pointless!

Kor grinned crookedly. He muttered something else and Dayn kneeled at his side in order to hear. "Every time you use your orishadai, the demons gain a foothold in this world. Your power weakens the barrier and lets them cross over."

Dayn's head sagged forward then snapped back up. "More lies?" he asked tiredly. "No more lies. You're just mad because you were beaten by a hu—"

Before he could finish his sentence, a streak of rusty gray metal flashed upwards and tore through his stomach, emerging from his back amidst a shower of crimson. Dayn stared in total shock at Agidyne and the god's gauntleted fist which gripped it.

"I would never allow a pathetic little whelp like you to defeat me," the god boasted. He reached down with one hand and effortlessly pushed aside the rubble pinning his legs, then drove the sword into the flagstones with his prey still skewered on the blade. Dayn sagged down the length of the blade, coming to rest with his back on the ground. "I know you, orishadaon. You will not die right away," Kor assured him. "You will live long enough to discover what happens to those who resist my will."

Numbing cold spread through Dayn, filling his entire body

with an icy chill. Shivers coursed across his skin, all the way from his toes to his fingertips. A deeper frigidity, one so cold it burned like fire, seeped out of the wound, draining him of everything.

He reached through the fog clouding his mind, grasping at anything beyond the numb emptiness that enveloped him. He found nothing to cling to. Most frustrating of all, Alis would soon be lost to him forever, a prisoner in her own body while his soul fell into the Aether for an eternity of torment. Not one thing remained to anchor his spirit to the world and he had to ask himself why he struggled so hard to survive. What made him cling so desperately to life when there was no reason to live?

Darkness draped itself across his awareness, shrouding him in blissful gloom. It called out to him, beckoning him to share in its dark embrace. His fading mind reached out hesitantly, then pulled back. Even now he dismissed the notion of surrendering to it. He pushed the shadows away from the faded center of himself that housed his soul. The darkness withdrew in confusion, allowing soothing light to flood his mind.

Dayn's eyes snapped open. He had nearly lost himself to that dark place. Only his natural instinct to fight had saved him.

Kor loomed overhead, finally within reach. "Still alive." It was not a question.

Dayn knew that this would be his only chance to strike at the god's soul, his intended target all along. Kor's body was beyond harm, but his soul was another matter. As long as he existed in the mortal world he must possess a mortal soul, or so the orishadaon hoped.

"Still alive," Dayn agreed, spitting out a mouthful of blood along with the words. Maybe not for long, but time would be irrelevant inside the weave. He reached forward, clamping his icy fingers around Kor's ankle, ready to take back his destiny and give Alis another chance at life.

37.
TO ANOTHER ABYSS

With that he slipped into the soul weave, allowing his mind to soar free of its earthly shell one last time. No euphoric sensation accompanied his initial release; there was only a feeling of unfulfilled longing. He noticed immediately, as he gazed down at himself, how badly damaged the physical shell was. Returning to it meant death for him, assuming he survived the weave long enough to inhabit the shell again.

He zipped across the shimmering, multicolored strands of the weave, barreling towards a distant speck of familiar light, with growing momentum and dwindling concern for his own safety. The speck grew steadily in size and brilliance, blossoming into a radiant sun that hovered on the weave's horizon, partially hidden by the surrounding tangle of strands. Alis' soul glowed like a beacon, made brighter in his eyes because he sought it out with such single-minded determination. He could have found her anywhere, against any odds.

As he drew nearer, Dayn saw something that gave him pause. Next to Alis' soul, a shadowy stain spread across the weave, like a glossy pool filled with water tinted so black it seemed impossibly deep and foreboding. On closer inspection, he realized it was no stain, but an empty void, a hole bored straight through the fabric of the weave. From the center of that abyssal gulf stretched a tunnel of pure redness that arched into Alis' soul. Bands of red curved around the scout's soul like the bars of a cage, imprisoning her, holding her tight in an oppressive embrace that she was powerless to break.

As he circled warily, drawing closer with each pass, Dayn eventually came to understand what he was seeing. The dark fissure was the gauntlet prison, trapping Kor within. The bridge was the god's link to Alis, his means of dominating her mind. Kor's immortal soul could not leave the prison, but it could unleash tendrils of influence outward to take hold of the scout's mind. The key to freeing Alis, then, was the severing of that bridge. However, before Dayn could attempt it, he had to awaken her mind and enlist her aid. Assaulting the god alone would only damn him to failure.

He moved closer, skimming across the surface of her soul, searching for a gap in the red ribbons encircling her that was large enough for him to squeeze his own soul through. After whirling around the scout's soul a number of times to carefully observe every detail, he settled on a spot where the god's defenses were less than perfect. A gap existed; small, but sizable enough for him to gain entry. He pressed through it into Alis, guilt-ridden for allowing her soul to be touched by his tainted one, and yet determined to find the spark of her mind so that he could lead her back to awareness.

A vast ocean of steaming crimson awaited him inside the scout. The expanse of blood red rage stretched to the horizons, bubbling and hissing with fiery intensity. Corpses bobbed amidst the scalding waves of hatred, thousands of them, all clawing at their surroundings in desperation. Most of the sufferers were human, but other, unidentifiable creatures drifted in the endless, churning sea, flailing and screaming madly.

This was not the scout's soul, he realized, but a fortress built by the god to keep her trapped inside. Kor was using his own heavy conscience and his memories of the legions he had slain or who had died because of him as a barrier to Alis' freedom. If she tried to escape, the endless despair inherent in those memories would bog her down long enough for the wailing sorrows of the god's previous victims to rip her mind apart in a flurry of shredded sanity.

Dayn flew above the galling scene, his soul pressing onward through the buffeting winds of contempt rising from the ocean below. The legions of dead reached towards him, calling for help, crying in agony or cursing him in a chorus of wailing voices. He increased his pace, taken aback by the horrifying display. The poor, miserable wretches were already dead and beyond his help. Nothing short of the god's death could set their tormented souls free, and that was a feat far beyond his abilities.

He searched the bleak vista for any sign of Alis. The spark of life that kept her going lay imprisoned somewhere amidst all this rage and sorrow. She would not be with the other shrieking victims; the soul of Kor's vessel was too valuable to be put in jeopardy. She would be in a place of ultimate security, at the very heart of this hellish soulscape.

Dayn sped over the seemingly endless sea, mindful not to look down lest he be overcome by despair. His flight path carried him deep into the prison of souls, towards its very center. He felt the emanations of Alis' presence from up ahead, weak but desperately alive.

In the distance, an inhospitable wall of treacherous mountain peaks jutted above the waves. Bloodstained mist coiled at the base of the spires, shrouding the thousands of moaning bodies floating at its borders in a haze of red. Those unlucky souls nearest the rocky wall of willpower wailed in frustration and pounded against the cliffs to no avail, only to be drowned beneath the press of bodies pushing forward to desperately grab at the rock face.

It was the perfect mental fortress and the perfect prison for Alis' mind.

Ignoring the screeching multitudes, Dayn passed beyond the wall into a steamy, primordial jungle of tangled emotions where no light shined and darkness prevailed. He landed in the shadows of a wide clearing, surrounded by knotted confusion, his soul's weak glow casting the only light.

Alis? he called out to her.

She did not respond.

Her ordeal with the god had dragged her mind into a desolate pit of hopelessness and he was going to have to pull her out forcibly. Dayn's awareness probed deeper into the emotional jungle. She was lost somewhere in this land of infinite darkness and he would find her.

Alis' private prison was a tumultuous and uncertain terrain.

Walls of fear rose up and blocked his path, some crumbling to nothingness as he passed, others burying him beneath their immense weight. Fanged chasms of confusion and doubt ripped the landscape apart, slamming shut to swallow the thin glimmer of hope he offered.

Dayn battled his way past the endless traps and pitfalls, driving ever deeper into the jungle until he found a spark of Alis' mind curled up in a dark, quiet corner where only desperation kept her going. He reached out and took hold of that tiny spark of light, leading her out of her own personal nightmare, away from the prison, beyond the sea of tortured souls and back into the comforting light of consciousness.

Alis?

He sensed her waking uncertainty. *Dayn?* Dayn! *What's happening?*

You are going to be fine. Everything is. I'm going to drive Kor back into the gauntlet, but I need you to help me. You have to fight him, resist his will, Alis. You have to distract him so he doesn't see me coming. Together we can beat him.

She hesitated, her entire soul shuddering in confusion or fear.

We can do this, he assured her, sounding truly confident.

Dayn, I—

Alis! He cut her off. *There's no time. I have to go after him now. He knows I'm here and he'll be coming. Fight him. Fight with everything you have, Alis, please.*

He left her at the edge of the sea of tortured souls and withdrew to the weave in search of Kor. She would awaken on her own without knowing that he had spoken to her for the last time.

He placed himself inside the tunnel connecting Alis' soul to the god's impenetrable prison and waited for a sign from the scout. He looked for any indication that she was fighting back, trying to retake control of her body. The instant he received that sign he would ambush Kor's emerging influence, force him back, smash the tunnel and free Alis before the god realized what was happening.

The outer edge of Alis' soul began to undulate. The motion started as a gentle wrinkling of her soul's surface, like the ripples created when a pebble is dropped into placid water. The ripples came more often, growing in size until they became huge, cresting waves. Her soul stretched one way, then another, pulling itself apart as she struggled against Kor's influence, strengthened by the knowledge that Dayn was waiting on the other side to lend her aid.

An immense crimson ball suddenly emerged from the gaping abyss ahead. It did not react to the orishadai user's presence as it approached. Either the god could not interact with the soul weave to defend himself or he simply did not care about being attacked.

Dayn altered his spiritual shape, reforming himself into a lustrous spear capable of punching a hole through any of the god's defenses. Once inside his foe's outer shell, he planned to tear Kor's soul loose and shove it back inside the gauntlet, leaving Alis' mind whole, undamaged, and once again in command of her body.

He hurtled across the connecting tunnel—a faded blue blur amidst the weave's dazzling rainbow of color—and drove ferociously into the side of the god's blinding redness. To his horror, he ground to an immediate halt against Kor's iron will. The jarring impact knocked him off balance, nearly tossing him from the weave. His mind tried to retreat, to recoup its senses, but before it could the fiery sun rolled towards him, a ball of unyielding death the size of a mountain. It crashed across the weave, snapping some strands while crushing others. It picked up momentum, moving inexorably towards him. Dayn was unable to halt its devastating advance, so he did the only thing he could: he launched himself at it.

The surface of the red sphere shifted with unexpected pliancy, dodging his clumsy charge. As Dayn sped past, his soul-spear form changed shape again, launching a barrage of hooked tentacles that caught hold of the god's undulating soul and dragged it closer. Kor's colossal size meant nothing on the weave. Size was a mere word in a place where words held no power.

The god was unexpectedly pulled off balance. He strained against his spiritual attacker.

As the tug-of-war continued, chunks of Kor's soul were ripped away as Dayn's tentacles tore loose, one by one. Dayn stopped resisting the pull and allowed himself to be yanked forward with tremendous force, straight towards the center of the god's blinding radiance.

Their souls collided in a flash of red and blue light. There they fought, both trying to smother the other. At first, Kor gained the advantage by wrapping himself around Dayn's soul and squeezing it in a crushing stranglehold. Dayn slithered out of the hold and doubled back on the god, enveloping him in turn.

Kor punched a hole straight through him and escaped, but not before Dayn grabbed his retreating form. They tumbled end over end through the emptiness, tearing open the very fabric of the soul weave with the intensity of their struggles.

Before Kor could counterattack, Dayn forced him into a tight ball and drove him back, away from Alis' mind, back down the tunnel and towards the gauntlet.

Kor sensed what was happening and surged towards Dayn with incredible ferocity, expanding to fill the entire tunnel. Both forms collided in an explosion that shook the weave, sending tendrils of death snaking outward in patterns that would be felt for hundreds of cycles of the seasons. The closest strands burst into nothingness. Those further away caught fire and burned, while others twisted into horribly scarred patterns.

Leaving Dayn dazed and struggling to recuperate, the god pulled back as two inky shadows appeared from within the gauntlet prison. They pulled themselves out of the abyss like a pair of monstrous shon rising from a pit of tar, soaked and dripping infinite darkness in their wake. Dayn recognized them for what they were: Kor's remaining pair of demonic annaru. The two of them advanced together, only slightly ahead of Kor's tunnel-spanning form.

Dayn retreated towards Alis' writhing soul, knowing he was outmatched by the trio of foes.

Both demon annaru attacked as one, arcing at the last moment to slam into him from opposite sides. Claws of pure darkness raked across his shimmering form, digging furrows that did not heal. Their corruption took hold, spreading through his soul. He tried to scream but had no mouth, confined to vent his pain and outrage in utter silence.

As Kor's shadow closed in to smother him, a beacon of blue-white light flickered into existence beside the orishadai user.

Ya need some help? it asked, then threw itself towards the demonic pair. The newcomer hauled both demon annaru away from Dayn and out of the tunnel, pulling the two minions into the nothingness that surrounded the weave. Though it quickly became apparent that his former friend was no match for his opponents, he fought on furiously, holding the demons back against all odds. The newcomer fought back bravely, latching onto the two creatures to keep them occupied. *Finish it*, he said while clinging desperately to a shadow, exposing himself to a barrage of attacks from the other one. The color of his soul faded with each blow.

Dayn launched into action with renewed vigor. He struck out at the god, hammering him with blow after blow. Kor shrugged them off and slammed into him, spinning him through the emptiness. By the time Dayn regained his senses, Kor was on him again, thrashing mercilessly at his exposed soul.

The god's mind was not trained for battle on the weave, though, and in the end it was this weakness that allowed Dayn to overwhelm him. He weathered the god's assault while slowly herding him towards the gauntlet prison.

For all the god's physical might, his soul was no more powerful than that of a mortal, a side effect, perhaps, of being separated from his powers. He failed to notice what Dayn was doing until it was too late. A mental wail of anguish reached out through the void as Dayn shoved the god back into solitude, where he would wait for all time, or until some other unfortunate took up the gauntlet and unleashed him on Urth again.

Dayn stopped, hesitating. He still had to smash the bridge connecting the prison to Alis. Without thinking, his soul took on the shape of Agidyne and started cutting. He made short work of the structure, reducing it to frayed bits of spiritual energy. That done, he turned to Alis' soul and peeled back the ribbons of red encasing it.

Get goin', his friend insisted, still holding onto the demons, though they were tearing his soul to pieces. *I'll give ya enough time for a few words*, he promised, dragging the pair of demons away.

It was the best he could hope for. *Thank you*, Dayn said solemnly.

Ryl's soul shuddered under the force of a particularly vicious attack. *Ya don't have too long, go to her now*, the former hunter told him urgently.

Dayn was about to release himself into the pain-wracked death throes of his own physical shell when the pair of shadows broke free from Ryl and latched onto his soul, anchoring him to the weave. He was too weak to resist as they dug into him, ripping apart what remained of his dismal essence, piece by piece.

Then his friend reappeared, lending his aid. The light of Ryl's soul was nearly extinguished, but he refused to let the demons have their way. Ryl's initial charge knocked one of them loose, and the other was quickly stripped away by his desperate attacks.

Go on back to her, his friend strained to say.

Dayn hesitated, knowing that his shell would not sustain him for long, if at all, when he returned to it. Once it gave out, his soul would quickly be torn loose and dragged down into the dark pits of the Aether for an eternity of nightmarish torment amongst the innumerable legions of shon.

Ryl struggled to keep hold of the demons as they flailed madly in a desperate attempt to free themselves and assault the departing soul.

With a final look at his tormented friend, Dayn regretfully relinquished his hold on the weave. The one he left behind had saved his life, as well as his soul. Ryl was a hero, and Dayn could not bear to witness the final fate of his friend's soul as the demons ripped it from existence.

38.
BREAKING THE HABIT

A pair of voices reached out to him from beyond the veil: one soft and melodic, like the rustling of leaves, the other tentative and indescribably sad.

"Who are you? What are you doing here?" asked the sad one, her voice brittle, as if it might break apart at any moment.

"I be calling myself Janeli, and I be protecting the orishadaon."

"Protecting? You could have done a better job of it."

"Is the orishadaon being dead?"

"He isn't breathing," the sad voice answered.

"He be dead, then?"

No verbal reply came, but Dayn sensed an outpouring of overwhelming sorrow.

The shock of re-entering his body nearly killed him. Only the desire to see Alis kept him clinging desperately to that last spark of life. His heart began to beat again, and his lungs flooded with breath once more. The overpowering, coppery tang of blood filled his mouth and nostrils, causing him to gag.

Then the pain returned, just as he knew it would, battering every last bit of his body with unrelenting force. He strained against Agidyne, gasping as the blade tore into his guts, opening the fatal wound further.

The weariness of his prolonged battle on the weave abruptly

overcame him and his heaving form went limp. Coupled with the pain from the gaping hole in his stomach, he barely managed to hold on to what little time he had left. He cursed his fate, eyelids drooping as he pressed both hands around the sword in his stomach to slow the bleeding and buy himself a few more precious moments of life.

"By the blood of the ancestors! You live!"

His eyes instantly snapped open at the sound of Alis' voice.

She looked better than he did, but only just. Her skin, now the pale white color of chalk, had grown back without the warding tattoos or the Swift Claw brand on her breast. All her hair was gone, and if her seared scalp was any indication, it might never grow back.

Forgetting about Agidyne, he tried to sit up, only to find himself caught in one of Alis' tight embraces before he could do himself any more harm.

"You weren't moving," she sobbed, wrapping her impossibly gaunt arms around him. "I thought . . . I thought you—"

"I know." His voice was a hoarse, barely audible whisper. He made no attempt to stop the tears welling up in his eyes from spilling across his cheeks. They were as much from his joy at seeing her alive as from the intense pain he felt throughout his body.

Her scent reached him through the stench of burnt flesh and blood clogging his nostrils. He breathed deeply, letting the intoxicating aroma fill his lungs. She smelled like the sun and the savannah, two things he would never see again.

She forced a smile and he did the same. A tense laugh escaped her lips. "Don't worry, orishadaon, I promise I won't think less of you for spilling a few tears."

Dayn did not have the courage to tell her he was no longer an orishadaon and would not be joining with the ancestors. He did not want to tell her he would never see her again, not even in the afterlife. These were their last moments, ever, and then the demons would have him.

Alis ran her gauntleted hand over his bloody stomach wound and shook her head in despair. The gauntlet remained fused to her forearm, but with the bridge inside her mind shattered, Kor would never again be able to exert control over her. She was safe, or, as safe as she could be considering the circumstances.

Dayn grasped her hand, squeezing weakly. "Forgive . . . me."

"Stubborn as always." She continued to smile for his benefit. "There's nothing to forgive."

It doesn't matter how they judge me, he thought to himself. It doesn't matter because I saved you, Alis. He had done the right thing by saving her, not the easy thing surely, but the right thing. No judging ancient, demon or god could ever take that away from him.

"Shhh," she soothed, the smile finally leaving her lips as she watched the life drain out of him. "Don't talk. Rest now, Dayn, you've earned it."

A dim shape appeared at the edge of his vision, casting its shadow upon him.

"The orishadaon is not being dead?" Janeli asked with a whistle.

She stood over him, clutching what remained of her right arm. From the shoulder down, nothing remained of the limb save crushed, wooden splinters dripping with sap. The amber liquid pooled on the flagstones at her feet. She wore an impassive look, clicking the huge claws on her toes in what might have been impatience, as if the wound was merely an inconvenience.

"You're hurt," he told her, wondering if she knew.

Janeli nodded curtly. "It is being nothing, orishadaon."

Somewhere in the distance he heard snarling and the sound of tough, leathery feet stomping against stone. What was going on?

He must have looked puzzled, so Janeli explained. "The annaru be coming," she stated, sounding bored.

His head lolled backwards in Alis' arms and all of a sudden he was staring straight up at the sky.

The stars glittered brightly through the hole in the ceiling, each one an ancestor calling him home. He had earned his rest, though the demons would afford him none.

The stomping grew increasingly louder and then annaru were crawling over the rubble all around them. One of the scaled ones spotted them the instant it reached the top of the mound, bellowing the group's position to its fellows before it scrabbled forward, three-toed feet kicking at the loose rock for purchase. A cascade of clattering debris followed it down.

The plant woman passed her calm gaze over the onrushing scaled one, never showing a hint of fear. She stood guard over Dayn, preparing to block the creature's approach with her own wounded body.

As she did this, the plant woman pointed a clawed finger towards the sky. "Look up there, you be seeing?"

Dayn noticed what she was pointing at immediately. A flight of winged karda soared blissfully past his field of vision, obscuring his view of the glittering stars. Everything was as it should be, as far as he could tell. Or was it? He could not shake the nagging feeling that something about the scene above him was out of place. The karda! Giant winged karda did not soar in flocks like the one flapping overhead. He had never seen so many of the creatures in one place before.

"Lirex is being here with the Fire Wing tribe," the huntress said just before the annaru bowled into her. It hit Janeli hard enough to lift her off her feet, driving its head forward to snap at her exposed midsection. The huntress lifted her remaining arm as the scaled one carried her towards Dayn. Moonlight glinted off her claws as she raked them across the scaled one's eyes. Blinded and screaming in pain, the annaru tripped, crashing to a halt mere paces from Dayn's head.

Alis leaped between the creature and her orishadaon, bashing its skull in with a heavy piece of rock. She hurriedly rolled its corpse off the plant woman and helped Janeli to her feet. "If those karda are friends of yours, we could use them down here," she told the huntress.

"They might be helping," agreed the huntress. She produced a small wooden trinket from some hidden compartment, the same instrument she had once used to summon the winged karda Lirex.

Before she could raise it to her lips an annaru sprang at her from the top of a rubble heap. For all Janeli's size and strength, the scaled one's massive weight smashed her to the ground like a child's reed doll, sending the wooden flute flying from her grasp. The annaru cared nothing for the instrument, which spun through the air to land near Dayn. Instead, it opened its toothy jaws wide and bent down, preparing to clamp them shut around the plant woman's throat. Saliva dripped in glistening strands onto her chest and face as it came closer, pinning her squirming form to the ground beneath its bulk.

Dayn reached out, straining against the sword in his guts that held him in place.

The huntress lashed out at the annaru with a vicious kick. Her toes—tipped with claws as large as the ones on her fingers—tore into the scaled one's midsection, slicing skin and muscle with equal ease. It arched backwards in surprise, opening itself up for another kick that ripped a hole in its stomach and spilled a steaming coil of its guts onto the cool stone. Janeli had little time to savor the victory before another annaru appeared, then another.

Alis moved uncertainly to help her, but Janeli waved her back. "Be using the axilis!" The plant woman gestured to the instrument for emphasis. Then the first annaru was on her and she was too busy defending herself to say more.

Dayn tried to speak, but blood bubbled up his throat, choking him.

Alis dove for the axilis, gingerly scooping it into her hands as she landed. Taking a deep breath, the scout raised the unfamiliar instrument to her lips . . . and was sent sprawling by a whip-like tail slapping her between the shoulder blades.

Dayn cried out and actually managed to grab hold of Agidyne's hilt before the strength in his arms gave out.

Before the annaru could hit Alis again, she rolled aside and put the axilis against her lips, blowing as hard as she could. No sound came out. She tried it again in desperation, and still it made no sound. Panicked, she threw the useless item aside and bolted for some nearby rubble.

In response to the silent call, a chorus of shrieks sounded from the flock of winged karda overhead. Numerous karda broke away from the rest, dipping their wings and descending directly towards the beleaguered humans and the plant woman.

A hail of expertly aimed javelins rained down upon the oncoming wave of annaru. Every one of the creatures within sight collapsed, clawing at their wounds as froth bubbled out of their clacking jaws. Those who were struck by more than one javelin died in a fit of muscle spasms that were powerful enough to snap bone, judging by the cracking and popping sounds filling the air.

With no way to reach the new flying threat, the annaru panicked, scattering in all directions. Their loyalty to their god seemed to last only as long as things went their way. Now that the tide of battle had turned they sought to escape by the fastest means possible. Dayn had never known the creatures to be cowards and he suspected that the sounds they made as they fled were not cries of fear, but rather curses and calls for vengeance. The Fire Wing tribe had made a dedicated enemy this lunar.

No longer having to worry about defending herself, Janeli raised her hand in greeting to a large karda circling above. It shrieked and banked, descending in a lazy circle that brought it down directly beside the plant woman. The beast's leathery wings kicked a storm of dust into the air and from that swirling storm emerged a tiny figure who waved excitedly at the huntress.

The man who slipped off the karda stood no more than five paces tall. His body was gaunt, with deeply tanned skin stretched impossibly tight over a thin, fragile looking frame. Chords of wiry muscle stood out against his skin, rippling as he strode forward with an uncomfortable, lopsided gait that made him look awkward on the ground. This was obviously a warrior who felt more at home in the skies, on the back of his winged mount.

"Lirex gave me your message," the tiny man said, patting his karda's scarred snout affectionately. He was naked and entirely hairless, his skin coated in some sort of fatty grease. "I came as soon as all my warriors were ready." He motioned to the flight of karda riders landing amidst the wreckage all across the temple top.

"My life is being yours, Agar." Janeli clasped his outstretched hand in her remaining one.

"Just repaying you for all the times your people have helped mine," he replied with a smile. The smile faded as he caught sight of Dayn. "Oh no." He kneeled beside him. "Orishadaon, I am sorry."

The blood in his throat prevented Dayn from responding.

"Brun!" Agar bellowed. Within moments a similarly featured man with tattoos that matched Dayn's appeared. "Is there anything you can do for him?" Agar directed the newcomer's attention to the dying orishadaon.

Alis held Dayn's hand throughout the exchange, waiting anxiously for an answer.

Brun, who was obviously an orishadaon himself, took one look at Dayn and shook his head. "The sword claims his soul," the little man said, gesturing to Agidyne.

The sword claimed his soul. Anyone struck down by a metal weapon had his soul taken by the weapon. Even in death, the demons could not have him! Dayn laughed, and coughed, spitting up more blood.

Alis gently wiped his face clean with the back of her hand. Oddly, knowing there was nothing that could be done for him seemed to be calming her. Dayn understood why she might feel this way, and did not resent her for it. She must have been content in the knowledge that his suffering would soon be over.

Janeli put a clawed hand on his shoulder and he turned to face her. "We be taking care of Alis," the plant woman assured him.

"She will be safe with us," agreed Agar.

Knowing Alis was alive and safe was all he needed. Janeli and the Fire Wing tribe would see to it that she was looked after. He could do nothing more for her.

There were so many things he wanted to say to Alis in his final moments. His chest shuddered with the effort of drawing breath and he felt the prolonged struggle as the very last gasp of air entered his lungs. All the things he wanted to say and only enough breath for one of them.

"I love you," he told her in as clear a voice as he could manage. It came out sounding more like, 'Uh luh yuh.'

She placed a hand on his shoulder and kissed him lightly on the cheek. "I love you too," she told him, understanding. Alis knew him too well.

His eyelids closed, plunging him into comforting darkness. He no longer feared the black abyss, but embraced it, welcoming the calm that settled over him as the world bled away. Each breath grew shallower. His attempts to draw more became weaker and less desperate with each passing moment. The erratic pounding of his heart slowed to a dull, peaceful rhythm as he relinquished his hold on life. It would all be over soon, he thought wistfully. He gave Alis' hand a final squeeze with the last of his dwindling strength. The rise and fall of his chest shuddered to a halt with a final hiss of escaping breath. Dayn's heart stopped pumping. His soul slipped away from the shell, with the image of the woman he loved as the last thing to flash through the dying embers of his mind.

ABOUT THE AUTHOR

Brandon RJ Bowling lives in Corunna, a small town in Ontario, Canada. When he isn't writing about dinosaurs, zombies, apocalyptic wastelands or people with bizarre psychic powers his time is divided between his girlfriend, Alicia, son, Zane, and his three conures, Spartacus, Wembley and Roxton.

For more on the author please visit:

www.brandonrjbowling.com

or

www.brandon-bowling.deviantart.com

www.ingramcontent.com/pod-product-compliance
Lightning Source LLC
Chambersburg PA
CBHW020439270626
47155CB00022B/646